The Haunting of Highdown Hall

Psychic Surveys
Book One

Shani Struthers

CROOKED CAT

Discover us online:
www.crookedcatpublishing.com

Join us on facebook:
www.facebook.com/crookedcatpublishing

Tweet a photo of yourself holding
this book to **@crookedcatbooks**
and something nice will happen.

To grounded spirits everywhere – don't be afraid, there are more adventures waiting.

About the Author

Born and bred in the sunny seaside town of Brighton, one of the first literary conundrums Shani had to deal with was her own name - Shani can be pronounced in a variety of ways but in this instance it's Shay-nee not Shar-ney or Shan-ni - although she does indeed know a Shanni - just to confuse matters further!

Hobbies include reading, writing, eating and drinking - all four of which keep her busy enough. After graduating from Sussex University with a degree in English and American Literature, Shani became a freelance copywriter. Twenty years later, the day job includes crafting novels too.

Psychic Surveys Book One: The Haunting of Highdown Hall is her second novel and the first in the series. All events depicted are fictitious – almost.

Acknowledgements

There are a huge many to thank during the writing of this book but first thanks goes to my husband, Rob Struthers, the whole concept of Psychic Surveys was your idea – I just took it and ran – here's to many more nights in The Rights of Man pub in Lewes (Ruby's favourite) discussing ideas.

And then there are the people I cringingly gave the first draft to to tear apart – in no particular order – Patrice Brown (Mum), Louisa Taylor, Lesley Hughes, Vanessa Patterson, Julie Tugwell, Gail Keen, Sarah Savery, Alicen Haire and Rachel Bell – you all saw something special in it and no tearing apart ensued. Jane Tyrrell, thank you for working so patiently with me on edits to get the book fit for submission – your input was invaluable and led to some crucial changes. Jill Blair – thanks for the proofread too.

Jane Dixon-Smith – thanks for creating a cover that makes everyone go 'Wow! You nailed it in record time'.

Thanks also to Laurence and Steph Patterson of Crooked Cat Publishing. It is an honour to be part of the team, alongside some of my favourite authors. And thanks to the Cats too for such a warm welcome.

Finally, to my children, Izzie, Jack and Misty – thanks for putting up with all the burnt dinners because I just couldn't tear myself away from writing the next sentence! Love you guys.

Shani Struthers
April 2014

The Haunting of Highdown Hall

Psychic Surveys
Book One

Prologue

Christmas Eve, 1958

"Pour me a glass of water, would you?"

"Yes, Ma'am."

The polished floorboards creaked as Sally walked across the bedroom to a small sideboard, on which stood an elegant silver and cut glass decanter. Emptying its cool, clear contents into an equally elegant tumbler, she returned to the dressing table and handed it to Cynthia Hart.

"Look at the headlines..." Cynthia breathed, taking the water almost absent-mindedly. "'The Most Beautiful Woman in the World', that's what they're calling me."

"Because you are," agreed Sally, continuing to fuss over her.

Placing the tumbler on her dressing table untouched, Cynthia leaned forward to check her reflection for the umpteenth time in the teak framed mirror in front of her. Sally was right, *they* were right – she was exquisite. Her sapphire eyes so much brighter than the violet of Taylor's, her mouth a perfect cupid's bow and her abundant Titian curls the envy of all.

As ever, she would be the belle of the ball tonight, a ball thrown to celebrate not only Christmas Eve, but also her birthday. Thirty-one today and not a line marred her face.

"Sally, my diamonds."

"Of course, Ma'am."

As Sally hurried from the bedroom, Cynthia stood up to appraise her hour-glass figure in the full mirror to the side of her dressing table. She swished her floor-length fuchsia dress from side to side; made exclusively for her by Dior it set off her colouring perfectly. As she continued to admire the glamorous vision in front of her, something caught her eye, something glinting in the dying light. Leaning forward, she had to squint slightly.

No, it can't be, surely not!

Cynthia felt rage boil up from nowhere and engulf her.

In amongst the red lay a single strand of steel, mocking her, *marring* her.

"No!" she screamed. "Not yet!"

Perfectly manicured fingertips flew upwards, desperate to locate it. Managing at last, she tore it from her scalp and threw it from her as though it were contagion itself.

How can I be the most beautiful woman in the world with grey in my hair?

Her breathing, previously calm and even, became erratic – as she gasped for breath her heart pounded violently against the walls of her fragile chest like some maddened wild animal seeking escape. Lytton had promised her, had said this wouldn't happen. But deep down she'd always known there were limits to that promise; that she would only be given so much, and for so long.

Damn that man! How she wished she had never met him. How she hated the still vivid memory of his face, how it haunted her dreams. But without him, what would she be, *where* would she be? Still on the scrapheap of life, being offered only the most meagre of parts? Just one chance, that's all she'd needed, one chance to show the world what she could do. And for that chance she would have done anything, *anything*, as he'd known only too well.

After Lytton had come the turning point, after Lytton had come *The Phoenix,* a Rank Organisation production all actresses had vied for, famous and struggling alike. Although she was offered a much coveted part – she had lines to say at least – Cynthia had refused it, insisting from the start that the main

4

role was hers, that she *was* Gayle Andrews, a woman of determination born into a life of grit, destined to make her mark in a harsh world. That the lead actress had suffered an accident just before taking up the role, that someone had then noticed her still waiting in the wings, were far from coincidence.

An award for 'Best British Actress in a Leading Role' had followed – her performance hailed by the critics as 'groundbreaking'. All manner of roles had poured in after that; intense, dramatic, whimsical roles, everything she had ever wanted, had ever desired. Two years later she'd picked up another award for Hitchcock's *Intruders,* and this March she'd finally secured her place as a screen legend with the ultimate: an Oscar for *The Elitists.* In the new year she'd be moving to Hollywood – not permanently, of course (no fancy Bel Air residence could compare to Highdown Hall, her first real home, her first real love), just long enough to star in *Atlantic,* which was set to surpass *Ben-Hur* as the most lavish film in cinematic history.

Sally's continued absence eventually drew Cynthia back to the present.

Where is she? What's taking her so long?

Walking over to the windows, two sets of them, floor to ceiling, Cynthia struggled to relax. These moods of hers, they were getting worse. One minute she was bursting with happiness, the next she had gone to pieces – and often with no warning. She knew all around her were growing increasingly nervous of her moods. But she also knew they would suffer them. Her entourage lived a dream life because of her, exalted from mere existence to a charmed existence. They would not rock the boat. They too had sold their souls – not to darkness, but to her, the irony of which she refused to dwell on.

How she loved the view from her window. In the west, the sun was beginning to set, casting an almost ethereal glow over the landscape. Her eyes rested on the lake in front of her, dark

5

and secretive in the dusk and shrouded by weeping willows. Ripples blew across the surface, but gently so – for December it was a clement night. Pride swelled up in her. This was *her* land, *her* house and hers alone. And to think she had come from nothing; a bleak, fatherless childhood spent sharing two rooms with her lowly drudge of a mother and a constantly whining brother. Neither of them had bothered to contact her since she'd left at fourteen. And neither of them had approached her in stardom, either. Although this suited her fine, she couldn't help but feel abandoned, despite having abandoned them.

Highdown Hall was regarded as one of the most beautiful houses in the south of England. She loved its almost regal approach down the private gravel drive, twisting and turning in a teasing manner before revealing a Gothic sandstone creation with imposing gables, stone mullioned windows and even a turret, the location of her bedroom. Ivy clung stubbornly to its ancient walls, creeping further and further upwards, but furtively so. Entering through weathered oak doors, suitably baronial in size, visitors were greeted by the Grand Hall, fully oak-panelled and adorned with a life-sized portrait of Cynthia, leaving no one in doubt as to whom this estate belonged to. As well as a drawing room, a sitting room, a dining room and a library on the ground floor, there was a ballroom too, blatantly opulent with its vintage chandeliers, its French windows leading onto a paved terrace and its sprung hard-wood floor. It was the scene of many an extravagant party – and tonight would be no exception.

She listened for sounds below. They were faint, but they were there, bringing the house to life. John Sterling, her American co-star in *The Elitists*, was one of the many famous names who'd crossed land and sea to attend. She had long been dazzled by his performances on the silver screen. On meeting, she had dazzled him. Their affair had begun quickly – she had never known such wildness in the bedroom, such imagination. But there was a surprising degree of tenderness too, something she was unused to. And, despite his serious public persona, his sense of humour was acute, delighting her with his behind-the-scenes wickedness. But she wouldn't fall too hard. It could lead nowhere. Frivolities such as marriage and babies were for others, mere mortals, not for her. Deliberately, she kept him at arm's length, allowing him only the occasional private audience; something she knew riled him terribly. In between, she ensured a constant flow of lovers, something else that incensed him. But she hated to sleep alone, hated the dark, even more so recently.

The view from her window had done the trick; Cynthia was breathing more easily again. Despite her earlier irritation with her maid, she was thankful now that Sally was taking her time, that she hadn't witnessed her momentary breakdown. It occurred to her sometimes that Sally cared for her as a mother should, despite being only two years older. She couldn't bear to see her mistress upset.

Banishing Lytton from her mind, Cynthia began to imagine the impact she was soon to make. All eyes would be on her as she swept down the oak staircase, she would hear sharp intakes of breath and then, as always, the vying would begin. Guests would elbow each other out of the way to reach her, some surreptitiously, others arrogantly, each and every one of them desperate to have her bestow on them even a cursory glance. Amusing really, considering how many years she had spent craving attention. And now it was *her* attention they craved; the film star, the diva, the most beautiful woman in the world.

She smiled at the thought, her face brightening further as she relaxed into a laugh. Returning to her dressing table, Cynthia picked up a silver compact – a gift from Chanel, her name engraved in swirling letters upon it, and reapplied blusher to the hollows of her cheeks. From a crystal bottle she dabbed *Phoenix* onto her wrists and cleavage; created in her honour by the House of Balmain, it was appropriately sensual with base notes of sandalwood, amber, patchouli and musk. Inhaling the heady scent, she listened again as excited chatter rose up from the floor below, electrifying the air in her bedroom.

Sally returned at last.

"I'm sorry, Ma'am," she rushed to explain. "The lock to the safe needed greasing; I had to call the butler to help me."

"No matter," Cynthia replied, indicating for her to fasten the jewels around her neck.

After she had done so, Sally took a step back.

"Oh, Ma'am," she said, pure devotion in her doe-like eyes. "No diamond could shine as bright as you."

Cynthia ignored the compliment. "Has everybody on the guest list arrived?"

"Yes, Ma'am."

"Including John?"

"Including Mr Sterling," Sally confirmed.

Checking herself one last time, Cynthia stepped forward, ready, yet again, to enthral.

Chapter One

"Good morning, Psychic Surveys. How can I help?"

As the caller started explaining, Ruby couldn't help but groan.

"Sorry?" said the caller, immediately picking up on it.

"Er, nothing," Ruby attempted to gloss over, "bad vibes you were saying? Cold spots? Yes, that's certainly something I can help you with. I'll need to do a survey first and then we can decide on a course of action. Are you in tomorrow morning? Say ten o'clock?"

Pencilling the appointment in her diary, Ruby wondered (not for the first time) why it was that such inviting house prices at the new housing estate in Horam, a nearby East Sussex village, never rang alarm bells with the buyers. It was well known that Brookbridge had been built on land that was steeped in an unsavoury past. Ever since it was finished residents had been calling her complaining of 'unusual activity', as they called it – in their living rooms, their bedrooms, heck, even their bathrooms at times! After performing a survey, followed by a cleansing, on one of the houses eighteen months ago, word of her services had spread. Since then, Psychic Surveys had visited several houses on the estate as family after family reported being spooked by "strange goings on". She replaced the receiver, testily. *What do they expect? It's the site of one of Britain's most notorious mental asylums; countless books and websites have been devoted to the horrendous practices that were carried out there. Of course there are going to be bad vibes and cold spots. It's only a matter of time before there's an actual manifestation with troubled souls galore unable to move on. Knocking down walls, putting up new ones and giving the whole place a fancy new name isn't going to change that fact.*

No, it wouldn't. But she, Ruby Davis, the latest in a long line of psychic females, could. She had a gift. A 'gift' her grandmother had taught her to utilise fully. As soon as she had been old enough to understand, Gran had drummed into her how important it was not to waste it; this precious gift had been bestowed on her, on *them*, for a reason. It was nothing less than her duty to help restless, earthbound souls to move on.

And Ruby took that duty seriously – as did her freelance team: Theo, Ness and Corinna. All psychically aware to varying degrees, she could call upon them at any time. Knowing that she didn't have to cope alone when her workload got too much, when a spirit became more challenging than normal, or she simply needed a bit of company on a job (living and breathing that is), made her life that much easier. Cool and level-headed all three of them, they were absolutely indispensable.

Assessing her diary; tomorrow looked set to be a busy day. After Brookbridge, she had a house in Hove to visit. Belonging to a young couple, it had become the scene of repeated nightmares for their young son, who kept dreaming that another little boy was attacking him. His parents couldn't understand it – he wasn't being bullied at school or anything – and were at breaking point, not having had a decent night's sleep since they moved in several months ago. She was their last hope, the mother had tearfully confided on the phone yesterday, they desperately needed her help.

"How did you hear about Psychic Surveys?" Ruby had asked, trying to calm Mrs Carter down.

"Word of mouth."

Ruby smiled to herself. This mysterious 'word of mouth' kept her very busy indeed. But at least it meant people were pleased with what she and her team were doing, that they could rest in peace again – a right that didn't belong solely to the spirit world. Although personal recommendations were great, she couldn't avoid the fact that in this day and age she needed a website, especially if she wanted to build up her business. To date, Psychic Surveys had mainly worked on cases in the South East, including London. But spirits didn't just confine themselves to one geographical area. The net needed to be cast wider and a website would help do that considerably.

Ruby knew there were other psychics doing what she was doing, but often in a more furtive manner, not out there, loud and proud as she was, as a bona fide high street business. In that, Psychic Surveys was unique. She wanted to unite as many psychic freelancers as possible under one umbrella, their aim to ease the minds of the living and convince the dearly departed it was time to move on. Not that they didn't do long distance healings, Theo specialised in them, from the comfort of her fireside armchair, and often with great success. But it would be good to have a physical presence too, perhaps more offices up and down the country one day, where people could pop in with their concerns, chat about them over a cup of tea, 'normalise' the paranormal, remove the taboo.

In pursuit of this vision, Ruby had already discovered it was possible to purchase a website off the shelf, virtually speaking, and to set it up with very little technological know-how. So she had tried – and failed, dismally, her very little technological know-how obviously way too scant. "We all have our strengths", her grandmother had soothed when Ruby had complained; but business was business, she needed a pro and fast. A shame then, that she couldn't afford one. Although she charged for what they did, she had to, it didn't seem ethical to charge too much, certainly not the fees surveyors of more earthly matters insisted upon. Theo, Ness and Corinna thought the same. Each of them agreed that theirs was a service as much as a business, hence their sliding scale of fees and the occasional client who wasn't charged at all. Corinna didn't rely solely on her wages from Psychic Surveys; she worked several shifts in a pub in Uckfield too. Theo was retired, and so had her pension. As for Ness, she seemed to have some private means of support, the source of which Ruby didn't know and didn't like to ask. Ruby had also worked part-time up until two years ago, in bars and shops mainly, even enduring a stint at Tesco stacking shelves. She'd never forget the store manager's words to her on her first day:

"Welcome to the graveyard shift," he had said. If only he knew.

Now, she was finally able to devote her time fully to Psychic Surveys, something she was grateful for, even if it did mean she had to rein in her lifestyle considerably: cut down on nights out, eat budget brands and only buy sale clothes, that sort of thing.

Thankfully, the rent was low on this excuse of an office of hers, procured from a friend of a friend. Set right at the top of a draughty old building that dated back to Tudor times (despite its more recent Victorian façade), she had to climb three flights of stairs for the pleasure of boiling in summer and freezing in winter. One day they would occupy more visible, ground floor premises on Lewes's historic high street, but for now they were stuck up under the eaves, in a room that, at best, could be described as 'cosy', although to be fair it would look much bigger if not for her desk. Made of yew, with an inlaid green leather top, she'd managed to get it for a bargain price at Ardingly Antiques Fair, due to its previous owners' clumsy or careless natures. Her office chair was equally impressive; a captain's chair, regal almost, even if horsehair did poke alarmingly out of its parched leather skin. She'd get the seat recovered when she could, but for now a cushion on top would have to do. Sometimes she wished she had chosen more compact furniture, but there was very little she could do about that now. It had taken two strong, obliging men from the solicitors' below to haul that beast of a desk up here; there was no way she was going to risk their wrath by asking them to take it back down again. Perhaps she'd attack her books instead, there were far too many of them lining shelves, stacked against the walls, on top of the filing cabinet. Most of them dealt with paranormal matters, but far too many were much-loved novels that she'd brought into work to read when things were quiet and had never taken back home. Ruby was the proud owner of a somewhat eclectic collection; Stephen King and Dean Koontz sat alongside Lee Child and Marian Keyes. Some books she couldn't bear to part with, some she knew she'd never read again. Culling the novels at least might make a difference.

Ruby's office was opposite the entrance to Lewes Castle, which was set slightly back from the High Street and reached via a small cobbled square. Sadly, the view from her tiny garret window was not of the grey and crumbling walls of the South and West Towers (all that remained of the imposing fortress built by the Normans after William the Conqueror's victory in 1066), but of the sky, also grey more often than not, and only fleetingly punctuated by birds. If she stood on her chair she could just see the verdant South Downs that lay beyond the town, but her more usual view was Rowland Hilder's *Morning Shadows over a Country Track*. 'Borrowed' from the family home, it graced the wall to the left of her desk – since childhood she had been fond of its oast house, autumnal fields and skeleton trees.

It wasn't only tomorrow that was going to be busy, today would be too. She had several reports to type up from various visits carried out last week, plus the team were coming in for their weekly meeting after lunch. Theo had been to assess a house in Sussex for a new client. Buried deep in the countryside, the house had once belonged to a famous film star, someone Theo had admired very much in her younger days. The current owner was spooked to say the least judging by his voice when Ruby had spoken to him on the phone last week. Theo had jumped at the chance of doing the initial survey and they were going to discuss her findings today. His was another word of mouth enquiry. It seemed, for the present at least, the lack of a website was hardly leaving them bereft. Psychic Surveys had never been busier. Which was worrying, really, when she thought about it; so many souls having trouble crossing the great divide, and for so many different reasons.

Sighing, she returned to her laptop and began typing.

***

"Hi, Ruby," Ness said as she wandered into the office, heading straight for the kettle which lived on top of a second, much smaller desk, pushed up against the rear wall. Their 'meeting desk' as Ruby grandly called it – not an antique this time, but a cheap and cheerful purchase from Ikea around which the four of them would huddle together.

"Cuppa?" she enquired.

Ruby nodded her head enthusiastically. Her office had no radiators, only a Calor Gas heater blasting valiantly away. Despite it, she still felt cold – the early December chill permeating the poorly maintained walls of this ancient building and burying itself deep inside her bones.

As Ness busied herself, Ruby typed the last few sentences of her report on a house in Southover Street, in the bustling city of Brighton, eight miles away. When they had visited, neither she nor Theo had sensed any 'paranormal' presence, so Ruby explained that after careful consideration it was their recommendation that the residents call in a plumber. Old pipes often explained the inexplicable, she typed – airlocks could be responsible for some very strange noises indeed. If that didn't resolve matters, Psychic Surveys would visit again, at no extra cost. Finishing the last sentence, she had no idea whether Mr and Mrs Gill would be disappointed or relieved that there was an apparently 'normal' reason for what was happening in their house. It surprised her how often it was the former, as though people actively *wanted* dealings with the supernatural, to be able

14

to boast to their family and friends that they lived in a haunted house perhaps – everyone loved a good ghost story after all. But dealing with supernatural matters was not what films such as *Ghostbusters* and *Casper* made it out to be. There were very few laughs involved and rarely any excitement – what there was, was a whole lot of sadness.

Turning to Ness, whose winter pale, heart-shaped face was framed by black bobbed hair, most of which was still hidden beneath a woolly cap despite being indoors, Ruby said "The others should be here soon."

Right on cue, the 'others' walked in – Theo and Corinna. Theo, as ever, was a sight to behold. In her late sixties and almost as wide as she was tall, she was bedecked in an assortment of colourful gossamer scarves and a purple padded coat. Her hair should have been snow-white, but instead it was pink, a soft, tasteful shade of pink, but pink nonetheless. Whenever Ruby saw her, she couldn't help but think of a line from Clement Clarke Moore's famous poem, *The Night Before Christmas*, the one that referred to St Nick as 'a right jolly old elf.' But Theo was no elfin-like creature; she was actually one of the most formidable women Ruby had ever met, an old-timer in the field. Although it was Ruby's business, they often tended to take their cue from her.

Corinna, by contrast, was the youngest of the group. Twenty-one, with a distinct penchant for black clothing, the only colourful thing about her was her long, almost Pre-Raphaelite auburn hair. Despite her preferred 'gothic' attire, she had a bubbly personality. Sensitive to the spirit world, she wanted to develop her psychic skills, to do her bit to 'help' the spirits when help was needed. Although her work at Psychic Surveys was not enough to support her financially, if Ruby's vision came to fruition, Corinna would be employed full-time one day, something Ruby knew she was eager for.

"Tea?" said Ness, jumping immediately into action.

Ness, short for Vanessa although they never called her that, was different to the other two. Much quieter, she reminded Ruby of her mother, albeit she was a few years older than her mother, early fifties as supposed to late forties, but both wore a world-weary countenance, very much so. Ness would sometimes work with Sussex Police, on an unofficial basis of course, and Ruby often thought that this must be the reason behind her somewhat subdued nature – she got the feeling some of the cases she had worked on had been extremely gruelling. Ruby had also been approached to help Sussex Police a year or so back but Ness had warned her off. Surely, Ruby had argued, earthbound spirits who had suffered heinously at the hands of others were the most in need of help, the most deserving? "You'd think so," Ness had replied, refusing to elaborate further. Instead, she had advised Ruby to concentrate on more domestic cases, making a very good case that they were the ones who were often overlooked. Having mulled it over for a while, Ruby had at last agreed. Maybe she'd reconsider in future, but for now, domestic cases were her forte.

"Love an Earl Grey," boomed Theo, cutting into Ruby's thoughts.

"Black for me," piped up Corinna, "trying to give up milk. Read some shocking stuff about the dairy industry recently, it's put me off completely."

Eager to get the meeting started, Ruby pulled up her chair. "Okay, what's to report?"

Although Theo was clearly champing at the bit to impart her own news, she let Ness, who had come straight from a house in Heathfield, go first. The couple living in the mid-terrace Edwardian house had complained of barking on their landing night after night, despite not owning a dog.

"Sounds travel, I told them. So I went to investigate, trying to ascertain who owned a dog in the local area. Well, quite a few of them do, but it's amazing how put out owners are when you even so much as hint that their beloved canine might be making a nuisance of his or herself. Apparently none of them so much as growls, not even at the postman."

"So?" nudged Ruby, intrigued. Animal spirits were new to her. Normally, four-footed creatures had no trouble moving into the light, even those who had experienced less than loving homes, their spirits able to remain pure and optimistic against all odds.

"So, having made sure that a real live dog was not the issue, I returned to the house and tuned in and I did sense something. And that something, this 'dog', seems to have one over-inflated sense of loyalty. From what I could gather, he still thinks his main function is to protect and serve the family living there. I tried to communicate with him, to impart that his work on earth is done, but to no avail. When I left, his presence seemed as strong as ever. I recommended to Miss Mills that we go back and perform a cleansing."

"Fair enough," said Ruby, wondering how she was going to succeed where Ness had failed. Perhaps together they would make an impact. "I'll ring her after our meeting to make an appointment. Now, Theo, what about you?"

"Weeell," said Theo, drawing out the word as much as possible, her blue eyes dancing. God, she loved the theatre of it all, did Theo. "I think we've got quite a case on our hands."

"Oh?" said Ruby, leaning forward. Corinna too looked fascinated, only Ness held back, guarded as usual.

"There is most definitely a presence at the Hall. I felt it most strongly in the master bedroom, but other parts of the house have a feeling about them too, particularly the ballroom. And yes, I believe that the spirit grounded *is* Cynthia Hart, the actress. She lived there for five years until her death on Christmas Eve in 1958, which, coincidentally, was also her thirty-first birthday. I was so excited to realise it might be her, I was tempted to ask for an autograph!" Theo laughed, another booming sound.

"Theo!" Ruby admonished affectionately, her awe-struck reaction really quite amusing.

"Her boudoir is quite something," Theo continued, oblivious. "It's kept as a shrine to her. Although Cynthia died many years ago, her estate was looked after by her maid, Sally Threadgold, whom she'd left it to, apparently as much to Sally's surprise as everyone else's. Mr Kierney, Alan, is Sally's nephew. She in turn left it to him upon her death, another surprise, but then Sally had no children of her own, so perhaps not so surprising after all. Cynthia's bedroom is the grandest, so it follows Mr Kierney wants it for himself. But Cynthia, she's having none of it. Every time he even attempts to enter, he fails – pushed out, as he describes it, by unseen hands, an impression of someone screaming in his face. That's usually followed by quite a bit of banging and crashing. She's still quite the diva it seems."

"How long has Mr Kierney lived at Highdown?" Ness asked thoughtfully.

"Only a couple of months. He sold his flat in London and moved down. After failing to gain access to the boudoir he resorted to sleeping in the bedroom next door, but the nocturnal noises proved too disconcerting. He sleeps downstairs now, in one of the living rooms, barely ventures upstairs anymore. And supremely pissed off about it he is too. He wants the whole place exorcised."

"Exorcised?" said Ruby, stiffening. "You did tell him we are not affiliated with the church, didn't you? That we use only holistic methods to guide spirits home?"

"Yes, of course I did," Theo shrugged her shoulders. "I don't think he cares either way to be honest, he just wants Highdown Hall to belong to him and him alone."

"Okay," replied Ruby, relieved. "Do you really think it's her, this actress, Cynthia Hart?"

"Definitely. I got an impression of a movie screen, an absolutely stunning dress, fuchsia in colour, silk if I'm not mistaken, and gleaming red curls – that's her alright. I was also given to understand she won't go easily. She seems... how can I put it? Very territorial."

"What caused her death?" asked Corinna. "She was so young."

"A heart attack apparently, and yes, she was very young to have suffered such a thing. But that was the verdict recorded, no foul play suspected." With genuine sorrow Theo added, "A terrible shame really, she was at the peak of her career too, about to star in *Atlantic*. Adele Hamilton, the actress who replaced her, was no match for Cynthia I can tell you; she just didn't have her charisma. The film didn't do nearly as well as expected."

"Do you think her sudden passing is the reason she's grounded?" asked Ruby.

"Either that or she literally can't get over missing the boat in *Atlantic* – although considering that particular boat sank, you'd think she'd be grateful!"

Once again, Theo laughed uproariously at her own joke.

Sneaking a surreptitious glance at Ness, who looked far from amused, Ruby announced she'd ring Mr Kierney after the meeting, to organise a time to go over and get a feel for the house herself.

"Tomorrow, though," she said, "I have to go to Brookbridge."

"*Again?*" Corinna was incredulous.

"Yes, again." Ruby raised her eyes skywards. "Theo, can you meet me in Hove tomorrow afternoon? We've got a little boy to send on his way."

"A little boy? Oh poor lamb, yes of course I can. At your service, my dear."

"And what about 'Rover'?" enquired Ness.

"Ah, yes, him too, perhaps I could squeeze him in between appointments. Heathfield is close to Brookbridge isn't it? I'll ring Miss Mills in a moment; maybe we can meet there around eleven or so if she agrees? Is that good for you?"

"It is," Ness nodded solemnly.

As Ruby pushed back her chair, intending to make a start on those phone calls whilst the others finished their tea, she was stopped in her tracks.

"I've got a feeling about Highdown Hall..." Theo's tone had changed, her furrowed brow highlighting her concern. "I think it may take a bit more than a simple cleansing to shift Cynthia – for whatever reason, she seems thoroughly intent on staying put."

"Hmmm..." Ruby's normally smooth features developed a frown of their own.

After all, if Theo said they had a problem, usually, they had a problem.

Chapter Two

After the meeting, various phone calls and typing up of more surveys, Ruby knew the sensible thing to do was to go home, have a hot bath and climb into bed. But the thing was she could murder a rum and coke. She grabbed the book she was currently reading from her desk, threw it into her rucksack, locked up the office and headed for The Rights of Man pub.

Next to the Law Courts, The Rights of Man was a favourite haunt of hers, run by the uber-efficient Gracie Lawless, an amusing surname considering the pub's location and the town's history. The pub paid homage to its most famous resident, Thomas Paine. Paine, who had lived there for several years in the eighteenth century and even married a local girl, was a radical free thinker whose political ideas and writing were highly influential in inspiring the American Revolution. Friends with none other than Benjamin Franklin, Paine had become known as 'The Godfather of American Independence'. One of the first places he'd expounded and developed his ideas in was The White Hart Hotel, just down the road from her office.

Ruby had always felt at home in Lewes, which is why she'd decided it was the perfect place to set up her business. She loved its anarchic side, its liberal attitudes, its highly varied history and particularly the annual bonfire processions on November 5th. Every year the town boarded up its shops and closed its roads to traffic so that different bonfire societies from the town and local villages could dress up in wonderfully ornate costumes and parade through the dark streets to the sound of primitive drumming and marching bands, before eventually setting off huge firework displays around the town. All to commemorate the successful foiling of the Gunpowder Plot to blow up the king in the Houses of Parliament in 1605. It was ironic that this should be such a massive part of the town's identity now, when the revolutionary Thomas Paine had also had his time here.

As she wandered through its historic streets and twittens, Ruby would often muse about the amazing number of interesting and influential people that had lived in this small Sussex county town: famous writers, artists, poets, musicians, physicians, scientists, even an Archbishop of Canterbury at one time. Sometimes she'd stroll through the ruins of Lewes Priory, on the outskirts of town, imagining the goings on in what had once been one of the richest monasteries in England; at others she'd take a walk up towards Offham Hill, picking up residual feelings from Lewes's famous battle of 1264 as she went. Thankfully, most people seemed to have passed successfully now. For such an ancient place, Lewes was surprisingly spirit free. Not even the souls of the protestant martyrs (who were burnt at the stake in the town for their supposedly 'heretical' beliefs during Catholic Mary Tudor's reign and whose sacrifice was also marked on Bonfire night) remained. Although again, residual feelings did – far too powerful to be erased from the atmosphere entirely, Ruby would regularly experience insights into a torturous death she could really do without.

Shuddering, and not entirely because of the chill night air, Ruby pulled her coat closer. She could rely on the pub to be warm, a log fire almost always burned in the grate during the winter months. She would sit beside it, plough through several chapters of her book, sip at her drink and then return home for that well-earned bath. A perfect evening by anybody's standards, she decided as she stepped through the door. The globe lights that Gracie had chosen during a recent refurbishment cast a golden glow, embracing her like an old friend. The pub was virtually empty inside, but then it was Monday. Lewes barely rocked on a Friday evening let alone the beginning of the week.

"Hi, Ruby," greeted Gracie as she walked to the bar. "The usual?"

"Yes, please, but the coke part, I'll have the full-fat version this time."

"Much nicer," agreed Gracie, winking at her.

Paying and taking her drink, she sat down at her favourite table, pulled out her book and began to read.

On the third paragraph of chapter eight she became aware that Gracie was speaking to her.

'Now isn't that odd?" she was saying. "You two, reading the same book."

"Sorry?" said Ruby, confused.

"You two..." Gracie repeated, nodding at her and then at a young man sitting a few tables away, also with a book in his hands. A young man who must have come in after her as she certainly hadn't noticed him on arrival. "You're both reading the same book."

The man in question looked up. Glancing at her book cover first, he then checked his own as though needing to reassure himself that Gracie wasn't in fact deluded.

"So we are," he muttered, surprised.

"Never heard of it myself," chirped Gracie, wiping down a beer pump. "Any good?"

"Yes," both readers chimed back in perfect unison.

Smiling now, the man turned towards Ruby. Holding up his copy, he pointed to it with one finger and mouthed, "Are you enjoying it?"

At least that's what Ruby thought he was saying; she wasn't quite sure. As if realising this was the case, the man picked up his book and his pint glass and walked over to her.

"*Drive Like Hell*, are you enjoying it?"

"Oh right, yes, the book," she replied. "Yes, I am actually. It's pretty good. Are you?"

"Yeah, so far so good."

There was a slight pause, only a second or two but Ruby felt the weight of it. Quickly, she shifted over, indicating it was okay for him to take a seat beside her.

"Dallas Hudgens," she said, referring to the book's author as her new acquaintance sat down, "he's not exactly No.1 in the Bestsellers list, is he? Who recommended him to you?"

"A guy called Wes Freed, have you heard of him?"

"No," Ruby shook her head.

"Oh, he's great. He does the artwork for a band called *The Drive-By Truckers*."

"Never heard of them either," said Ruby, a little confused.

"Well, Wes Freed, he's a fan of Dallas Hudgens, gave his book a big shout out on his website. That's how I heard of him."

"Oh, I see," replied Ruby, even though she wasn't sure she did. "I found him by accident, in a charity shop, £1.50, a bargain I'd say."

"Too right," he said and then, offering her his hand, "I'm Cash, Cash Wilkins."

"Hi," said Ruby, noting what a firm grip he had, "Ruby Davis."

"Pleased to meet you, Ruby."

"Likewise."

Taking a sip of her drink, Ruby couldn't resist asking: "Cash, that's unusual. Is it some sort of nickname?"

Cash shook his head. "No, it's my actual name, after that bad boy Johnny. My elder brother's called Presley – our mum's mad about Elvis too."

"Aha!" said Ruby, enlightened. "Good names... I like them."

"Yeah, not too bad I suppose. I dread to think if we'd had a sister what she would have been called though, Dolly perhaps? Not so good."

Another quiet moment passed.

"Do you come here often?" said Cash, attempting to fill the gap. "Sorry, that's such a cliché! I just meant I haven't seen you in here before." He looked mortified.

"That's okay," Ruby rushed to reassure him, "it's as good a question as any, and yes, I do come here quite often. It's my local; I work just up the road."

"Oh right, I'm usually at the other end of town actually, at The Snowdrop, thought I'd pop in here for a change tonight though. I work locally as well. What do you do?"

And here it was, so soon, the question she always dreaded. How should she reply? The answer: '*I see dead people*' rarely enamoured her to strangers even if they had seen and enjoyed the film *Sixth Sense*. Rather, it tended to make them look at her with barely concealed horror before making some excuse, any excuse, no matter how trivial, and hightailing it from her, condemning her mid-flight as some sort of fruit loop. Until they encountered a problem of the spiritual kind that is. Then they flew right back.

Refusing to be embarrassed, however, and reminding herself that her profession was just as valid as any other, she replied confidently, "I'm a surveyor, a psychic surveyor."

"A what?" he asked, clearly baffled.

Holding her head high, she continued, "I run a company called Psychic Surveys, just a short walk from here up the High Street, opposite the castle. I survey houses for paranormal presence and, if such a presence exists, I work either alone or with a team of psychics to send that presence into the light, where it belongs."

"You're a ghost hunter?" gasped Cash, his eyes wide, not with horror she was quick to note, but fascination.

"We don't call them ghosts, we call them spirits," she pointed out. "And we certainly do not go hunting for them."

"Wow! I never thought I'd be sitting in a pub on a Monday night talking to a ghost hunter!"

"As I've just explained," Ruby replied, a little peevishly this time, "I am not a ghost hunter, I'm a psychic surveyor. There's a difference."

Nodding towards their empty glasses Cash said, "Well,

whatever that difference is, I'd love to hear about it. Another drink?"

Ruby contemplated declining. It had been a long day and that hot bath she had imagined earlier, filled to the brim with bubbles, poured from the green bottle, the one that promised to ease her aches and pains, was calling to her. But there was something about Cash that intrigued her and it wasn't just their mutual taste in books.

"Okay," she conceded, reaching for her purse, "a rum and coke, please."

"No, I'll get these. It's a shame this is a Harveys pub and not a Shepherd Neame. If it was Shepherd Neame I'd get a pint of Spooks, as it is Bonfire Boy will have to do." He winked cheekily at her before heading to the bar.

With his back to her, Ruby was able to scrutinise Cash more closely. He was tall, six foot at least. His skin light caramel in colour and his black hair closely cropped, giving him a clean, streamlined look. In jeans, Timberland boots and a jacket, he was dressed casually, but not without style. Attempting a stab at his age, she'd put him at around twenty- eight – four years older than her.

When he came back with their drinks, Ruby endeavoured to change the subject.

"So, what do *you* do for a living?" she asked breezily.

"I'm a website designer, freelance."

Ruby sat abruptly up. "A website designer, seriously, you're not kidding me?"

"Er, no, I'm definitely not kidding you." Clearly he was amused by her somewhat extreme reaction.

"It's just, I need a website," she attempted to explain her enthusiasm before adding somewhat dejectedly, "but I suppose you're expensive. You guys always are."

"Hey, not so fast, I'm very reasonable actually. We could come to some sort of deal, I'm sure. But enough about my profession, it's not exactly mind-blowing, not like yours. Tell me more about Psychic Surveys."

Ruby sighed. She did think his profession was pretty mind-blowing actually, the wonderful world of computers as mysterious to her as the paranormal world was to others. Still, at least he wanted to know more, this man beside her; at least he wasn't running in the opposite direction.

"What do you want to know exactly?" she asked, slightly defeated.

Cash ran his hand across his smooth, stubble-free chin. "God, where do I start? Actually..." he continued, suddenly looking rather pleased with himself, "that's as good a place as any – God. Do you do all this spirit banishing on behalf of the church?"

"It is not banishing," she corrected once again, wondering how often she would have to do so during the course of their conversation. "It's sending spirits to the light, home in other words, where they belong and where sometimes, for a variety of reasons, they are reluctant to go. And no, I am not working on behalf of the church nor do I affiliate myself with any type of organised religion. The church carries out exorcisms; that is their domain and quite different to what I do."

"In what way?" quizzed Cash, his eyes reminding her of melted chocolate.

Striving to remain professional under his gaze, she continued, "Let's just say Psychic Surveys promotes a more holistic approach to paranormal problems. In my experience, humble though it may be, trapped spirits are far from demonic, they are simply confused and upset, frightened even. They need a helping hand, compassion, a little reassurance. They tend to go quite peacefully then. There is really very little drama involved."

Taking a swig of his ale and leaning back in his seat, Cash was obviously warming to the subject.

"So, what about gadgets? Do you take lots of gadgets with you when you go to a haunting?"

27

Gadgets? Ruby was baffled. *What is it with men and gadgets?*

"No," she replied, exasperated. "There's really no need for EVP recorders, EMF metres or indeed ambient thermometers, despite what you may have seen on *Most Haunted*. And anyway, that kind of equipment is usually used to detect presences. We don't need to do that. We use psychic connection to detect. Afterwards, when a spirit has been sent home, we use crystals, herbs and bells to cleanse the atmosphere, to renew it."

"Are you psychic?"

She was taken aback by his bluntness. "Yes, yes I am."

"You actually see ghosts?"

"On occasion, but more often than not I sense them. Very few spirits are able to summon up enough energy to manifest. That's more the stuff of horror movies."

"Cool..." he said, taking another long swig.

"Believe it or not, most people have some sort of psychic ability; but the tendency is to suppress it."

"Really?" said Cash, clearly unconvinced. "I can quite honestly say I've never had a psychic experience in my life, not once, ever."

"I said *most* people. We're not talking about an exact science here."

"It's annoying though," continued Cash, undaunted. "You know, when people start telling you about a ghostly experience they've had and then everybody starts chipping in with spooky tales of their own? Well, I'm out on a limb, I can't contribute at all. I've got nothing to say. It's dead boring," and then realising the pun, he laughed.

Ruby was really warming to him. He seemed harmless enough, relaxed around her, which counted for something. She also liked the fact he was totally closed to the spirit world, accustomed as she was to being in the company of other psychics, it made a refreshing change.

"Believe me," she said, finishing the dregs of her second drink, "being psychic is no picnic. When you're standing in line at the post office, that's all you want to be doing, not dealing with some spirit tapping you repeatedly on your shoulder, begging you to give a message to the person standing in front of you."

"Has that really happened?" Cash was aghast.

"It has," Ruby nodded.

"And what did you do?"

"I waited until we'd left the post office, went over to the person in question and imparted the message. She, however, threatened to call the police. Thought I was mad, even though I'd told her something I couldn't possibly have known, that only her aunt – the spirit tapping me on the shoulder – could have known. But what could I do? The message she had to relay was important. I couldn't *not* say anything."

"Tough call." The expression on his face was suitably grave.

"On occasion, yes," Ruby agreed. "But at least I've had expert guidance in how to deal with my ability. It runs in my family. Through the female line."

"Guided by your mum you mean?"

Keeping her voice steady, she replied "No, not my mum, my grandmother."

"Oh," said Cash, leaning forward slightly, clearly interested in hearing why – Ruby, however, was not about to go into details with a complete stranger.

Cash must have sensed her reluctance because, to his credit, he didn't pursue the matter. After a few moments, he said, "Can it be taught, this psychic ability?"

"Taught? Not exactly. Developed perhaps."

"Even in me?"

"Even in you."

Seeing the doubt cross his face, she continued, "You say you have no psychic ability at all, but how many times have you thought of someone, your mum say, and the next minute she's ringing you? Or perhaps you've left the house one morning feeling uneasy? Because you need to be somewhere fast, you dismiss it as paranoid nonsense. You drive to work and a car comes out of nowhere, narrowly avoiding you. You remember that feeling of unease; you think perhaps I'm not paranoid after all. Any of that sound familiar?"

Looking surprised, Cash thought a moment. "Yeah, yeah, I can identify with that."

"Well, that's *your* sixth sense – an ability to tune into the unseen world around you. And you do have it, Cash, even you."

"Hmmm," said Cash, tongue-in-cheek now. "I'm psychic after all!"

Ruby returned his smile, noting as she did so how white and even his teeth were. She liked good teeth in a man. And a good set of strong, wide shoulders. Just like his.

"Another drink?" he asked after a while.

"Are you trying to get me drunk?" she teased.

"Maybe..." he batted right back. "Another rum and coke?"

"Okay," Ruby capitulated the relaxing effects of the first two drinks kicking in. "But this will have to be my last, I've got a busy day tomorrow. Here, my shout."

"No, you can pay next time."

Next time, thought Ruby as Cash returned to the bar. *How come he's so sure there's going to be a next time?* Annoyingly, her intuition remained silent.

Returning with the drinks and settling himself in beside her once more, Cash asked, "So why do you do it? This job you do. Why spend a lifetime dealing with the dead?"

"Because they need help; every bit as much as the living. Because... it's my duty."

"Your duty? How come?"

"Look," said Ruby, picking her drink up then placing it back down without taking a sip. "The spirit world is not full of crazed ghouls, it's populated by those who were once human, ordinary people like you and me, who have found themselves caught between this world and whatever lies beyond. They can't move on, for so many reasons – perhaps their death was

30

sudden, unexpected, perhaps they can't bear to leave a loved one behind, a child perhaps; very often a child. But they have to. Their time on earth is over. The next adventure calls. If I can help them on their way, then it's my duty to do so."

"That necklace you're wearing, it's nice. What stone is it?"

Her hand reaching up to touch her throat, she was surprised at how swiftly he had changed the subject. Had her talk of other-worldly matters finally unsettled him?

"Erm... its obsidian," she replied after a few moments.

"Unusual," he said, still eyeing the purply black stone in its solid silver setting.

"It's..." she hesitated and then, thinking *Sod it,* she continued. "It's one of several stones used to protect against negative energy. It can come in handy sometimes."

Cash was grinning now, quite openly, definite amusement in his eyes.

"What?" Ruby said, unsure whether to be offended by his reaction or to laugh along with him.

"Nothing," he replied, breaking eye contact to finish his pint. "So, you need a website do you?"

"I do, yes." Ruby finished her drink too.

"I'll strike a deal with you then."

"A deal? What...?"

"I'll design and build a website for you if you let me accompany you on one of your... surveys."

Surveys? Not a haunting? He was learning the lingo at least. But no, she couldn't possibly take him to a survey, what would Theo say? She was about to protest when he started again.

"I promise I won't be a nuisance or anything. I'll just observe. I could, I don't know, hold a crystal or something. Please, I'm really interested."

Please? It was nice he had added that at least. Tired as well as lightheaded, she sensed he'd be difficult to turn down. And, in a way, she was flattered. No one had ever asked her if they could come along as politely as that. And she might even get a website

31

out of it.

"Okay," she said at last. "Not tomorrow though, Wednesday. I'm going to visit a large house up country a bit, near Framfield. It's presided over by the movie star who used to live there, apparently. One of my team has already surveyed it; I'm going along to get a 'feel' for the case myself before deciding on a course of action. You can come with me if you like."

"It's lucky that December's a quiet month for me, I'll rearrange my work so I can join you, I'd hate to miss out," he answered, smiling at her – a rather spine tingling smile, she had to admit.

After giving him the address of her office and telling him to meet her there at nine sharp on Wednesday morning, she stood up, swaying she was sure as she bent to collect her coat. Forcing herself to get a grip, she squeezed round the side of the table furthest from him, saying goodbye as she did so.

"See you Wednesday!" he called after her, his rich, deep voice sending shivers down her spine once more.

Chapter Three

The next morning, as she twisted her long brown hair into a neat chignon and pulled some tendrils down to frame her face on either side, Ruby could not believe what she had done. She blamed that third rum and coke entirely for clouding her judgement, for making her think it was okay to allow a non-psychic, an almost complete stranger, to accompany her on a survey – and one that might draw public attention too. But Cash had been persuasive, she'd give him that, dangling the carrot of a website in front of her nose. He certainly knew how to tempt a girl.

Slicking mascara onto her already long enough lashes, she wondered what harm it could do, him tagging along. None really, she supposed, it was a survey, nothing more. He'd get an insight into what she did and hopefully she'd get something more concrete from him.

And she had to admit, Cash was nice – very nice. It had been a long time since she'd met someone as nice, a member of the opposite sex that is. Aside from a few awkward moments at the start, they had got on well. She couldn't deny it; it felt good to think she'd be seeing him again. But she hoped he wouldn't get the wrong idea about her. As attractive as he was, she wasn't in the market for a boyfriend. The last serious relationship she'd had, a couple of years ago, hadn't ended too well. Although she always tried to keep her professional and personal lives separate, sometimes they overlapped; she couldn't help it, particularly if she had to deal with an emotionally traumatised spirit. Cases like these not only drained her, they upset her too. Although initially they had got on well, Adam had always found her job hard to come to terms with and certainly never wanted to deal with any fallout from it. He had preferred to ignore it, brush it under the carpet, and would get annoyed with her if she even so much as hinted to any of his friends what she did. She'd always suspected that he was embarrassed by her, though Adam had never admitted it. After a while, she'd grown tired of his attitude – she had nothing to be embarrassed of – and they'd spilt up. It was easier to be alone.

Applying lipstick, a plum shade, only slightly darker than her natural lip colour, Ruby checked her appearance before heading, once again, to Brookbridge. Dressed in boots, smart jeans and a fitted v-necked sage green jumper that leant warmth to her skin tone and hazel eyes, she decided she looked just the right side of 'smart' – not office-type 'smart' but casual 'smart' – a look carefully cultivated over the years to put her clients at ease. She was sure most of them expected some raging 'New Age' hippie to turn up, complete with flowing skirts and tie-dye bandana. She could see the relief in their eyes when she arrived and they saw that she was not some nut job after all; that she was, in fact, just like them.

Grabbing her navy three-quarter length coat off the hook beside her and shrugging it on, she left her ground floor flat, the lower half of a Victorian house in De Montfort Road, set one street back from the main thoroughfare through town. Almost immediately outside was parked her dark blue Ford Focus. Not a glamorous car, by any stretch of the imagination, but a reliable one and, more importantly, cheap to fix when it broke down, which to its credit and her relief, it hardly ever did.

Brookbridge was thirty minutes from Lewes: a pleasant drive, down a succession of country roads, some narrower than others, flanked either side with green fields and trees, many of them bare, having shed their leaves as autumn deepened into winter. Passing through the tiny village of Cromer, which had given the old asylum its name, Ruby turned left onto another country road, a road that eventually led to Heathfield if she continued along it. Instead, she turned off at the estate, bypassing a billboard which proudly informed anyone interested that highly desirable houses were still available to buy, with 2, 3, 4 or 5 bedrooms to choose from. *Highly desirable?* It was not how she'd describe them, and not just because of their former residents. The estate looked hastily thrown up, profit being the obvious motive. Windows and doors in cheap white plastic – no character whatsoever, just a series of bland boxes built side by side. What's more, old asylum buildings still lay dotted around the estate's fringes. They were boarded up now, except for the odd gap where local kids had torn down the chipboard panels looking for cheap thrills – and no doubt sometimes getting more than they'd bargained for. And there were usually billboards outside these buildings too – this time advertising the site's development potential. Future work at least, mused Ruby, and it wasn't the developers she was thinking of. Beside the estate lay extensive woodland, part of what was known as the ancient Forest of Anderida during the Roman occupation of Britain. Cool and leafy, Ruby had been for a walk there once but the atmosphere was oppressive; nothing to do with the Romans, more the pain of the asylum inmates reaching far and wide.

Turning into Rowan Drive and noting some of the residents had already placed heavily decorated Christmas trees strategically in their windows, Ruby parked neatly in front of No.13. She was standing on the pavement, admiring No.15's Christmas tree, the lights switched on despite it being daytime, a warm red and green glow reaching tantalisingly outwards, when a woman with dyed-blonde hair scraped mercilessly back into a ponytail came rushing at her, shouting, "At last! At last!"

Grabbing hold of Ruby's arm, the woman, her client Ruby presumed, practically dragged her up the garden path and into her house.

Shivering dramatically as she closed the door, Sarah Atkins

spoke hurriedly.

"I don't know what's in this house, but I *hate* being alone here. Not that I ever am – alone that is – he watches me, everywhere I go. In the shower or when I'm getting undressed, that's when I sense him the strongest, the bloody pervert. I used to love horror movies I did, the scarier the better. You know them *Hellraiser* films, *Saw*, that sort of thing. He's put me right off them!"

Ruby could tell as soon as she entered the house that there was no spiritual presence whatsoever and she was surprised. On this estate, calls to Psychic Surveys were normally well founded. So many of the people incarcerated at the Cromer Asylum had ended their pitiful lives on this ground and, on passing, had found themselves trapped between two planes: unable to believe that only love waited for them from hereon in, they were still reeling from the pain and terror that dominated their former existence. In dealing with them, she, Theo or Ness would often call upon spirit guides to come forth, to encourage them home – the battle-scarred, as she often thought of Cromer's former inmates, limping onwards, bloodied and bowed by the horrors and confusion of mental illness and the surprising many who had chosen to abuse rather than help them. The atmosphere at No.13, however, was unusually light and unencumbered.

"So, what or who do you think it is?" Mrs Atkins continued. "A former inmate or something? A schizo, perhaps? A mass murderer?"

Blimey, thought Ruby, *she really has watched too many horror films.*

Finishing the tea that had been offered to her, Ruby said, "I really can't say Mrs Atkins, at least not right now. I need to do a walk-through first, if that's okay, examine every room in the house, see if I can sense something."

"Oh, you'll be able to sense it alright," Mrs Atkins declared, "he's relentless!"

It didn't take long to do the walk-through, Mrs Atkins's

house was one of the smaller ones on the estate; two bedrooms only, the second bedroom a guest room, plainly furnished, so no evidence of children either. Walking into the main bedroom next, Ruby winced. Not so plainly furnished, it resembled a tart's boudoir: three walls painted deep red, plus a wallpapered feature wall; its flocked monochrome pattern a somewhat stark contrast. A pair of black fluffy handcuffs had been left brazenly on the dressing table alongside a packet of condoms – the ribbed variety, for extra sensation apparently. As Mrs Atkins shivered downstairs, Ruby shivered upstairs at the thought of the antics that went on in here.

Returning to the kitchen, Ruby calmly met Mrs Atkins's almost gleeful eyes. "I can sense no presence in your home at all, Mrs Atkins. You are not being haunted."

"Rubbish!" the woman screeched, as though she'd been expecting Ruby to say such a thing all along. "I feel him everywhere, I'm telling you. Do it again."

Normally, Ruby would do everything she could to appease a client: burn sage sticks in every room, recommend the use of crystals and the regular burning of candles or oils – eucalyptus, pine, lavender, all meant to cleanse and purify. Windows too, she would tell them, open them regularly; let the stale air out and fresh air in, keep the energy in the house moving. But she didn't like Mrs Atkins's attitude, it was no better than those who had failed the emotionally disturbed all those years ago.

"Mrs Atkins, there is no need to do it again. I have carefully surveyed every room and there is no spiritual presence in any of them. I'm sorry to say I think your imagination might be the culprit here – perhaps from viewing one too many horror films? If you're not happy with my assessment, I apologise, but there are plenty of other psychics you can call on for a second opinion. In my opinion, however, all is clear. As for today, I won't charge, call it a goodwill gesture."

"Charge? Of course you won't charge," Mrs Atkins seemed to be unravelling before her, "you haven't bloody *done* anything!"

"The reason I haven't done anything," Ruby countered, edging her way towards the door and freedom, "is because there's nothing *to* be done. Something to be grateful for, I should think."

Mrs Atkins quickly followed after her, her voice shrill in Ruby's ear. "But other houses on the estate, they have ghosts. Why haven't I?"

Ruby faltered at her words. It was never the dead that bothered her, always the living.

"Goodbye, Mrs Atkins," she sighed, before getting the heck out of there.

***

"Hi, Ness," said Ruby, pulling up outside the house of the ghost dog in Heathfield.

"Hi, Ruby. Bad morning at Brookbridge?"

"You could say that, but nothing to do with the dead."

"Oh, a wannabe." Ness was immediately sympathetic.

"Yep, a wannabe," confirmed Ruby, also using the nickname she and her team had for those who 'wannabe' haunted. "Anyway, next up. Let's go and see if we can send 'Rover' to join his friends at the Rainbow Bridge."

Knocking on the front door, solid oak this time she was glad to note, it was a couple of minutes before it opened rather hesitantly.

"Psychic Surveys?" said the occupier, another young woman, but this one looked embarrassed rather than manic – a slight improvement.

After confirming their identity, Ruby and Ness were ushered in; following Miss Mills to the kitchen, they were offered more tea. Depending on how many houses she visited in a day, Ruby sometimes felt awash with the stuff, unable to face any more once the working day was over. After explaining the procedure and asking a few questions, Ruby and Ness drained their mugs and made their way upstairs to the landing.

"This is it," said Miss Mills, lingering behind them, "where the noise comes from."

"Have you ever seen him?" asked Ruby, wondering about the dog's energy levels.

"No, of course not," blushed the woman before beating a hasty retreat downstairs.

Ruby turned to face Ness. She could definitely feel a presence – a wagging tail, a wet nose, a creature that sensed her right back. Initially worried it may have been a Rottweiler or a pit bull, she was relieved to sense a Labrador instead, a usually more amenable dog.

To test if she was right, she murmured, "Black?"

"Aha," nodded Ness.

"Labrador?"

"That's what I'm seeing."

"Male?"

"Male."

"Hey boy," whispered Ruby, closing her eyes and tuning in, "stop barking at me and listen up instead."

The dog immediately hushed, although its tail continued to wag expectantly.

Surprised by his obedience, Ruby continued. "You've been a good dog, I can tell; a cherished family pet. But the family you were a part of, they don't live here anymore. A new family live here and they're not exactly appreciating your efforts."

Sensing confusion, she kept talking. "Yes, I know that seems strange. But it's their house now, the new family, and their wishes count. You're a great guard dog, one of the best, but you don't have to guard anymore. You can rest awhile, in the light. You'll love it there. Listen, Jed is it, is that your name?" Ruby looked at Ness who nodded that she thought it was too. "Listen, Jed, the light that's shining, go towards it. That's home now."

"His tail's stopped wagging," Ness pointed out.

"I know, I think we're getting through to him," Ruby replied, somewhat amazed.

"He's turning to go," continued Ness, "he's walking away from us. He's still not wagging his tail though."

"He will, once he's in the light."

"He's looking back, he's unsure."

"Go on, boy," Ruby encouraged, "it's okay, there's nothing to worry about. Walk on."

After a few moments, Ness said, "He's gone."

"Good," said Ruby, hoping Jed was indeed furiously wagging his tail again and that he'd be amply rewarded on the other side for his gentle and loyal nature.

They rejoined Miss Mills in the kitchen and told her what had transpired.

"Oh, thank goodness," Miss Mills exclaimed. "I can't bear dogs, dead or alive."

After handing them a cheque, Ruby and Ness were promptly shown the door. Clearly Miss Mills wasn't overly fond of mediums either.

Walking to Ruby's Ford, which was parked next to the older woman's equally insalubrious Vauxhall, Ness said, "Our first encounter with an animal, huh? Went well, didn't it?"

"It did indeed," said Ruby, as pleased as Ness was, "surprisingly well."

"Are you off to meet Theo now?"

"Yes, in Hove. And then that should be it until Highdown Hall tomorrow."

"Oh yes, I'll be interested to see what you make of Highdown."

"What we'll all make of Highdown soon enough."

After saying goodbye, Ruby drove on to her next appointment. The journey, via Lewes, then past Brighton and on into Hove, was trouble-free, the roads clear, but still she felt uncomfortable, unable to shake off the feeling that she wasn't travelling alone. She knew it was possible for spirits to attach themselves to humans but such an occurrence was rare – normally they preferred to attach themselves to places rather than people. Rare, but not impossible – hence the need to visualise yourself wrapped in a blanket of white light before a cleansing, a protective shield to ward against such things happening, psychic armour almost. Ruby and her team never failed to do so; they had done so today, what had gone wrong?

Confused, Ruby chanced a surreptitious glance at the seat beside her; she then looked into the rear view mirror but could see nothing, no outline, no manifestation enjoying a scenic ride, just empty space. Or was it the illusion of empty space?

Driving past the Greyhound Stadium, past the traffic lights at the intersection of Old Shoreham Road and into Sackville Road, Hayes on the corner selling an abundance of Christmas trees, glorious even in their pre-adorned state, Ruby continued under the railway bridge before taking a right into a popular residential area known as Poets Corner – a series of streets named after Shelley, Wordsworth, Livingstone and their ilk.

Pulling up behind Theo's rather more stylish Fiat 500, pearlised white with Italian side stripes even though Theo claimed not a drop of Mediterranean blood, she felt the sensation of something wet brushing her hand. Surprised, she looked down and there he was, only just visible – Jed, the black Labrador, looking up at her eagerly with love, adoration and, yes, she was sure of it, unswerving loyalty in those soft canine eyes of his.

"Oh, Jed," she said as his manifestation faded, "what am I supposed to do with you?"

Chapter Four

Jed had in fact come in very useful during the cleansing of the house in Hove. As in life, so in death; children respond well to animals and this particular child had been no exception, playing enthusiastically with his new-found friend. Jed dutifully rolling over, allowing his tummy to be tickled, jumping back up again, nuzzling the boy, licking his face profusely. The spirit child had laughed and laughed – a wonderful sound. But, as heart-warming as it was to hear, Ruby had reminded herself that this was not a happy child they were dealing with, far from it. He was sad, lost; he wanted his mother, a mother he couldn't have again, not in this world anyway. A mother who, according to the new owners, had moved away shortly after his death from meningitis, unable to bear these four walls without her living child there with her. The owners had been quick to point out that the boy hadn't died at the house, but at the local hospital. It didn't matter though, if spirits returned, they tended towards places significant to them, places they were happy in during life, places where they felt they belonged.

Timothy, the boy, understood nothing of this.

I want my mummy. Where is she?

All he knew was that he was alone.

"How old are you, sweetheart?" Theo had asked him, her voice as soft and soothing as a favourite aunt's.

Five! The boy had announced his age proudly. *Five and three quarters.* A clever boy, if a little precocious. *Who is that other boy?*

"He's called Dylan." Ruby had spoken next. "He lives here

now. This is his bedroom."

No! A stomp of the foot. *This is my bedroom. Where are my toys? I don't like his. Tell him to go.*

Timothy was beginning to get cross, the energy around him building. On the floor, Lego and cowboys started to vibrate, as if he were getting ready to throw them. The atmosphere became heavier, denser. Theo and Ruby did their best to placate him, but not even Theo's soothing voice could calm him. It was only when a great ball of fur had suddenly thundered in, rushing past them, straight to the child's side and distracting him, that the increasingly dangerous situation had been defused.

As the child began to laugh, Theo seized the chance to explain to Timothy that he had passed; a hard thing to get across at the best of times, let alone to a small child. Timothy, however, steadfastly ignored her, too absorbed in Jed.

I always wanted a dog, he said, to no one in particular, probably to Jed.

Patiently, Theo tried again. "Do you see a light, Timothy? A beautiful, bright light? It's there if you look. Tell me, can you see it?"

No response.

"It's sparkling too," Theo continued, "like a beam from a magic lantern."

That got his attention.

What is it? He couldn't resist asking.

"It's home."

As the boy stared, Theo spoke again.

"Touch it," she encouraged, "feel how lovely it is, Timothy. It's like the warmest, the softest, the fluffiest blanket you've ever known, wrapping itself around you."

But the boy did not move.

"Timothy?" Ruby prompted.

A shake of the head.

I want my mummy, he repeated, his hand, previously deep in Jed's fur, faltering.

43

Theo ventured on.

"I know you do, sweetheart. And she wants you too, so very much. But she's not here anymore. She had to go and live in another house. A new family live here and this is their home now. Your home is in the light. There are people there, people who know and love you, people who will look after you until mummy can be with you again."

Ruby could see tears running down the boy's cheeks, tears that caused her own eyes to blur. Dealing with spirit children was always so damned hard.

"Darling..." but before Theo had a chance to say anything more, Ruby quietened her.

"Wait..." she whispered, laying a hand on her arm.

Jed was nudging the boy now with his nose, nudging him, Ruby presumed, towards the light. The boy was resistant at first, pushing the dog away, lost in sorrow again, thinking only of his mother – but Jed was relentless. Finally, the boy looked up.

Grandad? There was surprise and delight in his voice.

Both Theo and Ruby watched as the boy rose to his feet.

Grandad! He repeated the name, no surprise this time, just pure and sweet delight.

Turning away from them, from Jed, the boy ran to his grandfather and, as the old man's arms encircled him, the atmosphere in the room immediately brightened. After a few moments, Timothy's grandfather pulled away and, taking the boy's hand in his, led the child home.

It was only when they had faded entirely that Jed returned to Ruby's side, looking, she had to admit, extremely pleased with himself.

"You still can't stay," she said sternly. Then, unable to resist, she favoured him with an indulgent smile before turning to Theo, "I could murder a Starbucks."

"Me too," Theo eagerly agreed, "one of those caramel macchiato things." And with that she was off downstairs to break the good news to the anxious owners waiting below.

***

After a fitful night's sleep (mainly because Jed had taken up residence at the end of her bed, scratching constantly at some imaginary itch), Wednesday dawned bright and cold.

Yawning, Ruby removed her earplugs first and then her eye mask – essential nightwear as far as she was concerned, sensory deprivation giving her the best chance of remaining oblivious to any spirits that happened to be wandering about. Any spirit, that was, except Jed, his fidgets were too regular to ignore.

Cash, she thought as soon as her feet touched the ground, *I'm meeting Cash today.*

She was also going to Highdown Hall to meet Alan Kierney and Cynthia Hart for the first time. Excited at both prospects, she made her way to the bathroom. After a long, hot shower, the jets of water deliciously warm as they pummelled her neck and shoulders; she entered the kitchen, in dire need of caffeine. After several cups of coffee and a bowl of rice pops, she was ready to go, alert, even if artificially so.

If she walked at a brisk pace, it would take less than ten minutes to reach her office. Later, she would walk back with Cash to collect her car. And it was a pleasant walk, a walk she never tired of – past The Pelham Arms, reputedly one of the most haunted pubs in Sussex – although Ruby had never sensed anything there at all, Trevor House, a beautiful Grade II listed building that she coveted, and Lewes Old Grammar School. Dating back to the sixteenth century, she'd very much like to look inside the school building one day – to see what lingered there – a lost child perhaps, sitting at his desk, still trying to solve that wretched maths equation, or a headmaster unable to relinquish control.

She arrived outside her office just before nine, Cash a minute or so later.

"Hey," he said, striding confidently up to her, "good to see you again."

Ruby wondered if he was going to lean in for a hello kiss on her cheek and was both relieved and disappointed when he didn't. Instead, he simply stood before her, a grin on his handsome face and cold hands stuffed in jean pockets.

"Follow me," she said, turning from him to open the door before climbing the three flights of narrow stairs to the attic.

"Wow, this is... snug," he said upon entering.

"That's one way of putting it," she replied, before offering him tea.

"Yeah, please, white, no sugar."

Flicking the switch on the kettle, Ruby nodded towards her computer.

"We're not due at Highdown Hall until after ten thirty so I thought perhaps we could spend half an hour or so looking at some websites of businesses similar to mine first, to give us a few ideas of what we could do and what to avoid."

"Sure," said Cash, rather presumptuously seating himself in her captain's chair.

Grabbing a fold-up chair from the meeting table, she opened it pointedly beside him and then returned to the kettle to make the tea she had promised.

Handing him the warm mug, she said, "If I type in 'spiritual cleansing' or 'house healers', quite a few people in the same business as me come up – thing is, their websites are a bit, I don't know how to put it, spiritual I suppose."

"Spiritual?" Cash raised an eyebrow. "How strange!"

She ignored his sarcasm. "I want my website to be more pragmatic, down-to-earth – accessible to the masses if you like, not just the spiritually inclined."

"Like an estate agent's?" he said, clearly enjoying himself.

"Oh, shut up," she too suppressed a smile. "I think you know what I mean."

"I do," he said, serious again. "And I agree, a more pragmatic approach seems like a really good idea. Bring it all into the 21st century. I'll get some ideas mocked up."

"Really?" She could hardly believe her luck. "That would be great."

Sipping at her tea, Ruby noticed the confused look that had suddenly appeared on Cash's face.

"What is it?" she asked. "What's the matter?"

"I'm not sure," he answered. "I can smell something. No, don't worry, I don't mean you – or me for that matter, but something. The best I can describe it as is 'wet dog'."

"Wet dog?" repeated Ruby, equally as perplexed for a moment before looking around. "Jed, Jed where are you boy? Are you here?"

"Er, who's Jed?"

"The dog. You said you could smell him."

"You've got a dog?"

"No. Well, yes. Sort of."

As Cash continued to look bewildered, Ruby greeted Jed. "Oh, there you are. Where have you been? What have you been doing? You are indeed wet, you silly boy." And then as realisation dawned, she turned back to Cash and said, "You can smell him?"

"I can smell *something*," was Cash's hesitant reply.

"But you said you weren't psychic."

"I'm not."

"If you can smell wet dog, I wouldn't be so sure."

Quickly, she explained. "There is indeed a big, hairy, wet dog standing right beside us, wagging his tail. A ghost dog if you like. And you can smell him."

Cash looked shocked. He looked as if he were about to fall off her captain's chair and land rather heavily on the floor.

"Easy," said Ruby, adopting Theo's soothing voice. "It's probably just a one-off or something. An anomaly. Nothing to worry about."

"You're joking with me, right?" Cash answered, far from soothed.

"Honestly, I'm not," replied Ruby, biting down on her lip

now to keep from laughing. "Ness and I did a house cleansing yesterday, to remove the spirit of a dog – and we did. Except he hasn't gone where he's supposed to go, he's attached himself to me."

Looking at Jed fondly she continued, "Not that I mind really, he's a friendly lad and he's proved himself to be very useful so far. But he's got to go soon; he shouldn't be here."

His eyes wide and yes, she was sure of it, ever so slightly alarmed, Cash turned back to her laptop, touching base with more earthly matters – ideas for her website.

***

A short while later, Ruby and Cash walked back to her car and bundled themselves into it. The weather was still nothing less than arctic, so she turned the heater to maximum, hoping it wouldn't take too long to warm up – sometimes it did, sometimes it didn't, it was getting temperamental in its old age. Jed, meanwhile, had disappeared again – where to, she didn't know. Putting the Ford into gear, she pulled out of the parking space.

As she drove, she explained to Cash about the background of Highdown Hall. He nodded dutifully throughout before asking, "Have you seen any of Cynthia Hart's movies?"

"I must have done, when I was younger, but I don't really remember them."

"I remember *her*," Cash said. "Gorgeous she was; a real siren, but the movies yeah, a bit of a blur." After a slight pause, he continued. "Hey, we should have a movie night; get to know Cynthia in the flesh so to speak. What are you doing tomorrow evening?"

Taken aback by his eagerness, she could only reply, "Erm... nothing. I don't think."

"Good, I'll see if I can get a DVD of one of her films from somewhere and I'll come round to yours. Is eight okay?"

"Yeah, sure," she replied, wondering just how persistent Cash was going to be. As fascinated as he was by her at the moment, or with her profession at least, it wouldn't last. It never did. In her experience, men were simple creatures at heart, they preferred simple, uncomplicated lives and hers could never be described as such. But Cash as a boyfriend? She mustn't jump the gun. All he'd done was ask if she wanted to watch a movie with him, nothing more than that. As she carried on driving, she couldn't help stealing a sideways glance at him. He had a good profile she noted: straight nose, firm jaw line. And that caramel skin of his, it was lovely, making her feel so pale in comparison.

"Here we are," she said, turning off just before the village of Framfield into a country lane, "it's just down here. Another mile or two."

Negotiating the lane, not quite big enough for two cars to pass each other, Ruby stiffened.

"What's wrong?" said Cash, noticing.

"Oh nothing, I can just sense there was a nasty accident on this stretch of road, a while back, a car crash."

"How do you know?"

"Residual feelings," said Ruby.

"Which are?" queried Cash.

"Sorry," said Ruby, reminding herself she was in the company of a... a what? A normal person? A muggle as Harry Potter and co might have said. She endeavoured to explain.

"Residual feelings are emotions so intense they don't easily dissipate. They become etched into the atmosphere; they become *part* of the atmosphere, replaying over and over again on the airwaves, as though caught in a loop. Does that make sense?"

"Kind of..." said Cash, although he sounded unsure.

"Anyone can pick up on residual feelings," Ruby continued. "You don't have to be a psychic to be able to. If you walk into a house, for example, and you get a bad feeling about that house,

49

well, that could be because you've tuned into residual feelings left behind by either someone or some dramatic event that has taken place there. Most people just dismiss such feelings, they push them to the back of their minds, desensitise themselves after a while, but some take note, some listen to instinct and don't hang around."

Cash was nodding his head, taking it all in.

"So, what you just experienced, it's just feelings, there's no ghost attached?"

"No, if the spirit was still attached, we'd call it an intelligent haunting."

Ruby smiled. It was a lot for a novice to take in.

"The thing is," Ruby mused, "they're a strange mix of feelings. There's triumph and joy, but dark joy, not the kind that lifts your heart, and at the very last, just before impact I should imagine, there's disbelief and anguish."

"Maybe the driver had just heard his lotto numbers announced on the radio and then, in the same instance, realised he'd forgotten to buy that week's ticket. Maybe that could account for that sense of triumph going pear-shaped?"

"Maybe," Ruby rolled her eyes good-humouredly. Despite her previous misgivings, she was glad to have Cash along for the ride. He knew how to keep things light.

At last they reached their destination, not the house itself, but the gates to it, attached either side to sturdy stone columns, gleaming black once she imagined, now rusted in places. Tall and ornate, they had thoughtfully been left open by Mr Kierney for their arrival.

Slowing the car to a respectful speed, Ruby cruised up the driveway, admiring the expanse of well-kept green lawn on either side, which softened and blended into the trees in the distance. Rounding a corner, the house came into sight. To one side of it was a lake.

"Whoa!" said Cash, his mouth wide open. "This is some pile. I can see why the owner's staying put, ghost or not."

"It's *not* a ghost, it's a spirit," Ruby admonished. "And Cash, please remember, Mr Kierney is extremely unsettled by events at Highdown Hall. This is not a joke to him."

"Sorry," said Cash, suitably contrite.

Parking the car, they walked up the last stretch of driveway, the gravel crunching beneath their feet like the rice pops she'd had for breakfast. Snap, crackle and pop. As Cash had been awed by the house, so was she. It was magnificent. Gothic in style with those stone mullioned windows Ruby had only ever seen on National Trust properties. It had a turret too, reminding her of a Scottish castle she had once visited as a child with her grandmother, somewhere in Perth, a castle beginning with a 'B' but whose name in its entirety escaped her for now. Although Highdown Hall was far from being a castle, it was certainly impressive, fitting for a movie star.

Reaching the main entrance, a pair of studded double doors in silvered oak, Cash whispered, "What do we do? There's no bell."

Ruby searched; there must be a bell. Fists banging on these doors would make no impact whatsoever.

"Oh, look." Cash pointed to a black iron rod, also far from gleaming, with a heart shaped loop at the bottom. "I think we give this a pull."

Before she could do so, however, the right half of the double doors swung open. Only half visible in the interior gloom was her client, Mr Kierney. As he stepped forward, Ruby got a better view of him. Not a tall man, he was rather delicate in stature, his dark hair peppered with grey and his brown eyes similarly faded.

"Thank God you're here." Ruby was used to such greetings.

Beckoning them into the Grand Hall, complete with timber panelling and sweeping staircase, Ruby tried not to gawp. Her entire flat could fit into this space alone, she was sure of it. Returning her attention to Mr Kierney, she noticed him wring his hands together. Clearly he was the nervous type, and even more so now thanks to Cynthia.

"Upstairs," he said, bypassing any small talk, "it's mainly upstairs, in what used to be her bedroom. But the whole top floor is, I don't know, *alive* with her presence, ironically. She hates me being here, that bloody woman. And it's not fair;" his manner was petulant almost, "this is *my* house now, not hers. God knows how Aunt Sally put up with it."

Her eyes travelling the length of the staircase, Ruby was curious.

"Did your aunt ever report any unusual activity?" she asked.

"Well, no," Mr Kierney looked surprised to realise this. "Not that I know of anyway. She just holed herself up here after Cynthia died, inconsolable apparently after the death of her beloved mistress. Probably a bit eccentric, like my other aunt, Esme. My mother was the only sane one amongst them."

"And your mother, is she...?"

"Dead," replied Mr Kierney.

That explained why Sally had left Highdown Hall to her nephew then, thought Ruby. If Cynthia's death turned her into a recluse, that was probably why she'd never married or had children. And if the other sister was 'eccentric' perhaps she had no one other than Mr Kierney to leave it to.

"My colleague said you tend to sleep downstairs now. Do you feel safe down here at least?"

"I'm not sure 'safe' is the word." He looked almost annoyed that Ruby could even suggest such a thing. "But she can't seem to get me down here. Stays in that bedroom of hers, or of mine I should say, makes a bloody rumpus sometimes."

"And you definitely think it's Cynthia Hart?"

"Of course I do. Who else could it be?"

It could be anyone actually, thought Ruby. A spirit passing through, perhaps, somebody who lived here a century or more ago; it was an old house after all – Victorian definitely, some parts of it perhaps older, she'd have to check. But, like Theo, like Mr Kierney, she had a sense it was indeed Cynthia Hart that they were dealing with.

"Mr Kierney,' said Ruby at last. "I will need to survey the whole house, not just the bedroom, to make sure her presence is confined. Is that okay?"

"Yes, yes, that's fine," replied Mr Kierney, "but I'm not going with you, up there I mean."

"No, you don't have to. In fact, it's best we do this on our own." Then, appalled that she hadn't done so before, she introduced the young man standing eagerly beside her. "I'm sorry. This is Cash, Cash Wilkins. He's my, my... assistant."

Mr Kierney looked as if he couldn't give a damn who Cash was, backing away from them as if they too were fearsome entities. Cash, however, looked very much amused.

"Your assistant?" he said as soon as Mr Kierney had disappeared. "I like it."

"Well I could hardly say that you're some sort of voyeur could I, just in it for the cheap thrills?"

Cash pretended offense.

"Hey, I am not some sort of voyeur, I'm genuinely interested."

"Really?" Ruby still wasn't sure.

"*Really*," Cash affirmed, his tone more serious now. Trying to explain further, he added, "I don't know, it just seems really noble what you do, helping grounded spirits to move on, unusual but noble. Talking of which," he clapped his hands together, "what's your theory on why Cynthia's still here?"

"Hopefully we'll find out soon enough but as far as theory goes her passing was sudden, unexpected. It could be she doesn't realise she's passed."

Cash was unconvinced.

"Even after all this time?"

"In the spirit world, I don't think time's an issue."

Ruby returned her attentions to the house; the interior was even more impressive than the exterior. Surveying her surroundings, she moved over to the far wall.

53

"A portrait of Cynthia used to hang here," she stated, as much to herself as Cash. "I'm sure she's not best pleased it's been taken down."

To the left of the Grand Hall was another room, partially panelled this time and not just impressive but magnificent in its sheer size and grandeur, even though not a stick of furniture inhabited it now, apart from a couple of hard-backed chairs and a side table, somewhat randomly placed. Cynthia may have left the house to Sally Threadgold, but either the star's family or friends had descended like vultures on its contents or Sally had sold them all off one-by-one to pay the no doubt vast running costs. It was also impressively clean. Had Sally kept it that way or had Mr Kierney brought in a team of professionals upon arrival to do the honours?

"What's this room?" breathed Cash, looking about him.

"The ballroom I think," Ruby answered, also awe-struck.

Crossing the floorboards, several protesting as she did so, Ruby stopped by the first of two sets of French windows. Even now, in the depths of winter, the light poured in through them, animating the room. Ruby could easily imagine the parties that had taken place here; memories of which must be ingrained in the very walls themselves. Lavish, exciting parties, everyone focussed on having a good time, the time of their lives for some. But there were troubled spots too, definitely. A sense of something dark, anger and frustration in particular. Residual feelings – faint now, but very real to someone once.

Moving out of the ballroom and back into the Grand Hall, they explored further; the study, bereft of a writing desk and cosy fire, the library, where just a few books stood guard on recessed shelves, and the dining room, heavy red drapes with a golden pattern, the only adornment. The living room did have a few home comforts, including a large-screened TV, a coffee table and a modern-looking sofa bed pulled-out to full capacity, the dark blue duvet on top a rumpled mess. Ruby could feel nothing out of the ordinary in any of them. The kitchen too, not cosy but functional, very much a workplace, was completely free of spiritual presence. Briefly, Ruby wondered if Cynthia had even known where the kitchen was.

"Let's go upstairs," she said to Cash, returning again to the Grand Hall and heading for the staircase. As she did so, she couldn't help but notice him blanch a little at her words. *Ah, you're not as confident as you like to make out,* she thought.

The staircase too was awe-inspiring. Built of oak that had darkened considerably with age, Ruby could just imagine the effort various maids must have put in through the ages to keep it in tip top condition. She half expected to see the shade of some young nineteenth or twentieth century servant sitting on a step rubbing feverishly at a barley twist spindle as she climbed the stairs. Instead, only dust motes danced in the air. Each newel post was adorned with a heavily carved, almost ecclesiastical urn-shaped carving. As Ruby passed the half landing, she couldn't resist running her hand over the carving, knowing that Cynthia must have done the same thing too, many times over.

At the top of the stairs was a corridor with several doors leading presumably into bedrooms. Putting that theory to the test, she counted seven in total. Only three had beds in them, surprisingly modern looking beds, and wardrobes too, again modern in style rather than antique, brought from Mr Kierney's flat perhaps or purchased since he'd been in residence. Perhaps he planned to turn the place into a B&B – an opportunity to stay in a dead movie star's home – that would bring the punters flooding in for sure. The turret, Cynthia Hart's bedroom, was located at the end of the corridor. As she approached it, Ruby could feel powerful waves of anguish rushing towards her.

"Stop!" she shouted. Cash did so immediately.

"Cynthia, it appears, is one very unhappy lady. And when a spirit is unhappy, that's when they can be dangerous. You can't come in with me. You'll have to wait downstairs."

"Dangerous?" said Cash. "Are you serious? In that case, I'm

definitely coming in with you. You can't go in alone."

His sense of chivalry made her smile.

"Don't worry," she said, "I've taken steps to protect myself. I need to establish a psychic connection with Cynthia and it will be easier to do so if I don't have you to worry about."

When she saw him about to protest further, she insisted "Cash, please, I know what I'm doing. I've been doing it for long enough. Seriously, you can't come in with me."

"Okay," said Cash at last, "but I'm not going downstairs. I'll wait here for you, on the landing. Within shouting distance."

Conceding, Ruby smiled at him again before entering Cynthia's domain.

Chapter Five

Who is she? What does she want? How dare she enter unbidden?

From the safety of the shadows in which she dwelt, Cynthia Hart stared at the intruder. It was not the man this time, that pathetic, little man who insisted he lived here now, that he was Sally's nephew, even though she knew damn well Sally didn't have a nephew, but a girl – young and presentable but not glamorous at all, with brown hair piled on top of her head in a most unkempt manner. Jeans she had on, jeans, boots and a jumper – a dreadful way to dress. No celebration of her femininity at all.

Out! Cynthia screamed. *Get out!*

"No," the girl replied calmly, startling her.

She could hear her! The man couldn't. Sally hadn't, despite her repeated attempts to gain her maid's attention. But this girl could. Instead of being relieved, however, Cynthia became angrier still. She had refused her. How dare she? Who did she think she was?

Aggression causing her lip to curl, she prepared to rush at the intruder, just as she had rushed at the man, to beat her back, to rid the room of her, to reclaim her sanctuary, but she was stopped in her tracks. The girl was speaking again.

"I'm Ruby Davis. I believe you've already met my friend, Theo. We want to help you."

Theo? Did she mean that ludicrous old woman who had violated her privacy too, when was it, a day ago, two days? She didn't know. Time was so hard to grasp suddenly.

"Cynthia. It is Cynthia isn't it?"

57

Of course it's Cynthia! This is my house. You are not welcome in it.

"Cynthia, I repeat, I mean no harm. I just want to help. Please, allow us to help you."

Help? How can you help? A chit of a girl! Nobody can help. Nobody.

Get out! She screamed again and then, more in despair than anger, *Get out.*

***

When feeling threatened, Cynthia did as she always did; she retreated into the comfort of memories, her last memory in particular – the party of course. It had been glorious, every detail planned meticulously; the champagne, vintage Laurent-Perrier, served in crystal glasses, the big band playing not the rock 'n' roll tunes so favoured of late, but beautiful songs from the 1920s, 30s and 40s – 'Blue Moon', 'Embraceable You', 'Sunrise Serenade' – reinforcing the sophistication of the occasion.

Despite so many beauties, all eyes in the room had been on her, as Lytton had promised so long ago. Not a man in the room could tear his gaze away, or a woman, their naked adoration breathing life into her limbs. How she had danced that night! Her feet had barely touched the ground. Would-be suitors fighting amongst themselves to partner her, whisking her round the dance floor as though she weighed no more than a child, whispering words of love and dedication into her ear, begging her for more than just one dance. And from the sidelines, John Sterling, the world's most respected actor, had devoured her with his impossibly dark eyes. Driving her wild inside with desire, a desire she refused to reveal, knowing her reticence to do so infuriated him. Would she take him to her bed that night? Show how grateful she was for the lavish gift he had had sent to her earlier in the day. She hadn't decided.

Possibly not. Drive him wilder still.

She remembered laughing, her head thrown back in consummate joy as she was held in a succession of arms and still John stared at her, not moving from where he stood, ignoring the multitude of sycophants who gathered around him, not just up and coming actresses but actresses at the top of their game, all desperate for his attention as so many were for hers. He ignored them, his eyes only for her. It was a wonderful night, a night full of magic and then... it was over. No big band tunes, no laughter or admiring comments, no more John pleading silently with her, nothing. Where had everyone gone? She couldn't understand it. Why was she alone? Except for Sally, who occasionally wept on the ground before her, clutching her fuchsia dress. But how so, when she was still wearing it?

She had drunk several glasses of champagne that night, but not enough to cause such confusion, surely? Usually it was her preference to remain sober at public events, refusing to allow one slur or stagger to mar her 'darling of the movie world' reputation. Perhaps she should have refrained on this occasion too? But it was her birthday, a private affair, *and* it was Christmas Eve. Everybody was allowed to drink on Christmas Eve!

Perhaps the haze she was in was the result of some hideous concoction. Some lesser starlet, insane with jealousy, had surreptitiously laced her glass with something. Yes! That had to be it, it made sense. But if so, why had no one realised she was missing and come rushing to her aid? She employed enough people to take care of her. Where were they?

Reaching a hand up to her temple, her head felt as the land had looked earlier from her bedroom window, wreathed in mist. How long had she been in darkness? Seconds, minutes, hours, longer than that? Years? Some days it felt like it. Not that she'd aged, judging from her reflection in the mirror when she had at last dared to look into it. A reflection that looked more distant than usual, but nonetheless, she had recognised herself –

her smooth complexion, her Titian curls, that part of the bargain upheld at least. The bargain? No, she mustn't think of that. To do so was dangerous. She had dues to pay; she knew she did, but so soon? Surely not! To be plucked from the spotlight when it was at its brightest, that was cruel, evil. But then wasn't evil what she had bargained with?

Cynthia felt cold again. As if icy arms had found her at last and wrapped themselves around her, holding her tight, entombing her. *No,* she whimpered, filled with terror, an emotion all too familiar now. *Hide, I need to hide. I'll be alright if I can hide.*

Crouching further into the corner, she made herself small, smaller still, shielding her eyes from the Devil searching for her. The Devil that she sensed was near. It was too soon to pay. She didn't want to pay. Not now, not ever.

Damn Lytton! She raged as sobs tore through her.

***

Lytton? Who's Lytton? Ruby wondered, careful to keep her thoughts shrouded for fear of enraging Cynthia further. And what was the bargain she had struck with him? So quickly the dead star's anger had given way to terror. A terror that seemed to be anchoring her, that was connected in some way to someone called Lytton. It was clear Cynthia had no recollection of her passing. She remembered the party it seemed, but not the heart attack or the events leading up to it. Perhaps an explanation was the key to releasing her.

Looking around the bedroom, Ruby could see what Theo had meant; it was most definitely a shrine. Kept that way by Sally presumably, the devoted maid.

Velvet drapes, deep red in colour, like the precious stone she herself was named after and sumptuous if dusty to behold, adorned two sets of floor to ceiling windows. In between the windows was a dressing table, art deco in style with an assortment of silver brushes and combs artfully arranged on top as well as crystal scent bottles, some full, and some half full. On each and every item lay more dust. She knew if she scrutinised further, she'd see cobwebs too. If Mr Kierney had employed a team of cleaners, Cynthia obviously hadn't let them into her bedroom either.

Double doors with ornate handles, also art deco in style, led to a walk-in wardrobe, empty but for a few padded hangers swaying slightly in the breeze that Ruby had created by opening the doors. Where were Cynthia's clothes? Lovingly placed in storage perhaps? In the attic above them? Or perhaps they'd been auctioned off or sold to a museum somewhere. There was another door, a peek around it revealing a large en-suite bathroom in shimmering white marble, a sizeable glass bottle that looked to contain bath salts standing beside a smaller empty bottle on a floating glass shelf above the dramatic claw-footed tub. Back in the bedroom, Persian rugs, predominantly red in colour, but with blue in them too and green, the colours once vibrant she presumed, now distinctly faded, were scattered across the oak floorboards, but the bed was the star of the show. Obviously custom-made, it was much bigger than king-size, it was enormous, the wood dark and sturdy, walnut perhaps? There were four intricately carved half posts at each corner, a silken cover in midnight blue with scatter cushions not thrown but arranged on top, some sequinned, although bare in patches. Walking over to the bed, she laid her hands upon it. Vibrations, not entirely savoury, could be detected, but Ruby ignored them. Cynthia's private life was none of her concern.

On either side of the monolith were two bedside tables, sturdy also and in matching wood – again custom-made she'd wager. Quickly, Ruby rifled through the drawers, they had been emptied too, home now to just more dust and cobwebs.

"Cynthia," she called out. "I'm leaving now but I'm coming back with Theo and some friends of mine. In the meantime, please remember, you are not alone. We are with you, my friends and I, and our intent is to help you. There's no need to be frightened anymore."

Nothing, zero, nada was the response. Cynthia was gone. Hiding again.

As soon as she left the room, Cash stood up.

"Are you okay?" he asked, genuine concern very much apparent in his eyes.

"I'm fine. But Cynthia, she's not. Far from it."

Walking side by side down the corridor, they returned to the staircase. "There was such a dark feeling coming from that room, it was almost, I don't know how to describe it... cloying somehow. And then it just went, disappeared. Have you... you know... sent her on her way?"

"Not yet, I'll need the entire team to do that I think. Fear tends to make a spirit resistant and for some reason, Cynthia is very afraid."

Descending the stairs, Cash replied "I'll help. I want to. In whatever way I can."

"What, you mean hold a crystal or something?"

"Yeah," he said, laughing. "Unless you promote me to smudge stick duty that is."

"Smudge sticks?" she replied, raising an eyebrow. "You know what they are?"

"Yep, they're herb wands, used predominantly to purify psychic space and create an aura of protection; I've been doing my homework."

"In that case," she laughed along with him, "promotion might just be on the cards."

***

"Did you sense her?" said Mr Kierney, materialising from the same shadows he had retreated into as they reached the bottom of the staircase.

"Yes," Ruby replied.

"And, what you do, this cleansing business, it works doesn't it?"

"Usually."

As soon as the word left her mouth, Ruby knew she had made a mistake. Proving her right, Mr Kierney seized upon it.

"Usually? What do you mean *usually*? It either works or it doesn't."

She rushed to reassure him.

"I mean usually we are successful, *very* successful concerning the removal of spirits, as many of our former clients would testify. In fact, I remember you saying, you heard about us through a former client didn't you?"

"I did," Mr Kierney agreed grudgingly.

"A Mr Warner, from Peckham in London? A friend of yours?"

"Look, I don't want to talk about him. It's my case I'm interested in."

Taking a deep breath, Ruby continued "I've made a connection with Cynthia, which is an encouraging sign. She knows who I am and who Theo is. I've stated our intent – which is, of course, to help her. Fear tends to make a spirit resistant. Now that she knows she's not alone, hopefully she'll feel less fearful next time we meet, more inclined to move on."

"I don't give a damn about her feelings. Just get her out of my house."

My house? Only by default.

Crossing the Grand Hall, Ruby was disappointed by Mr Kierney's attitude. Cynthia was as scared as he was, more so, a little sympathy for her plight wouldn't go amiss.

Before leaving, curiosity got the better of her. "Mr Kierney, where are all Cynthia's personal things, her clothes, things like that? The drawers and wardrobes in her bedroom are empty."

"Don't look at me, I can't get in there, remember?" Less defensively, he continued, "What I do know is that Sally sold a lot of stuff off, broke her heart according to my mother.

Cynthia may have left her the house but she didn't leave any funding to pay for it."

Ruby nodded in understanding. It was as she thought. No matter. Although personal possessions were handy when trying to connect with a spirit, they weren't the be all and end all. She had connected well enough with Cynthia just being in her precious surrounds.

Reaching the door, Ruby asked "Is Monday okay for my team to visit?"

"Monday? You can't do sooner?"

She could juggle her week to fit in with his demands but she didn't want to – she wanted instead to find out as much information about the movie star as possible before she returned. Knowledge was armour too; it would help them further, she was sure.

"I'm sorry, Mr Kierney, Monday is our earliest slot. Would you like me to book you in?"

"If you really can't do better than that, I suppose so," he replied, seething.

Just before she and Cash stepped back into the winter sunlight, Mr Kierney spoke again.

"What if it doesn't work, if she refuses to budge?"

"Then we go deeper," Ruby replied.

"Deeper? At what cost? Financial I mean."

"We can come to an agreement regarding cost. What truly matters is sending Cynthia to the light."

"And my peace of mind!" Mr Kierney pointed out aggressively.

"And your peace of mind," Ruby acknowledged.

"I hope you're right. I hope you can get rid of her. That you're not just a bunch of charlatans."

"We're not," said Ruby, bristling at the accusation, "and we'll prove it."

"You'd better," Mr Kierney replied stiffly before adding, "You do know I'm a journalist, don't you? For a much respected national newspaper?"

"I do," said Ruby.

She also knew a threat when she heard one.

Chapter Six

Cash was proving to be very punctual, turning up on her doorstep as promised at eight the next evening, waving a DVD at her.

"It's *The Phoenix*, Cynthia's signature film according to the woman on the till at Asda."

"You actually bought it?" said Ruby, motioning for him to come in.

"Yeah, but don't worry, it was only three quid, along with other greats from the era."

"Like what?" Ruby led him down the hallway to the kitchen.

"*Gone With the Wind, Cat on a Hot Tin Roof*, do you want me to go on?"

"No, no, I get the picture."

"Literally," he said, winking at her.

In the kitchen, she was about to ask if he wanted red or white wine at the exact moment he proffered a bottle of red.

"Red then," she said, laughing.

"Is that okay?" enquired Cash, worry crossing his face. "Or do you prefer white? If you do, I can always pop back out and get some; the off-license isn't far."

"No, not at all, I like both to be honest," she said, taking the bottle from him and examining the label. "This looks really nice."

The Australian Shiraz promised plenty of spice and bursting berry flavours. Extracting the cork, she poured them both a generous glass and handed one to him. The nerves she had been trying to keep under control all day suddenly getting the better of her, she took two huge gulps, wishing she'd had the foresight to have a glass of something relaxing before his arrival.

"Are you okay?" he asked, a little too intuitively she thought.

"Fine," Ruby mumbled, thinking all the while: *Get a grip, girl!*

Looking around, he asked, "Is, er, Jed with us?"

"No, not right now. I haven't seen him all day."

"So it's just the two of us?"

"It is," she confirmed, leading him through to the living room.

Heading for the sofa, she tried to seat herself comfortably but was amazed at how awkward she felt, her limbs behaving as though they belonged to someone else entirely. Cash, however, was clearly at ease, kicking his boots off and settling cheerfully beside her.

How she wished she hadn't worn her tightest pair of jeans. Flattering they may be, but the waistband was digging into her stomach, making her feel even more uncomfortable. She'd have to make an excuse later, say she was popping to the bathroom or something and swap them for a slightly looser pair. Hopefully Cash, like your typical male, would remain oblivious to such a costume change.

"Have you got the DVD?" said Ruby, hoping her voice sounded more confident than she felt.

"Yeah, here it is," he said, passing it to her. As he did so, his fingers brushed hers, causing her to tremble slightly. Quickly, she focused on the blurb in front of her.

Cynthia Hart pours her heart and soul into the determined and feisty character of Gayle Andrews, not only portraying one of literature's most stirring heroines but becoming her in a truly effortless performance. Her first award-winning role, it is one that cements her place in the hall of fame, inspiring not just her generation but generations of women to come.

"Wow!" said Ruby, impressed. "And all for just three pounds."

"I would have paid a fiver if pushed," replied Cash, tongue in cheek.

"And have you seen it? *The Phoenix*?"

"I think so, when I was a kid. Around Christmas time probably. From what I remember, it was good. Or rather she was good. The film's a bit corny really."

"Shall I put it on?" Corny or not, Ruby was intrigued.

"Sure," he replied, leaning further back into the sofa.

At just under three hours, the film *was* good, it was excellent. Several times the harrowing story of Gayle Andrews nearly reduced Ruby to tears and she'd had to reach for a hanky to dab discreetly at her eyes and nose. Ploughing through a second bottle of red wine together, this time one she had in stock, had done nothing to help her emotional state, she was sure. Thankfully, Cash didn't seem to mind the copious sniffing and sighing going on beside him. Glancing at him every now and then, she thought his eyes looked suspiciously misty too on occasion.

The young and vibrant actress on screen was so different to the spirit full of dark brooding emotion she had encountered at Highdown Hall only yesterday. It was hard to reconcile the two. What had happened to Cynthia Hart during her lifetime? Why was she so frightened? Finding out 'what' wouldn't be hard. There was a mountain of stuff on the internet about her. The 'why', however, could prove more difficult.

At the end of the film, the credits started to roll and dramatic music befitting such an epic production blared out, almost deafening them. Reaching quickly for the remote, Ruby pressed the off button, the ensuing silence almost as loud she noticed.

"Well, that was a bit more heart-wrenching than I thought it was going to be," Cash admitted, looking really quite shell-shocked. "Bloody good actress, wasn't she?"

"Phenomenal," Ruby said, sighing.

Placing his empty glass on the coffee table in front of the sofa, Cash sat in repose for a few moments, as though trying to recover from the traumatic onslaught. Eventually, he started speaking again.

"I'm not sure how it's supposed to work, but did you feel any sort of psychic connection with Cynthia during the film?"

"No, not psychic," Ruby replied. "Emotional, well, as you can see..."

Smiling at her comment, Cash continued to look at her. Having relaxed completely during the course of the film, Ruby felt flustered again. Nonetheless, she found it surprisingly hard to look away. It was as though Cash were drawing her into his very being, those molten eyes of his penetrating her. Music, she decided, that was what was needed, something contemporary and frivolous to break the spell between them. Hauling herself up from the sofa, she walked to the CD player, beside which was an alcove filled with shelves, the bottom two not home to more books like the others, but her entire music collection.

"What do you like?" she asked, relieved to be talking about more mundane matters.

"Surprise me," he called from the sofa.

Strangely, Johnny Cash's 'Hurt' album came to hand. She was about to put it back and then stopped. Turning, she said, "So, you're named after Johnny Cash, right?"

"Right," he answered, his gaze still intent.

"Because your mum is a fan of his?"

"Correct."

"Do you listen to his music too?"

"Sometimes," he said, rising and moving towards her.

Kneeling down, he ran his fingers along the long lines of CDs, scanning them with his eyes.

"I see we've got similar taste in music," he said at last.

"Have we?" replied Ruby, damning that squeaky note in her voice.

"No *Drive-by Truckers* though or *Richmond Fontaine.* I'll

have to introduce you to them."

Will you now? His close proximity was making her feel decidedly clammy. If only Jed would come bounding in, she could use him as an excuse to tear her gaze away. In fact, she'd be grateful for any passing spirit right now, shame her flat was usually bereft of them. Instead, she stared right back, as though caught in a vice.

Suspecting that he would, Cash reached out a hand to touch her hair. As he did so, she couldn't help it, she started shaking, praying she was the only one to notice.

In the silence, he leaned forward and his lips touched hers. His full, soft lips, lips that if she were honest, she had fantasised about kissing since meeting him in the pub on Monday. *Was it really only four days ago?* To be pressed against them now felt good and she relished the feeling, for a few seconds at least.

Drawing back, she started to speak, but words failed her.

"It's okay," he said, gently tilting her face upwards, "it was a bit forward of me I suppose. We have only just met."

"It's not that," she rushed to explain. "It's just that... I'm not looking for a boyfriend right now. Relationships are often difficult for me."

"Why?" he asked, genuine curiosity in his voice.

Such a simple question. Not such a simple answer. Where did she start? Yes, he was fascinated with her right now. But how long would it be before fascination turned into something else? Contempt, perhaps? A desire to live only in the 'real' world? She had seen it happen too many times; not just with Adam but with other boyfriends too, every boyfriend in fact. And not just boyfriends, men in general, she had never known her father or grandfather either – they had also bailed out from their relationships. It was widely said that celebrities tended only to date fellow celebrities, someone who could perfectly understand the pros and cons of their profession. Well, following their lead, perhaps she should find herself a psychic boyfriend. Trouble was, the only other psychics she knew were women. Psychic men didn't happen along very often. *Fanciable* psychic men that is.

Desperately she wanted to explain all this to him, felt like she *owed* him an explanation, but the right words simply wouldn't come.

Attempting to say *something* at least, she said, "Can we take it slowly? Be friends for a while, see how we go."

Cash looked disappointed but he didn't let that expression linger.

"Sure," he said, just stopping himself, she knew, from touching her hair again and then, "Blimey, it's five past one. I'd better get going. Work tomorrow."

Checking the clock, she couldn't believe it either. Where had the last few hours gone?

Cash slipped his boots on and grabbed his jacket en route to the door.

"Haven't you got a proper coat?" said Ruby, shivering. "It's freezing out there."

Good God, she thought, *now I sound like his mother*.

"I have, but this is fine for now," he said, looking actually quite touched she was fussing over him.

"Thanks for coming over, for bringing the movie," she smiled shyly at him.

Standing there in her bare feet, she felt tiny in comparison. If she kissed him now, she'd have to stand on tip toe to do so.

"So, Monday, Highdown Hall. Can I still come?"

"Of course," Ruby exclaimed. "And my website, can you still help with that?"

"I promised, didn't I?" he replied, the timbre of his voice mesmerising to her ears. "What time shall I be there, and where?"

"Nine thirty at my office. Is that okay?"

"Nine thirty is perfect," he said, walking backwards a few steps before turning, devouring her again with his eyes before allowing the night to devour him.

Returning to the living room, Ruby noticed that he had left the DVD behind. She picked it up and considered running after him to return it but decided against it. There was no hurry. She'd see him on Monday, she could return it then. Hopefully, she'd see him a lot more after that, if she hadn't scared him off entirely. Going through to the bedroom, she let the jeans she hadn't bothered to change after all fall to the floor and slipped into pyjama bottoms, sighing with relief as she did so. As she was climbing into bed, Jed came hurrying in and barked a couple of times before curling up beside her.

"Oh, so now you show up?" she said, sighing.

Reaching for her eye mask and ear plugs, she turned off the lamp and fell asleep – the memory of Cash's lips on hers accompanying her deep into dreamless realms.

Chapter Seven

"Everybody ready?"

Three heads nodded whilst Cash simply beamed; reminding her of a little boy who'd just been told it was his birthday. Theo had been simply bemused by his presence. Ness, however, hadn't looked best pleased. Ness took their 'work' very seriously, as they all did, and clearly she didn't see the need to have some sort of enthusiast tagging along. Normally Ruby would have agreed with Ness, never before had she brought a 'friend' along to a cleansing, it was inappropriate. But Cash, he was different. Just as she connected with spirits, she had connected with him. She felt good when he was around, and something else, something she couldn't quite put her finger on – safe, perhaps? As for Corinna's reaction to Cash, she too had looked taken aback at first, but then she had started giggling, particularly whenever Cash happened to make a remark. Although she knew it was ridiculous, Ruby couldn't help feeling slightly irritated by Corinna's girlish, flirty behaviour. Even more annoyingly, Cash didn't seem to mind it at all.

Ruby had spent practically the entire weekend researching Cynthia Hart. Born in Brighton in 1927 and from apparently humble beginnings, she had lived with her mother and younger brother in a flat in a street that no longer existed, that had been demolished in the late 1940s, part of an eradication programme to get rid of Brighton's worst slums. Having famously left home at fourteen, she had climbed on board the non-stop stardom express and ridden it all the way to the stars, becoming the brightest of them all, surpassing even those who had shone in

73

Hollywood – not bad for an ordinary local girl, thought Ruby. *The Phoenix* had been her breakthrough film. Although there had been several theatre and film roles before that, it was the first one she'd bagged a starring role in. Still, the others were good films; her early performances often described as commendable by the critics. From 'commendable' to 'spell-binding', though, was quite a leap and one that must have stunned her as well as those in the film industry. A well-deserved award had followed for *The Phoenix* and then again for *Intruders.* It was *The Elitists* that had won her an Oscar – a film about a group of high society revellers involved in murder and espionage across several continents; she had co-starred in it with the delicious John Sterling. By 1958, Ms Hart was hot to trot, smokin' – in demand the world over and then, boom! It was over. Just like that.

The night she had passed, Christmas Eve, which was also her birthday, a party had been held at Highdown Hall. Not an unusual occurrence, it seemed. Ms Hart was quite the socialite, forever in the media, an ever-changing string of admirers on her arm, not least John Sterling. Concentrating particularly on pictures of them together, Ruby thought they made a dynamite couple, the spark between them almost tangible. It was Sterling who had found her the night of the party, collapsed in her bedroom. It was he who had held her body close as she took her last breath. Sterling had been inconsolable afterwards, according to reports in the papers, and had never returned to acting. Retiring to the South of France instead, he had passed in his mid sixties; cirrhosis of the liver.

Throughout her research, Ruby had found absolutely no mention of anyone called Lytton. She was still none the wiser. Who was he and why was he as significant in death as he was in life – to Cynthia anyway? Or maybe his significance would fade? Once they'd explained to her how she had passed, helped her to accept the suddenness of it, maybe the hold he had on her would diminish. Be forgotten about. They'd find out soon enough.

***

"And where should I go whilst you're conducting this... this cleansing?" Mr Kierney said, looking quite put out about it, despite having engaged them to carry the work out.

"You can either stay downstairs or go to a nearby pub, it's up to you," Theo replied, a slight edge to her voice informing Ruby she wasn't too enamoured of him either.

"The pub? Yes, of course, I'll go there," Mr Kierney replied. "Call me when my house is my own again."

All five of them stared after him as he hurried to his car, all five unimpressed by his brusque manner. Ruby almost felt like leaving Cynthia be, after all, this had been her house first.

"We can't," said Ness, tuning into her thoughts, an ability of hers Ruby still found alarming. "She's been here too long already. It's time to move on."

Nodding her head to show that, of course, she agreed, that it hadn't been a serious thought, Ruby led the way. Climbing the oak staircase, Corinna marvelled at how grand it was.

"I can just imagine Cynthia in all her film star gorgeousness wafting down these stairs," she giggled.

Unfortunately, all Ruby could imagine was Cash bestowing another indulgent smile on Corinna.

At the door to Cynthia's bedroom, Ruby turned to face him.

"Are you sure you want to come in?" she asked.

"I'm sure." There was no hesitation in his voice at all.

Contemplating the wisdom of it for a few moments, Ruby conceded.

"Okay, but if you feel even slightly uncomfortable, let me know and we'll get you out."

Cash nodded his understanding.

Before entering, they initiated the protection ritual. Each of them, including Cash, were to visualise themselves surrounded

75

entirely by white light. Ruby had also given Cash her obsidian necklace to wear for extra protection. The black stone, she thought, looked rather good against the smoothness of his throat.

"Ready?" she asked after a few minutes.

"Ready," the group chorused.

"Cash, you're absolutely sure?" Ruby double checked.

Before he could reply, however, Corinna piped up.

"Don't worry, Ruby, I'll keep an eye on him." And she took hold of his arm.

I bet you will, thought Ruby peevishly.

She noticed Ness raising an eyebrow at her. She was quite right; it wouldn't do to bring negative feelings into the room, it was important to remain in a positive and loving frame of mind when dealing with a spirit, particularly one who was distressed. It helped to redress the balance.

When she was sure the green-eyed monster had retreated far enough inside her, she closed her hand around the handle of the door and pushed.

***

Motioning for everyone to stand in a circle, Ruby said, "Let's tune in first and see if we can make a connection."

Theo, Ness and Corinna nodded. Cash, however, couldn't resist looking around him, his eyes wide with awe. Ruby didn't blame him. It wasn't everyday you found yourself in the inner sanctum of a world-famous movie star.

Once they were all in a circle, she took a deep breath.

"Cynthia, it's me again, Ruby. I came to visit you recently, as did Theo, standing to my right. Do you remember us? Today I've brought along my other colleagues as well."

Gesturing to each of them in turn, she continued, "This is Ness, Corinna and Cash. As I said to you before, we are here only with the intention of helping you."

There was no response.

"Cynthia," continued Ruby, injecting firmness into her voice. "I know you're here, in this room, and I know you're frightened. You don't understand what has happened to you. But we can help you understand. You have passed Cynthia – your spirit left your physical body the night of your party, Christmas Eve, 1958. You left the party sometime after ten o'clock and went upstairs to your bedroom. Could it be possible you were experiencing the start of chest pains and wanted to be alone? Whilst in your bedroom you suffered a fatal heart attack. It was sudden and it was unexpected, leaving you confused, disorientated and, of course, very frightened. I understand how attached you are to this house, that you feel safe here, but it's time to leave, to return to the light, which is your true home."

Still nothing.

Ruby nodded to Ness, who took it as a signal to start lighting smudge sticks. Handing one to Corinna and one to Cash, she motioned for them to go to the corners of the room and start waving the smoke around. Normally a cleansing was performed *after* the spirit had successfully passed, but because of Cynthia's reluctance to show herself, they would start now. Ness lit her own smudge stick and started to walk clockwise around the room. Later she would open doors and closets to cleanse every inch of those spaces too. The floor-to-ceiling windows, Mr Kierney had told her previously, were sealed shut so they couldn't open them, which was a shame. Not only did an open window or door offer the spirit a physical exit, the air in Cynthia's room could do with freshening up, it was stale.

Theo tried next to establish a connection with Cynthia.

"Cynthia, it's Theo. I've seen all your films. Do you remember me saying so? I admired you greatly; you were an amazing actress – and the most beautiful of your generation."

A flicker in the darkness. Clever Theo, appealing to the spirit's vanity – evidently still intact, even on the other side.

"*The Phoenix* was my favourite, you were remarkable in it. I

77

think it was everybody's favourite to be honest. But *Intruders, Translation* and *The Fledgling* were superb too, and, of course, *The Elitists,* with John Sterling, what a handsome couple you made."

It was the mention of John that emboldened Cynthia. She came rushing forward.

John! Where is he?

"Cynthia," said Ruby, seizing the moment, "John isn't with us. He passed in 1969, peacefully I'm told. The night that you passed, John was the one who found you. He was with you as you passed. He's in the light now, waiting to be reunited with you."

As Ruby was speaking, Ness beckoned for Corinna and Cash to come and join the circle once more.

"Join hands," she whispered, expecting action stations now that the 'news' had been imparted.

At first though there was nothing. All was still again. Ruby wondered if they had 'lost' Cynthia, if she had retreated back into the shadows. And then there came a scream, a scream that ripped through her body as a tornado might rip through a mid-American town, through Theo too, and Ness, both of their bodies shuddering with the impact. It was so intense; Ruby was sure Corinna and Cash must have felt it on some level too.

The energy that was Cynthia started to gain momentum. Overhead, the chandelier swayed as though caught in a strong gust of air. At the window, the heavy curtains fluttered as though they were not made of velvet but of some much lighter material.

"Cash, I think you'd better leave..." started Theo.

"It's okay," he insisted. "I'm fine."

As if to reinforce this fact, his hand tightened around Ruby's.

Theo looked uncomfortable. She glanced at Ruby, who gave an almost imperceptible nod of her head.

"It's your call," said Theo finally. "But stand firm and remember there's nothing to be afraid of."

"Cynthia," Theo spoke again, "I implore you, please remain calm," but Ruby knew her words would fall on deaf ears. The truth, instead of setting Cynthia free, had only served to enrage her.

The bed started shaking next, almost imperceptibly at first but the movements quickly became violent, the sheer weight of it clearly no obstacle. The dressing table started to shake too, its various contents and mirror rattling.

"Imagine white light!" Theo had to shout to make herself heard above the din. "All of you, as strongly as you can, and I don't want any chinks in it either. Imagine a solid blanket of white light surrounding you, impenetrable as steel."

As everyone did her bidding, Theo re-addressed Cynthia as loudly as she could.

"Cynthia, I want you to focus on my voice. I know you can hear me. There's a light shining in the distance, look at it, go to it, there are people who know you and love you in the light, who are waiting for you. Go towards the light, Cynthia. Go home."

This is my home!

The doors to her walk-in wardrobe suddenly burst open. At the same time, Ruby felt Cash jump beside her. Darkness from within began to seep out like ink spilled on blotting paper, edging its way forwards.

"Stand firm!" shouted Ruby, echoing what Theo had said earlier.

She knew well enough what Cynthia was doing. She was trying to manifest, hoping perhaps to frighten the living into leaving and never coming back. It was rare for a spirit to manifest. An actual sighting was usually nothing more than a hollow image replaying on the airwaves, like a DVD stuck on repeat play. Because Cynthia was grounded, however, because her soul was still very much present, her manifestation would be considerably more substantial, perhaps even visible to the non-psychics amongst them, to Cash and Corinna.

Quickly, Ruby envisioned the last scene from *The Phoenix,* the one in which Gayle declared that she would rise again from the ashes, reclaim her life once more, her Titian-curls wreathing wildly around her tear-stained but determined face. Taking this vision she bathed it in pure white light, the light of love, yet still the crashing and banging around her continued, the dark mass drew closer. She stole a glance at Cash. She should never have brought him along. It was irresponsible of her. This experience must be terrifying for him, he'd be scarred forever. But to her surprise, he looked far from terrified. His face was smooth; his brow distinctly unfurrowed. He was witnessing one of the most dramatic cleansings the team had ever encountered as a collective, and yet he remained cool and calm throughout, doing exactly as he was told to do: project white light.

With a final ear-splitting scream, the energy around them imploded. Cynthia hadn't been able to manifest after all. She would be quiet for some time now, depleted.

"Corinna," whispered Ruby urgently, "scatter eucalyptus drops. I'll place crystals all around. Rose quartz I think, to help promote love and peace. Ness, the bells."

"Bells?" whispered Cash, his eyes open once more.

"Yes, bells," Ruby whispered back. "Sound is a frequency; we use it to break up lower frequencies, to dispel any negativity that may still be lingering."

"Oh, right,' Cash nodded. "And she's gone has she, Cynthia?"

"No, she hasn't gone. She's still here and she's still angry."

"So, what do we do?" asked Cash, his use of the word 'we' not lost on Ruby.

"Remember I said to Mr Kierney if this doesn't work we go deeper. Well, we do just that, we go deeper."

"Deeper? How do you mean?"

"I'll explain when we're out of here."

***

Cynthia huddled in the shadows, exhausted, drifting in and out of consciousness. Dead? She wasn't dead! But if not, what was she? This existence she endured, it could not be called living. A heart attack, the young woman had said, the one who called herself Ruby, the girl who looked no better than a street urchin. She'd had a heart attack the night of her party? Insane! She had just turned thirty-one; there was nothing wrong with her heart. She was perfect, both inside and out. And John had found her, held her as she took her dying breath? If that were true, she would have remembered. Instead, all she knew was the thrill of the evening, the love and admiration in everyone's eyes. But wait – there *was* something else. She *had* removed herself from the crowd, but only for a few moments surely? A flame of memory lit up the darkness, but just as quickly it fizzled out. Everything was black again. If it were true, if she *had* left the party, for what purpose had she done so? Not for sex; that would come later. A select few invited into her sanctuary until the break of day.

Was John responsible for her death? He had a temper; she knew that, he blamed his Irish origins for it. Before sailing to America, his mother had lived in Carrickfergus, a small village on the north shore of Belfast Lough. Often he compared Cynthia to her.

"You've got hair as red as hers," he would say.

"Got a thing for red heads have you?"

"Don't." He hated it when she was crude. He saw her as something pure, how wrong he had been.

When had they last rowed? Cynthia tried to remember. Not long before the party. He had flown over to visit her in between shooting his latest movie. Yes, that was it. Just two or three weeks before, she was sure of it. He was angry again because she had refused yet another proposal.

"But why, Cynthia? Why won't you marry me? Give me one good reason."

They had been in bed at the time; he had just ravaged her,

bringing her to climax time and time again as only John could. Effortlessly.

Sitting up, the silk sheets slipping down to reveal his strong, muscular body and those gorgeous shoulders, smooth and golden in colour, he had let his head fall into his hands.

"You love me, I know you do."

How did he know? She had never told him so.

"Cynthia," he had turned to her then, his voice beseeching. "Why won't you marry me?"

Again, she hadn't answered. Instead, she had slipped from the bed, intending to make her way to the bathroom, to shower. She had only taken a few steps when he was by her side again, naked also, grabbing at her wrists. Encircling them with his hands.

"God, Cynthia, you're infuriating."

She knew she was. She also knew he found her attitude towards him arousing. That was something John Sterling had liked – the chase. Too easily women fell at his feet.

He was beginning to stir again; she could feel him pressing against her thigh.

Lowering her eyes, deliberately demure, she had smiled at him, fully expecting to be thrown back onto the bed, to be ravaged all over again. To hell with her shower.

He had looked into her eyes – she remembered it clearly – holding her with his gaze as firmly as he held her wrists. Her breath had caught in her throat. Any minute now, his lips would be on hers, his tongue exploring deep inside her, first her mouth and then more sensitive, secret places. She braced herself, waiting. But he had surprised her. He had thrown her from him as though she were poison itself.

"John... !" she had started. No, she would not beg. She would never beg again.

John had grabbed at his clothes, torn off him hours ago and thrown to the floor.

"I can't do this anymore!" he had muttered under his breath.

Fury had ignited in her; she remembered that too, another black mood rapidly descending.

"Can't do *what* anymore?" She grabbed at his wrist now.

How easily he had flung her off.

"I can't share you, Cynthia. I *won't* share you."

"In that you have no choice."

"I do." His voice had been low, a growl. "I can walk out of this room right now and never return. I can leave you, Cynthia, to become a parody of yourself, which is what you'll be if you don't stop doing what you're doing, believing in the hype that surrounds you. Commit to me, Cynthia, without me..."

She hadn't let him finish.

"Without you I'm nothing? Is that what you're trying to say? Don't make me laugh! I belong to no man, do you hear me, John, no man. Least of all you. Without me, *you* are nothing. *I* am the world's darling, *I* am the one they adore, you are pale in comparison."

"The world's darling today, tomorrow second best. I've seen it happen, Cynthia, I've seen how it destroys people. Don't let fame be the only thing you have in your life."

"Fame is enough!" she had screamed at him.

Again he held her gaze. She had read the contempt in his eyes; contempt and despair. Without another word, he pulled on his clothes and left the bedroom. Not even a backwards glance.

She had fallen onto the bed – alone. Reeling from what he had said to her. At how quickly the mood had turned sour. *How dare John try to cage her, to own her? She belonged to no one, no one.* A shiver ran through her as she realised this wasn't strictly true. She did belong to someone. Lytton had made sure of it. Lytton! Why had she allowed herself to fall under his spell? So many times she had asked herself that question. She had been young and naive, she had been desperate – so different to the person she was today. And the man she belonged to, if you could call him a man, he was here, she was certain of it. Not

83

John, the antithesis of John. He watched her every move, blocking her path to the light that she could see shining in the distance, a light that looked so inviting but she knew was also a trick. As soon as she tried to reach it, he would step forward; drag her down with him to an existence even worse than this. The girl, the old woman, they did not know what they were talking about; who they were dealing with. She *couldn't* go to the light. She belonged to the Devil and perhaps always had done – since she had first felt that desire for stardom burn in her belly. All Lytton had done was to facilitate that bond.

No, she would stay here: in *her* house, in *her* room, in the shadows, where it was safe. And if they came back, those wretched people, that man that squatted below, they would regret it. But for now she would rest. Gather her strength. She would need it.

Chapter Eight

"What do you mean, she's still here? I was given to understand you people were professionals, that you'd rid me of her."

"Mr Kierney..." Ruby started to appease, but Theo interrupted.

"Mr Kierney, we have completed stage one of our investigations and in very many cases, stage one is sufficient. Sometimes, however, spirits dig their heels in, refuse to depart. There can be a number of reasons for this, which aren't always obvious and so we need to delve further. But believe me when I say our concern is not just for Cynthia's wellbeing but for yours too. We plan to go away, conduct more research and find out the reason behind her resistance. Armed with this knowledge, we will return to perform another cleansing, endeavouring to achieve a conclusion that is satisfactory for all."

Mr Kierney didn't seem half as inclined to argue with Theo as he was with Ruby.

"And what am I supposed to do in the meantime?" he muttered, his eyes refusing to meet the old lady's, his mouth a grim line.

"I believe you're sleeping downstairs at the moment," Theo continued, "and that you feel relatively safe doing so? I suggest you continue in that manner until we return."

"Or I could get another team in," said Mr Kierney, rallying.

"Indeed you could," sanctioned Theo, "but Psychic Surveys has made significant progress with your case, whereas another team would have to start from scratch. I believe your best bet is to stick with us, although, of course, it's your decision entirely."

His pallid complexion flushing red with fury, Mr Kierney conceded but not with good grace.

"I want the entire use of my house!" he thundered. "And I want it soon. One more chance, that's all I'm prepared to give you and at no extra cost to me."

"Mr Kierney, I..." Theo began, a rise in her voice signalling it was time for Ruby to butt back in.

"One more chance is all we need Mr Kierney, we're very grateful to you. I intend to devote myself personally to this case, to find out what the problem is, what grounds Cynthia. We'll be back as soon as possible to try again – later this week or early the week after."

"You'd better!" Mr Kierney growled before indicating he'd like them to leave.

Outside, Corinna turned to Ruby.

"Bloody idiot! Why didn't you just tell him to get lost?"

"First, because it wouldn't do Cynthia any good, and second, Mr Kierney's a journalist. If we fail to evict Cynthia, he could use the media to harm our reputation considerably. We've spent two years getting people to take Psychic Surveys seriously; we don't want the work that we do devalued by an arrogant arse like him."

At the thought of everything she'd worked so hard for suddenly being under threat, Ruby started to feel emotional and – psychic, sensitive or not – all around her felt it.

"Mr Kierney said there's a pub somewhere close?" Cash reached out his hand to rest lightly on Ruby's shoulder.

"Yes," confirmed Ness, "I passed it on my way here, The Rainbow Inn it's called. Follow me, I'll lead the way."

***

A typical Sussex country pub, the taller among them had to duck as they entered The Rainbow Inn, its doorway was so low. Inside, the ceiling, complete with blackened oak beams, was also low. The sense of enclosure, however, ensured an intimate and cosy atmosphere, a respite from the weather. The bar shone like a beacon in the gloom, and on the chalkboard menu a member of staff with an artistic bent had drawn holly leaves and berries in the top corners, green and red a festive contrast against the black. Cash took orders whilst the others settled themselves round a large, battered table, not too far from the fire that danced in the grate.

Seeing the drinks lined up on the bar, Corinna jumped up to help Cash bring them over. A coke for Ruby and her, a half pint of bitter for Cash, gin and tonic for Theo and tomato juice for Ness, heavy on the Tabasco and Worcester Sauce.

"Well, that was interesting," she said, returning.

"That's one way of putting it," Ness mumbled, clearly savouring her drink.

Ruby was about to speak next but movement at the bar caught her attention.

"You can see him too?" said Theo, leaning towards her.

"Yes," said Ruby, smiling again at last. "But I don't think he's earthbound. He looks too content. I get the impression he just enjoys propping up the bar every now and again."

As Corinna and Cash looked to the bar intrigued, Theo changed the subject.

"So, what next?"

"Next, we find out who Lytton is."

"Lytton?" enquired Ness, pushing a rogue strand of black hair behind her ear.

"Yes, Lytton," answered Ruby. "When I first made contact with Cynthia, she mentioned someone called Lytton, she wanted to know where he was. She sounded desperate at the mention of his name. We need to find out who he is. What relationship he had with her."

"And his name hasn't come up in the research you've done already?" enquired Ness.

"No, it hasn't," said Ruby. Lowering her head, she continued.

"Obviously I didn't look hard enough. To be honest though, her passing was sudden, unexpected. I thought once we'd explained to her what had happened, helped her to understand, she'd go peacefully enough. Big mistake. There's more than that holding her here."

Cash leaned forward too. "Is that what you mean by going deeper? More research equals more knowledge equals the key to her being stuck here? Unlocking the secret equals all round-success?"

"Something like that," confirmed Ruby.

Sipping at her coke, she continued "I'll spend the next couple of days looking into it, shall we meet up again at my office on Thursday? Does that suit everyone?"

Even if it didn't, Ruby knew they'd rearrange whatever they had planned to ensure that it did. A surge of affection for these people sitting around her, her team, her friends, rose up in her. She was lucky to have found them. Maybe Cash too as it was turning out.

That settled, their conversation turned to more mundane matters.

"Wonder if Lucy and Joey are going to get it on in EastEnders tonight?" wondered Corinna, an avid fan of the soap opera.

"How you can watch such rubbish, I don't know." Ness looked truly shocked. "No one ever talks to each other in that programme, they just shout. It's full of such negative energy."

Corinna smirked as she took another sip of coke.

"The present pile," Theo joined in. "That's what I'll be wading through tonight."

That's all Theo ever seemed to spend her evenings doing lately. She had three sons and each son had at least two children. If Ruby remembered correctly, one of them had five – an impressive if excessive number in the modern world. Nonetheless, Theo adored each and every one of her grandchildren and delighted in spoiling them. All year she'd stock up on toys and then spend practically the whole of December wrapping them.

Drinks finished, everyone started grabbing their coats and saying their goodbyes, making ready to go. Whilst they did so, Ruby seized the opportunity to pop to the bar. Standing beside the outline of the man she had noticed earlier, she turned to look directly at him, trying to form a connection with him. Tuning in, she gathered he had been in his seventies; that his name was Albert, but he was known more commonly as Burt and that, in life, The Rainbow Inn was not just a pub to him but a home-from-home.

Are you stuck here or can you come and go? Ruby asked, not in words, in thought.

I can come and go, love, the old man replied good-naturedly enough. *For a while anyway.*

What are you drinking?

Harveys Old, that's my tipple. He was grinning at her, she could sense it. *There's nothing like it.*

Not even on the other side it would seem. It was one heck of an endorsement. The company that brewed it, Harveys Brewery in her home town of Lewes, would be pleased to hear that.

You're okay then?

I'm fine. Burt winked at her.

Ruby couldn't tell when he had passed exactly, but fairly recently, something to do with his liver. Although he had gone to the light with no problems, Burt was having trouble relinquishing his earthly pleasures – a beer with friends in a pub he loved. She didn't know what happened on the 'other side', but from experience she had gleaned there were those who were allowed a certain amount of time to come to terms with leaving the physical world in which they had been so happy. As long as they didn't make a nuisance of themselves, they could visit places or people every now and again until they felt ready to move on entirely, to wherever it was they were supposed to go – the next leg of their spiritual journey. Such visitations could not be considered hauntings as such as the spirits in question rarely needed help; they would do what they had to do, just in their own time.

Enjoy your pint, Ruby said, leaving him to it.

Cash had waited behind for her.

"Are you okay?" His voice was low, his eyes gentle.

"I'm fine," she replied. "What about you? After what happened back there, all that banging and crashing?"

"I'm fine. Honest. I've never been better."

She shouldn't believe him, but somehow she did. He seemed genuinely unfazed by the more obvious elements of Cynthia's tantrum, astonishingly so.

"Well, it's over now," she continued. "You don't have to set foot in Highdown Hall ever again."

"Are you kidding?" Cash looked genuinely put out. "I'm looking forward to it. But I can't wait until the end of the week to see you again. Fancy a curry tonight? My shout."

Chapter Nine

The atmosphere at Chaula's, a local Indian restaurant near Waitrose in Eastgate Street, was quiet. *Quietly perfect,* thought Ruby, she'd had enough drama for one day. Looking at the man sitting opposite her, she was glad she had agreed to go, if only to give him the chance to offload about what had happened earlier that day. As she expected, Cash broached the subject of Highdown Hall within minutes of sitting down.

"This spirit stuff, it's real, isn't it?"

"As real as you and me," agreed Ruby, wondering why Jed, who was sitting by her side looking longingly at her, had chosen this precise moment to show up.

Jed, you don't eat anymore. And especially not curry. Stop staring!

Jed wasn't buying it though. He wagged his tail expectantly and his eyes were almost heartbreaking, they were so hopeful.

Since there was nothing she could do about the dog's phantom hunger pangs, she decided to ignore him and concentrate on Cash instead. The waiter had delivered their food, a chicken jalfrezi with extra chillies for him and a prawn dhansak with boiled rice and a side of chilli pickle for her. His eyes widening, Cash lost no time in wading in.

"You like it hot too?" he noted, watching her dollop a spoonful of pickle onto the side of her plate.

"I'm addicted to the stuff, chillies I mean. I can't get enough."

"Me too," he replied. "Raised on them."

"Have you tried the food at Wham-Bam?" he continued,

referring to a food vendor that set up regularly in the pedestrian square that ran from the bottom of School Hill to the old bridge that crossed the river and took you to the beginning of Cliffe High Street, a pretty stretch of the town dominated by Harveys Brewery, antique shops and cafés.

"No," replied Ruby intrigued. She had always meant to try the food from there, vegetables deep-fried in spicy batter, a sort of Indian tempura she supposed. The smell whenever she passed by made her mouth water.

"The chilli pickle there, it will blow your head off. I've tried to cajole the recipe out of them several times, but they won't give it, it's a closely guarded secret."

Before she could reply, he was back on the subject of Cynthia again.

"So, Cynthia, do you think she's evil?" he said, in between mouthfuls.

"I've told you before; I choose not to believe in evil. Cynthia's frightened, that's all, and a frightened spirit can be dangerous to deal with, in much the same way a frightened living person is. The way she acted today, lashing out, it's got something to do with Lytton."

"Yeah, the mysterious Lytton. I wonder who he is."

"Was," Ruby reminded him, and then, more to herself than him. "I'll have to check."

For the next few minutes they ate in companionable silence, the food really too good not to give it their full attention.

Cash was the first to finish, pushing his empty plate to one side.

"So," he said, picking up the threads of their previous conversation, "this choosing not to believe in evil business, I'm really not convinced you know. I could name some pretty evil people out there, an endless list of them."

Ruby pushed her plate aside too; she was too full to eat any more.

She paused a few moments before attempting to explain.

"Have you ever looked at a newborn baby and thought, crikey, you're an evil little sod, aren't you?"

Cash looked horrified.

"No, of course not."

"No, me neither. There is only innocence in their eyes, a purity."

"Until they reach teenage years that is."

"Ah, teenagers," Ruby couldn't help laughing too. "The less said about them the better. Seriously though, people aren't born with a propensity for evil, whatever they become in life, whatever choices they make along the way, perhaps as a result of injustices they've suffered, perhaps not, once they were good and that goodness remains at core, even if it does become buried under layers and layers of crud."

Cash raised an eyebrow at this but remained silent.

Ruby finished her half pint of lager. "Look, I'm no expert on what happens on the other side, Cash; I don't really know to be honest. But from what I've seen, what I've *felt*, love is the ultimate force. Evil doesn't stand a chance against it. The light, or home as we call it, is pure love, with no conditions attached. We come from it and, at the end of our human journey, we go back to it. Despite what we get up to in between, there's no judgement in the light, no fear or damnation. What there is, is unconditional love and understanding."

"So, everyone gets away with it you mean? Murderers, rapists... politicians."

Ruby smiled again as she shook her head. "No, I don't think anybody gets away with anything. There are always consequences to actions. I'm sure murderers, rapists and yes, even a fair few politicians, have to undergo intensive re-education of some sort; a form of rehabilitation if you like. My feeling is that wrong-doers have to suffer every suffering they've ever inflicted; not just on their victims, but the families of their victims, their friends, everyone their actions have touched, no matter how remotely. In doing so they take responsibility, experience the sorrow – and the weight of that sorrow must be horrendous. Hell enough I should think."

Coming to the end of her sentence, she noticed that it wasn't only Jed staring at her.

"What?" she said, feeling her face start to burn.

"You," said Cash. "You're amazing."

"No I'm not!" snorted Ruby, crimson now.

"You are," Cash insisted. "I've never met anyone like you before. Not only are you gifted but you're compassionate too. I don't know, you shine with it."

Ruby was glad the waiter chose that exact moment to come over and clear their plates. His compliment had rendered her speechless.

Having ordered coffee for both of them, Cash said, "So, reincarnation, I presume you believe in that too?"

Ruby nodded her head. "Don't get me started on reincarnation," she said, "we'll be here all night. It just makes sense to me, that's all, to have more than one life; we've so much to learn."

"You mentioned your mum was a psychic too, does she believe as you do?"

Ruby stiffened. Had she mentioned that? She must have done, when they first met.

"My mum is psychic and my grandmother, and her mother before that. In fact, my great-grandmother was quite renowned in Victorian times. Rosamund Davis. Google her, there's quite a bit about her on the internet. She documented meticulously all her psychic experiences. Quite austere she was to look at but Gran assures me she was as soft as a kitten inside. It was my grandmother who brought me up though, she taught me to respect the gift we have, to use it wisely and to help. And yes, I tend to agree with my grandmother's beliefs, not just because she taught me, but instinctively."

Cash continued to hold her gaze, a talent of his she decided.

"Tell me to shut up if you want, that it's none of my

business, but is... is your mum okay?"

Ten out of ten for perceptiveness. As tempted as she was to tell him it was indeed none of his business, she felt she should say something, to stop future prying if nothing else.

"My mum is fine," she said carefully, "my grandmother looks after her."

"Where do they live?"

"Hastings, they live in Hastings."

Knowing she should elaborate at least a little bit, she continued "Like me, my grandmother taught my mother to use her gift wisely. Unlike me, my mother didn't listen. She was a real live wire when she was younger." Ruby smiled at the memory. "I remember her always laughing. Unfortunately, she had a bad psychic experience, when I was still a child. She didn't protect herself properly. She retreated into herself after that, had what you might call a breakdown. Rarely laughed again. I miss that sound."

"I'm sorry," said Cash, reaching across the table and covering her hand with his.

"Don't be," said Ruby, surprised at how comforted she was by his touch. "I don't know the ins and outs of what happened to my mother – my grandmother says it wouldn't help me if I did – so, I can't tell you much more than that I'm afraid. You know as much as me."

His hand still on hers, Cash said, "That's fine. I feel privileged you've told me what you have. I'd like to meet your grandmother and mother one day."

"Really?" said Ruby, it was the last thing she had expected him to say.

"Really," he replied. "They sound as special as you are."

Feeling a stirring inside her chest, a sensation that both scared and excited her, they paid the bill and left the restaurant, Jed less hopeful but ever loyal, trotting behind them.

Although Cash lived close to Chaula's, he had a flat in Fullers Passage, he insisted on walking her home. Instead of cutting through back streets, they decided to take the more scenic route, through the heart of town. Linking arms as they walked, he quizzed her about various historical buildings, eager to know if they were haunted or not.

"Bull House, where Tom Paine lived," he said, "is he still there?"

"I've never been inside," Ruby replied. "Maybe, maybe not."

"But what if he is?" Cash pressed further.

"Then maybe the current owners are happy to live alongside him."

"That happens?" Cash was incredulous.

"It happens."

"What about The White Hart Hotel, that's *got* to be haunted."

"I know one of the managers there; they know what I do but they've never contacted me. I think that answers that question."

"And The Judges Inn, it's as haunted as The Pelham Arms apparently."

"A rumour the landlord encourages," Ruby confided. "It helps bring the punters in."

Ruby burst out laughing.

"What?" Cash came to a halt.

"You," she said. "You look so disappointed."

"I'm surprised, that's all," he replied a little ruefully.

"You're more likely to find a spirit in Waitrose than in The Judges Inn, I'm telling you."

"Really?"

"No, not really!" Ruby giggled again. "What I'm trying to say is that spirits don't conform to stereotype, they're not always to be found in the most obvious of places."

Picking up pace once more they soon reached the top of the High Street. Cash nodded over the road at St Anne's church, raised up above the pavement on its own hillock it made an imposing silhouette against the night sky with its surrounding graveyard.

"Now, that, you have to admit, by moonlight at least, is spooky."

"Peaceful, I'd say," replied Ruby wistfully.

Again they stopped, this time to stare across at the various stone markers depicting lives long gone.

"Peaceful," Cash repeated after a few moments, "Yeah, that's another way of looking at it."

The beginnings of understanding, thought Ruby, before turning into Irelands Lane towards home.

Chapter Ten

Ruby and Cash put in an early appearance at her office the next day. Before saying goodbye the previous night, they had made plans to spend the morning together. He was ahead of schedule at the moment, so he could spare a few hours to work on ideas for her website. She, meanwhile, would continue to try and find out about Lytton. If they managed to make enough headway they might even nip up to the Pelham Arms for lunch.

Cash sat down at the meeting table and pressed his laptop into action. Ruby, meanwhile, switched on the kettle. As soon as the room started to warm up, Jed sloped in and settled himself in front of the heater. As he did so, Ruby noticed Cash look up, albeit briefly.

Waiting for the kettle to boil, Ruby wandered over to her desk calendar. Christmas was just three weeks away. It'd be nice to have the Highdown Hall case done and dusted by then. She could then look forward to a week off over the festive holidays, spending it with her mother and grandmother in Hastings, fantasising already about the evocative smell of homemade orange and cinnamon mince pies, a family recipe passed down through the ages.

Settling herself down, she was just about to type 'Cynthia Hart, Lytton' once again into Google when the phone rang.

"Hello, Psychic Surveys," Ruby answered.

"I need your help. I can't stand it anymore."

After urging the distressed man to calm down, Ruby ascertained that he lived in a flat in Brighton, his name was Paul Ashton and he believed he was being haunted. Not only did his flat have a 'nasty' feel to it, he had experienced somebody pressing down on him several times as he attempted to sleep, as though trying to suffocate him. What's more – and this was the last straw, Ruby gathered – his cat, Lips, now had to be fed outside, refusing to enter the house.

"My brother phoned me yesterday," the man continued, hardly drawing breath, "and he could hear screaming on the line. Of course he asked me what the heck was going on at my end but I didn't know. I heard nothing, just my brother's voice. He told me he had a really bad feeling about what was happening in the flat and to get out quick. He said the screaming sounded evil. But I can't just leave; my brother lives miles away in Leicester, I live in Brighton, I work in Brighton. I have to stay. Please, I'm not imagining this. Help me."

"When was the last time you experienced an attack?" asked Ruby, all thoughts of Lytton temporarily suspended.

"Last night. I'm hardly sleeping. I'm too afraid."

"And did you know the former occupant?"

"No, but I've heard about him from the neighbours, a right wrong 'un he was apparently, into drugs and all sorts."

Grabbing a pen, Ruby said, "Look, give me your full address, I can be with you in less than an hour, is that okay?"

"Less than an hour? Oh, thank you, thank you so much."

"No problem," said Ruby. Before he could ring off, however, she remembered to ask how he had heard of Psychic Surveys.

"My friend in Hove, his son had a ghost in his bedroom; you managed to get rid of it. The Carters. Look, I don't care how much it costs. I'll pay anything. Just help me."

"The Carters, yes of course," said Ruby, replacing the receiver, more determined than ever that Mr Kierney would not tarnish in any way their growing reputation.

"Lytton, Lytton..." mused Cash in the background. "I can't find any mention of him in relation to Cynthia Hart. It would help if we had a first name I suppose."

"Aren't you working on my website?" Ruby said, surprised.

"I am, but I thought I'd have a quick look for information whilst you were on the phone, see if I could find anything that might help."

"Oh, right, thanks. The search for Lytton, however, will have to wait. I need to go into Brighton to do an urgent survey and possible cleansing. The man that just rang, Mr Ashton, he's pretty distraught, he can't wait."

"Okay, I'll get my things."

"Why?" queried Ruby.

"I'm coming with you, of course."

"You don't need to," Ruby assured him.

"Yes I do. You know, Ruby, sometimes I think your job is really quite a risky one."

"Look, I've told you," said Ruby, reaching for her coat, "I always make sure I'm fully protected before I make contact with the other side."

Cash pulled on his own coat. "I'm not talking about pissed-off spirits; I'm talking about the real live people complaining about them. You rush round to their houses, often alone it seems, and you've no idea who they are, not really. They could be waiting for you with a pickaxe or something, more dangerous than any ghost."

"You really are quite paranoid aren't you?" said Ruby, hunting for her car keys.

"And you're not paranoid enough."

Before descending the stairs, Ruby turned to look at him. Who did Cash think he was? Some sort of protector? The genuine concern in his eyes, however, softened her reply.

"I've been okay up until now. But thanks for caring."

"I know we've only just met, but I do care, Ruby Davis. Honestly. I worry about you."

His words startled her. He *cared* about her, in what way? As a friend? As something more? Damn her intuition for stubbornly remaining silent on the matter.

Reminding herself that someone urgently needed her help,

she carried on down the stairs. At the bottom, she delved into her pocket for her mobile phone.

"Hang on, I've just got to phone Theo," she said, more to herself than Cash.

A few minutes later, Theo had promised to find out as much as she could about Cynthia Hart and Lytton and to report back as soon as she could. Suggesting that Ruby continued with online research, Theo would go instead to East Sussex Record Office, recently named The Keep, near the Falmer university sites. She'd rope in Ness too – Ness was big chums with the person in charge there, often negating the need to make an appointment to visit.

As they reached her car, Ruby stopped briefly.

"If you're going to insist on accompanying me to surveys, I'm going to end up owing you much more than the price of a website!" she said, not entirely joking.

"Its payment enough just being with you," he replied, still deadly serious.

***

"How come you haven't called the team in for this one?" quizzed Cash as Ruby just about made it through the lights at the Kingston Roundabout.

"Psychic Surveys is my company, so it follows I do the lion's share of cases. I only tend to call in the team when the workload gets heavy or when a spirit is resistant."

"What do the others do the rest of the time?"

"Corinna works in a pub, Theo and Ness are largely retired. Well, as much as you can retire from being a psychic. Ness used to work with Sussex Police, but she quit that a while ago."

"Any particular reason?"

"Not that I know of, but she warned me off working for Sussex Police when they approached me, so I'm not sure her experience with them was entirely positive."

"They approached you?" Cash looked impressed.

"Yeah, but I've decided to specialise in domestic cases for now."

"Hmm..." Cash appeared to contemplate this. "It could get heavy with the police I suppose."

"I imagine so."

"Corinna, is she as psychic as the rest of you?"

"No, she's more of a sensitive."

"A sensitive? And the difference is?"

"It's hard to explain," answered Ruby, passing Sussex University to her right and the city's much loved Falmer Stadium, home to Brighton and Hove Albion football club, on her left. "In general though, a sensitive is able to feel when a spirit is around. A psychic, on the other hand, can communicate with spirits. For some psychics, it's a one-way communication; they can hear spirits but can't reply to them, for others, like me, Theo and Ness, it's more of a two-way thing. There's no hard and fast rule though, psychics, mediums and sensitives, they don't tend to slot into neat grooves; occasionally skills cross over."

Her explanation seemed to satisfy Cash.

After a while, another question occurred to him.

"This spirit, in the house we're going to, what if it's resistant?"

"Keep everything crossed it isn't," said Ruby, and then looking into her rear view mirror she added, "Oh good, Jed's here."

***

Pulling into Compton Road, close to the Seven Dials area of Brighton, Ruby found a place to park and pumped coins into the meter. It was three pounds fifty for the privilege instead of the normal two pounds; yet again the council had seen fit to increase charges without notice. Slightly perturbed, she returned to Cash and led him to Ashton's flat; pressing the lower doorbell marked Flat 1, the one with his name tag sellotaped above it.

The door opened swiftly. Hurriedly, they were invited in.

Straightaway Ruby could sense a presence in the flat, there was anger, confusion and despair by the truck load. As Mr Ashton started to go into great detail once again about what he had experienced, Ruby took note of his pallor. It was ashen, unhealthy – a common symptom of an 'intelligent' haunting. The spirit who resided there was feeding on his life force, draining him – no wonder the cat had moved out, eager to avoid the same fate.

After he had finished speaking, Ruby asked Mr Ashton if he would like to stay whilst she attempted to make a connection, or whether he'd prefer to leave them to it.

"I should probably stay," he replied. "But not inside, I'll wait in the garden. Is that okay?"

"That's fine," nodded Ruby.

"How long will it take?" Mr Ashton asked again.

How long is a piece of string?

Instead, Ruby answered, "There's no hard and fast timescale, an hour or so, sometimes less, sometimes more. Look, it's not very nice outside, it's starting to drizzle, why don't you wait in the kitchen?"

"The garden's fine, honestly," said Mr Ashton, backing towards the kitchen where, presumably, the exit to the garden was. Ruby wondered if Lips would be waiting for him, equally as nervous.

After he had left, Ruby turned to Cash.

Noting he was still wearing her necklace, the one she had given him at Highdown Hall, she pointed to it and said, "You might as well keep that, its effective protection."

At once, his hand flew up to his neck. "Oh, sorry, I meant to give it back."

"No, really, it's fine, keep it; it looks better on you than me

103

anyway."

A smile lit up his face.

"Are you sure?" He looked almost shy, endearingly so Ruby decided. "I do like it."

"I'm sure, now get the smudge sticks burning and start cleansing every corner of every room like I showed you. A lot of negative energy has built up in here."

"Then the bells?" he asked, raising an eyebrow.

"Then the bells," she couldn't help but smile. "You'll find a range of oils in the bag too, eucalyptus, pine, lavender and citrus – pick one, it doesn't matter which, they all cleanse, scatter a few drops in every room. And see if you can open a few windows, change the air."

As Cash unzipped the black holdall they had brought in with them, Ruby made her way into the living room. Here the atmosphere was much denser than in the rest of the flat, and a degree or two colder. This was obviously the room the spirit favoured, perhaps it was where he'd spent most of his time when alive.

Looking around, it was obvious Paul Ashton was a bachelor; there were no feminine niceties at all, no photos in frames of happy faces smiling, no trinkets on the mantelpiece, no flowers to give colour. It was purely functional with a sofa, an armchair, a coffee table, plasma TV, PlayStation and little else. The walls were an unprepossessing magnolia and looked chipped in places, in need of a fresh coat. Only one piece of artwork graced them: a lake scene, which also managed to be bland and anonymous despite the artist's deft hand. And, despite it being so close to Christmas, the house was bauble and tinsel free. Mind you, so was hers at the moment, so she could hardly hold that against him. Briefly, she wondered what Cash's flat was like, whether it had more personality than this one. If rooms were a reflection of the person who lived in them, she was certain it would.

Closing her eyes, Ruby kick-started the process, introducing

104

herself to the spirit and informing it, as she had informed Cynthia, that she meant no harm, she was here to help.

It took a few moments, but eventually a connection was made. A mental image of a man popped into her mind, so thin he looked ravaged.

"What's your name?" she asked.

David.

Another image: this time a hypodermic needle, empty, discarded. Heroin, she guessed. But it was not the heroin that killed him, Ruby sensed, not directly anyway. It was an illness not his drug addiction – an illness that had attacked his brain as well as his body.

Far from a 'wrong 'un', Ruby pitied his wretchedness.

"David, I've come to help you, to explain to you that you have left your physical body and have passed into the realm of spirit. Although you'd been ill for a while, I think your passing was sudden, unexpected. I get the impression you felt you had more time. But David, I'm sorry, you didn't. Your life here has come to an end; you need to move on, the next part of your spiritual journey awaits you."

Allowing David time to consider her words, Ruby paused. An ashtray, full of cigarette butts on the arm of the sofa moved slightly. After a few moments she spoke again.

"Can you see a light David? It's shining before you. The light is home. Don't be afraid, go towards it. There are loved ones waiting for you in the light, eager to see you again."

A growl of anguish echoed around the room; the living room grew colder still. If she breathed out now she was sure her breath would form a cloud in front of her.

Ruby remained undaunted.

"David, you *must* pass, you cannot stay here. This flat, it belongs solely to the living now. It's of no use to you anyway; walls cannot confine you any longer. Let it go David, take the next step. Make your way to the light. There is only love and comfort in the light. There is no judgement, there is no pain or heartache, such things have no place there."

The ashtray flew off the arm of the sofa, its contents rudely scattered. At that exact moment, screaming erupted, agonised screaming, perhaps the screaming Paul's brother had heard down the telephone, bouncing off every wall, encircling her. Although dramatic, she wasn't startled. Far from evil, Ruby recognised its pure despair.

As she braced herself, Jed appeared by her side, his nose sniffing the air, curious.

"Go on, boy," said Ruby, noting the sound of bells coming from another room in the flat, Cash hard at work. "Go and see what you can do."

Ever obedient, Jed sloped forward. Unfortunately, David was not as enamoured by him as the child spirit, Timothy, had been. Quickly he returned to Ruby's side, yelping.

Slowly, in the corner of the room, behind the black screen of the TV, a shape began to make itself known. Desperation could lend spirits strength and that seemed to be the case with David. He was faint at first, but quickly he grew stronger, his ethereal features contorted, his eyes glaring – a frightening sight to some. Ruby sincerely hoped Cash wouldn't choose this moment to return to the living room. She was pretty sure he wouldn't be able to see David; that he would remain oblivious, but she didn't want to risk it either.

Without warning the spirit flew at her. Ruby had already visualised a white shield around herself and Cash before entering the flat, standard protection stuff. And, as she had every faith it would, it held firm, David unable to penetrate. Frustrated, he hurled himself against it, over and over again, increasing in force each time. The shield rippled slightly she noticed, frustration and anger a potent mix.

Jed, meanwhile, had fled. Alone with David, she concentrated on pouring forth light and love.

Still David resisted. She found herself growing tired; her own energy draining. David was feeding off her too, a psychic vampire. Behind her she heard movement.

"Cash, is that you?"

"Yeah, everything okay?"

"Er, soon hopefully."

David's head snapped sideways, he too had noticed the newcomer.

"Cash, quickly, hold the necklace in front of you."

"The necklace...?" Cash began, but then thought better about questioning her.

"David," Ruby tried again, as reassuringly and calmly as she could. "You are suffering and you don't need to be. All you have to do is go to the light, there is love in the light; understanding, all the things you craved on earth but which eluded you. You endured a terrible disease for years, a disease that isolated you from public life. You felt adrift, abandoned. You still do. But, David, you haven't been abandoned, you came from the light and the light wants you back. It is waiting for you David; it has *always* been waiting for you. Don't resist it anymore."

As hard as Ruby tried to make David understand, she knew he wasn't listening to her; instead he was racing between her and Cash, reminding her of a crazed dog, rabid even, trying to find a way to penetrate their shields, to devour them whole. But just as she was tiring, so was he. His movements were not as quick, his expression less fierce.

Patiently, she waited. Cash did too; not moving a muscle, barely even breathing.

"David," Ruby spoke gently. "Move on."

Another scream, no wonder Jed had fled, the Rainbow Bridge an altogether more pleasant place to be than here at the moment.

And then a second voice broke in, an older voice this time. Help at last?

David, stop that.

The voice was firm, parental. It was also effective. Immediately, David stopped screaming but his eyes remained frantic, sweeping from side to side.

Listen to what she says.

David turned round, the lampshade above him swaying.

Who are you? What do you want?

The light around the second spirit dipped.

Have you forgotten me already?

Although wary, David could not deny his curiosity. Tentatively, he moved closer.

Do you see David? I haven't changed so much.

Col?

Yes, David, it's Colin.

A shriek from David.

You abandoned me!

No.

You did, you left me.

I've been here all along.

David seemed to contemplate the second spirit's words. In him, Ruby sensed a desperate need to believe.

Quickly she urged, "Listen to him, David, *trust* him."

David trembled. Rage, the emotion he was holding onto, the emotion that kept him grounded, was beginning to drain away, bit by bit. Distrust, however, remained.

I couldn't see you.

You see me now.

Colin closed the gap between them, the light around him no longer dim, but shining like countless stars.

David could resist no more.

As he staggered forwards, Ruby suddenly understood. She knew they had been lovers. Colin had perished from AIDS too, possibly even in this flat, leaving David distraught and even more heavily dependent on drugs, turning to heroin shortly afterwards in an attempt to negate the pain. As images of David's life flicked through her mind, she realised that loss, for the large part, had characterised his life. His mother had passed when he was young, his father too. From thereon in it had been a series of foster homes, abuse, mainly physical but sexual too she gathered, alcohol, soft drugs, heroin and, finally, disease. Colin had been the only genuine source of affection David had known in life – his love amongst the ashes.

David placed his hands in Colin's. For a while the two men simply stared at each other. Then slowly, they began to fade.

At their departure, the atmosphere in the room lightened. Cash, still holding the obsidian necklace obediently in front of him, said, "Are we done?"

"We're done," Ruby answered.

She turned to look at him; he didn't look even slightly ruffled.

"Are you okay?" she checked.

"I'm fine," Cash lowered the necklace.

Questioning further, she asked, "Did you... did you see anything?"

Cash shrugged his shoulders. "I didn't see anything, no," he looked disappointed. "It felt a bit lively in here though, funnily enough – the feeling 'lively' I mean, kind of ironic under the circumstances. It doesn't now though, it just feels normal. Has the spirit gone?"

"Yes, David's gone," Ruby replied, smiling at him.

"Good, because I'm famished. Can we go and get something to eat?"

Her smile widening into a grin, Ruby went in search of Mr Ashton first.

Chapter Eleven

Mid-morning the next day, Ruby got a call from Cash.

"Hi, how are you?" he asked.

Ruby stifled a yawn. "I'm fine. I was up late last night on the internet, trawling through any and every site even remotely connected to Cynthia to see if Lytton was mentioned too. I'm a bit tired today to be honest."

"Me too, I was working on your website 'til gone midnight."

"Is it going okay?"

"Did you find anything significant?"

Their questions clashed.

Laughing, she insisted he answer first.

"It's going very okay. I also spent a bit of time checking out a few online psychic forums with a view to you advertising on them. On one particular forum, a local one, there's a lot of talk about a place called Tide Mills, do you know it? It's out near Newhaven, there's loads of psychic activity there apparently. Do you fancy a jaunt there this afternoon?"

Ruby looked at the clock.

"Hmm, I'm not sure. I've got a report that needs typing up. And no, I didn't find anything significant; I just hope Theo and Ness have at the record office. I'll find out tomorrow."

"A breather today might do you good; it might help to clear your head. I'm only talking a couple of hours. More of an extended lunch break really."

Ruby was tempted; some fresh air would be nice. And, she couldn't deny it, she wanted to see Cash again. A feeling she knew was mutual. Whilst he was still on the line, she Googled

110

the place he had mentioned. She had heard of it but only vaguely. She discovered the mill itself had closed in 1883 but a village had continued to thrive around it until the late 1930s when it was condemned as unfit for habitation. Abandoned, it had fallen into serious disrepair.

Cash came to meet her just after lunch. As Ruby drove them to their destination, he found out more about Tide Mills via the Google app on his iPhone.

"Hey, this place was featured in a novel by Lesley Thomson, *A Kind of Vanishing* it was called. Have you heard of it?"

"No, I haven't," replied Ruby. "What's it about?"

Reading further, Cash said, "It's about two girls playing hide and seek amongst the ruins during the late 1960s, one of the girls, Alice, goes missing and isn't found again. It's a kind of murder mystery I think."

"Sounds good, I'll have to check it out."

"Do you think it's haunted?" Cash asked after a while. "Plenty on the forum think it is."

"A derelict village, the ruins of which still remain?" Ruby mused. "It certainly fires the imagination, as Lesley Thomson would no doubt agree."

Pulling off the main road into a small parking area, they left the car behind and set off along a narrow pathway, which would lead them to the village, with hedgerows and acres of empty fields, brown in colour rather than golden, on either side. As they crossed a train track, a breeze started to blow, toying with Ruby's hair, she pushed aside any tendrils obscuring her view. They were alone but for one or two dog walkers weaving their way, heads down, through tumbled down walls that led, ultimately, to the shingle strewn beach.

History boards were scattered throughout the crumbling stonework, some still attached to their metal frames, whilst others, unable to withstand the corrosion of the salt air, had long since become detached. Instead, they lay propped up against their stands, as forgotten as the place itself. Quickly,

Ruby became engrossed in them. Before today, she had never heard of Tide Mills, never realised such history was on her doorstep. She learnt that flour was big business back in the eighteenth century and exporting it by sea was much cheaper than doing so by land, hence its location, close to a natural estuary. Cottages had been built for its workers and soon a thriving community had built up. In the late 1800s, however, the development of the railways had set the beginning of the end in motion. Stormy weather hadn't helped either, causing some very costly damage. But the development of nearby Newhaven harbour had been the last nail in the coffin, preventing high tides entering the channel west of the mill. The mill, unable to withstand either natural disasters or man-made progress, finally closed.

Coming up beside her, Cash's eyes scanned the board she was reading.

"Strange how people continued to live here long after the mill closed down."

"They'd made lives I suppose, forged friendships, fallen in love, reared children. Once people put down roots, normally they want to stay."

"In the material world as in the spirit world?" Cash wondered aloud.

"Sometimes."

"Look, there's a poem by a former resident on this board, Arthur Davis. Any relation to you?"

"I don't think so." Ruby smiled at the intimation. "Read it out."

As he did so, Ruby relished the sound of his voice.

Now all is quiet and so still,
Gone forever the dear old Mill.
Even now people speak,
In reverence of the Old Mill Creek.
Goodbye Tide Mill. Rest in Peace.
Memories of you will never cease.

"Simple words, but it sums up so much, makes it seem real." Ruby wasn't sure if Cash was speaking to her or himself.

Picking her way through more ruins, only a few shingle walls still standing, built with stones that no doubt had lain only a few yards away, Ruby pointed to the remains of a ceramic toilet. Cream in colour, broken at the base, its jagged shards could quite easily cause an injury if you happened to stumble and fall upon it.

"That makes it seem real too," she said.

Cash smiled wryly. "Yeah, toilets tend to have that effect." Looking around, he continued, "Can you sense anything, *anyone?*"

Ruby stared over at the station house, the only building whose structure could still be clearly identified, and tuned in for a few moments. She shook her head.

"No, I can't. It looks like everyone's moved on at last."

"Hmmm..." Cash frowned. "Forums then, they're not all they're cracked up to be?"

Ruby thought for a few moments. "Sometimes they are, depends what they're for. In psychic matters though, they tend to whip up hysteria. That's why I've avoided them in the past." Her head to one side, she added, "And why I'll avoid them in the future too."

"Fair enough," muttered Cash, slightly downcast.

Walking further up the path, closer to the beach, Ruby stopped abruptly.

"What is it?" whispered Cash, stopping too.

"A plane, flames, two officers killed." Ruby shook her head. "Ugh, dreadful way to go."

"Officers, during World War I you mean? I read there was a seaplane base here during that time."

"It must be then, World War I or II," Ruby nodded.

"Are they here, the pilots?"

"No, but evidence of the agony they suffered is. It may have been brief but it was horrific."

"Residual feelings?"

"Residual feelings," confirmed Ruby.

"Bummer," said Cash gravely.

"Come on, let's go," said Ruby, rubbing her arms with her hands. It was only a few minutes after four o'clock but the light was fading and with it any last vestige of warmth.

"Back to work?" Cash asked, the eagerness in his eyes telling her it was the last thing he wanted. She hesitated, but only for a moment. That report she had needed to type up she'd done in double quick time and emailed off. All else could wait. Heck, she could work into the evening again tomorrow if she had to, as could he she supposed.

"I don't mind," she said at last. "Back to mine perhaps. I'll cook?"

On the way home, they stopped at a supermarket to stock up on ingredients, organic mince, spaghetti and bags of salad. By the time they had drawn up outside De Montfort Road, night had fallen in its entirety. Ruby let them into her flat and walked straight to the kitchen to dump the bags. Grabbing a bottle of white wine from the fridge, a Chilean Sauvignon Blanc, she gave it to Cash to open. As she chopped and fried, they talked about more earthly subjects. Or rather Cash talked, Ruby his willing audience.

Perched on a kitchen chair, full glass in one hand, he told her about his mother. She'd brought him and Presley up single-handedly, his father having left the family home when Cash was little more than a baby. Ruby sympathised, she didn't know her father either. Jessica, her mother, had given birth to her at twenty-four. Having had a string of lovers beforehand, her mother wasn't even sure who Ruby's father was. Whether that was true or not, it had effectively prevented Ruby from ever making contact, not unless she wanted to end up like the daughter in *Mamma Mia*, grilling several men at once to find out who the culprit was – which, she laughingly assured Cash, she didn't.

"I went in search of my dad," Cash confided, both of them sitting at the table now, wine glasses refilled, spaghetti bolognese heaped on plates and accompanied by a watercress and rocket salad. "But he had re-married. Had another family, two girls this time."

"That must have hurt," Ruby replied, sensitive to his reaction.

"Not as much as I thought it would." Cash seemed genuinely unaffected. "We're a tight-knit family, my mum, brother and me; I don't feel as though I've missed out by not having a father figure around." Perking up he continued, "I'll introduce you to her soon, my mum, she's a fantastic cook too, does a brilliant jerk chicken. If you like spicy, you'll adore it."

After dinner they had watched *The Elitists* and both thought it was every bit as good as *The Phoenix*, but thankfully not as heart-wrenching or as long. As he got up to go, Cash suggested working on her website in her office again the following morning. "It would be lovely to have the company," she grinned.

Watching him retreat once more up the pathway a few minutes later, she couldn't help but feel disappointed at how compliant he was. She had told him she just wanted to be friends for the moment, but she had also wanted him to take the lead and kiss her again. *All in good time,* she reasoned as she shut the world out, *all in good time.*

***

On Thursday, they both actually managed to do what they had supposed to do the previous day – Cash working beside her on her website, Ruby typing up another report as well as answering the phone and booking in more surveys – space clearing mostly, dispelling negative energies that had built up within domestic walls, energies that were responsible for headaches, lethargy and a general lack of wellbeing. She also had another go at finding out some information about the mysterious Lytton online but failed dismally.

Cash had to leave just after lunch, he had a client to meet, but before he went he showed her his proposed design for her home page. Ruby hadn't really known what to expect but she was impressed with what he'd done. Clean and crisp, it was welcoming too, and very user-friendly. 'Psychic Surveys', as a bold heading, and their phone number were prominently placed at the top of the page. Underneath there was some Latin text showing where her introductory blurb about the company would go, and various buttons for people to press for further information on the different services they offered – home consultation, business consultation, space clearing, cleansings, distance healing and, last but not least, spirit release.

"It's... brilliant," she managed, thrilled.

"It's getting there. I'll get the other pages knocked up soon but you'll need to provide me with the copy for them too."

"Yes, of course," nodded Ruby.

"And forums," he continued. "We'll forget about them, shall we?"

"For now," confirmed Ruby.

Shutting down his laptop, Cash grinned at her.

"What?" she couldn't help but quiz.

"PsychicSurveys.com," he said, drawing out the words. "It's got a ring to it hasn't it?"

Reciting it a couple of times in her head, she had to agree. It did.

***

Jed has just settled himself cosily beside her when Theo burst in, her larger-than-life personality immediately filling the room. Behind her came Ness, so much smaller in comparison. Moments later they heard Corinna bounding up the stairs and the team was complete once more. They squeezed themselves around the meeting table, Ness, as usual, taking on tea duty.

Raising an eyebrow at Jed, Theo asked Ruby whether she'd managed to find out anything about Lytton.

Faltering slightly, Ruby admitted, "Well, I've searched and searched, but I still can't find anything about Lytton online that might help us. There's no mention of him at all in connection with Cynthia Hart. Like Cash said, it would help if we had a first name."

"Cash?" said Theo, raising an eyebrow yet again.

Feeling her cheeks redden, Ruby was relieved when Theo quickly continued.

"The reason you've had no success – well, one of the reasons – is the man you're looking for isn't called Lytton at all, he's called Rawlings, Geoffrey Rawlings."

"Rawlings?" Ruby was confused.

"Yes," continued Theo, adjusting her aqua blue gossamer scarf, a fetching contrast to her hair. "Rawlings was a man of many personas it seems, Clive Lytton being just one of them. A good name for the times I have to admit, very debonair."

"And?" prompted Ruby, eager to know more.

"Liked to sniff around up and coming starlets, did Rawlings. They were a speciality of his; the younger and more naive they were, the better. He led them to believe he could help them achieve their dreams."

"How?" said Corinna, fascinated.

"By selling their souls to the Devil."

Ruby balked. "Are you serious?"

"Absolutely," replied Theo, enjoying the stir she was creating. "Hallucinogens helped him to convince his victims he was best friends with a certain you know who. He would feed them cocktails which, unbeknown to them, had been previously laced with something, mescaline probably. Whilst under the influence of the drug, he would suggest that the person who stood before them was the great Lucifer himself, no less. He would then try to initiate sex, an essential ingredient of the ritual he would tell them; it would help to cement the pact. Sometimes he was successful in getting his wicked way, sometimes he was given a well-deserved clip around the ear."

"How do you know? About how successful he was I mean?"

"Because Cynthia wasn't the first starlet to succumb, there were others. It all came to light when his last victim, Darlene Grayson, furious at what had happened to her, how she'd been duped, exposed Rawlings, or Lytton as Cynthia knew him, by tipping off the police about one of the parties he liked to throw. Several underage girls happened to be in attendance. Rawlings was caught in the act and arrested. The case went to court and he was sentenced to two years for gross indecency. He spent it banged up in Lewes Prison, funnily enough, right on our doorstep."

"When was this?" Ruby continued to probe.

"In 1960, after Cynthia had passed. Too bad she wasn't around to realise what a charlatan she'd got herself involved with."

Ness took up the reins. "Cynthia was involved with him before she shot to fame. She must have been in her late teens/early twenties at the time. Impressionable."

"And desperate," added Theo.

"Certainly that," conceded Ness. "Although officially Cynthia's name was never mentioned in connection with either Rawlings or Lytton, putting two and two together I think it's safe to assume her fear of passing over has something to do with him and the Devil he conjured up for her, courtesy of drugs and alcohol."

"Erm, excuse me," Corinna piped up. "Mescaline, I've never heard of it, what is it?"

"Ah, so young," sighed Theo, looking fondly at her. "Mescaline, my dear, was the forerunner to LSD. A psychedelic drug, it was brought to the public's attention thanks to authors such as Aldous Huxley. He wrote an essay about it in 1954 called *The Doors of Perception* and another one two years later entitled *Heaven & Hell,* topically enough. Both documenting experiences he had whilst high on drugs. Perhaps Rawlings was a fan."

Ruby shook her head in wonder.

"How did you find all this out?" she said, "I couldn't find a thing."

"Simple really," said Theo, draining her mug of tea. "Not everything's online. Ness and I found a picture of them together in an old newspaper at the archives – 'Cynthia Hart and Clive Lytton', the caption ran, the pair of them were attending a play in the West End in which Cynthia had bagged herself a small role. She looked every inch the movie star, even back then when she was still a struggling actress. He, on the other hand, looked very much in lust."

Placing her mug on the table, Theo continued, "I recognised him straightaway, Lytton I mean. In the mid-sixties he was busted again for his behaviour. He formed a black magic cult, a popular thing to do at the time. However, he didn't bargain for the fact that some of his disciples really were into black magic – heavily so, drawing rather a lot of attention to themselves with their practices. You can get away with that sort of stuff in the Nevada desert, but not in South London. The police were called in yet again, and back he went to court. It was all over the papers at the time, I remember it well, most amusing. Far from being a scary Aleister Crowley type character, he was a gibbering wreck, asking to be imprisoned, to be kept safe from the 'nutters' as he called his devoted followers. He wasn't given a sentence this time, just cautioned. Kept himself to himself after that."

"So Lytton, Rawlings, or whatever he was called, he wasn't in league with the Devil at all?" Corinna double-checked.

"No more than you or I," scoffed Theo. "One of life's fakers I'm afraid, a sorry specimen of a man. I expect he's getting quite worried about everything now he's nearing the end."

"Nearing the end?" gasped Ruby. "Do you mean he's still

alive?"

Theo tossed aside a few rogue strands of pink hair. "He may well be."

"How do I find out?"

"According to 192.com, there are 40 Geoffrey Rawlings living in the United Kingdom, three of whom live in Brighton. Of those three, one is in his fifties, which, of course, rules him out but the other two are in their eighties. I'll bet you a pound to a penny one of those is him."

"But why would he be living in Brighton?" Ruby was puzzled.

"Oh, he's a local man. He was born in Brighton, hence his spell at Lewes Prison. I know he spent time in London in between but chickens come home to roost usually."

"I'm on to it," Ruby nodded, eager to find him. Looking admiringly at the old lady in front of her, she added, "Thanks so much, Theo. I don't know how you find out these things."

"It's called research, darling," Theo replied, somewhat pointedly Ruby thought. "You know, that little thing you've been busy doing as well?"

Ruby looked away. Just like Ness, Theo could often see straight through her.

***

Ruby rang Cash after they'd all gone. He was busy with a client, so rang her back just over an hour later. Quickly, she told him that Lytton's real name was Geoffrey Rawlings, that he was a charlatan and a rapist to boot, or as good as, that it looked like he had tricked Cynthia Hart into believing she had sold her soul to the Devil – the probable reason behind her reluctance to move on – and, the best bit, that there was a possibility he was still alive and living locally.

"What do you mean a possibility?" Cash asked.

Ruby explained Theo's theory.

"So, what are you planning to do? Visit them both?"

"Absolutely. If one of them is our Rawlings, he can damn well explain to Cynthia himself what he did. She might not believe us but she *will* believe it from the horse's mouth."

"You're not going alone," warned Cash, "it could be dangerous."

Ruby couldn't help laughing. "I hardly think I've got anything to fear from someone in their eighties!"

"No, no way Ruby. I'm coming with you. When do you intend going?"

"Tomorrow. Can you make it?"

"If it's the afternoon I can."

Agreeing, Ruby hung up, amused at the insistence of her 'protector'.

Chapter Twelve

As they drove into Brighton, parking was not the only issue on Cash's mind.

"Are you sure this Rawlings bloke isn't into black magic anymore? I've seen *The Devil Rides Out* you know; those Satan worshippers, they can be pretty scary people."

"Now, Cash," Ruby looked at him in mock-earnestness, "you shouldn't watch films like that if they're going to upset you. You're better off sticking to Disney."

"Humph!" was Cash's less than impressed reply.

As Cash had suspected, they had trouble parking. Both Rawlings lived close to the centre of Brighton, one in Kemp Town, the other not far from Western Road, the main shopping thoroughfare. A busy seaside city, second only to London in popularity, it was rammed at the best of times, but in the run up to Christmas it was bordering on the manic. After cruising the streets around Kemp Town for more than twenty minutes, Ruby eventually found a space, about a ten-minute walk to the first Mr Rawlings flat in Mount Pleasant. Expertly squeezing her car between an Audi and a Land Rover, she and Cash walked the rest of the way. As they drew close, Cash couldn't help pointing out that Mount Pleasant was anything but.

"The views are nice though," shrugged Ruby. "You can almost see the sea."

"With binoculars perhaps," was his surly reply.

Ruby smiled.

"Are you still cross with me?"

"Cross with you, why?"

"For the Disney remark."

"Oh, that. No, I'm getting used to your wisecracks," he answered wryly.

Stopping in front of a red brick semi-detached house, Ruby said, "This is it."

"How are we going to explain who we are?"

"We'll say we're film students, from the university or something, studying the life and times of Cynthia Hart. We're canvassing information on her from people likely to have been fans."

"And you'll think he'll buy that?"

"Probably not, no."

Ruby rang the doorbell.

When the door opened, an old man with blue eyes the exact shade of his denim shirt stood before them.

"Hello," he said pleasantly.

"Hello," said Ruby, adopting what she hoped was a gracious smile. "I'm Ruby Davis, this is Cash Wilkins. We're students from the university. We're carrying out some research on Cynthia Hart, the movie star. We found your name in the local archives. It seemed you might have known her at one time? We were wondering if you could perhaps spare a few minutes of your time to talk to us about her."

"Cynthia Hart?" the old man looked confused. After a few moments his furrowed eyebrows relaxed. "Cynthia Hart. Oh yes, of course. Yes, I knew her."

Ruby looked at Cash, her eyes alight. Bingo! She could hardly believe their luck.

"Oh, great, erm, well, we don't have to come in or anything, but we would like to ask you a few questions."

"Nonsense," Mr Rawlings was having none of it, "come in, come in, it's far too cold to be standing on the doorstep."

A part of Ruby despaired at how trusting this gentleman was, inviting a pair of complete strangers into his house. She also marvelled at his friendliness. If this *was* the Mr Rawlings they were looking for, he didn't seem at all roguish; he seemed very nice.

Following him into his living room, surprisingly warm and cosy, Mr Rawlings waved for them both to sit down. Then he lowered himself into an armchair, a slight stiffness to his actions belying his youthful character.

"Cynthia Hart," Mr Rawlings sighed. "A wonderful actress, a wonderful woman."

Ruby nodded her head enthusiastically. "Oh, absolutely, I couldn't agree more. We've seen all her films, haven't we, Cash?"

"Yeah," Cash lied, "every one of them."

Leaning forward in an almost conspiratorial manner, Mr Rawlings said, "Tell me, which one was your favourite?"

"*The Phoenix*," Ruby said at precisely the same time as Cash said, "*The Elitists*."

Mr Rawlings laughed.

"Both wonderful films, but *my* favourite was *Intruders,* I love anything by Hitchcock, I do."

"Mr Rawlings," Ruby pressed ahead. "You said you knew Cynthia."

"What's that dear?" Mr Rawlings tugged at his ear to indicate slight deafness.

Ruby raised her voice a couple of notches.

"You said you knew Cynthia?"

"Of course I did, lovely girl, one of the best."

"You got on with her?"

"Didn't everyone?"

Ruby decided to get serious.

"Mr Rawlings, despite what you're telling us, we know your association with Cynthia Hart wasn't entirely of a savoury nature." Blunter still, she added, "We know what you did."

"What I did, dear? I don't understand."

It was Ruby's turn to be confused. She wondered briefly if Mr Rawlings suffered from some form of dementia – he seemed to have no idea what she was talking about. Deciding it wasn't worth beating about the bush, she came straight to the point.

"We know you tricked young girls, Mr Rawlings, up and coming starlets mostly, those that were desperate for fame. You threw parties, fed them drugs, promised them the fame they craved if they would sell their souls, via you, to the Devil. We know sex was your motive."

"Are you alright, dear?"

It was Ruby's turn to be nonplussed.

"Erm... yes... I'm fine thank you. Sorry, did you not hear what I just said?"

"I heard." Mr Rawlings replied, looking bemused rather than offended.

Cash tried next.

"Mr Rawlings, you said you knew Cynthia."

"I did," Mr Rawlings smiled.

"In the flesh?"

"In the flesh?" Mr Rawlings laughed heartily at such an idea. "Oh, I wish."

"You wish? So you didn't?"

"Not in the flesh, no, of course not," the old man laughed even louder. "Oh, but she was breathtaking, wasn't she? She set the screen on fire did Cynthia. She and that Sophia Loren, oh and Gina Lollobrigida too, I mustn't forget her. Gorgeous women, all three of them, cracking figures too, they don't make them like that anymore, do they?" His eyes resting on Ruby, he added: "Sorry, dear, no offence."

Shaking her head to indicate none was taken, Ruby said, "So you knew *of* her rather than *knew* her."

"That's what I said," the old man beamed happily.

Ruby's shoulders slumped in defeat. No, that wasn't what he had said.

Settling back into his chair, making himself quite comfortable, Mr Rawlings continued. "Now, *The Phoenix*, I've got a tidbit for you, something you might find interesting. Did you know that Louisa Taylor was originally cast in the lead role, not Cynthia? Sadly for her, Louisa that is, she met with an accident just before filming started, fell off her horse, broke her leg and collarbone, nasty stuff. Tell me, do you think that film would have been just as successful with her in it or do you think Cynthia was the reason it broke all box office records? Her performance really was outstanding after all."

It was an hour later before they managed to extricate themselves from the first Mr Rawlings. After accusing him of such heinous acts, Ruby hadn't felt she and Cash could just up and leave. And so they had listened, not only to his musings on Cynthia Hart's merit as a film star, but also his views on the world in general. In a nutshell, to Mr Geoffrey Rawlings of Mount Pleasant, Brighton, the world was not as gracious a place as it had once been.

Out on the street, Cash looked at his watch.

"It's nearly half past three," he sighed, "we'd better visit Rawlings number two."

The natural light was dimming as they approached their second destination. Finding a parking space close by was not such a problem this time, the Christmas shoppers having thankfully started to thin out.

"What if this Mr Rawlings isn't *the* Mr Rawlings either?" asked Cash, his hands stuffed in his pockets as he walked.

"He has to be!" Ruby knew she sounded more confident than she felt.

Turning into Oriental Place, Cash looked around him.

"This is a dump too. Brighton's looking a bit run-down lately, isn't it?"

Ruby had to agree. Once, Oriental Place had been considered one of Brighton's most fashionable streets, set as it was in a prime location a few steps from the seafront. In recent years, however, it had fallen on hard times. The many houses in this once-grand Regency terrace no longer belonged to wealthy, upper class families; rather they hid a world of bedsits, as many people stuffed into each house as possible if the bewildering

126

number of bells beside each worn front door was anything to go by.

The house the second Mr Rawlings lived in was covered in scaffolding, as were several others either side of it – an attempt to restore the fading grandeur of yesteryear perhaps, or at the very least to mask its decay with a coat of paint.

"Are we going to say we're students again?"

"To begin with," replied Ruby, "but if it's him, we'll quickly get to the truth."

"I hope he doesn't set his dog on us," worried Cash.

"His dog? How do you know he's got a dog?"

"I don't, it's just a feeling."

Ruby raised an eyebrow.

"Be interesting to see if you're right."

His flat, 1a, was located in the basement. As they descended the narrow stairs, harsh barking could be heard from within. He did indeed have a canine companion.

"I wish Jed were here," muttered Cash and, before he could even finish his sentence, Jed appeared.

"Wow!" said Ruby astonished. "Wish for him and he comes. Another protector."

"Another what?" queried Cash.

"Oh, nothing," Ruby replied airily, ringing the doorbell.

It took an age for the door to open, the dog still barking and a gruff voice inside telling it to "Shut the fuck up."

All three waited patiently outside.

Finally, the second Mr Rawlings stood before them. Slightly stooped and wearing distinctly shabby clothes, every one of life's excesses showed in his face, in the grooves surrounding his eyes, his nose and mouth, in his expression even. Ruby knew without a doubt they had found their man.

"What do you want?" his voice was cracked and sore sounding.

"Good afternoon, Mr Rawlings, my name is Ruby Davis and this is Cash Wilkins. You used to know an old friend of ours, I believe; I'd appreciate it if we could talk to you about her."

"An old friend?" Mr Rawlings was clearly suspicious. "Not bleedin' likely. Buzz off."

Ruby tried again. "Mr Rawlings, it really is imperative we speak. Our friend's wellbeing depends on it."

"I couldn't give a toss about your friend's wellbeing," said the old man, preparing to slam the door in their faces.

"Mr Rawlings, or Mr Lytton if you prefer, we would really appreciate a few words."

As Ruby had suspected, her use of his old alias brought him up short.

"Are you the police? I don't want no bother with the police."

Ruby was quick to assure him. "No, we are not the police. We simply want to help our friend and we believe that you can help us do so."

Geoffrey Rawlings stared at them for a while longer, a mixture of emotions flickering across his rheumy eyes, blue just like the first Mr Rawlings but nowhere near as bright.

"Come in," he said at last, his resentment evident.

Tentatively, Ruby, Cash and Jed entered the flat. The stench of old food, of dust and dirt long forgotten, made her want to gag. She could see Cash grimacing too. It was such a stark contrast to where they'd just been.

Rawlings opened the door to the living room. As he did so, a mangy looking brown terrier rushed out, no longer barking but wagging its tail, seemingly glad of visitors. It came to an abrupt halt, however, at the sight of Jed, retreating backwards, whimpering. Jed looked disappointed at such a reaction. He wanted to play.

The living room was dark with a damp smell to it, the curtains shut tight. The floor was strewn here and there with litter, a tin of beer, some cheap, generic brand, a rolled up piece of newspaper, presumably meant as a ball for the terrier to fetch, any interest in it, however, long gone. The only furniture was an old sideboard, an armchair that looked every bit as worn as its owner and a TV, a surprisingly modern one. There was a table too, up against the far wall and a couple of dining chairs. It was these Rawlings motioned to when asking them to take a seat.

Sinking down into his armchair, Ruby couldn't help but feel sorry for Geoffrey Rawlings, despite his somewhat lurid past. Whatever he had done, he had done as a young man. He was elderly now and vulnerable by the looks of it. Why weren't social services or a relative, if he had any, keeping an eye on him? If they had been, she was sure he wouldn't be living in quite such squalor. Too many people ended their days this way, she reflected ruefully. It was a sad exit from the world.

"This friend," said Mr Rawlings, interrupting her thoughts, "who is it?"

Ruby braced herself; he wasn't going to like her reply.

"Cynthia Hart," she said finally.

Rawlings' already pale face drained completely of colour.

"But... but she's dead."

"Yes, I'm aware of that."

"She has been for years and years, you can't possibly know her. What is this all about?"

"Please," replied Ruby, "keep calm. I can explain – if you'll let me."

Rawlings fell silent but his whole demeanour had stiffened. Ruby shot a sideways glance at Cash, who looked uneasy too, before pressing ahead.

"I'm a psychic, Mr Rawlings. Do you know what that is?"

"Of course I bloody do. I'm old, not an idiot."

Chastised, Ruby pressed on. "My company, Psychic Surveys, is involved with, amongst other things, spiritual clearance. We've been called to Highdown Hall, Cynthia's former home. The current owner feels it's haunted. We've visited the hall and verified his claim. It *is* haunted. By Cynthia Hart."

If Rawlings was shocked by this statement, he hid it well. He simply continued to look at Ruby, his face a mask.

"In death, Cynthia is distressed. Considerably distressed. She is unable to leave this realm and pass into the next. And we believe the reason for this is that she thinks she has sold her soul to the Devil and so she hides." *Ah, ha!* Ruby detected a visible start at this revelation. "Now, please believe me when I say we are not here to judge you or your past actions, but we do know that Cynthia Hart was a friend of yours from many years ago and that, at one point, the two of you were close." Although she and the team could only surmise what had in fact happened between Rawlings and Cynthia, Ruby ensured she spoke her next words with absolute conviction. "We also know about the ritual you performed with her and that she shot to success soon after. Tell me, was this ritual merely a ruse on your part in order to sleep with Cynthia Hart?"

"Of course it bloody was!" Mr Rawlings burst out, confirming their theory. "She was young, she was pretty, I wanted her, who wouldn't? I wanted lots of them. And the wannabe film stars, they were always the prettiest. They'd never have looked at someone like me though, not unless I could think of some ingenious plan to make them."

He stopped then, as though lost in memories, a smile, not a pleasant one, creeping across his lips.

"Mr Rawlings..." Ruby prompted.

Fixing his faded but steely eyes back on her, he continued, "I needed a bit of magic in my life, who cared if it was black? I never took any of it seriously, anyway. I was surprised they did. I met Cynthia when she was still treading the boards. Did you know she used to live in Brighton, before she moved to London? We had that in common at least. Her mother was a char or something. Cynthia was embarrassed by her, hated talking about her. She had much grander ideas, did Cynthia, wanted stardom she did. Never seen anyone want it as much as her and I saw a few, believe me. I spun the usual line, told her I could make her dreams come true and she believed me. I told her she could have all the fame she wanted – at a price. She obviously thought the price was worth paying at the time."

"And so you tricked her?" said Cash. "To get her to sleep with you, you tricked her?"

"Cash," whispered Ruby, wincing at the look on his face. "Leave this to me."

Cash shut up but reluctantly, she could tell, champing at the bit to say more. Jed, meanwhile, continued to look hopefully at the terrier. The terrier, however, was refusing all eye contact. He remained hidden behind Rawlings armchair, his small body trembling.

"So what if I did? The woman was a whore anyway. Women like her, they'd sleep with man or beast if they thought it would further their careers. And she did, sleep with the beast I mean, or rather me," he said, actually chuckling to himself, inflaming Cash further. "Used to give them mescaline, feed their imaginations more like, worked like a charm. But I'll tell you something you don't know – Cynthia gave the Devil his money's worth, before she passed out that is!"

Again he chuckled. Ruby shot Cash another warning look.

"I can't believe the old girl bought it though, not really. Most of them played willingly along, enjoyed the game, most of them except that bloody Darlene that is, frigid she was."

"Mr Rawlings," said Ruby firmly, tiring not only of him all of a sudden, but the stench in the room and its thick, oppressive atmosphere, "Cynthia *did* believe you. And she's tormented in death because of it. I want you to help me help her."

"Help *her*?" Mr Rawlings snorted. "Why should I help her? I don't give a damn about her. She dropped me after that one encounter she did. Shame really, cos like you said, she hit the big time soon after, I would have liked a share in that. Hell can have her for all I care."

"Come on, let's go," started Cash, obviously finding him unbearable too. "We're wasting our time here." But Ruby wasn't going to give up so easily.

"Mr Rawlings," she began, "how old are you?"

Clearly taken aback at the change of subject, Rawlings faltered before replying sharply, "Mind your own bloody business."

"Okay," said Ruby, maintaining a deliberate coolness. "I'm guessing you're in your mid-eighties. Whatever, there can't be many years left in you. You've done a lot of harm in your life; hurt a lot of people. There's such a thing as karma you know."

"Karma? I don't believe in karma," he snorted.

"Even so, it exists; there are consequences to actions, always."

"I want you to leave," Rawlings started to rise from his chair but Ruby sat still.

"Do you ever feel afraid Mr Rawlings? As though someone is watching you?"

"No." His denial was emphatic as he dropped back down, but fear had begun to dance in his eyes.

"But what if someone *is* watching you, someone who wants to make you pay for what you did? Darlene, perhaps?"

Incensed, his nostrils flared as he spat back, "I went to prison because of Darlene, I've paid already."

"Two years for what you did to her? It was tantamount to rape, wasn't it? Do you really think Darlene would agree that two years was payment enough?"

Before he could answer, she carried on. "You need to do something to redress the balance while you can. Counter bad with good. It will stand you well at your life review."

"Life review? What the..."

"I can see her, Mr Rawlings, Darlene, as clear as day, she's standing behind you. She was a pretty young thing, wasn't she? Lovely brown hair. But, oh dear, she's not happy with you, what you did to her, what you did to the others. She's not happy at all."

His eyes flickered nervously, first to his left and then to his right.

"She's probably going to be the first person you see when you pass over and, believe me, I don't think you're going to enjoy your encounter with her so much this time."

There was a slight turn of his head.

"But, Mr Rawlings," Ruby spoke more softly now. "I could explain to her how sorry you are, that in the end you tried to make amends. It will stand you in good stead. It will make her go away."

As he contemplated her words, Ruby was surprised to note that actually there wasn't anybody waiting in the shadows for Geoffrey Rawlings, no Darlene, no other wronged starlet, not even the Grim Reaper. She'd tell him so, but only after he'd helped her.

"Mr Rawlings..." Ruby was beginning to run out of patience.

Clutching onto his cardigan with gnarled hands, there was a tremor in his voice as he replied.

"What do you want me to do?"

"Come with me to Highdown Hall. You've got some explaining to do."

Chapter Thirteen

"I didn't think you could do it, but you did, you swung it good and proper," said Cash, standing outside in the fresh air again, bitter now that evening had descended and, like her, breathing in great gulps of it, trying to remove the stench of the flat that clung not just to the outside of them, to their clothes, but to their insides too, contaminating them.

"I have my ways," said Ruby, smiling in mock allure.

"I'm aware of that," replied Cash, his eyes sparkling.

More thoughtfully he asked, "So, come on, *is* Darlene waiting for him in the shadows?"

Ruby shook her head. "No, she isn't. There's no one, on this side or the next it seems."

Rawlings had agreed that they could come back and pick him up first thing on Monday for the drive to Highdown Hall. Ruby would have preferred to go sooner, but Theo and Corinna had weekend commitments and she didn't want to interrupt them. Besides which, she was pretty sure she'd spooked Rawlings enough that he wouldn't change his mind in the meantime, if anything the extra time would give him longer to dwell on things.

Taking shelter from the icy sea wind, in the doorway of a nearby hotel, Ruby called Mr Kierney to tell him when they would be with him.

"I should bloody hope so," he snarled. "That thing's been making a racket up there, banging and crashing at all hours. I'm sick of it."

Concealing her dismay at his attitude, she then called Theo,

Ness and Corinna in turn to tell them what time to meet them at the Hall on Monday. Theo, she could tell, was unsure at the prospect of bringing Rawlings along, but Ruby had insisted he would only be brought into the room as a last resort. Theo eventually conceded, reluctantly.

Walking back to the car, Cash vented his frustration. "Geoffrey Rawlings, though, what a bastard. I'm not surprised he hasn't got anyone waiting for him, someone nice I mean."

"I know what you mean, Cash, and I don't condone what he's done, but it's not our place to stand in judgement."

"I can't help it, Ruby. That man is vile."

"What he's *done* is vile. I think deep down even he knows that."

"I wouldn't be so sure," Cash replied derisively.

"Mr Rawlings was an ordinary man who worked out a way to bed extraordinary women – albeit an horrendous one." Ruby countered. "If he doesn't fully realise the impact of his actions on this side, he will do when he crosses over, of that I am sure." Shaking her head, she continued. "And let's face it; they don't come more extraordinary than Cynthia. She would never have looked at someone like him – even before she was famous – if he hadn't enticed her with promises of what he could do for her. Her desperation and greed was what he tapped into to satisfy his own urges. It's really very sad."

Having reached the Ford, Cash turned to look at Ruby.

"Aren't you getting in?" she asked.

"Yeah, I'm getting in."

"What's the matter then?"

"I just wish I could see what you see."

Ruby was perplexed. "See spirits you mean?"

Cash laughed. "No, nothing quite as grand as that. I meant in human terms. I wish I could see what lies below the surface, just like you do."

"I'm not so sure you don't," Ruby replied, meaning every word.

On Monday morning, at ten o'clock prompt, the Psychic Surveys team and Cash met as arranged on the gravel drive in front of Highdown Hall.

"Did everyone open their advent calendars today?" Corinna asked.

As Cash nodded enthusiastically, Ruby raised an eyebrow at him.

"What?" he rushed to his own defence. "They're not just for kids you know."

Even Ness suppressed a chuckle at this.

Standing beside them was Rawlings. He looked very subdued indeed, his eyes downcast, but every now and again he was unable to resist glancing up nervously at the house. He had been silent for most of the journey from Brighton to Highdown too, pulling nervously at the tie around his neck. The fact that he had dressed up for such an occasion, in a two-piece brown suit, a shirt the colour of nicotine and a brown tie, touched Ruby in a way she hadn't expected. She wondered how often he had such a chance to dress up or whether the suit spent most of its time confined to the back of his wardrobe. Probably the latter, she suspected from its rumpled appearance.

"Did you know Cynthia lived locally?" she asked him, laying a hand on his arm, hoping to portray in some way how grateful she was that he had agreed to come with them.

"No, of course not," he growled. "I forgot about the bitch after she dumped me."

Theo visibly stiffened at his words.

"I don't think it's helpful to address Cynthia as a bitch, Mr Rawlings," she admonished. "I'd rather you refrained from using such language."

Rawlings muttered something in reply, but whether it was an apology or not, Ruby couldn't tell.

Cash picked up the bag containing the smudge sticks,

crystals and oils and followed Ruby to the front door. She'd noticed her necklace still round his neck earlier; it didn't look like he'd taken it off since the day she had given it to him. Almost involuntarily, her hand reached up to her own neck and the replacement necklace that graced it, a tourmaline one this time. Also effective at repelling negative energy, her grandmother had given it to her several years ago. This necklace was something of a family heirloom, having once belonged to her great-grandmother, Rosamund, and as such it was extra precious.

When Mr Kierney opened the door to them, a mixture of relief and distaste played across his face.

"The car keys," was his greeting, "I can't find the bloody car keys. I'm sure she's responsible for that as well, she keeps bloody moving things."

Ruby was equally sure Mr Kierney's own absent-mindedness was responsible for the regular loss of his car keys, as well as any other items that happened to go amiss, but she didn't say so. Instead, she was relieved when at last he located them and headed outside.

"Call me when it's over," he shouted before scarpering.

Before they made their way to Cynthia's bedroom, Ruby turned to her team. "I think we should take a few moments to ground ourselves, to reinforce our protective shields. Cynthia probably won't be happy to see us again, not at first anyway. Cash, I'll fix your shield. Theo, perhaps you can include Mr Rawlings in your visualisation too?"

"I thought you said he wouldn't be coming into the bedroom with us?" started Theo.

"He won't be unless absolutely necessary. It's just a precaution."

Theo did as she was bid, looking far from pleased as she did so.

A few minutes later, they were ready to tackle the upstairs. Although not exactly light and cheerful downstairs, it was

137

distinctly preferable to the atmosphere that reigned the further up they climbed. Close to the turret, it was akin to wading through treacle.

Pointing to a chair on the landing, the same one Cash had occupied the first time they had visited Highdown Hall, high-backed and ornate with an upholstered seat, obviously an antique, Ruby said, "Mr Rawlings, perhaps you'd like to sit there and wait for us."

Rawlings mumbled another unintelligible reply as he shuffled over.

"Are you ready?" said Ruby to the others.

All four assured her they were.

"And, Cash, are you sure you want to come in with us?"

"I'm sure," he replied, his face stern with determination.

Ruby took a deep breath. "Let's go then."

The door was resistant. Ruby had expected this. She struggled slightly to get it to open, but at last it gave way. Once everybody was in, she closed the door behind them while everyone took up position in the centre of the room and closed their eyes. She had already explained to Cash that standing in a circle reinforced them by combining their strength. She had also advised him that, unless she or Theo said otherwise, he should remain holding hands with those on either side of him, especially once a connection had been made.

Satisfied that all was in place and everyone knew what to do, she began. "Cynthia, it's Ruby. My colleagues and I are back again. Please don't be angry with us, you know why we've come back, not to pester you but to help you. You're stuck in the dark, Cynthia, and you don't belong there."

The air around them was still. The only sound that of Cash shuffling.

"Cynthia," continued Ruby, "we know why you're hiding from the light."

Taking another deep breath and squeezing Cash's hand, she spoke Lytton's name.

Lytton! A voice beside her screamed. *He sold my soul. I want it back!*

Neither Corinna nor Cash could hear Cynthia's words but Theo and Ness stiffened immediately.

"Lytton has *not* sold your soul," Ruby's voice was resolute. "Neither he nor any other human being has the power to do so. Lytton was a fraud, Cynthia, a charlatan. He was exposed as such not once, but twice. You wouldn't have known, because it happened two years after you'd passed, in 1960. He tricked you, Cynthia, and not just you, other women too. He used your desire for fame to trick you. Your soul is your own."

There was silence again. Was she listening, Ruby wondered? Taking in what had been said? Trying to comprehend? Or perhaps she was already moving towards the light, the lie that tethered her in fear to this realm revealed at last.

Ruby opened her eyes and glanced around. The atmosphere was calm. Too calm.

Suddenly Ness's eyes flew open too.

"She's still here, Ruby, she doesn't believe you, she's..."

Before Ness could finish what she was saying, a bulb in the chandelier above them exploded; then another and another. The sound making Corinna and Cash jump.

"Visualise light and love," Theo advised. "Don't be distracted by theatricals."

In a repeat of last time, the dressing table and bed started shaking – the atmosphere around them darkening considerably, and not just because of the loss of electric light.

"This isn't working," whispered Ruby to Theo. "We're just irritating her further. I've got no choice; I've got to get Rawlings in."

"I really don't think you should," Theo whispered back but urgently.

Ruby stood her ground.

"It's the only idea I have right now. We need to send Cynthia to the light, not only for her sake but for Psychic Surveys too.

You know the damage Mr Kierney could do us."

Before Theo could retort, Ruby let go of her hand and Cash's, joining them together instead. Making for the door, she had to use her hand to feel her way, unable to believe how dark the room had become despite the natural light streaming in through the tall windows.

The door was stuck again, keeping them in this time instead of locking them out. She didn't know if she'd be able to yank it open by herself or whether she'd need Cash to come and help. Gradually, it relented.

"Mr Rawlings," shouted Ruby, startling him. "Would you please come in?"

Although he looked wary, he obeyed. Ruby surrounding him with more white light as he shuffled forward.

"It's okay," she said, taking hold of his hand. "You'll be safe, I promise. I just want you to explain what happened, that Cynthia did *not* sell her soul to the Devil. That her fame was due to her talent and persistence, nothing more. Speak loud and clear. And, Mr Rawlings," she added, "it might be an idea to say you're sorry."

Leading him to the safety of the circle, Ruby prompted him to speak.

"Cynthia," he said, his voice quivering at first but gaining in strength the more he spoke. "It's me, Raw... Lytton."

Abruptly, all activity seized.

"I... I've come to apologise for duping you all those years ago. I never thought for one minute you would believe me. I... I just wanted to... to be with you. You were *so* beautiful."

"Go on," Ruby encouraged.

"It was a bad thing I did, a very bad thing, I know that now. But I want you to know, I was never in league with the Devil. Of course I wasn't. I tricked you. I'm sorry."

"Cynthia," Ruby took over, "your rise to fame, I believe it happened soon after the incident with Lytton. But it had nothing to do with him or with any satanic force. You were, quite simply, a talented actress, one of the finest the world has ever seen. That was the reason for your success, nothing more, nothing less. Stop hiding, Cynthia. Come out."

Nothing. No response at all. Where *was* she? Was she even listening?

"Has it worked?" Rawlings asked, but as soon as he opened his mouth, the dressing table chair flew across the room, landing just short of the bed.

"Get him out!" yelled Theo, referring to the old man, but she needn't have bothered. He was already running on surprisingly nimble legs towards the room's only exit, disappearing into the safety of the corridor.

Grabbing hold of Theo's hand, Ruby closed the circle yet again.

"Cynthia!" she yelled, but in her mind only.

Liar, came the acrid reply. *You're all liars, him as well as you!*

"Cynthia," Theo tried to remonstrate. "Cynthia, we don't want to upset you, believe me, that is not our intention. We brought Lytton here only to help you realise that you do not belong to evil, that you belong to all that is good, whatever he made you think then. Please, I implore you, linger here no more. Look to where the light is shining and go to it. You are quite safe."

This is my home! I will not leave.

"But why, Cynthia? Why won't you leave?" It was Ness this time.

Because he's there, in the dark, waiting for me. I cannot leave.

Ruby was nonplussed. Who was waiting for her in the dark? Not the Devil, they'd established that.

"Cynthia," she beseeched, "look again, there is no one waiting for you in the dark, no one at all."

Yes there is!

As Cynthia flung these words at them, the room was plunged into complete darkness. Ruby could only feel the others now, and she could also feel the energy around her building to catastrophic proportions. Suddenly another agonising scream

141

rang out, but one that was all too human.

As the daylight began to edge its way warily back, Theo was the first to step forward, shouting Corinna's name. Looking over, Ruby could see Corinna, slumped in a heap on the floor, blood pouring from the side of her temple.

"Oh God," she breathed, rushing to Corinna's side also.

"Be careful, don't touch her, not until we know what's wrong," said Ness, calm and level-headed.

It was Cash who found the perfume bottle, lying just a few feet from where Corinna lay.

"Could Cynthia have thrown this?" he asked, alerting the others to it.

Ruby nodded. "Yes, I think she could have done."

"A ghost can do that?" replied Cash in horror.

"Only when severely provoked," said Theo, her accusatory tone not lost on Ruby.

Corinna was coming round.

"Ugh," she said groggily. "What happened?"

Her hand reaching up, she touched her head gingerly with her fingertips.

"Blood," she said. "Why am I bleeding?"

"Don't worry, sweetheart, it's okay," Theo replied tenderly. "Cynthia got a bit upset, that's all. We need to get you out of here though, to a hospital, straight away."

"No, I'm fine..." started Corinna, trying to get to her feet but quickly becoming overwhelmed by wooziness, she sank back down again.

Cash hooked his hands underneath her arms and raised her gently to her feet. Lifting Corinna into his own arms, he cradled her there whilst looking at Theo.

"Take her to my car," instructed Theo. "And Rawlings too; take them both."

As Cash carried Corinna out of the room, Theo and Ness turned to Ruby.

"You should *never* have brought him in here," said Theo, her brown eyes blazing.

"I thought it would help," replied Ruby, feeling small suddenly.

"Well, now you know," said Theo, turning abruptly and leaving the room. Ness, who had said nothing but looked decidedly more sympathetic than Theo, followed her.

Alone in the grand, empty room, Ruby looked around. Everything was normal. Well, as normal as it could be in a haunted shrine. She knew Cynthia had used up all her energy in that strike against Corinna, she'd be exhausted now, drained completely.

"I'm not done with you, Cynthia," Ruby shouted out, anger temporarily replacing any sympathy she might have previously felt for her. "What you did today, attacking Corinna, was not acceptable. You don't belong at Highdown Hall, not anymore. Face up to it. And you are wrong. There is *no one* waiting for you in the shadows. You belong in the light, Cynthia, and make no mistake; I will be the one to send you there. I won't rest until I do."

As she turned to go, Ruby was sure she could hear the sound of weeping.

***

How dare they bring that man in here, the man who insisted he was Lytton. How could he be? Lytton was younger than her, a year or so, not an old man almost at the end of his days. He was further proof they were lying, that they hadn't got a clue what they were talking about. Via Corinna, she had shown them she was a woman not to be messed with.

A cry of anguish escaped Cynthia. Did they *really* think she would believe them? Lytton, his face, she would never forget it, or his legacy. The very first time they had met she had known there was something about him. He seemed to walk alone, tall and straight, a confident air about him. She had been appearing

143

in a play at the Strand at the time, *Summer's End*, as the daughter-in-law to the main character, and Lytton; he had waited outside for her, at the stage doors. Many people would wait outside the stage doors, pencil and paper in hand, poised to ask the stars for their autographs; but never *her* autograph, they didn't want the signature of someone who uttered less than ten lines in just under two hours. Of course she'd been flattered by his attentions.

"You're the real star of that show," he had said, catching up beside her as she hurried along the Embankment. "You knock the others into a cocked hat."

"Go away," she had replied lightly. How she wished she had meant it.

"It's a lovely night, let's go for a drink, I'll buy."

When she had started to protest, he'd turned on the charm. "No, really, it would be such an honour if you did."

He wasn't a bad looking man. He had a twinkle in those blue eyes of his. A certain charisma, she supposed. Besides which, she was lonely. Since arriving in London she had made numerous friends but many had fallen by the wayside over the years, often citing her ambition for driving a wedge between them.

"You think of nothing else," one friend, Elsie, had said to her once. "It's... it's stifling."

Stifling it may be, but she held onto her dreams and one day she would show them, she had promised herself that.

One drink with Lytton had turned into two, one night into another. He appeared to be her greatest fan, constantly telling her how beautiful she was, how talented, how damned unfair it was that the world would not wake up and take notice. He seemed to understand her; he also said he could help her. She couldn't deny it, she had been intrigued.

He had a flat in Central London, in the Lancaster Gate area. When he had told her, Cynthia had been impressed. She rented a room from a lady in the East End, in a house no better than the one she grew up in, something that irked her terribly, particularly when she lay awake in the lonely hours of the early morning. That evening she had finished work and hurried along to the address he had written down for her on a scrap of paper.

"There might be others in attendance, you don't mind, do you?" he had asked her.

Of course, she didn't mind. In fact, she thought she might prefer it. Even though she craved attention, she found him overbearing at times. Perhaps it was the way he licked his lips when he spoke to her or the way his eyes flickered constantly to her bosom. Lascivious was a word she had just learnt. It had been used to describe a character in a new script she was reading, and it seemed to suit Lytton perfectly. Still, he said he could help her and how he could do so, she was keen to know.

Arriving at his flat, just around the corner from the Bayswater Road, she had been disappointed by what she had found. It was not grand at all, but positioned at the top of a once grand but now run-down Victorian town house. Less than salubrious characters peppering the streets about it.

The front door had been left open. She let herself in and climbed three flights of stairs, trying not to breathe in the stale smell of urine, sweat and something else, something vaguely familiar.

Reaching No.8, Lytton's flat, she found the door to that open too. Before entering, she listened carefully to see if she could hear anyone inside, but all was silent.

"Mr Lytton?" she had called upon entering. And then, more daringly, "Clive?"

The room was empty. Looking around, she had noted a large bed in the far corner, grubby curtains hanging at the windows and little else. Had it not been for the tempting promise of what he could do for her, she would have turned on her heels right then. Where *was* he?

"Ah, my darling," said a voice to her right. Mr Lytton emerged from the bathroom, clad in a silk dressing gown.

"There you are. Come in, come in. Just us tonight, I'm afraid. Lucinda and Arabella couldn't make it. Terribly disappointing, I know."

Briefly, Cynthia wondered who Lucinda and Arabella were; she had also wondered at their names, they seemed to belong to creatures far more exotic than her. Walking towards her, Lytton reached out an arm, shutting the door behind her. She was in his lair. A fly caught in a spider's web.

Lytton must have noticed how nervous she was.

"Relax," he had said, "have some of this."

It was the smell she had noticed in the hallway, the smell that sometimes drifted out from the dressing rooms of the back street theatres she worked in, making her feel lightheaded whenever she breathed it in.

"Go on," he had noticed her reluctance, "it won't hurt you."

She did as he wanted her too, took a few drags of the cigarette offered to her, wanting very much to relax; it was something she didn't allow herself to do very often.

After a few moments her head started to spin but she found herself giggling too, suddenly everything seemed funny; she remembered that, gloriously funny.

She continued smoking, one cigarette perhaps or was it two? She had drunk vodka too, not her normal tipple, shot after shot. She couldn't remember having so much fun. Mr Lytton was clearly having fun too.

How many hours had passed? She didn't know. Time was as hazy then as it was now. Finally, she had asked him the question she had longed to ask him all night.

"How can you help me?"

She remembered his words.

"Your dreams, I can help you achieve them. It's what I do."

Beating back a faint wave of nausea, she had leaned forward, eager to hear more.

"Tell me..."

And he did. About the Devil he served, the dark lord who

made all things possible. Cynthia remembered giggling even more at his words, taking another shot of vodka, her head lurching violently as she did so.

Recovering herself, she had scoffed, "And the Devil's going to help *me*?"

"The Devil is on your side."

Which was more than God was, she remembered thinking. She had prayed so hard for recognition, her fervent pleas falling on deaf ears.

"And how do I get in touch with the Devil?" she was still only teasing, or so she had thought, her mind swimming by this time.

"Through me," had been Lytton's reply, reaching for the bottle and pouring the contents straight into her mouth, some of it missing, dribbling down her chin, onto the dark green dress she had been wearing.

Darkness had claimed her then. Not the all-consuming darkness that held her in its grip now, but a patchy darkness she had woken from to find herself riding Lytton, sitting astride him, completely naked as was he, her dress discarded. Peering closer she realised it wasn't Lytton. It was the creature he had been talking about, the Devil himself, impossibly handsome but with depthless eyes, eyes she could drown in. And then he had smiled; a smile that had both scintillated and terrified her, his mouth a cavern which she had to stop herself falling into. His hands had come up then to grab at her breasts, sharp claws leaving trails of blood behind them she was sure. She had ridden him harder, harder still, realising after a few moments that it was she who was the one laughing, a wild sound, joining him in madness. She had – and she shuddered to admit it now – enjoyed rutting with the creature below her. She had wanted all he had to give, at whatever price.

Again blackness consumed her; again she had come round. Lytton was nowhere to be seen. She remembered sitting up in bed, the carnage surrounding her jolting her fully awake; empty vodka bottles, several of them, cigarette ends, clothes strewn everywhere, hers not his. Moving slowly, she had felt sore, violated in places she hadn't thought possible. Testament to the evil she had courted.

Gathering her clothes, she had hurried from Lytton's flat, vowing never to return. For days after she had lain low, sobbing, aching and refusing to move from the dismal confines of her tawdry room. She had lost her part in *Summer's End*; they couldn't afford to wait for her. Life had seemingly fallen apart; but then it had blossomed, unexpectedly, spectacularly, the Devil true to his word, despite the fact that she had doubted him.

And now it was payback time. Now he had come to collect. The Devil didn't forget.

Chapter Fourteen

Back at his flat, Ruby and Cash continued to soothe a highly agitated Rawlings; Ruby terrified that today might spawn another casualty. She suspected that at his age his heart might be weak, perhaps prone to angina which could easily lead to a heart attack. However, after keeping a careful eye on him, he gradually calmed, eventually asking them to go.

"Are you sure you'll be alright?" Ruby was worried still.

"Fine, I'll be fine," he said, but his voice was subdued.

Having settled him in his armchair with a fresh cup of tea, she found a tartan blanket in his bedroom, thrown on top of a hard-backed chair in the corner. Sniffing it, it didn't smell too bad. She returned to the living room and tucked it round his legs. Next she switched the TV on.

"Leave it on BBC1," he ordered, "always rubbish on the other side."

Doing as she was bid, some drama in full flow, she turned to him. "I'll phone you tomorrow and perhaps I'll come by later in the week? Check you're okay."

"Suit yourself," the old man grunted in reply. Before she and Cash took their leave, however, he spoke again.

"I know what I did," he said, his voice so low Ruby wasn't actually sure he meant them to hear. "I know what I was, I'm not proud. And I *am* sorry. I hope she finds peace soon."

"Me too," whispered Ruby, gently shutting the door behind her.

***

Outside on the street, Ruby phoned Theo.

"She had to have four stitches," Theo bluntly informed her.

Theo and Corinna often worked together; there was a strong bond between them, almost like that of a mother and daughter.

"Tell her... please tell her I'm sorry. Where is she now?" asked Ruby.

"At home, with her parents. Resting. She's exhausted."

"Yes, of course she is, I'll call her tomorrow."

"Do that," said Theo before adding, "I think we need a meeting soon, set a few things straight."

"Yes," said Ruby meekly. "I'll speak to you tomorrow too."

After hanging up, Ruby felt the burden of guilt weighing heavily upon her.

"Hey," said Cash, putting his arms around her and drawing her close. "What happened to Corinna, it's not your fault. You were doing what you thought was best."

Comforted by his embrace, she felt tears prick at her eyes but she would not let them fall. She was stronger than that. Unfortunately, her emotions refused to cooperate with her steadfast thoughts and several tears escaped, spilling rebelliously onto her cheeks. Quickly she pushed Cash away, wiping roughly at her eyes with the back of her hand.

"I need... I need to get back to the office," she said hastily. "I've got admin to do. I'll drop you back home."

Cash must have sensed she meant it; he didn't push further. Instead, he walked with her back to the car; the subsequent drive from Brighton to Lewes a silent one.

"I'll call you tomorrow." Cash's voice was concerned but firm as he got out of the car. "Okay," was all she could manage in reply.

Ruby was already dreading tomorrow. Not because of Cash, but because of the conversations she would have to have with Theo and Mr Kierney.

Sitting for a few minutes in her car, her hand on the steering wheel, she decided not to go to her office after all. She would go home. Not to the flat in De Montfort Road but to Hastings; her real home, back to her grandmother. She desperately needed validation for her actions, reassurance that she had done the right thing in bringing Rawlings to Highdown Hall, even if the right thing had made things worse. Only Gran, a woman whose passion for helping grounded spirits she had inherited, could give her that support. Putting her foot down on the accelerator, she sped out of Lewes and onto country roads.

***

Ruby's mother, Jessica, and grandmother, Sarah, lived together in a cottage in the Old Town of Hastings. Theirs was a modest 3-bedroomed house, the bedroom that used to belong to Ruby kept much the same as it was when she had left at the age of eighteen, eager to strike out on her own. Sarah always kept a vase of fresh flowers in Ruby's bedroom, not just because she loved them, but because she believed their bright beauty kept alive a room that lay mostly empty, preventing it from stagnating or drawing attention.

It was just after six when Ruby arrived in the Old Town. She parked her car in the free zone, about a ten minute walk from the house.

Although she had lived in Lewes for several years, Hastings – the town she had grown up in – was still very much a part of her. She loved it here, it *felt* like home. She was particularly fond of the Old Town, with its mixture of houses and cottages vying for space amongst its tiny, winding lanes; some dated back as far as the thirteenth century, while a few distinctly more modern ones were at odds with their surroundings. The High Street ran the length of the Old Town and was traffic-free. Like her adopted town of Lewes, it boasted an interesting assortment of shops, rather unique one-of-a-kind shops, selling antiques predominantly, but also second-hand books, jewellery and clothes. Dotted in between were several warm and welcoming coffee shops, as well as cafés and a couple of fish restaurants. There were pubs too, some of the finest in Hastings many would say – The Jenny Lind, The Hastings Arms, The First In Last Out – frequented not by the people who lived in the more modern part of town but the residents of the Old Town themselves. People she had grown up with, people who remembered her well, who always welcomed her back with open arms.

Drawing closer to Lazuli Cottage, the cry of seagulls loud above her, Ruby wondered if she should have called ahead. But she needn't have worried. As she walked up the cobbled path, weeds poking determinedly between the stones, the door opened.

"Ruby! Lovely to see you, darling," said her grandmother, her voice like velvet, as comforting as home itself. "I've just put the kettle on. Come in. You can tell me all about it."

Entering the narrow hallway, Ruby couldn't help but smile. Of course she didn't need to ring ahead, she never did with Gran. Following her, she bypassed the living room where a log fire burned, the smell of smoke and wood capturing the very essence of winter.

"Where's Mum?" she said, taking a seat at the kitchen table, a table that like her grandmother and mother before her, she had camped under as a child, lost in a world of her own making, a world just as removed from this one as the next.

"Upstairs, sleeping," said Sarah, pouring hot water into a teapot. "She's not feeling well."

Jessica hadn't felt well for as long as Ruby could remember. No, that wasn't strictly true, she chastised herself. If she reached back through the years, to when she was six, perhaps seven, she could remember her mother laughing, always laughing it seemed, full of life, exuberant. Not so pleasant memories of that time were the rows between her mother and grandmother, lots of them, the worry in the older woman's voice striking a chord with Ruby. Her mother had been headstrong, reckless even. She

152

must have been, it was the only explanation for what had happened to her, for the way she was now. Reckless when dealing with the spirit world for sure, opening herself up to forces she could have easily avoided. But what forces exactly? Ruby didn't know.

According to Sarah, every person's soul, without exception, was precious, no matter what heinous act they had committed; there was atonement, certainly, but in the form of re-education, not burning pits of brimstone and fire. Fear was often at the root of heinous acts. Fear, loneliness and rejection. Never just a propensity for evil alone. Once you understood that, believed that even the worst amongst us was magnificent at core, you began to understand the way the universe and everything in it worked. That everybody, *everything* was part of a much greater good. Ruby wanted to believe her grandmother. What she said made perfect sense. But if it were true, if evil as such did not exist, if demons weren't real, only the product of a creative mind, what had frightened her mother so much, rendering her little more than an empty shell for nearly eighteen years? Gran would never say. *It won't help you to know, Ruby,* she had told her once after Ruby had summoned up the courage to ask. *What is a part of your mother's world does not have to be a part of yours. Carry on with your work, stay in the light and you won't go wrong.*

Won't go wrong? Perhaps not, until now. Now she had veered off the path, big time.

Sitting opposite her, Sarah filled both their cups and then pushed a plate of homemade fruit cake towards her, a slice already cut and ready for her to take. Ruby hadn't seen her slice the cake, briefly she wondered how long her grandmother had known she was going to turn up. Before she'd even known herself?

Sipping at her tea, Sarah asked, "What's troubling you, dear?"

Ruby hesitated. She still felt so guilty about Corinna,

Rawlings, even Cash – putting them all in the line of fire. Behaving, perhaps, as recklessly as her mother had, inheriting yet another family trait.

"No, dear," said Sarah, her green eyes still bright, still sparkling despite the fact she wasn't far off eighty. "You are *not* like your mother, now tell me."

The tears she had fought so hard to keep at bay when Cash had wrapped his arms around her outside Rawlings flat, could not be thwarted any longer. As they fell in torrents down her cheeks, Ruby explained what had happened at Highdown Hall.

***

Sarah had never met Theo; she hadn't met any of the team, although Ruby had told her plenty about them. She admired Ruby, and them, for what they were trying to do: to dissolve the fearsome reputation still attached to dealings with the spiritual world by bringing the whole process out into the open. Despite this, she had made it clear to Ruby when she had first set up Psychic Surveys, that this was something her granddaughter must do independently of her family. Although Sarah would help anyone who asked her to, for many years now her main focus had been caring only for Jessica.

Focusing her soft eyes on Ruby now, Sarah considered her words carefully before she spoke.

"Now, I'm not saying I agree with Theo, I'm just saying I can see her point. However, I'm sure she knows, as I do, that you acted from good intention in bringing Rawlings to the cleansing, even if that intention was somewhat flawed."

Ruby's head came up abruptly.

"Flawed? In what way?"

"Geoffrey Rawlings in his guise as Clive Lytton was obviously a significant character in Cynthia Hart's life, but only in a negative sense. It therefore follows that despite his remorse he can only introduce further negativity to the process, stirring

154

up painful emotions within her. Emotions hard to deal with."

"But she wouldn't believe me when I told her that whole thing about selling your soul to the Devil was rubbish. I had to find some way to *prove* it to her."

"But you didn't prove a thing it seems. She still believes something is blocking her path to the light, something menacing – and it is causing her great distress."

"But there is *nothing*!" Ruby almost shouted. She felt so frustrated.

"It is not your place to decide that." Sarah's voice became sterner too. "You are *not* Cynthia and you do not know what she is experiencing."

Trying to keep her emotions under control, Ruby muttered, "So what do I do now?"

"More research for a start. Find out what else could possibly be keeping her there."

"If I'm allowed to," Ruby replied, downcast. "Mr Kierney's not going to be impressed we failed a second time. He may not let me try again."

"Find a way to persuade him. You can't leave Cynthia in the state she is in. Arm yourself with as much information as you can before you try again. Go prepared."

A tired smile crossed Ruby's features. "Psychic Surveys? Psychic Investigations more like."

"All part and parcel, my dear," Sarah smiled back at her. "Now, I think I'll wake your mother, dinner will be ready soon."

Ruby steeled herself as Sarah left the room, having to bolster herself before coming face to face with Jessica again; she always looked so lost it was hard to bear. Thank God her grandmother rose brilliantly to the challenge of looking after her, fussing over her as though she were a small child still, wrapping her tightly in her own special brand of love, doing her best to make an unbearable life bearable. But what would happen when Gran passed? It was a question she would only ask herself occasionally. The baton would pass to her of course and it filled her with dread. There was no way she could do as good a job as Gran did, she just wasn't as selfless.

Whilst Sarah put the finishing touches to dinner, boiling peas to go with the shepherd's pie she had made earlier in the day, and warming plates, Ruby sat and did a jigsaw with her mother. When Jessica had first entered the room, she had smiled at Ruby, kissed her on the cheek and then looked away. Ruby knew what to do to engage her though.

Jessica adored jigsaws, had always done apparently, since she'd been a small child. She did them avidly, day in, day out. Sarah said they helped to keep her mind occupied. Getting up and going into the living room, Ruby stopped to admire the small Christmas tree in the corner, how bright and jolly it looked. Next, she found the board upon which was scattered the pieces of her mother's latest project, a picture detail from the Sistine Chapel in Rome – God's finger pointing. Bringing it back to the kitchen table, her mother's eyes lit up. Both she and Ruby got to work, her mother's hands working swiftly, Ruby's excruciatingly slow in comparison. Unlike her mother, she wasn't keen on jigsaws.

"Dinner's ready," said her grandmother, smiling indulgently at both her daughter and granddaughter. *My two favourite people in the world,* she would often say.

Pushing the board to one side, Sarah started to dish up. Jessica's portion was meagre compared to Ruby's but both ate what they were given, Ruby not realising until the plate of steaming hot food was put in front of her, just how ravenous she was.

Afterwards, Sarah made coffee and the three of them retired to the living room to sit in front of the fire, Sarah and Ruby chatting, careful to refer only to mundane everyday matters, whilst Jessica stared into the distance – at what, Ruby didn't know.

Chapter Fifteen

Ruby rose early the next morning, intending to be at her desk by nine sharp. On the doorstep of her childhood home, Sarah took hold of her hands and clasped them tightly.

"You're special, Ruby," she said, a light shining in her eyes, "truly deserving of the gift you've been given. Great-gran Rosamund would have been so proud of you. I'm proud of you. So is your mother. What you do is good, really good. Remember that."

"I will," said Ruby, bolstered by her words, by her unwavering belief. Ready to tackle, once again, Cynthia Hart, or any spirit trapped by fear.

Walking away, she glanced up at her mother's bedroom window and was surprised to see her standing behind the glass; she didn't normally wake so early.

Ruby raised a hand to wave at her but Jessica did not wave back, she just continued to stare down at her, a slight frown on her face.

***

Back in the office, the heater turned to maximum, her fingerless gloves and woollen scarf kept on for extra warmth, Ruby restrained her hair in a pony tail before calling Mr Kierney. He was, as she had predicted, far from pleased.

"Last night was the worst ever. I didn't sleep a wink, not a bloody wink! And I've got an important meeting today. I blame you entirely," he shouted down the phone.

"Mr Kierney, I apologise, but we are making progress I assure you. Some cases just... well, they just take a little extra effort, that's all."

"Extra effort? You've been here three bloody times."

"I know, I know." Ruby didn't need reminding. "And all the procedures we have carried out to date usually meet with great success. Sometimes, however, a spirit is resistant and the reasons why aren't immediately obvious. I need to investigate further, which of course, I intend to do."

"Investigate further? Everything you need to know about her must be on the net; she was world-famous for God's sake."

"I know," Ruby tried to appease. "And we've searched the internet as well as historical records, but so far to no avail. We'll continue checking, obviously, and we'll need to visit Highdown Hall again too."

"Again? You want to come to my house again? You'll be moving in next!"

If that's what it takes, Ruby was tempted to reply. Instead, she said, "Please, Mr Kierney, I intend to solve this case and at no extra charge to you. I truly believe I am close to releasing Cynthia's spirit. Allow me to see it through."

After a long pause during which Ruby found herself holding her breath, Mr Kierney at last graced her with a reply.

"I'm moving out, going to stay with a friend in London until this nonsense is over. I'll give you time, Ruby, but not much, a week, no more. I plan to return to Highdown Hall with friends on Boxing Day, they're really looking forward to spending the rest of the festive season in the country; I don't want to let them down. Make sure she's gone by then or mine will be the last case you work on. Do I make myself clear?"

"Perfectly," replied Ruby through gritted teeth. Drawing a deep breath, she continued, "What about access to the house? Would you be willing to loan me a key?"

"If you want it, come and get it. I'll be gone by lunchtime."

Replacing the receiver, Ruby let her head fall into her hands.

All other Psychic Surveys cases would have to be dealt with by Theo, Ness and Corinna whilst she concentrated on Highdown Hall. There was no way she could afford to let one failure overshadow their achievements. More than that, she couldn't abandon Cynthia, no matter how cross she was with her right now for hurting Corinna. She'd have to dig deep, and be fast about it.

Thinking of Corinna, she phoned her next.

"Hi, hun," she said, "how are you?"

"Hey, Ruby," Corinna sounded chirpy enough. "I'm good, really, don't worry about me."

"But I am worried, I've never known a spirit attack before, not physically I mean. In many ways, I didn't think it was possible. I'm so sorry."

"No need to be, no need at all. How are you?"

Tired, she wanted to say, and not just because of lack of sleep. Instead, she responded, "I'm good too. Listen, Corinna, if you don't want to continue working for Psychic Surveys, I'd totally understand. What happened to you at Highdown, it was awful."

"Ruby," Corinna's voice was serious now. "I know I'm not as psychic as you are, as Theo or Ness, but I'm as committed. Don't ever doubt that."

Ruby felt contrite that she had done so.

"I won't, Corinna, and thanks, thank you so much. Rest today. I'll be in touch tomorrow. I'll pay you for today. Is that okay?"

"A duvet day sanctioned by the boss? Of course it's okay! See you tomorrow."

Two down, one to go – Theo.

***

Theo hadn't been quite as accommodating as Corinna, but she didn't sound as angry as she had done the day before. Ruby

159

explained that Mr Kierney was giving her the key to Highdown Hall, that she was picking it up today and that he would be absent for a week.

"Which leads us up to Christmas Eve – Cynthia's birthday and the night she died."

"So it does," replied Ruby, glancing at her desk calendar. "Interesting."

"If you're thinking of going there alone, Ruby, don't. This spirit is the strongest we've encountered; I don't want you getting hurt too."

"I won't," said Ruby, but she knew as much as Theo did that it was a lie. She *did* intend to go there alone. It may be the only way of finding out what really happened that night in 1958. With no one else's wellbeing to take into account, she could push Cynthia to remember, harder than she had done already.

"What about other cases, are there any you'd like us to help you with?" asked Theo, bringing Ruby back to the present.

"The answer machine's beeping furiously, so on that basis, I'd say yes please."

"I'll pop in later this afternoon with Ness so we can sort out some kind of rota; leave you free to research Cynthia, an actress, who I'm afraid, I'm not quite as enamoured with as I used to be."

"I'll be back around three o'clock," said Ruby, relieved that Theo too had no intention of abandoning her. But how much more they wanted to take of Cynthia she didn't know.

Chapter Sixteen

Mr Kierney wouldn't let Ruby past the front door when she turned up at Highdown Hall later that morning.

"You can do what you have to do when I'm gone," he had said, "I want no more of it."

Handing her a brown envelope with the key in it, he continued, "There are instructions inside on how to use the alarm system as well as the gate code. Under no circumstances leave the house unalarmed or the gates open."

Assuring him she wouldn't, she turned to go, glancing fleetingly up at the turret where Cynthia still resided as she did so. She was not a fan of horror films, found the scream-inducing tricks they used to frighten their audiences predictable and pathetic, but even she had half-expected a face to appear suddenly at the window, glowing white features transformed into a twisted grimace, claw-like hands reaching up to frantically scrape at the glass. She rarely felt fear, but a frisson made itself known in the pit of her stomach and refused to go away. Despite it, or maybe in spite of it, she still intended to come back – but to say she wasn't looking forward to it was something of an understatement.

***

When she arrived back at the office, Cash was waiting outside as they'd arranged by text earlier. Ushering him in, she quickly updated him on Highdown Hall as they climbed the stairs.

"Okay, but you're not going there alone are you?" his thoughts obviously echoing Theo's.

After contemplating lying for a moment, she decided to come clean instead.

"Yes, yes I am."

"Are you mad?" Cash exploded, his voice bounding off the walls. "Cynthia is dangerous, she hurt Corinna, she'll hurt you too. You *can't* go back alone."

"I have to." Ruby was resolute. Trying to lighten their exchange, she continued, "But don't worry, I won't go back in the dead of night or anything. I'll go during daytime."

"You won't go there at all, not without me."

"Cash," Ruby was getting irate too, "you can't come with me, not this time. I *have* to go alone. Research only ever offers so much; in fact, it's offered us barely anything in this case. From everything I've read, Cynthia was whiter than white. But if that were so, if it were true, how come she's stuck here, afraid to move on? We've exposed Lytton but still she's afraid. What of? We're not going to find out by looking on the internet or in old newspapers, that's for sure."

Running one hand over his close cropped hair in a gesture of exasperation, Cash said, "Well, it's obvious. She doesn't believe you, that's all. She thinks the Devil's still after her."

"But *why* does she think that?" Ruby felt exasperated too. "And why can't she remember what happened the night of her death? I mean, I know it must have been awful, but was it *that* awful? I need to find out and the only way I can do that is by connecting again – if I'm alone, maybe, I don't know... *maybe* I can get her to cooperate."

"And there's really nothing on the net or anywhere else? Nothing at all that could give you an insight?"

Ruby shook her head. "You know as well as I do, we've exhausted every website, book and record of her there is. Like I said, her public persona, it's impeccable. There's not even a hint of scandal."

162

"Okay," Cash finally conceded. "I understand you need to go back but I'm coming too. I'll wait downstairs, even outside if you insist, but at least I'll be there if you need me."

Knowing he was adamant, she changed the subject.

"Show me this website then," she said, turning to the computer.

"Haven't you seen it yet? I told you when you emailed me the photos and final copy that I'd put it up live as soon as I'd finished."

"I thought we might look at it together," she replied, almost shyly.

Raising an eyebrow at her, he seemed amused by this but touched also, his features definitely softening.

"A grand unveiling you mean?"

"Something like that," she replied, unable to quite meet his gaze.

Doing as she was instructed, she typed Psychic Surveys into the search engine. Straightaway her company came up, at the top of the listings. There was the bold header: PsychicSurveys.com, under that the sub-heading 'Surveys and Holistic Spiritual Clearance' – their final chosen typeface not gothic in any way, but clean and crisp. There was also a picture of the team, one she already had that had been taken for free for promotional purposes by a photographer friend of Corinna's. It showed the four of them standing outside the office building in Lewes, looking professional but relaxed – approachable. Also on the home page was general information about the company, introducing the team and what they did, as well as the links to more detailed information on the services they provided. There was also a twitter link, a Facebook link, an email contact form and easy-to-find telephone numbers. The whole site looked fresh and modern.

"Well?" said Cash, slightly nervously she thought.

"Well..." repeated Ruby, deliberately drawing the moment out. Turning to face him, she smiled widely. "It looks great, really great. It looks fantastic."

Before he could reply, she continued, "I have to be honest, I was a bit worried you might make it all dark and spooky with pictures of phantoms and the like, but you've done no such thing. You've done what you said, you've brought us out of the dark ages and smack bang into modern times. You've made us look as though we know what we're doing."

"I did think you knew what you were doing," an edge had returned to Cash's voice, "it's only now I'm not so sure."

Ignoring what he was referring to, Ruby turned back to the computer, clicking on various links on the website instead, trying to imagine herself as a potential client reading the blurb, what she would make of it. She had to admit, she'd be impressed.

"Check your emails," Cash said, his voice still a little tight. "See if you've had any enquiries yet."

She did. "Look, there's an email from a Mrs Potter in Leeds!"

Mrs Potter explained that she had seen the website and thought Psychic Surveys might be able to help her. She went on to explain she wasn't sure her house was haunted as such, but she did think it held some sort of negative energy as everyone had been feeling lethargic since moving in. She wondered if a long distance healing could be performed first, as the website suggested, then, if things didn't improve, perhaps a house visit. While Cash looked on, Ruby responded immediately, saying that she would get her colleague, Theo, who specialised in distance healings, to call her within twenty-four hours to discuss how best to proceed with her case.

Pressing 'send', Ruby turned to Cash and said, "Thanks to you, the crusade is already beginning to reach far and wide."

Well, as far as Leeds anyway.

***

Having finally finished responding to her telephone

messages, Ruby drew up a work rota for Theo and Ness when they popped in later that afternoon. The meeting was perfunctory and soon Ruby and Cash were on their own again.

Glancing at his watch, Cash said, "Seeing as we missed lunch, how do you fancy an early dinner?"

"Okay," agreed Ruby, not sure how dinner was going to go exactly.

Cash had become increasingly distant during the afternoon. Several times she had caught him staring at her, well, frowning at her would be a more accurate description, but she had left him to get on with his work, building another website, this time for an up and coming structural engineering company in Brighton, whilst she got on with hers.

They decided to have a drink in The Rights of Man pub first, Gracie greeting them both enthusiastically, temporarily lightening the atmosphere between them with her chatter. After a glass of wine each, they headed to a family-run Italian restaurant. A few minutes' walk away and a favourite of Ruby's, she would often meet friends there for dinner. Cash was subdued over their meal, a delicious seafood linguini for both of them, the restaurant's speciality, and Ruby wondered if this was it – the beginning of the end. What she did for a living was just too much to handle for the average person.

The walk home had been as quiet as the streets themselves, past shop windows dressed-up tantalisingly for Christmas, some of them glittering and bold, others self-consciously tasteful. Both of them came to a standstill outside her front door. Ruby knew it was cold but she could not quite feel it somehow. She felt numb. Stealing a glance at the man in front of her, she had to admit, there was nothing average about Cash.

Lost in thought, it was a second before she realised he was speaking.

"What are you doing tomorrow?" he asked.

"It's Wednesday, working of course." Inwardly she winced; she hadn't meant to sound as snappy as she did.

"You're not going to Highdown?"

"Not tomorrow, no."

"Promise?"

"Promise," she said, keeping her fingers crossed behind her back. A childish gesture, she knew, but one she hoped still carried weight.

Leaning over to kiss her on the cheek, he whispered in her ear, "Don't, just don't," before walking away.

Rather than striking dread into her, his words ignited a glimmer of hope. Maybe, just maybe, his withdrawal from her today had nothing to do with not caring about her anymore, maybe it was just the opposite, because he *did* care.

Entering her flat, she realised, on her left hand at least, her fingers were still crossed.

Chapter Seventeen

Driving to Highdown Hall the next day, Ruby felt guilty again. She hadn't wanted to lie to Cash but she'd had no choice, she couldn't allow him to accompany her, not this time. He, like Corinna, was more vulnerable to the spirit's anger; she didn't want him injured in some way too. She pondered over what she knew of Cynthia once more, of her oh-so-dazzling life. Her struggle to become successful and how in demand she'd become after *The Phoenix* had smashed all expectations, no longer having to suffer the indignity of begging for bit parts ever again. They had found some information concerning her early background, it was relatively humble it seemed, but so what? A lot of famous people came from modest beginnings, certain members of The Beatles immediately sprang to mind, as did Marilyn Monroe; it wasn't a clue. Frustrated, she told herself she had no choice but to try and connect with Cynthia again, in the privacy of her boudoir. Cynthia was the only person who could tell her what she needed to know. Before she ventured upstairs though, she would check out the ballroom again, try and make sense of the anger and frustration she had felt there on her first visit. Who did those feelings belong to? Were they significant? They must have been, to have endured.

Reaching the gates to the hall, she found them locked. Punching the code Mr Kierney had given her into a small box located on the right hand side stone pillar, the gates swung open tentatively. Driving through, they closed again, taking an age to lock her in. Slowly, she drove up the gravel drive, wishing the sky on this mid-December day was blue, not dull grey. Bright skies always helped, if only in a psychological sense.

At last the house presented itself to her, even greyer than the sky and definitely more foreboding. A house that may have once been a happy family home, but which had been devoid of innocent laughter for too long. Drunken laughter? Oh yes, plenty of that had seeped into the walls over the years, but it was not the same thing, not the same thing at all.

Parking her car and walking to the entrance, Ruby could feel Cynthia's anger before she had even opened the front door. There was no doubt about it, she was increasing in strength. Fear could do that to a spirit. Before stepping over the threshold, Ruby took a few moments to reinforce the white light that protected her, imagining it not only enveloping her, but shooting upwards in a long white ribbon, connecting her to the very fabric of the universe itself. Her tourmaline necklace was firmly in place around her neck and in her pocket she carried an obsidian stone, shiny, round and black, which she retrieved now and held for a few moments in the palm of her hand – the equivalent of a comfort blanket, she supposed.

The grand hall was gloomy. Ruby considered turning the lights on but decided against it as it was daytime. It was also quite empty apart from an old table with barley twist legs, upon which stood an earthenware jug filled with dried lavender, their once glorious lilac colour long since faded. Had it been put there by Mr Kierney himself as an attempt at brightening the house or was it a leftover from Sally? She couldn't tell. Once again Ruby stared at the wall where Cynthia's portrait had been, the air around it seemed bereft.

Turning right, Ruby re-entered the ballroom. Another grand room, the grandest the house had to offer. The atmosphere was still but Ruby could easily imagine the decadence of evenings spent here, famous names in showbiz who had come to see and be seen. She lost herself in the glamour of it all for a moment before bringing herself back to the present, reminding herself sternly she was not here to dream, but to work. The emotions she had encountered before, male emotions she'd wager, had been at the far end of the room. She went there again. A cold spot, yes, but it was residual, nothing more. Who had been feeling such a powerful emotion and why? Her lover? There had been so many, that was the problem, but none as prominent as John Sterling, her co-star in *The Elitists*. He was Richard Burton to her Elizabeth Taylor, albeit without the wedding ceremonies. Could it be John who had stood on this precise spot on that Christmas Eve in 1958, looking on whilst Cynthia danced with everyone but him? Feelings of anger, frustration and jealousy emanating from every pore, making their mark. It made a certain kind of sense. John was also the last one to have seen her alive. He had followed Cynthia upstairs, for what reasons Ruby didn't yet know, perhaps reasons bordering on the murderous? At the inquest, a heart attack had been the verdict recorded, but *was* it? Could John, in a fit of rage, have found some way to have killed Cynthia, some clever way that escaped detection? Poison, perhaps? One that left no trace? She was sure she had read about such things in an Agatha Christie novel, or perhaps it had been a Lee Child. Potassium chloride sprang to mind – she'd have to Google it later. If such a scenario were true, could it be John waiting for her in the shadows, still in the grip of that mad, jealous frenzy, unable to let his lover go? Tormenting her as well as himself? Deep in contemplation, a loud bang from upstairs brought her sharply back to the present.

Relax, Cynthia, she thought, *I'm coming.*

***

As she approached the door to Cynthia's room, walking down the corridor that had become so familiar to her of late, Ruby began to doubt her judgement. Maybe Cash was right, she shouldn't have come alone. Theo would be furious about it too. Striving to remain positive, however, she entered the room, the door slightly ajar although Ruby was sure she had shut it behind her when she had last left. Mr Kierney professed never to venture upstairs, so who had left it open?

Cynthia was definitely present; Ruby could feel her, staring at her from the safety of the shadows. Walking to the centre of the room, to the exact spot where she had felt Cynthia fall to the ground, clutching at her heart, Ruby looked around her. The room felt so lonely, it felt forgotten – terrible feelings for a person like Cynthia to endure. Although there was no need to talk out loud – she could communicate perfectly well with spirits by thought alone – Ruby did so anyway, more for her own comfort than anything else.

"Yes, Cynthia, it's me again and yes, I know you're not happy to see me," she began, "but I'm not giving up on you. I told you that. I'm not leaving you here alone."

Silence again. Ruby expected nothing less.

"I know you're frightened, Cynthia," she continued. "And perhaps you're right; perhaps there is something, *someone* waiting for you in the shadows. If so, I'm going to find out who he is and send him home too."

Him? How do you know it's a him?

Cynthia was talking at last; talking, not screaming. It was a good sign.

"I can only go on hunches with that I'm afraid, but I feel it's a 'him'. And I can't help wondering if it's John Sterling, a man you were intimate with in life."

Not John! John wouldn't do this. Followed by an agonising howl of anguish. *How I miss him!*

"If it's not John, then *who* is it? You must know, Cynthia, you must have an idea. If you can remember what happened the night you passed, we can solve this. I know John found you but could he have been involved in any other way? In your passing I mean."

John loved me.

Remembering the emotions she had felt downstairs, Ruby continued, "But he was jealous of you too, wasn't he? He hated sharing you with other men."

He understood!

Ruby wasn't so sure.

Walking over to the bed, tuning into the vibes still present, Ruby knew Cynthia had been far from faithful to John. There had been many lovers on this bed.

Knowing she was goading her, but unsure what else to do, she replied, "Perhaps he didn't understand as well as you think he did, Cynthia? Everybody has limits, even John."

Steeling herself, Ruby waited for Cynthia's reaction and was surprised when there wasn't one.

"Cynthia," she tried again, "do you think you pushed John too far the night of your party? That his temper finally snapped? Could he have killed you? Tell me what happened."

No, no, NO! Cynthia screamed.

Quickly, Ruby reinforced the white light around herself, one hand on her necklace, the other still clutching at the stone in her pocket. What little light was entering the room through the windows fell back, retreating, as though it too were afraid. Suddenly Ruby thought of her mother, had she experienced something similar years ago? Had she goaded a spirit, when really she should have left well alone? Was she, Ruby, now making a mistake, doing the same thing her mother had? She may be psychic, she may be able to connect with the spirit world, but really, she admitted to herself, her knowledge of what lay beyond was scant. All she knew, and this her grandmother had taught her, was that the light was good, the light never judged, it welcomed you back, glad to have you home again. But if that were true, why were so many reluctant to go towards it? Why choose torment over relief? What did they know that she didn't?

Cynthia spoke again, the anger having left her voice.

John wouldn't hurt me.

Had Cynthia reacted differently, Ruby might have been more inclined to believe in her own theory. As in life, so on the other side, violent denial can sometimes mean you'd touched a sore spot. That this particular spirit remained calm in the face of such allegations suggested Cynthia had known her man, had known just what he was capable of: endless devotion, by the sounds of it.

Deciding not to irritate her any further over this point, Ruby apologised.

"If I've done John a disservice, I'm sorry. But might it still be him waiting for you in the shadows, Cynthia? Not intent on harming you, but simply trying to reach you?"

I, I... Cynthia seemed uncertain now. *I don't know...*

"I'm here, Cynthia, I'm with you. Don't be afraid. Look into the shadows. It may be John; it may be nothing bad at all."

I... Cynthia started again. But this time Ruby could sense her moving forward, slowly, wanting so very much to believe.

"Who is it?" asked Ruby. "Can you see?"

No answer.

"Cynthia, is it John? Is John waiting for you?"

Ruby held her breath, praying for a happy ending. In truth, just an ending would do. Was she right? Had Cynthia been hiding from her protector all along? Her own fear the only thing keeping her prisoner? Losing contact briefly, Ruby began to wonder if Cynthia had finally gone to the light – if she hadn't, if she was still present, then contact would usually be maintained. *Go on, Cynthia, go on...* she urged with every fibre of her being. Starting to feel a glimmer of hope at last, she relaxed. Too late she realised her mistake. From out of nowhere, she was suddenly hit square in the stomach and sent flying backwards onto the bed, her feet leaving the ground entirely, her arms flailing either side, desperate to find something to hold onto, to break her fall.

Her mind scrabbling to comprehend, Ruby attempted to clutch at her necklace, needing the comfort of the trinket's heritage, of Rosamund, more than the stone itself. She couldn't move, however, she was pinned down, a pressure upon her, oppressive, choking.

"Cynthia," she managed. "Stop."

But as soon as she said it, she knew it wasn't Cynthia. Cynthia was hiding again, whimpering. This was the one who waited in the shadows.

"John?"

That didn't feel right either. But if not John, who the hell was it? Or *what* from hell was it?

Desperately, she forced herself to remember what her grandmother had taught her. That evil did not exist, only acts of evil, and always at the root of those acts was fear. This 'being', doing its utmost to drain her life force, was not evil, simply frightened, as frightened as Cynthia was, or perhaps even more so. Fear was the reason it attacked, she told herself. In such a situation, she should feel only empathy for the spirit, immense love. Love triumphs over everything.

Doing her utmost, she had to admit it was hard to feel immense love under such dire circumstances. She did her best, but to no avail – the grip around her neck was getting tighter. Ruby was convinced her windpipe wouldn't be able to withstand such pressure. She knew she should remain calm, but it was no use, panic was setting in. Nobody knew she was here, nobody living that is, there was no one to help her.

If she lost consciousness the fight would be over – for her anyway. She had to concentrate. But she couldn't think straight, let alone visualise; her mind was becoming filmy at the edges, detaching itself. As she was about to surrender to oblivion, she heard a faint noise. It grew louder, more urgent, bringing her back to full awareness the more insistent it became. *Barking?*

Jed, is that you? She couldn't turn her head to see, but the barking became more furious, startling the malign entity that had hold of her. For a moment the presence faltered, only for a second, perhaps two, but it was just enough for Ruby to redouble her efforts, sending light and love to wrap itself around this tortured being. As she did so, its grip loosened. As

173

though scalded, it started to retreat, shrieking hideously all the while. She poured forth more light and love, sending it from the very core of her own being, outwards like a tidal wave, reaching higher and higher, getting stronger and stronger, relentless in its flow. When she was sure it had retreated far enough, that she had achieved a measure of safety, she pushed herself up from Cynthia's bed, coughing as she did so, one hand reaching up to support her bruised throat and chin. The atmosphere was once again subdued. Her attacker was gone – for now.

Turning to where Jed stood beside the bed, looking at her with bright eyes worried, his tail wagging only intermittently, she whispered "Cynthia? Cynthia, are you okay?"

Get out! Cynthia's reply lacked its usual venom; instead her voice was anxious. She was obviously as concerned for Ruby's safety as Jed was.

Chapter Eighteen

"You *did* go, didn't you?"

"No, I didn't."

"Yes you *did*, admit it!"

"Oh, for goodness sake, Cash, yes I did go, but I wasn't alone. Jed was with me."

"A ghost dog?" Cash almost spat. "What good is a ghost dog?"

"A lot of good, as it turns out. It seemed the last thing my attacker was expecting was a ghost dog attacking him right back. His surprise at Jed doing so gave me the break I needed to regain control."

"Your attacker? What the..."

But Cash didn't get to finish his interrogation as just at that moment Theo, Ness and Corinna marched into the office, ready to do business.

***

All four faces looked shocked as Ruby revealed what had happened at Highdown Hall the previous day, even though she was sure she had played down events considerably. As she got to the bit about Jed, he came moseying into the room and settled himself in front of the heater.

"He's attached himself to you good and proper, hasn't he?" said Ness, eyeing him.

"He has indeed, he's part of the team now – and a welcome addition he is too, isn't he, Theo?" said Ruby, referring to how the dog had helped send the young boy, Timothy, to the light.

"He can't stay," was Theo's sober reply.

"I don't think he does stay," said Ruby, looking fondly over at him. "I think he comes and goes between our world and the next whenever he wants to. I'm not sure who's given him leave to do so, but one thing I do know, I'm very grateful to him. He saved my life."

"Your life?" Cash was incredulous now. "Are you saying that spirit, the one that attacked you, could actually have killed you?"

"No, no, no," Ruby was eager to placate him. "At least, I don't think so. The point is, he, whoever *he* is, didn't do any lasting damage. I'm fine, really."

"You're not going back to Highdown Hall alone again." It was Theo this time, just as concerned as Cash. "I forbid it. When we go back, we go together or not at all."

"And what would happen if we decided upon the latter, if we didn't go back at all?" As Corinna spoke, Ruby saw a nervous glint in her eye.

"That's not an option, we *have* to go back, but we keep in mind we're dealing with two spirits now, both of them angry and confused. Double trouble if you like."

Her attempt at humour fell flat. No one was smiling.

Ruby continued, "We need to do our utmost to uncover the exact events leading up to Cynthia's heart attack; doing so may give us a clue as to who the other spirit is."

"And you don't think it's John Sterling?" asked Ness.

"No," said Ruby. "And more to the point, neither does Cynthia. It's not some sort of devil creature either, I sensed all-too-human emotions. Blind rage being the most obvious."

Corinna couldn't resist chuckling at Ruby's second stab at humour, although it was Theo who spoke next.

"We *will* go back, but just you, Ruby, you, Ness and me. In my opinion, it is not safe to take Cash and Corinna with us."

Corinna stopped chuckling.

"Hey, not so fast, Theo. I am part of this team and I'd like to remain so, thank you very much. Just because the going gets tough doesn't mean I want out."

"Same here," chimed in Cash. "I was there at the start of the Highdown Hall case and I want to be there at the end." Looking intently into Ruby's eyes, he continued, "Make no mistake, Ruby, I'm here for you." Turning to the rest of the team, he blushed slightly as he added: "For all of you, of course."

Ruby had to blink to quell the emotions this heartfelt show of support – from Cash as well as her colleagues – had stirred within her. Cash was there for her? She liked that, she liked that a lot. And Corinna, dear, sweet Corinna – so ready to take up arms and fight, despite the danger to herself. She tried to speak but couldn't, no words were enough to express the gratitude she felt.

Sensing Ruby's predicament, Theo piped up. "But you know what? Before we delve further into the enigma that is Cynthia Hart, why don't we go and have a bit of fun? Call it the office Christmas party if you will. Bowling and pizza anyone?"

***

Squeezing into Ruby's Ford, Theo in the front with Ruby, the other three extremely cosy in the back, the team headed to Brighton's Marina, home of the Bowlplex.

"I haven't bowled in ages," said Ness, looking actually quite excited at the prospect. She had a lovely smile, thought Ruby, catching sight of her in the rear view mirror. It made her look younger, it was a shame she didn't smile like that more often.

Parking in the multi-storey, they made their way to the Bowlplex, opposite the cinema, Corinna complaining the whole time about the dreadful shoes they would have to wear to play.

"They're just so damned unflattering," she moaned. "And God knows who's had their feet in them before. Ugh."

It turned out there were new rules. As long as you were wearing flats, you didn't have to wear the offending shoes on offer; all five breathed a sigh of relief. The Bowlplex was packed; several other Christmas parties clearly in attendance, but after only a short wait they were able to secure a lane. Theo insisted on paying for it. Knowing it was no use remonstrating with the older woman, Theo could be very determined when she wanted to be, Ruby gracefully gave in, wandering over to their designated alley as money was handed over and punching in the team's details on the computer screen. She could hear Corinna following behind her, giggling with Cash but, unlike last time, she didn't mind a bit. Instead, she felt warm inside, happier than she had done in a long time, which was strange considering she'd nearly had the life choked out of her the day before. Or maybe it was because of it? Although she didn't fear death, she was certainly glad to be alive.

The team played three games in total, Theo, despite her age and size, proving herself to be a fearsome opponent, winning one game and scoring highly in the following two. Corinna had beaten Theo on the second game, whilst Cash had brought home the third. Ness had scored fair to middling on all three games, whilst Ruby had ranked consistently low.

"Never mind," said Cash, putting his arm round her in a show of mock sympathy.

Swiping playfully at him, she couldn't help but laugh too.

"I detect hunger pangs," Theo suddenly declared, her arms wrapped round her ample stomach. "Pizza Express beckons."

Leaving the Bowlplex, they passed various small children's amusement rides, rendered silent for the evening, as well as Santa's Grotto – a somewhat plastic-looking igloo guarded by several life-sized reindeers, one whose red nose blatantly marked him out as Rudolph and another who looked like he had a serious case of mange. The grotto was also closed; Santa having departed for home, to Patcham, perhaps, or Whitehawk rather than the North Pole, for a well-earned rest. McDonald's, on the other hand, was doing a roaring trade, stuffed with the 'before' and 'after' cinema crowd as well as families no longer constrained by the time limits of school nights. As they passed it, Corinna declared a passionate distaste for the fast food chain.

Leaning into Ruby, Cash whispered, "I can't help it, I love Big Macs!" She did too, but she wasn't about to admit that right now.

At Pizza Express, they were greeted by a smiling young man dressed smartly in a blue shirt and black, pleated trousers. He selected a table for them towards the front of the restaurant, overlooking the crowded waters glistening in the moonlight and bobbing with yachts belonging to playboy millionaires Ruby imagined, their masts swaying and rattling gently in the breeze. Iced bottles of Peroni were swiftly ordered by Theo and just as swiftly delivered to their table.

"Hey, look," said Corinna, gleefully eyeing the menu. "There's a turkey and cranberry pizza on special, I'm having that!"

Cash and Ruby both opted for the American Hot and requested extra jalapeños simultaneously. So close to Christmas, the atmosphere in the restaurant was buzzing and it was infectious. Although she couldn't help but do a quick sweep of the dining room, Ruby knew there'd be no lost soul haunting a place such as this tonight, no child sitting pitifully alone at a table, yearning for birthday jubilations, no chef still in pristine whites, hovering over the juniors, making sure they arranged circles of pepperoni or strips of Cajun chicken 'just so'. Pizza Express was just too damned lively for the spirit world.

Back at the table, Theo was holding court, cracking joke after joke, a comedienne as well as a psychic marvel. All were content to let her take the lead, knowing that in the wit stakes at least, they couldn't compete. Whilst she entertained them all, Ruby looked over to where Cash was sitting. He immediately returned her gaze, as though he'd been waiting to do so all evening. As his mouth widened into a smile, Ruby knew, suddenly and without doubt, that any resistance she might have had towards him was fading fast.

***

Crouching low into her corner, Cynthia wished she could make herself smaller, disappear entirely, become nothing at all. But she couldn't. She couldn't do anything except cower in terror. The man, the one who waited for her in the shadows was raging, screaming as though he were in agony, his dark mass beginning to solidify, to take on shape. Again she thought she recognised him. Again she refused to look – her only defence. She wouldn't listen to him either, despite him calling her name, over and over, beseechingly at first but with increasing fury.

Then suddenly, with one almighty scream of frustration, the man, the *creature*, grabbed at her precious items on the dressing table – her crystal bottles, her silver comb, her hairbrush. One by one he threw them across the room, even the perfume bottle she herself had thrown at the red-headed girl, the girl with curls so like her own. This time, however, it smashed across the floor – *Phoenix* seeping deep into the rugs, the smell enticing once upon a time but acrid now. Her bed too, the spirit targeted, removing the rose quartz crystal the last girl had placed upon it and lifting it up, smashing it against the far wall, renting the cover in two, scattering the cushions.

Where __are__ you, Cynthia? You can't hide forever!

Trembling, she wondered where Ruby was, the girl who had promised she wouldn't give up on her, the girl who had been so viciously attacked by this monster. Would she give up on her now? Had he succeeded in frightening her off for good? She hoped not.

Help me, Ruby, Cynthia whispered into the abyss, *please help me.*

Chapter Nineteen

Looking at her watch, Ruby decided she would drive into Brighton to see Rawlings during the afternoon, perhaps take him a little hamper of food for Christmas that she would put together courtesy of a trip to Waitrose beforehand. She had promised the old man she would visit now and again, hating to think of anyone alone, even him, and especially at this time of year. But first she had more research to do.

Although she'd had a great time with Cash and the team yesterday, she hadn't slept well for the second night running. Cynthia had dominated her thoughts and dreams last night, both as the glittering figure she had once been and the terrified wreck she had become. Ruby sensed that, forthcoming anniversary or not, events were coming to a head at Highdown Hall – and neither spirit could be allowed to linger for longer than they already had, the situation was becoming too intense. First though, she intended to trawl through the internet one more time to see if there was anything she might have missed, no matter how insignificant. She needed to unveil who it was that held a grudge against Cynthia, a grudge so extreme it grounded them both.

Thankfully, Theo, Ness and Corinna were working on the other cases, including yet another call to Brookbridge. A resident, this time from Oakleaf Drive, had called to say they were having terrible trouble with their TV. At seven o'clock every evening – no matter what channel they were watching, it would flip to ITV for the start of Emmerdale. Sky engineers had been called out several times but none of them could find a fault. Fed up to the back teeth, the homeowner had called Psychic Surveys instead.

"A former resident of the asylum with a fetish for soap operas..." Theo had mused. "It takes all sorts, I suppose."

The new website was working a treat, prompting enquiries from as far afield as Orkney about the services they provided. In fact, when she checked, there were several from Orkney – just what was going on up there in the mystic Highlands? If even half the enquiries came to fruition they'd be working non-stop well into the new year. She'd have to think about the previously unheard of question of travel expenses now, it seemed – there was no way the team could fund trips as far afield as Scotland themselves.

Before getting onto Google, Ruby made a mug of tea and then returned to her desk, stepping over Jed who had taken up his favourite spot in front of the fire. She knew, technically, she didn't have to step over him, she could walk right through him, but she didn't want to offend his sensibilities. She also replied to a text from Cash saying she'd meet him at three o'clock outside Rawlings' flat. He was working in Brighton until then and would go straight there when he was finished.

Flexing her fingers, she began typing Cynthia Hart's name alongside various phrases into the search engine, wondering how many times she had done so during the month of December, dozens at least she estimated. Top of the list as usual was Wikipedia, chronicling every detail of the movie star's life. There were also a couple of Cynthia Hart fan sites with similar biographies, gossip and newspaper articles, and various YouTube clips of her accepting her Oscar, resplendent in a turquoise Dior ball gown according to the blurb accompanying it, and in the hallowed presence of other award-winning actors and actresses such as Tony Curtis, Paul Newman, Susan Hayward and Shirley MacLaine. Ruby could just imagine the after-show party for that one, how glamorous it must have been, and Cynthia, a Brighton girl, right at the heart of it.

Several pages of search results in, rather ghoulishly, she discovered a site entitled *The Death of Cynthia Hart* which devoted itself entirely to detailing the events of the last party ever held at Highdown Hall: how she was found dead from a heart attack in her bedroom, several photographs of grieving friends and party guests, and a description of the funeral held two weeks later at a church in London, St Mary's in the West End, mourners spilling into the streets apparently. Theatre lights around the country had been turned off for an hour on the evening of her funeral; a mark of deep respect from the film and theatre world, mourning her untimely demise. Images galore of the actress peppered the net, film stills as well as more personal pictures, some formal, others capturing her in more natural, less stylised poses. Always she was smiling; always she was accompanied by leading lights of the day, not just John Sterling, but Gregory Peck, Alec Guinness, and a particularly sweet one with Cary Grant, the pair of them giggling, as though sharing some private joke. It was in the pictures with John Sterling, however, that she shone the brightest, her eyes glittering – but with what exactly? Lust? Love? If the latter, why had she kept him so determinedly at arm's length? Why not give into him? It was well documented that Sterling had asked her to be his wife on several occasions, but she had never accepted. Why not? She seemed to yearn for him in death and, certainly, her end had been the beginning of the end for him, so it was obvious the bond between them was real.

Scouring through acres of virtual pages for the umpteenth time did not yield any new information. Cynthia's public life genuinely appeared to be without stain, everyone seemed to adore her and her private life had remained just that, private – a remarkable feat for one so famous. She had moved to London in 1941 to seek fame and fortune aged just fourteen, young by today's standards but more the norm in those days it would seem, leaving her mother and younger brother, Jack, behind in Brighton. Apart from that, not much else was known about her early years. Ruby wondered if Jack might still be alive, after all Geoffrey Rawlings had been. So, as Theo had done with Rawlings, she spent some time checking through the records of all the Jack Harts that resided in England; there were dozens and dozens of them. Locally, in East Sussex, there were three, but being in their thirties, fifties and sixties, age ruled them out as *the* Jack Hart. More than likely, Ruby surmised, Jack had followed the usual route, a job as a mechanic perhaps, or an insurance man, marriage and kids. Or perhaps he had emigrated to Australia, a lot of people did in the 1960s and 70s – taking advantage of the 'ten pound passage' to find a better life. If he was still alive, he could be anywhere in the world and, again, their resources didn't stretch to the phone bills or man hours that checking up on every Jack Hart would incur. Cynthia's mother had been called Mary, but on Cynthia's birth certificate, which Theo had checked earlier at the record office, her father had been listed as 'unknown'. Mary had never married nor, it seemed, been on good terms with the father of her children, if indeed the same man had fathered both.

Tapping the fingers of her right hand on her desk, Ruby wondered if Cynthia had become estranged from her immediate family. Certainly she had not come across any photographs of them together. Had her mother outlived her? There had been no mention of her as being at her funeral, or her brother for that matter, the papers had focused only on the famous in attendance. Perhaps she hadn't outlived her; perhaps Mary had died before Cynthia? It was feasible and easily checked, she supposed, at the record office, if only she could find the time to visit. Whatever had happened, neither mother nor brother figured heavily in her life; figured at all.

Cynthia's spectacular career and determined rise from humble beginnings had been amazing, and was something Ruby found fascinating in its own right. Her first role of note had actually been in the West End, playing the maid, Rosalie, in Oscar Wilde's *Lady Windermere's Fan*. She had trodden the boards quite a bit when she was younger and reading about it Ruby could almost smell the greasepaint, almost feel the excitement that must have charged the air before going 'live' each night. Gradually, Cynthia's stage roles had became more prominent and she moved into film at the age of twenty-three, supporting parts still, but in a variety of comedies, dramas and thrillers, proving herself versatile at least. It wasn't until the early 1950s that she had landed the starring role in *The Phoenix* and her first major award for Best Actress. America invited her to Hollywood after that. A second award was won for *Intruders,* and then the biggie – the Oscar – for *The Elitists,* in which she starred alongside John Sterling. That was in 1958 – the year she died. In 1959, she would have been moving to the USA, although she had stated quite clearly in the press that she'd be doing so only for as long as it took to complete her next starring role in *Atlantic,* which was being touted as the most ambitious film in cinematic history, based as it was around one of the deadliest peacetime disasters in modern history, the sinking of the Titanic. At the time of her death, the media-hype for *Atlantic* was at boiling point; the world wanting not only to see such a cinematic feat, but the great Cynthia Hart in the leading role of Lady Agatha Darnell in particular. Worldwide disappointment that she never boarded that ship was often cited as one of the reasons the film had bombed.

Poor Cynthia, thought Ruby. To be felled at the height of her career and by a heart attack of all things, it *was* unfair. Little wonder she was having a hard time coming to terms with it. Sudden passing was something Ruby dealt with often. Just last month she had been asked to make contact with a man who had been sitting up in bed, responding to emails. When he had finished, he had closed his laptop, placed it on his bedside table, turned to his wife to say goodnight and promptly died. A year or so after his death, his wife had called Ruby, seeking help. According to her, her husband was still sitting beside her in bed, occupying the exact same spot in which he had died.

"I can't see him, you understand," she had endeavoured to explain. "But I can feel him. Do you know what I mean?"

At first she had found it comforting, but as time wore on and her heart had begun to heal, it became less so.

"It's off-putting. If I want to bring someone home, you know, another man, I can't exactly take them to the bedroom, can I? Not with him there."

Ruby could see her point.

When she had arrived at the woman's home to carry out the survey, she had sensed him immediately. James, aged fifty-one, was indeed still very much present.

Asking his wife if they might have some time alone together, Ruby had settled herself on the edge of the bed and gently explained to James that he had passed, that, according to his doctors, an aneurysm had been the cause of death, lying dormant for years before erupting as spectacularly as Mount Vesuvius. Gently, she had explained to him that this stage of his spiritual journey was over and it was time to move on. James had not welcomed the news.

But I love life. I don't want it to be over. Our first grandchild has just been born.

Ruby had bowed her head at his words. She understood. She enjoyed life too. Even more so now that Cash was in it. And like most people, she'd prefer some notice before it came to an end. But recent grandchild or not, James had been earthbound for long enough, it was time to go home, to his real home that is. Ruby believed people were born with a 'sell-by' date – when you had learnt the lessons you were supposed to learn, when you had played your part in the bigger picture, it was time to move to a higher plane, or perhaps to return to the physical world again in some other guise, ready to learn new lessons. Some lives were unbearably short, some were extraordinarily long. Perhaps it depended on the lessons you had to learn.

Although James was resistant at first, gradually she had made him understand he couldn't stay. Whilst he absorbed this they sat in silence, Ruby listening to the sound of the clock ticking on his wife's side of the bed – counting the seconds, the minutes along with it. Eventually, he had made a show of pushing the blankets back before stepping out of bed. Then he made his way slowly to the far wall where the light was shining. Ruby watched him go, a strange mix of emotions vying for attention in her, happy emotions mostly, but slight melancholy too. If she could wave a wand, she'd give him the extra years he wanted to spend with his wife, his grandchild; she'd do it for all of them. But just before he faded from view, James had done something which had surprised her. He had turned to Ruby and mouthed the words: *Thank you*. There had been no sadness in his eyes at all, just acceptance she was glad to note, acceptance and something else – something that looked very much like excitement. She hoped so. Rarely was a spirit so polite. If his wife was looking for another man, she would have a long way to go before she found her husband's equal.

Comparing this case of sudden death to Cynthia's, Ruby was sure that although Cynthia's abrupt passing had also left her bereft, she would have been able to move on by now if it hadn't been for the malevolent entity in the shadows. That was the key to success at Highdown Hall, finding out just who her tormenter was. Sadly, it was that very information that was continuing to elude her.

Chapter Twenty

"Find out anything new today?" said Cash, after turning up ten minutes late outside Rawlings' flat, cursing the horrendous Christmas traffic.

"Not a bloody thing," Ruby replied, more dismayed than irritated. "Everybody loved Cynthia, or so it seems."

"What a bummer. We've got so little time left."

"Don't remind me," Ruby sighed.

"When are we going to Highdown again?" asked Cash as they descended the stairs to the basement.

"On Monday. Christmas Eve."

"The anniversary of her death? Spooky."

"I'm not sure about spooky, but meaningful certainly. Theo thinks the energies in the house will be more prevalent then and possibly more pliable to work with."

"To shift you mean?"

"You've got it," Ruby nodded.

While they waited for Rawlings to open the door, Cash peered at the bags she was carrying.

"What have you got there?"

"Mostly ready meals, a few tins of soup," she answered, "stuff that's easy for him to cook. I don't think he's capable of spending much time in the kitchen."

"I'll go halves with you," Cash offered immediately.

"You don't have to," Ruby protested.

"I want to," he insisted.

The minutes passed as they stood patiently at the front door, smiling into each other's eyes. Too many minutes, Ruby realised with a start.

"Where is he?" she queried, ringing the doorbell yet again.

Still there was no reply, only the sound of the dog from deep within, barking frantically.

"He does know we're coming today, doesn't he?"

"Yes. I rang him first thing this morning to say we'd come by, he said it was fine, he wasn't going anywhere. Apparently, he *never* goes anywhere."

"Well, he hasn't taken the dog for a walk, that's for sure. The poor thing's not happy."

"Something's wrong," said Ruby at last. "I can feel it."

"Me too," agreed Cash. "Do you think he's fallen or something?"

"Or something." Ruby's face was grim. "Can you push against the door, Cash, try and open it?"

"Shouldn't we just call the police?" Cash looked worried too now.

"If we call the police, we might not be allowed in. And I... I want to make sure that if he's passed, he's passed successfully. I don't want him left there alone anymore."

"Passed? You think he's dead?"

"I think he is," Ruby replied solemnly.

"Okay," Cash said after a few moments. "Stand back, I'll see what I can do."

Flexing his right arm first, he threw his full weight against the door. It remained steadfast. Taking a deep breath, he did so again, this time it gave a little. A third crash sent the door flying open. The carrier bags forgotten, Ruby rushed in, down the hallway, opening the door to the living room where she found Rawlings sitting in his armchair, his dog barking at his feet.

"Easy boy," said Cash, edging slowly towards the dog, one hand held out in supplication. "It's okay, we're here now."

While Cash took care of the dog, Ruby rushed over to him.

"Mr Rawlings, Geoffrey!" she yelled. "It's me, Ruby, are you okay?"

Stupid question. He was clearly not okay, she knew that.

Kneeling beside him, his whiskered face was completely devoid of colour, not even a hint of grey in it now; his rheumy eyes were open and stared back at her blankly. His expression surprised rather than shocked; a good sign she decided. She closed his eyes gently before briefly taking hold of his gnarled hand, the one still clutching at his chest.

A heart attack, Ruby presumed, and a sudden one at that. The television was still blaring, his beloved BBC1 airing what looked like some family quiz show. She switched it off quickly, wanting to silence the inappropriate canned laughter. Walking over to the curtains, she allowed what scant winter light there was outside to come in. Next, she grabbed hold of one of the chairs that lived under the table; the same chair she had occupied during her first visit to Rawlings' flat, and dragged it over to sit beside him.

"I'm so sorry," she said, once again taking his hand in hers.

"Why are you sorry?" Cash stood a few feet from her, holding the dog to his chest.

"Because I probably hastened his death, taking him to Highdown Hall. Because when he passed, he passed alone. Because I didn't get here sooner."

"It's not your fault. He was old; it was his time to go."

"But he hasn't gone," Ruby said. "He's still very much here."

Ruby sensed the dog knew his master was in residence too, but couldn't understand why now there were suddenly two of him.

Glancing at the poor creature, Ruby said, "Can you keep hold of the dog; I need to speak to Geoffrey."

Without another word, Cash retreated to a far corner of the room and sank down against the wall.

"Geoffrey, I can see you." Ruby spoke out loud. "And I'm really sorry I didn't get here earlier, that I arrived too late."

Standing just behind his favourite armchair, Rawlings nodded at her. He looked sad, unbearably so.

190

"I... I brought you some things for Christmas," she continued, tears pricking at her eyes. "Things I thought you might like."

Thank you.

"Why are you still here? Why haven't you gone to the light?"

I waited for you.

"For me?" Ruby tilted her head.

Yes.

"Because?"

Because I'm scared.

"Of what?"

You know what. I'm not a good man.

"You're not a bad man either, Geoffrey, really you're not. What you *did* in the past was bad, but that's not the same thing."

There was a pause before he spoke again.

What's going to happen to me?

"You'll be welcomed, you'll be going home."

Cynthia? Will she be there?

"No, not yet, but I'm working on it."

She'll be angry with me.

"No, she won't. She cannot take anger into the light, nor can she take vengeance."

It's my fault she's stuck here.

"It's not your fault," Ruby's voice was firm. "I thought it was but I was wrong."

Another pause as Rawlings considered her words.

She wasn't a bad lass, you know, just ambitious. I took advantage.

"I know, but you won't be judged, re-educated perhaps but not judged."

I took advantage of so many. I'm sorry.

"And it's good that you're sorry. It means you've learnt."

Her family abandoned her.

Ruby was taken aback by this revelation. What did he mean?

191

She didn't have to wait long for him to explain.

Inside, she felt worthless. If her family didn't want her, who would? I recognised that in her because it's in me too. Nobody wanted me either. Just what they thought I could give them.

In her recent research into Cynthia's family, Ruby had quickly realised that very little connected daughter to mother, or sister to brother. But that had been Cynthia's choice, surely? After all, she was the one who had left home so young to seek fame and fortune. Had she really never been welcomed back, her achievements celebrated around the family hearth? It seemed incredible if not. Before her mind could wander further, she reminded herself that now was not the time to think of Cynthia, it was Rawlings she needed to focus her attention on.

"Geoffrey," Ruby explained, "you have *always* been wanted, by the love and the light from which you came. Call it God, the Universe, the Higher Power, it doesn't matter; they're one and the same. And the light wants you back, Mr Rawlings, you are part of it."

Rawlings looked at her steadily as she said these words, the misery that had filled his eyes for far too long slowly dissolving. He then looked right through her, to the far side of the room, the opposite side to where Cash and the dog waited. Hesitantly at first he moved forward, his gait as awkward as it had been in old age, painful almost, but with every step he gained in confidence. The closer to the light he got, the younger he became, the ravages of time reversing. Suddenly, he stopped.

Will you take care of my dog?

The dog? She already had a ghost dog to contend with, now she'd have a live one too? Neither of whom she'd asked for. Looking at the canine clutched in Cash's arms, his eyes still trained on his master, his little brown body quivering, she relented. That dog loved his master, refuting his claim that nobody wanted him, the dog obviously did, very much so and his heart was breaking. Rawlings seemed to sense that and the smile on his face widened.

Ruby?

"Yes," she said at last. "I'll take care of the dog. What's his name?"

Daisy.

Oh, a girl then. Pretty name.

Goodbye.

"Goodbye, Geoffrey," she whispered after him.

"Has he gone?" said Cash, rising with Daisy, whining inconsolably, still in his arms.

"He's gone."

"And you've inherited another dog?"

"Looks like it."

"Shall we call the police now?"

"Yes," said Ruby, retrieving her mobile phone from her jacket pocket and starting to dial. "We'll stay until they arrive and then I'll head back to Waitrose, get some dog food."

Chapter Twenty-One

After introducing Daisy to her new home, Ruby turned her attentions to Jed, warning the happy, excited Labrador that he had to give the new addition some space – Daisy had had a hard day and the last thing she needed was a ghost dog sniffing around her, but not to worry, she'd come round, in time. Jed's wagging tail faltered slightly at her words but he obligingly went and settled on Ruby's bed, leaving Daisy safe and snug on Cash's lap in the living room. Opening a bottle of red wine, Ruby grabbed two glasses and went through to him.

"I hope Jed isn't going to be jealous of her," Cash worried.

"I don't think there's a jealous bone in Jed's body. They'll rub along together just fine in time, I'm sure."

Ruby poured a generous measure into both their glasses, handed one to him then clinked hers against it.

"Cheers," Cash smiled back at her.

"I know I shouldn't be sad," she said after taking a sip, "I know he is where he's supposed to be, but I wish we'd visited him sooner. Just to let him know that we cared. That we appreciated what he'd done for us."

"I know what you mean," Cash nodded. "He may have done some dreadful things, but he seemed so, I don't know... so abandoned at the end, not just by people, but by life itself."

"Abandoned?" said Ruby, her head to one side. "That's how he said Cynthia felt, even though she was the one who left the family home in search of fame and fortune. From what I can gather, her mother and brother didn't have anything to do with her after she left. You'd think they would have, wouldn't you, if

194

only to congratulate her on her success."

"Maybe they thought it would give the wrong impression if they did, who knows. Or perhaps fame just didn't impress them; they simply wanted to get on with their own lives without the fuss that being related to Cynthia would inevitably bring. Besides, families don't always stick together, we know that."

"I suppose," said Ruby, knowing he was referring to the absent fathers in both their lives.

Cash interrupted her thoughts.

"How old would Cynthia be now if she were still alive?"

"Eighty-eight," Ruby replied.

"Not excessively old these days," Cash mused. "There must be someone alive who knew her, somebody who can give us an insight into the real Cynthia."

"Quite a few of the acting elite I should imagine, but I don't think they'll grant us an audience somehow."

"No, shame that."

"Her brother was younger than her by two years; he may well still be alive. But even if he is, we don't have enough time left to wade through all the Jack Harts I've found."

"Besides which, we need someone who knew Cynthia post-childhood, really."

"Hmm... yeah, that's true."

Cash thought for a second.

"Didn't Mr Kierney say he had another aunt as well as Sally? She must have come down to Highdown Hall at some point to visit her sister – perhaps she's still alive?"

Ruby wracked her brains.

"Yes... I think he did. Esme wasn't it? Though from what he said she sounded a bit out of it, probably why she didn't inherit the Hall."

"Let's find out. I know it's a long shot but it could prove significant."

"You're right; I don't know much about Sally either, except

195

that she became a bit of a recluse after Cynthia passed, shutting herself up at Highdown Hall. A bit more information about her could be useful."

Cash looked suspicious.

"You don't think it's her, do you? The second rogue spirit? Beneath her devotion a woman obsessed."

Ruby laughed.

"That had crossed my mind too; Sally, by all accounts, was almost unnaturally devoted to her mistress, but no, I don't think so. The second energy is definitely male. Sally's not the culprit here."

"But she might have known who was and she might have told someone close to her."

"It's possible," Ruby nodded, slowly at first and then more eagerly.

She couldn't help herself; she leaned over and pecked him on the cheek. "You're a genius sometimes, Cash, you know that?"

***

Despite it being early on a Saturday morning, Ruby phoned Mr Kierney.

"I hope this is good news," was his curt greeting.

"Mr Kierney," Ruby entreated, "I believe we're closer to ridding Highdown Hall of Cynthia than we have ever been. I just need... erm... some more information from you."

"From me? Why?"

"Your aunt, Sally Threadgold, does she have any other surviving relatives? Apart from you that is."

"What the hell has that got to do with anything?" Mr Kierney exploded.

"Mr Kierney, please," Ruby held firm, "humour me, it may be relevant. Does she?"

Perhaps impressed by the conviction in her voice, he complied, if begrudgingly so.

"I've told you before, my mother, Sally's sister, is dead. But there is another sister, the youngest of the three, Esme, who is still alive. She used to work at Highdown Hall too on occasion. She lives in London, but I don't see how she can help, she's practically senile."

Worked at Highdown Hall? "She could be very helpful indeed," Ruby tried to keep the excitement out of her voice. "She might be able to shed some light onto a particular situation we're investigating. Would it be okay for us to visit her?"

"She still lives at home, in the East End. I suppose I could ask her. But don't go upsetting her. Like I said, she's fragile."

"I promise I won't, I just want to ask her a few simple questions, the answers to which could be very useful to us."

"I don't see what good it will do – but it's on your time, not mine, so why should I worry? God knows, she rarely gets visitors; I just don't have the time. When do you want to see her?"

Knowing there was no time to waste, Ruby said hopefully, "As soon as possible, basically. Today?"

There was silence for a few moments and then Mr Kierney spoke again. "Look, I'll call to check first and ring you back."

***

They could indeed see Mr Kierney's aunt later that day. Ruby called round at Cash's flat and together they took Daisy for a quick walk beside the River Ouse, which winds through Lewes on its way to the sea, before depositing her at Cash's mum's, also in Lewes. Ruby waited round the corner while Cash handed the dog over and told her they'd be back to collect her later that day. She didn't want her first meeting with his mum to be a hurried one. Catching the noon train to London, Ruby estimated they should be at Mrs Esme Harris's house around two o'clock that afternoon.

"I hope we're not on a hiding to nothing here," Cash said as they took their seats on the surprisingly empty train.

"Like you said, it's a long shot but one worth exploring."

Noting he still looked worried, she elaborated. "We've got no choice but to explore every avenue. Theo, Ness and Corinna haven't been able to come up with anything other than generic information regarding Cynthia either. She really was squeaky clean, publicly at least. Even her dalliance with Lytton was never made public. If Sally's sister worked at Highdown Hall on occasion, she might be able to give us the insight into Cynthia's character we need, an insight into those around her too with luck. At this point, any bloody insight will do. We have to find out what lay beneath that perfectly smiling face of hers."

"The diva beneath the princess you mean?"

"Exactly. A diva who trod on some toes on her way to the top it seems, particularly hard on one person's at least. We know it isn't John Sterling lying in wait for her, despite the fact she maddened him by refusing to commit to him, but it's definitely someone who feels wronged by her for some reason. Despite her reputation, I don't think she was entirely made of sugar and spice."

"The attack on Corinna certainly doesn't suggest she was," said Cash grimly.

"No, nor does the energy surrounding her bed. Cynthia was a woman of extreme tastes I think."

"Ugh," said Cash, shuddering. "Seriously, there are times I'm glad I'm not psychic."

Laughing, Ruby relaxed back into her seat, gazing out of the window as the Sussex and Surrey countryside gave way to the suburbs of London and finally, the city itself.

Her calculations had been correct; they arrived at Esme's address, a humble Victorian terrace in the East End of London, during early afternoon. Ringing the doorbell, Ruby felt nerves flutter in her stomach. She hoped their enquiries would only stir up good memories for the old woman, nothing that would cause her distress. She'd had it with heart attacks.

Instead of someone frail and supposedly senile, as Mr Kierney had suggested, a spritely woman, obviously in her eighties but looking very good for it, opened the door.

"Hello," she said, a slight waiver in her voice. "My nephew phoned to say you were paying me a visit."

"Hello," said Ruby, extending her hand. "Yes, I'm Ruby Davis and this is my colleague, Cash Wilkins. Thank you so much for agreeing to see us."

"It's a delight, dear. I don't get many visitors nowadays. Come in."

The small, bird-like woman ushered them down a narrow hallway – which appeared even narrower because of the floral wallpaper – into a living room, also very floral and packed to the hilt with ornaments. They were on the mantelpiece, the window sill, the sideboard, everywhere.

Indicating for them to sit down on the two-seater sofa, thankfully plain in colour, Esme enquired how she could help them.

"We're investigating Cynthia Hart," Ruby began.

"Investigating, dear?" Esme looked confused. "My nephew didn't say you were the police."

"No, we're not," Ruby quickly reassured her. How much had Mr Kierney imparted to Esme about what was happening at Highdown Hall she wondered. Probably nothing at all.

Not wanting to exploit the 'I'm a psychic trying to help a grounded spirit move towards the light' angle, she opted for the explanation she had given to the first Mr Rawlings instead, that she and Cash were students documenting the life of Cynthia Hart.

"Mr Kierney said you worked occasionally at Highdown Hall, alongside your sister, Sally."

"Highdown Hall? Yes indeed I did, a long time ago now though, dear," sighed Esme, somewhat misty-eyed. Brightening, she continued. "Isn't it strange that the Hall belongs to our

199

family now, who'd have thought it? Not me, and certainly not Sally, I can tell you. You could have knocked her down with a feather when she learnt Cynthia had left it to her."

Offering them tea, Esme tottered off to the kitchen, returning a few minutes later with a tray laden with biscuits as well as a china pot and three china cups.

"Here, let me take that," said Cash, jumping immediately to his feet.

"What a lovely young man," Esme winked at Ruby, handing the tray over to him. "Never much liked foreigners, so many of them in London nowadays, but you're rather intriguing, my dear, a pleasing colour."

Cash looked slightly taken aback. Sitting back down, he said "Er, thank you, I think."

Biting down on her amusement, Ruby examined further the mantelpiece. On it were pictures of Esme, she presumed, in her younger years. One on her wedding day, standing formally beside a much taller man, he dressed in a dark suit, she in a knee-length cream dress that nipped in at the waist and then flared out again into a flattering full skirt. In contrast, there was a much more relaxed picture of her standing in between two women, their arms thrown about each other's shoulders, all of them with big grins on their faces. Her two sisters perhaps – Sally, and Alan Kierney's mother.

"Yes," Esme continued to muse. "And now the Hall belongs to Alan, though what he'll do with such a vast place I don't know."

"Did Sally not have children of her own?" Ruby couldn't help but enquire. She had surmised as such in the past but had never actually asked Mr Kierney directly to confirm it. If she had, she was sure he'd have given her a mouthful for being so nosy.

Esme shook her head sadly. "No, neither Sally nor myself. Alan was the only child between us. We doted on him, my sisters and I, we spoilt him really, well, when he was a child anyway." Her head to one side, she added: "And it shows."

Shaking her head again, almost despairingly Ruby thought, Esme returned to the subject of Cynthia. "She was quite the one was Cynthia, quite the movie star. As big in America as she was in England, you know, our finest export."

"She most certainly was an amazing woman," agreed Ruby whilst Cash ploughed through the proffered chocolate bourbons. Ruby couldn't help but marvel at his appetite, he had already put away a ham and cheese Panini, a packet of salt and vinegar crisps and a Danish pastry since they'd left Lewes.

"And from such humble beginnings too."

"Ah yes," said Ruby, eager to keep Esme chugging along that train of thought. "Her humble beginnings, as researchers, that's what we're particularly interested in, the Cynthia behind the spotlight. She didn't come from a wealthy background, did she?"

"Cynthia? No, dear. Not at all. Quite the opposite. Her mother was... what did they call them in those days? A charwoman I suppose – she worked for local families, cleaning, child-care, that sort of thing. Shopping and ironing too no doubt – the kind of chores that people from the upper echelons didn't like to dirty their hands doing."

"How do you know?" Ruby was intrigued.

"Used to say to Sally, she did, 'Look at me, my mother always at the beck and call of others, and me the biggest movie star in the world', said it all the time. Not in public of course, she refused to be drawn on her background in public, but to Sally, all the time."

"She was ashamed of her mother?" It was Cash this time, torn between his interest in Cynthia and what had to be his third bourbon biscuit.

"She must have been," Esme concurred. "I suppose if you're putting on airs and graces, you don't want people to know you're doing just that, do you? *Putting* them on I mean. Although perhaps her mother was content to be a char, not everyone wants fame and riches. From what Sally gleaned, Mary worked for some big noises in her life, was held in high esteem. Do you remember Aston's, the famous Brighton milliners? She worked for them for several years as well as the Carr's, who manufactured gloves – not just anybody got a job with those types of families, you had to have proved your mettle beforehand."

"It might have been enough for Mary," Ruby mused. "But for Cynthia, it clearly wasn't."

Esme shrugged. "My sister used to think that comparing what she'd achieved to what she perceived her mother *hadn't* achieved, gave Cynthia a sense of self-worth. Sally didn't seem to think she was confident, inside I mean. I disagreed though. I thought she was too confident for her own good sometimes. It didn't do to cross her, you know."

"Was Sally fond of Cynthia?" asked Ruby, sensing Esme wasn't overly so.

"Fond? She was devoted. Dazzled by her, as so many were. There was no doubt she was a fine actress, but Sally, she believed Cynthia was a lost soul too; she wanted to take care of her. Look after her. She was like that was Sally; one of life's carers."

"Cynthia must have been grateful for it though, after all she left her house to her."

"Who else was she going to leave it to, dear? She had no husband or children."

"I know," consented Ruby, "but to make Sally the inheritor of her estate, that's quite something. There must have been a special bond between them."

Esme nodded.

"If she'd had children or a husband I'm sure Sally wouldn't have got a look in, but yes there was a bond between them. Sally wouldn't have a bad word said against her."

"Do you know anyone who did say a bad word about her? Cynthia I mean?"

"No, dear," Esme was adamant. "Nobody would have dared."

"Dared? Why not?"

"I told you, it wouldn't do to cross Cynthia. She had a temper, particularly in the last year of her life; she was always flying off the handle for some reason or other. Even Sally, whom she was usually civil to, came in for a verbal lashing every now and again, although Cynthia was always very apologetic to her afterwards. One of the few people Cynthia ever apologised to, mind. She was a powerful woman, if you upset her, she could destroy you."

"And did she?" Ruby probed further. "Destroy anyone?"

"Not to my knowledge, dear, but then I kept out of the way of both her and her entourage."

"Her entourage?"

"Yes, the band of sycophants she kept around her at all times, hung on every word she uttered they did. If she said the sky was green not blue they would have agreed with her. Sickening really."

"Why didn't Cynthia leave the house to one of them?"

"I don't know," Esme shrugged. "Perhaps she knew that's what they were; sycophants. Perhaps she knew Sally would look after the house properly. She was meticulous was Sally, a perfectionist. Cynthia was as well, they had that in common. Deep down, and this is only my theory, I think Cynthia might have realised Sally was the only person who genuinely cared for her, not the movie star her, but the real her, the person, as you say, behind the spotlight. The people she surrounded herself with, oh they paid lip-service alright, but only because they wanted a share in her glory. Any fool could see that."

"She should have sacked the lot of them," Cash piped up.

"But she wouldn't," Esme continued. "She needed them. Sally said she kept them round her because she was desperate to be loved, because she wasn't loved by her family."

A tingle ran down Ruby's spine.

"Wasn't she? Do you know that for sure?"

"That's what Sally said; that she was a lost lamb in the wilderness was Cynthia – more like a bloody Bengal tiger in the suburbs I'd say!" Esme laughed at her own joke.

Although she was smiling too, Ruby couldn't help thinking what a waste of time their trip to London had been. Time they just didn't have any more. It was lovely to meet Esme, she was a charming lady, and not at all demented as Mr Kierney had suggested, but she hadn't learned anything new concerning whom might have held a grudge against Cynthia. It couldn't be someone from her family. If they had abandoned her in life, they probably weren't around for her in death either. The man in the shadows, he could be anyone.

Attempting one last question, Ruby asked, "When was the last time you saw Cynthia?"

Esme didn't need to think, straightaway she answered, "The night she died. I was there, at Highdown Hall, helping out. Got paid well for working on Christmas Eve we did, made it worth our while. I'll say this for her, Cynthia didn't stint when it came to wages."

"You were there the night she died?" said Cash, his attention wholly captured now.

"Yes, I was; what a tragedy, eh? Only thirty-one and at the height of her career too."

"Can you tell me exactly what happened that night, Esme?" said Ruby, trying to keep her voice neutral, to stifle the urgency in it.

Esme was only too happy to oblige.

"It was a lovely night," she was misty-eyed once again, "and she looked beautiful in that dress of hers Cynthia did; a dress Sally kept so nice after her death, despite cradling it to her chest sometimes, as you would a child. Even though there were so many lovelies in attendance, Cynthia was the loveliest; there was no doubt about it. John Sterling was there too, her on-off lover you know, well, on for his part, off mainly for hers." Esme chuckled. "Dashing he was; her match in looks, I can tell you.

All us maids were quite agog at the sight of him, and some of the waiters too," she winked. "But she didn't dance with him, snubbed him I would go so far as to say. She danced all night but not once in his arms, being swung round and round the dance floor by handsome man after handsome man, breathtaking in her happiness. It was her birthday, you know, Christmas Eve, she was radiant, the world at her feet. And then she disappeared. One minute she was there, holding court, Queen of all she surveyed, and the next she wasn't. I don't know why. John Sterling found her upstairs a while later; she died in his arms, a heart attack of all things. Destroyed him it did."

Again Ruby's heart sank. They knew all this; it wasn't going to help them. Starting to rise, she was about to thank Esme for her time, when she was stopped in her tracks.

"Two deaths that night... tragic. And it started off so well too."

"Two deaths?" Ruby could feel the blood draining from her face. "What do you mean two deaths?"

"There were two deaths. David Levine left the party around the same time that Cynthia had the heart attack I believe, maybe a bit before, I can't remember exactly; it's all so long ago now and my memory isn't what it used to be. Said he wasn't feeling well when he asked me to get his coat. And he didn't look great, I remember that, he was all hot and bothered under the collar. Anyway, he must have been feeling awful, because he crashed his car, not far from the house, a few minutes later. Ran off the road and hit a tree. Died instantly."

"David Levine? Who's he?" said Cash before Ruby had the chance.

"He was a film director I think, dear. Not big fry, like some at the party, but up and coming. Who's to say he wouldn't have gone on to be a big noise had he lived? Another glittering career wiped out, just like that. A crying shame."

Unlike Ness, and sometimes Theo, Ruby couldn't read thoughts, but as she looked at Cash, she knew what he was thinking. Could David Levine be the man in the shadows? The one who waited for Cynthia? And, if he was, why? What had Cynthia done to upset him?

Chapter Twenty-Two

Esme was getting tired; Ruby could see her paper-thin eyelids growing heavy, her almost painfully thin shoulders, formerly upright, sagging. No doubt the rare treat of having visitors was draining her. Armed with their new information, she thought now would be a good time to take their leave and indicated as much to Cash with a nod of her head. Wiping imaginary crumbs from the side of his mouth, he nodded back.

"Thank you so much, Esme..." Ruby began.

But it seemed Esme wasn't quite done yet.

"I've got a box you might be interested in; it's full of newspaper cuttings of Cynthia."

"A box?" Ruby sat back down again.

"Yes, it was found beside her on the night she died. Sally found it. She had no idea how it had got there, never seen it before in her life. She brought it to me for safe-keeping. Daft old Sally, she seemed to think keeping the box at Highdown Hall upset Cynthia in some way, said it was best if it were removed from the house entirely. I haven't a clue what she meant, how could it upset Cynthia when she was dead? Would you like to have a look through it? It might help."

"Yes, please," said Ruby, once again glancing at Cash. His eyes sparkled with excitement.

"It's in the spare bedroom. In the wardrobe. Run up and get it would you, dear? I don't think I've enough energy to negotiate upstairs at the moment. It's a brown box, has some gold engravings on it. Not real gold, you understand, it's nothing special I can assure you. You can't miss it, there's barely anything else in that wardrobe."

Ruby did as she was told, squeezing past the chairlift before taking the stairs two at a time in her eagerness. At the top of the landing, she turned right into the spare bedroom. From the lack of furniture – just a wardrobe and a bed with a faded pink counterpane on it – she gathered Esme didn't have many overnight visitors. She opened the wardrobe doors and found what she was looking for straightaway, a box, lying forlorn at the bottom.

Bending to retrieve it, she brought the box close to her chest, tuning in for a few moments to see what vibes emitted from it. Although faint, she could detect anger and bitterness, but also surprise – the latter confusing her. It was definitely the odd one out.

Aware that she shouldn't keep Esme and Cash waiting, she dashed back downstairs with the box.

"Is this it?" she asked Esme.

"Yes, but don't give it to me, I don't want it. You take it."

"Are you sure?" Ruby was struggling to hide her delight.

"Of course I'm sure. I'm thrilled to help with your research."

"Thank you," said Ruby, impulsively leaning forward and kissing the old lady on the cheek, her lips touching skin as soft as clouds.

Esme looked surprised initially and then delighted, one hand reaching up to linger where she had been kissed.

Saying their warm goodbyes, Ruby clutched the box to her. When the door had been closed on them, she imagined Esme tottering back to her armchair for a well deserved nap.

Back on the street, the day starting to fade, Cash said, "Well, that was productive."

"It certainly was," agreed Ruby, looking down at the box. "And I can't wait to look through this. But before we do, do you remember me saying to you, the very first time we drove to Highdown Hall, that we'd passed the scene of a car accident?"

Cash's brow furrowed as he cast his mind back.

"Yeah, that's right. I remember now. You mentioned a crash, something about residual feelings..."

"Yes, really heightened emotions, not just the shock of realising death was imminent but anger and triumph too, bitter triumph. You made that joke about the lottery. I assumed the crash had been recent, in the past few years or so. After all, residual feelings don't come with a date stamped on them. But it could just as easily have been from many years before, from 1958 in fact."

"David Levine, you mean?"

Nodding, Ruby continued, "I think it's where David Levine passed. Esme said he had looked flustered when he left Highdown Hall. I wonder why? And also, why the dark feelings? Were they to do with Cynthia? Had she crossed him in some way?"

"How do we find out?"

"Research again, but also by mentioning his name to Cynthia, to gauge what sort of a reaction we'll get."

"It could be as extreme as last time," said Cash, wary.

"It could be. It's a chance we'll have to take."

While Cash mulled over what she had said, Ruby made a quick phone call to Theo, eager to tell her what they had learnt from Esme.

"David Levine? I'll Google him, see what I can find out."

Ruby explained about the box.

"Have you looked through it?" asked Theo.

"No, not yet, but I intend to soon."

"Let me know if you find anything significant."

"I will, thanks, Theo."

"Shall we meet up tomorrow morning to discuss our findings?"

"Tomorrow morning would be perfect, say half past ten?" said Ruby. "I'll text Corinna and Ness and let them know. After the meeting though, we should rest, no more work."

"Absolutely," agreed Theo, "rest is imperative. We need to

209

face Highdown Hall with all cylinders firing. All else can wait until after Christmas, except emergencies of course."

"Of course," said Ruby, remembering the pact they'd made when she'd started the business, never to turn down a distress call. And there was no doubt about it, Christmas could be a busy time, a time when energies in this world and the next stirred themselves even more than usual, an emotional time for so many, not just the living, and not always joyful. But for now, all other cases would be on hold, for a short time anyway.

As she ended the call, Cash came up behind her.

"Did I hear you say there's no more work until the big one?" he murmured into her ear.

"You did indeed," she turned to smile at him. "We need to save ourselves for Highdown."

"Well, for the rest of the day, can we save ourselves at a pub I know in the West End?"

"We can, but let's head to that café we passed on the way first. What was it called? The Mock Turtle or something? I'd like to have a quick look through the box."

The café was indeed called The Mock Turtle and it promised not only the finest cakes in the East End of London but also delicious Lavazza coffee. It was also shut.

"Where now?" sighed Cash.

Ruby looked around. There was no other café within sight. Unable to wait any longer, she opened the box and looked inside.

"Anything interesting?" Cash's voice was eager.

"Hmmm, not really." Ruby couldn't help it, she was disappointed. "Just more magazine and newspaper clippings, I've seen most of them before already." Her shoulders slumping, she continued, "I suppose it's to be expected Cynthia would have collected such things."

"Maybe she was looking through them, just before the party? A little reminder of how famous she was?"

"Maybe..." Ruby conceded.

Stepping closer, Cash pointed to one of the cuttings in Ruby's hand.

"Who's that?"

Ruby looked again. This piece didn't appear to concern Cynthia at all; instead it featured a head shot of a rather glamorous man, another actor by the looks of it.

Reading the caption, she discovered he was indeed an actor called Ron Mason who had the same sort of distinguished, serious air about him as his contemporary Sir Laurence Olivier. Although Ruby had never heard of him, he looked familiar.

Cash seemed to think so too.

"He reminds me of someone," he said. Not even two seconds later, he added, a note of triumph in his voice: "He reminds me of Cynthia."

Yes! Ruby's excitement stirred again. Mason had the same shape face as Cynthia, the same dazzling smile. Although the cutting was black and white, she would have bet anything he had also had the same red hair and blue eyes – twinkling blue eyes in fact. The cutting was dated 1941 and the man looked to be in his late thirties.

Stuffing the rest of the articles back into the box but holding that particular one aloft, she turned to Cash. "We need to do some research on this man, Ron Mason."

"He looks like a relation, what do you think?"

"He could be, perhaps even Cynthia's father – maybe he wasn't 'unknown' after all."

Cash had already got his iPhone out and was Googling the name but unfortunately the search engine was having trouble loading. "Damn," he swore under his breath.

"Look, don't worry about it for now." Ruby carefully folded the newspaper cutting and slipped it into her coat pocket. "We'll look into it when we get back to Lewes. We've got our work cut out though; we need to find out about him *and* David Levine now."

"Whoever *he* is," replied Cash.

Ruby nodded. "Well, if Google can't tell us, perhaps Cynthia can."

Cash looked at his watch. "Pub?"

"Are you trying to get me drunk again, Cash Wilkins?"

"Ruby Davis... it's not just ghosts you can see through, is it?"

***

"Here it is," Cash announced proudly. "The Angel and Crown. One of the finest hostelries in London."

"Really?" Ruby was unconvinced. "It looks a bit of a dive to me."

Its once grand Victorian facade had indeed fallen on hard times, many of its dark green tiles were chipped and its rusty old hanging baskets, which might have cheered it up in spring, dangled sad and empty. Only the golden lanterns, placed at intervals around the exterior, looked as though they were taken pride in, they had obviously been recently polished and sent out a soft glow into the winter gloom.

Cash was undeterred by her general lack of enthusiasm.

"This is a real old London boozer this is," he continued, beaming at her. "Your typical gin palace. How a real pub should be. Come on, let's go inside."

As numerous shadows at the windows suggested, the inside was heaving, full of people revving up for the Christmas holidays. So authentic in its 'London-ness' it was almost a parody of itself, Ruby did indeed love it – despite being a bit on the tatty side it had atmosphere in buckets, and the fairy lights strung around the bar in honour of the looming holiday gave the whole place a somewhat surreal feel. Laughter filled the air.

"There's actually a seat over there," said Cash, having to shout to make himself heard. "I'll get the drinks. They've got mulled wine on the go; do you fancy some of that?"

"Ooh, yes please," replied Ruby, squeezing past various revellers towards the corner Cash had pointed at. Seating herself on the end of a long burgundy velvet seat, the rest of it occupied by a huddled group of friends, she pulled a vacant stool close to her. Placing the box on her lap, her hands hovered protectively over it.

When Cash eventually returned, he took up residence on the stool. As there was so little room, he had to lean in close, snaking his arm around the back of her. Although she knew it was mainly for reasons of balance, she couldn't deny she liked the feel of it. He had opted for mulled wine too, both of them clearly relishing its spicy warmth – cloves, cinnamon and nutmeg, shot through with orange and ginger.

After a few more sips, Cash suggested they take another look through the box.

"No, not here, it's far too busy. Like I said, we'll have time later."

"Fair enough," said Cash. "Hey, I never asked you. Did you finish that book?"

"What book?"

"*Drive Like Hell.*"

"Oh yeah," laughed Ruby, recalling the way they'd met. "I loved it, it was really good. Did you finish it?"

"Almost, not quite. Got a few pages to go still. Glad to note Wes Freed didn't let me down with his book recommendation though."

It felt nice talking about 'normal' things. And she could do that with Cash. He was just as happy to talk about books and music as he was about the paranormal. He seemed to take life, death and everything in between in his stride. Perhaps it would be okay to take their relationship further. Perhaps he wouldn't run. He might be the one to stick around.

They shared a bottle of wine next, a surprisingly good Shiraz considering it was a pub. Cash then declared he was hungry.

"I don't know where you put it," Ruby said, eyeing his lean frame.

"Hollow legs, that's what my mum says. Shall we go and

eat?"

The mention of his mum reminded Ruby of Daisy.

"Oh God, the dog. We need to go and get her."

"She'll be fine with Mum, she loves dogs, she'll be spoiling her rotten, believe me. I'll text to let her know we'll be back a bit later than we thought."

Still Ruby hesitated.

"We should really get back now. Start finding out what we can about Levine and Mason."

"Theo's got Levine covered," Cash was persuasive. "She'll find out all there is to know."

"Hmmm," said Ruby, still contemplating. He was right though, one of Theo's fortes was research, ferreting out facts and figures. Levine was in capable hands and they could look up Mason tomorrow.

"Okay," she conceded, feeling hungry herself all of a sudden, though for what exactly, she wasn't sure.

"Just don't let me drink too much; I don't want to end up mislaying this box."

"You won't, I'll make sure of it," replied Cash, winking at her.

***

They ate at a French food restaurant in the theatre district. Although part of a well-known chain, the atmosphere was good and the food above average. Choosing the normal menu over the festive one, Cash ordered a rib-eye steak; she ordered the risotto, both of them declaring their dishes delicious. After some comfortingly mundane chat, Cash started telling her more about his background: his absent father, his wonderful mother, 'the best cook in the world' apparently, and his older brother, Presley, a motorcycle courier by day and a guitarist in a band by night, their mother's obvious love of music running deep in his veins too.

"And what about you," she asked, "do you play any instruments?"

"I used to play the drums. Played in a band too, just locally, pubs and stuff. The band broke up a couple of years ago; I haven't played much since then."

"Do you miss it?"

"Yeah, a bit. I might find myself another band soon."

"What sort of music did you play?" asked Ruby, bursting with questions, suddenly wanting to know everything there was to know about the man sitting opposite her.

"Prog rock but with a harder edge."

"And what was the band's name?"

"Eagle Rare," he said, smiling shyly at her.

"Unusual name," she said, loving this new coy side to him.

"It's after an unusual whiskey, available by mail order from America."

"Now that I'd like to try," she replied, unable to keep her flirty nature at bay.

"For you, I'd crack it open anytime," he countered, just as suggestively.

Feeling herself blush, she brought the conversation back round to music.

"Presley's band, are they good?"

"Thousand Island Park? They're brilliant. They've got a gig coming up in February, in Essex, do you fancy going?"

"I'd love to," said Ruby, chuffed he was making plans for them so far ahead.

Cash managed to squeeze in a chocolate mousse but Ruby opted for a cappuccino instead. Woozy from the wine they had drunk, she felt unsteady as they rose to go. Seemingly unaffected by his quota, Cash reached out a helping hand, a hand she wanted him to keep in place, to never take away. He seemed to realise this; his expression became more serious, his eyes intense, the way they had looked on that night they had first kissed – all-consuming. A night that seemed so long ago

215

now – not just mere weeks.

Realising it must look odd; the pair of them, standing in a packed restaurant, staring at each other, Ruby broke the connection. As she tried to make a steady exit, Cash called after her.

"Ruby? Haven't you forgotten something?"

Confused, she turned back.

Looking at the box, she muttered, "Honestly, Cash, what would I do without you?"

"You've got me; you don't need to worry on that score."

His words, although delivered casually, felt like they had set off bubbles of happiness inside her, rising up like champagne. Taking the box from him and turning on her heel, she practically floated outside.

They decided to walk to Victoria Station, Ruby claiming she needed as much fresh air as possible before the train journey home. Cash put his arm around her and she leaned into him, as he had leant into her in the pub. She sensed this was a ground breaking night for her, for them and one that was thankfully far from over yet.

Walking through the lively streets, packed with smiling crowds of people – friends, couples, families – all negotiating the still busy roads, Ruby couldn't remember a time when she had felt happier, like a regular girl on a date with a regular boy. Normal.

The next train to Lewes was a slow one and didn't leave for another hour or so, so they decided to get the Brighton train instead, sprinting across the concourse when Cash pointed out that it was just about to leave. Breathless with laughter, they managed to bag themselves the last two empty seats. Once again, she placed the box safely on her lap.

Ruby knew why she was so eager to reach home and hoped Cash felt the same. For a second, worry consumed her. What if he didn't? What if he was looking forward to nothing more than a good night's sleep in his own comfortable bed? What if she'd read him, *this,* all wrong? She needn't have tortured herself though, because as soon as the doubts set in, he quashed them, leaning across to kiss her, gently, on the lips – lingering only as long as it was seemly, restraining himself because of the commuters around them.

Looking up at him, she smiled, hoping to silently convey that it would be okay to kiss her again later, and more. He seemed to get the message because he grinned back at her, happy, excited and, dare she think it, just a little bit in love? A chuckle escaping her at how sentimental she was being, she snuggled into him, relishing the feel of him, the smell of him, desire going into overdrive on the 21.06.

When they reached Brighton Station, rather than wait for a connecting train to Lewes, Cash said, "Shall we get a taxi? I'll pay."

Just as keen as him to reach her flat as quickly as possible, she ran with him to the taxi rank in front of the station, bypassing as many people as they could to ensure a short wait.

In the back of the cab, Cash leaned over and kissed her again, for longer this time, deeper.

"Are you sure?" he whispered, so low only Ruby could hear.

"I'm sure," she whispered back, wishing there weren't so many damn traffic lights between here and her front door.

As Cash paid the driver, Ruby exited the cab. When he came round to her side of the pavement, she pulled him close with her free hand, giggling as she did so before exploring his mouth once more with her tongue and simultaneously walking him slowly backwards to her front door. He was laughing too as she handed him the box and rummaged around in her bag for the front door key. Finding it at last, she lifted her hand up to the lock. But just as she did so, a figure stepped forward from the dark shadows of the alcove, startling them both.

For a moment, Ruby was speechless; then, with great effort, she managed to utter one word.

"Mum!"

Chapter Twenty-Three

It took Ruby and Cash a few moments to get over the shock of seeing this woman, her mother, standing before them.

"Why are you here?" gasped Ruby when she had recovered enough to string more words together.

"To see you, of course." Her mother's voice was so low it was barely audible.

Her mind still reeling, Ruby could only manage: "Does Gran know?"

"Yes, if she's read the note I left her on the kitchen table."

"She'll be frantic."

"She'll understand."

Suddenly remembering the man beside her, the man she couldn't get enough of just a few seconds before, Ruby introduced Cash to Jessica.

"It's nice to meet you," said Cash, a strangled quality to his voice Ruby thought.

Ruby wasn't sure what her mother would make of his outstretched hand. Without a moment's hesitation, however, Jessica shook it. Not timidly, as Ruby would have expected, but firmly, whilst flashing an equally unexpected smile at him; a smile that said: *Nice to meet you too.*

Turning to Ruby, Cash said, "Look, I'd better be going, it's late. I'll see you in the morning, okay?"

"What about Daisy?" Ruby asked, not just out of genuine concern but because she was looking for excuses to keep Cash with her, it hurt to let him go.

"I've texted Mum. She's happy to keep her for as long you

like. I think you'll have trouble getting her back."

Ruby was only slightly relieved. Lingering for a few moments more, she could tell he didn't want to leave and she definitely didn't want him to go, but they had no choice, their unspoken plans were well and truly scuppered. Reaching up to kiss him, she stared after him as he walked away, every inch of her aching for his touch. Then she turned round to face her mother – a large part of her also intrigued to see what had brought Jessica to her doorstep for the first time ever without Gran.

"Come on," Ruby said, "let's get you inside. It's freezing."

Ruby put the box on the table in the hallway; she wouldn't get a chance to sift through more of its contents tonight. It would have to wait until tomorrow. Quickly, she glanced at the answer machine, the red light wasn't flashing. It was her assurance that Gran did understand after all.

"Hey, boy," said her mother, smiling down at Jed who'd been waiting eagerly in the kitchen for them. He seemed to like her too; he even seemed to be smiling back.

Straightening up, Jessica asked, "That young man, Cash is it? Is he your boyfriend?"

"Erm, yes," replied Ruby, "potentially."

"I like him, he has a good aura."

I like him too. A lot.

"I know you do," said her mother, startling her, "and I'm glad."

Recovering from her mother's insight, Ruby said, "Tea? Would you like a cup?"

"That panacea for all ills," responded Jessica, a somewhat wistful tone in her voice. "Yes, please, I would."

Glad to have something practical to do, Ruby rummaged through her cupboards for the necessary accoutrements, the wonderfully mundane task allowing her time and space to come to terms with her mother's surprise visit.

As Ruby swirled hot water around the teapot to warm it up, Jessica looked around her.

"This flat, it's lovely, safe."

Safe? A strange word to describe a flat, but yes, Ruby supposed she was right. Certainly she always felt safe here. Apart from Jed, no spirit had ever seen the need to take up residence within its walls, no matter how fleetingly. Instead it was a haven, a place of retreat, somewhere to retire to when the world and those not quite in it became too much.

"I could be happy in a flat like this," continued Jessica.

At Ruby's alarmed face, she emitted a small laugh. "Oh no, dear, don't worry, not with you. I mean when... when..."

She didn't have to continue, Ruby knew what she meant. *When Gran passed.* Something neither of them wanted to contemplate. Gran was strong. Gran was sturdy, a rock to both of them, but Gran was also getting old. She couldn't go on forever, not in this world anyway.

"Here you go," said Ruby, handing her mother's tea over in a plain white no-nonsense mug, unlike the dainty china cups her Gran and Esme favoured.

As her mother cradled the mug and sipped tentatively at the hot liquid, Ruby quietly took her in. Jessica's face looked even paler than normal, dark rings encircled her eyes – was her mother not sleeping? Normally, that was all she ever did, since the breakdown. And she was thin. Too thin for a woman of forty-eight, it made her look older than she was. Jessica's hair was still dark but flecked with grey, another sign of ageing she took no interest in hiding. She looked beaten, downcast. She *was* beaten and downcast. Once she had been anything but; she had been beautiful, to the young Ruby anyway. With luxuriant hair and sparkling eyes – a young woman with a zest for life but an ability to see beyond it too, an ability that had very nearly destroyed her. Nearly, but not quite, Ruby reminded herself. There was strength in her mother; she could sense it, even if her mother, and sometimes her grandmother, couldn't.

"Mum, why are you here?" asked Ruby at last.

"I heard you, when you came to visit, talking about

Highdown Hall."

"Oh, right," Ruby faltered. She had thought her mother was asleep when she'd confided in Gran.

Seeking to reassure her, Ruby said, "Yes, it's a bit of a tricky case, but we're on it, Mum, we've nearly cracked it."

"When are you going back?" was her mother's blunt response.

"Christmas Eve."

"Christmas Eve?"

"Yes, Mum, but I'll be home Christmas Day, if that's what you're worried about, I wouldn't miss being with you and Gran for the world."

"Ruby," Jessica's voice was not as patient as before. "I am not worried about Christmas Day. I'm worried about you. I don't want you to go back."

"I have to," Ruby countered.

"No you don't," Jessica reached across the table to hold her hand, an urgency to her actions. "Despite what Gran has told you, what she's drummed into you from the day you were born, whatever resides at Highdown Hall, it is *not* your responsibility."

Ruby stared across the table at her mother. She was right. Gran *had* always drummed it into her that it was her responsibility to help grounded souls; that she, or rather they, had been given the ability to do so for a reason, a purpose, which they must fulfil. Gran would have drummed the same message into Jessica too, but clearly it had fallen short.

"Mum," said Ruby, reluctant to upset her further but not wanting to lie either, "I am going back. I *want* to go back. Cynthia... she needs me."

Jessica simply stared at her.

After a moment, she said, "She attacked one of your team. Has she attacked you too?"

"No," Ruby hung her head. "Not Cynthia."

"But someone? Someone attacked you?"

Still looking down, Ruby mumbled "Yes."

"Who?"

"That's what I'm trying to find out."

There was silence again, Ruby almost not daring to breathe.

"You don't know what you're dealing with," Jessica said at last, almost spitting the words out. "Know when to admit defeat, Ruby, before you yourself are defeated."

"Mum!" said Ruby, shocked by her reaction.

Since her breakdown, Jessica had been placid, withdrawn, lost inside herself – shunning the world, seeking refuge in her childhood home, hardly ever leaving it, only to visit local shops, never anything more. This angry Jessica, who had just scraped her chair back and stood before her now with eyes blazing, Ruby had never encountered before.

"Your grandmother thinks love is the ultimate force, the *only* force. That evil does not exist. But it *does* Ruby. And I have stared into the face of it."

Ruby held her breath. Was this the moment her mother revealed just what she had seen, the moment she would learn at last the reason for her breakdown?

Leaning on the table now, her face only inches from Ruby's, Jessica continued.

"Where there is construction, there is deconstruction, where there is light, there is darkness, the two exist side by side, Ruby, in a strange and twisted sort of harmony. We are given freedom of choice, all of us, we can follow the light, or we can follow the dark. There are many who choose the latter, who walk so far down that path they change, become something else entirely. Not everyone, *everything,* can live in the light."

"Mum, what has this got to do with..."

But Ruby didn't have a chance to finish.

"Whatever it is that waits for you at Highdown Hall, who's to say it's even human? Who's to say it was *ever* human?"

"Mum, that's ridiculous," Ruby breathed out at last. "Of course it was human."

"Why 'of course', Ruby? Do you think you know everything that exists out there in the universe? Do you think Gran does? Have you not read all of Rosamund's papers? She hints at it too, the existence of demons. Gran is wrong. She's taught you there's nothing to fear. But you *should* fear, Ruby. You're as open to it as I was. There is danger at every turn and it's waiting, patiently waiting, for you to walk right into its clutches."

Ruby's head was spinning. What her mother was saying was difficult to comprehend. Of course she'd read Rosamund's papers, even those that hadn't been published, which Gran kept in a bureau at home. Never had she read about demons. Had Gran taken some of the papers and hidden them? Had Jessica found them? Were *they* the key to her breakdown?

A picture of Sarah's face popped into her mind, the light inside her evident on her face. Gran wouldn't do such a thing. She wasn't capable of deceit. Ruby would not doubt her.

Rising to her feet, she faced her mother.

"Hell is a human myth," she began, her voice faltering at first but getting stronger with each word that left her mouth, "nothing more. Demons do *not* exist. No soul, no matter what they've done, is ever beyond redemption or damned for eternity. Every human being, every animal, every insect, every plant, every damn pebble on the beach is a part of the light and one day they *must* return to it, no matter how meandering that journey is."

Jessica held her gaze.

"Ruby, there is more between heaven and earth than you can possibly know."

"More good things," Ruby insisted.

As though all fight had left her, Jessica slumped back down on her chair. Her face for a brief moment wizened, as though she'd lived a hundred lifetimes in the space of one.

"If only I had one ounce of your conviction," her voice was broken again, sad.

Kneeling down beside her, Ruby took hold of her hands,

they were chill to the touch but Ruby suspected that was from poor circulation, nothing more.

"But I've seen them, Mum," Ruby continued to argue, but gently, "I've seen spirit after spirit return from beyond, to collect their loved ones. I've seen how magnificent they are."

"And I've seen something different," was Jessica's bleak reply.

Ruby wondered if it was right to press her, to ask her to elaborate. Gran would say no, to leave well alone, but Gran wasn't here. It was just the two of them, for the first time in so long.

"Mum," she said eventually. "What have you seen? I *want* to know."

Jessica looked up sharply and in her eyes Ruby could see a desperate need to share, to try and make sense of the horror she had experienced – real or imagined. Perhaps, in the end, even she didn't know. Jessica tried to speak, attempted to form words, her hands balled into fists so tight her knuckles were white, but quickly she stopped; a violent shake of the head.

"No, Ruby, I can't... I can't contaminate you."

Her voice cracking, she continued, "You don't know how much I want you to be right, you and Mum, how much I long to believe you. If you are right, then I have created my own world, my own demons, and only I can destroy them. And I try, Ruby, really I do. I try."

Tears streamed from Jessica's eyes.

"Mum," whispered Ruby. "It's okay, I'm here."

Still kneeling, Ruby wrapped her arms protectively around her distressed mother's fragile frame, her heart breaking as she rocked her gently, their roles reversed.

After a while, the tears subsided.

Pulling up a chair so she could sit close beside her, Ruby said, "I know you're worried about me and I'm touched that you are, but I'm strong, I can do this, I *can* help Cynthia."

"I used to think I was strong once too..." Jessica reached out a hand to smooth Ruby's hair. "I used to think I was invincible.

But I quickly found out how weak I am."

"No!" Ruby almost shouted. "You are *not* weak. I don't know what happened to you, Mum, I hope someday you'll tell me, but what I do know is this: you live with fear that's very real to you, every single day you live with it, yet still you live, you battle on, you don't give in, not entirely. Your life, it's not how it was perhaps, but it is still life, a valid life, a life with love in it. Beneath your fear you're as strong as Gran, as me, as all us Davis women."

"But I'm scared, Ruby," Jessica whispered. "Scared of dying, of what's waiting for me."

"Then you'll understand how Cynthia feels and why I have to help her."

Ruby did indeed see a flicker of understanding in her mother's eyes, a flicker replaced almost at once by abject sadness as she asked, "But who will help *me*?"

"I will, Mum," Ruby was resolute, "and Gran and Great Gran too, all us Davis women."

A slight smile softened Jessica's features, as though Ruby's words were sinking in.

"Protect yourself, Ruby, stay strong. Whatever happens at Highdown Hall, stay strong."

"I intend to," Ruby replied, chasing away any fears her mother's words may have stirred in her. It was true; she didn't know what waited for Cynthia – and for her – in the shadows. And perhaps it would attack again, just as viciously as before. But surely going in with good intention, with love in her heart for *all* things, would protect her? Her beliefs defined her world and she would not let them waiver, could not afford to let them waiver, to let darkness get a foothold.

Hoping very much she would bring home only good news on Christmas Day, Ruby decided it was time to change the subject. All this talk of the world beyond, good, bad or otherwise, had tired her mother, she needed something to eat and then sleep, both of them bedding down in her room perhaps, snuggled together like they used to do when Ruby was young. It would be nice to do so again – comforting, and not just for her mother. In the morning, she would drive Jessica home, postponing the meeting with Theo and the team til later in the day. They wouldn't mind, not at all, not once she'd explained.

Less than two hours later, Ruby and Jessica were cosy in bed, relishing the warmth and closeness of each other. Just before sleep claimed them, Jessica pointed at Jed, who had also made himself comfortable on top of the covers.

"Take him with you," she said, "promise me you will."

"I promise," said Ruby, yawning widely.

"And Cash too. It's no coincidence they've found you."

Although momentarily startled by her words, the relief of temporary oblivion was too strong to resist. *Yes, you're right,* she thought, drifting off, *they're both a part of me now.*

Chapter Twenty-Four

Ruby and Jessica slept surprisingly well, waking much later than intended. Noticing it was nearly nine o'clock, Ruby jumped out of bed and made a beeline for the phone.

"Theo, I've overslept, my mum's here, I have to take her back home to Hastings. I'm going to be late for our meeting."

"No worries," replied Theo, somewhat amused, Ruby could tell, at the babble of words being thrown at her. "We'll meet later, that's all. Will you be back by noon?"

Ruby mentally calculated the time it would take to drive to Hastings. "Make it just after one to be on the safe side."

"Fine with me, I'll let the others know."

"And I'll text Cash. Thanks, Theo, see you then."

Cash responded almost immediately saying that delaying their meeting was fine too and not to worry about Daisy, she had settled in well at his mum's, who loved having a dog around again.

Relieved, Ruby walked back to the bedroom. Jessica was up, dressed and sitting on the edge of the bed, Jed once again making a fuss of her.

"Hi, Mum," said Ruby, brightly.

"Hello, darling." Jessica replied, but there was an absent-minded tone to her voice. "I think I'd like to go home now."

"What about a cup of tea first? I'll put the kettle on."

"No," Jessica was emphatic. Tightly, she added, "Thank you though."

Ruby smiled gently at her.

"No worries, Mum. I'll be ready in ten."

It was actually fifteen minutes later that Ruby was showered, dressed and ready to go. Jessica, meanwhile, had put her coat on and was waiting in the hallway.

The drive to Hastings was silent. Jessica sat staring passively at the passing countryside, which looked nothing less than bleak. Ruby knew she'd lost her again, but was surprised to note that she didn't feel the usual sadness about it. Instead she was grateful they had found each other, had actually *seen* each other, for the first time in years. Although it had been fleeting, it was something. Leaving her mother to her own thoughts, Ruby's mind wandered too. It was hard to believe tomorrow was Christmas Eve. Ruby was well aware Christmas happened at the same time every year, but even so, it always took her by surprise. She hadn't even begun to think about it, hadn't purchased a single present. Idly, she wondered if there'd be time later on, after the meeting, to dash around the shops that were open in Lewes, purchase some gifts from Wickle perhaps: a fragrant candle for Jessica, with cleansing eucalyptus, ideal for guarding against bad dreams. And maybe one of their lovely woollen blankets for Gran – perfect for wrapping round her for a doze in front of the fire. Should she get Cash a present too? Would it seem a bit forward? Presumptuous even? And then she checked herself. They'd very nearly fallen into bed together last night; it was okay to be a little presumptuous. At the very least he was a friend, and friends tended to buy each other gifts; it wouldn't look odd at all. Having convinced herself, she resolved to pop into Sussex Stationers to buy him a book, another by Dallas Hudgens if she could find one, or something similar. If she couldn't find something suitable, she'd go to Union Record Store in Lansdowne Place, their music selection, particularly the country stuff that Cash seemed to like, was impressive.

As Ruby entered Hastings, the sparse Sunday traffic ensured their swift passage through the town. Driving along the seafront, she passed the ruined pier to her right (she was still upset by its wanton destruction by arsonists several years back).

To her left was a series of houses, flats and B&Bs, some well maintained, others had obviously fallen on hard times – very hard times by the look of some of them. The new town, set further back, could just be glimpsed, its high street shops no doubt packed already. Shame she couldn't join the shoppers in a last minute festive fever but there was no chance this morning. Rounding the bend at Rock a Nore, she caught a glimpse of the black fishing huts, unique to Hastings and iconic because of it. They stood like sentinels, tall and proud, overlooking fishing boats and huts where the day's catch was sold. Reaching the Old Town, she parked the car and walked with Jessica to their family home.

Gran must have been hovering behind the door because no sooner had Ruby raised her hand to ring the bell, it flung open and Sarah rushed straight to Jessica.

"Are you alright, dear?" she fussed. "Come inside, let's get some tea."

Tea – that panacea for all ills as her mother had wearily called it.

Following the two older women inside, Ruby could tell Gran had been busy baking, the air redolent with cinnamon, a smell that characterised Christmas and immediately ignited a spark of childish excitement within her. Gran always made such an effort at this time of year, putting up decorations, not garish, but sophisticated, silver and gold the predominant colours. Christmas cards from friends the world over were proudly displayed on every mantel and carefully wrapped presents waited patiently and tantalisingly under the tree.

Whilst Gran got Jessica settled, seating her in front of a roaring log fire with a cup of tea and some home-made shortbread, Ruby wandered into the kitchen. Spying the polka dot tin Gran kept her biscuits in, again home-made, she helped herself, hoping she could take a few home too. Cash would love them.

"Thank God she's alright," said Sarah, coming up behind her.

229

"I was so worried."

"But she left you a note didn't she? Explaining."

"Yes, she did," said Sarah, still clearly agitated. "But I... I don't know, it's been such a long time since she's been out on her own, that far I mean. Not since the... the..."

"The breakdown."

"Yes," Sarah sighed.

"What prompted her to undertake such a journey?" she continued.

"She was worried about me," Ruby made sure she closed the kitchen door firmly this time so they couldn't be overheard. "She heard me telling you about Highdown Hall, about how Cynthia attacked Corinna; she thinks I'm in danger too."

"Do *you* think you're in danger?" Sarah asked, surprising her.

Gran didn't know that she'd been attacked too. Should she tell her?

Ruby hesitated. "I... I don't think so, no."

Motioning for her to sit down, Sarah looked into Ruby's eyes. "Remember what I've taught you, Ruby. Even the blackest heart has cracks in it. That's how the light gets in."

"I know," Ruby nodded her head in fervent agreement, "but Mum's convinced otherwise. She believes some souls are beyond help. That hell and damnation do exist."

"Ruby..." Sarah's voice was low but firm. "Your mother made mistakes when she was younger; got in with a crowd of people who weren't good for her. She... how can I put it, dabbled with drugs, drank too much, she... she flaunted her gift, used it entirely in the wrong way, to impress the living rather than help the departed. When you behave like that, it *is* possible to encounter negative influences."

"What influences?" Ruby asked, sitting to attention.

Sarah thought for a few moments.

"Human beings are capable of great good; they are also capable of bad thoughts and deeds. We know deeds are physical but thoughts are energy too. These thoughts, they have no place

230

in the light, but as a form of energy they must go somewhere, and they do. Into a band that surrounds our world, pulled there as though magnetically – a sort of dumping ground if you like. In this band, thought forms can sometimes manifest. I think your mother inadvertently tuned into this band, that she did indeed see something dreadful. In reality, such manifestations are weak; they cannot exist outside of darkness. They are part of a much lower frequency, a frequency we leave behind when we leave this world. Their sole purpose is to terrify, to frighten, but they can only do that if you let them."

Ruby tried to take in all her grandmother was telling her. Mum had dabbled with drugs? There was a dumping ground for less than pleasant thought forms? That Jessica had looked into it, had glimpsed something terrible, a thought form made manifest?

Could it be that what waited for Cynthia in the shadows wasn't real but rather some force that Cynthia herself had created? Rawlings' Devil? But no, it couldn't be. It had felt very real when it had attacked her; it had felt human. Levine, perhaps? Or even Mason? But why?

"Ruby, tell me what you're thinking."

Ruby duly complied, imparting all she had learnt from Esme Harris.

"If it is this film director Levine, openly identifying him should cause a reaction. It may also prompt Cynthia to remember what happened the night she passed."

"But what if it isn't him, Gran? What if it is...?"

"A demon?" Sarah laughed. "Darling, no demon could touch you. They wouldn't dare. It sounds like it is Levine – their mutual deaths are too much of a coincidence to ignore. If it *is* him, remember, he's hiding because he's frightened, not for any other reason. So many are afraid that only retribution awaits them – it's our job to help them understand it doesn't. Keep the faith, Ruby. Chase away any lingering fears. Love will never let you down."

Ruby swallowed hard.

"Thanks, Gran," she said at last, "I needed to hear that," and then on a laugh, "again."

"Always happy to help. Now come on, let's check on your mum."

Jessica had fallen into a deep sleep. Her face, in repose at least, peaceful.

Staring at her, Ruby caught sight of the clock on the mantelpiece.

"Crikey, is that the time already? I've got about an hour to get back to the office. Listen, Gran, I have to go, I'll see you on Christmas Day."

"You will indeed, Ruby, and perhaps skip breakfast? I've made a mountain of food here."

"I will," laughed Ruby, determination spurring her forwards.

Chapter Twenty-Five

"Sorry I'm late, guys," said Ruby, hurrying along the street towards the familiar team waiting patiently outside the entrance to her office.

"No worries," said Corinna, ever cheerful. "We've only just got here ourselves."

Retrieving her key from her bag, she chanced a glance at Cash. He was looking straight at her, a slight naughtiness to his grin she thought.

Feeling her face burn, she opened the door and stood aside. In single file they walked past her up the stairs. Ruby followed, having trouble taking her eyes of a certain part of Cash's anatomy as he ascended before her.

"Bloody hell, I wish they'd install heating in here," she complained on entering her office.

After briefly rubbing her hands together, she fired up the Calor Gas heater, its orange flame attracting Jed to his usual spot beside it.

"Hello, boy," she whispered fondly.

The rest of the team settled themselves around the meeting desk, Corinna taking their requests for hot drinks this time. As she busied herself by the kettle they talked briefly about the weather, how cold it was, how miserable, everybody lamenting the lack of blue skies. Taking the mug Corinna handed to her, Ruby relished its warmth, encircling her hands around it. Once everyone else had theirs she kick-started the meeting.

"First off, thanks for coming in on a Sunday, guys."

"Needs must," Ness pointed out.

"You're not wrong there," Ruby conceded. "Okay, what have we found?"

Four pairs of eyes, five if you included Jed's, looked hopefully at Theo.

"Well, this David Levine, there's really not a lot on him."

"So he wasn't another movie star?" enquired Ness.

"On the Z-list if he was," Corinna butted in. "I've never heard of him."

"No," said Theo, shaking her head. "He wasn't an actor, he was a director. Not up with the big boys of his day, the projects he was involved in were far more modest. And I say director, but really he was more of an assistant director. The highlight of his career seems to have been working on a film called *Later in the Day*, in which Cynthia starred."

"Before or after *The Phoenix*?" asked Ruby.

"It was after *The Phoenix*, between *Intruders* and *The Elitists*. It was another Rank Organisation production I think, nothing to do with Hollywood. Levine is British."

"What I find strange," Ruby interjected, "is that all the time I was researching Cynthia Hart, I found no mention of a second death at Highdown Hall."

"There is some mention," countered Theo. "I found a short newspaper article concerning his death yesterday. His car veered off the road not far from the house, apparently the night of the party. The article mentioned the party, and that it was held to celebrate Cynthia's birthday and forthcoming move to America, and said that it wasn't long after leaving her house that he'd crashed. So their names were linked, but only briefly and in a piece that barely merited more than a few lines. Reports concerning Cynthia's death, as we know, were abundant at the time, but they focused on her and her alone."

"So," said Ruby, trying to make sense of it. "Cynthia *did* know Levine, but only in a work-related sense. There's absolutely no information linking them together in a more personal sense?"

234

"None that I could find," replied Theo.

"It's not much to go on, is it?" Ruby was downcast again. "Perhaps Levine isn't our man after all."

"There's no such thing as coincidence," Ness muttered, echoing Sarah's sentiment.

It seemed Cash agreed too.

"Remember what Esme Harris said, that Levine left the party looking red and flustered. He was obviously agitated, but why? Had someone said or done something to upset him? Perhaps he and Cynthia were having a clandestine affair? Maybe she teased him like she did John Sterling?"

"Maybe," replied Ruby, "but the only way we'll find out is through Cynthia. Talking of which..." Ruby paused as she went to fetch the newspaper article about Ron Mason, which she had slipped into her coat pocket the day before. "The box Esme gave me; I've left it at the flat, but I found this in it." Nodding at Cash, she said, "Or rather *we* found it."

"What is it?" Ness leant her head to one side.

Handing the newspaper photograph over to Theo, Ruby explained hers and Cash's theory.

"I recognise him, a bit of a rogue Ron Mason, if I remember correctly, a ladies' man. Have you heard of him, Ness?"

"Vaguely, but I've never seen any films with him in I don't think."

"There is a resemblance though, isn't there?" continued Theo. "A pretty strong resemblance I'd say."

"There is," Ruby agreed. "I thought I'd look into his background this afternoon; see if I can find a link with him at least."

"Good luck with that." Theo raised a cynical eyebrow. "We've read just about everything there is to read on Cynthia and not once has Ron Mason been mentioned."

"I know, and it is just speculation on our part but you never know, it's within the realms of possibility. Cynthia's father on her birth certificate was listed as 'unknown', but the very fact she kept a cutting of him suggests he was significant to her in some way."

"Was he her brother's father too?" Corinna enquired.

"I don't know," admitted Ruby. "And it's not as if I can just pop down to the record office to check either. They're closed until after the holidays now."

"But it's possible," Ness interjected. "Mason could have hung around just long enough to get Mary pregnant again and then taken off."

"Anything is possible," Theo sighed, "that's the problem. Anyway, Ruby, research what you can about this Mason character just in case, but remember you must get some rest."

Ruby was just about to promise she would when the phone rang. She answered it quickly while Theo, Ness and Corinna started putting on their hats, gloves and coats. Only Cash remained where he was. Replacing the receiver, Ruby turned to the imminently departing crowd, wincing as she did so.

"Erm, you'll never guess what?" she said, hoping she sounded suitably apologetic.

"What?" responded Corinna chirpily.

"We've got ourselves an emergency."

***

All callers to Psychic Surveys sounded distressed to varying degrees, but on a scale of one to ten, Ruby would say the call she had just taken ranked around the nine mark. The fact the woman had felt the need to phone on a Sunday nudged it up to ten. After apologising profusely for doing so, the woman, Angela Lawrence, then went on to tell Ruby that she'd only been resident in her home for six months, but ever since moving in she had felt nervous and anxious, as though she was being watched – not just intermittently, but all the time. Then, she'd confided further, the night-time noises had started: footsteps on the stairs, when she knew damn well her husband

236

and two teenage sons were in bed; a door banging at intervals downstairs. Often, just as she was drifting off, she'd hear a grunt-like noise in her ear, deep and guttural, inhuman. She was the only one in the house who experienced such phenomena; the others remaining blissfully unaffected, alternating between teasing her and becoming irritated whenever she mentioned it. More and more irritated in fact, she told Ruby. Normally, she hated to get out of bed at night, once beneath the covers she would remain there, her eyes stubbornly shut until morning. But last night she'd suffered a raging thirst that just wouldn't abate.

Fed up of feeling bullied in her own home, she had eventually got up. It was pitch black outside, she told Ruby, and silent, but not an easy silence, it seemed ominous instead. Steeling herself, she had made her way downstairs and drank an entire pint of water before returning to bed. And that's when she had seen him, an outline of a large man, solidly built, standing halfway up the stairs, blocking her route back to safety, leering at her, reaching out to her, his features fixed in a threatening grimace.

"Well, I screamed the house down, didn't I? I just screamed and screamed. My husband rushed out of the bedroom towards me and passed straight through him, didn't even know he was there. He thought I'd seen a spider or something. A spider? If only! I really feel I'm going out of my mind, Miss Davis. Please help. Even though it's Christmas in a couple of days I feel like running away. Leaving them all to it. I can't take this any longer. I simply can't."

Ruby knew the team should rest but there was no way she could ignore the distress in Mrs Lawrence's voice. She sounded desperate.

After promising they would come straight away to her address in Crawley, Ruby asked how she'd heard of Psychic Surveys.

"Your website. There's quite a few of you on the net, isn't

237

there? Psychics I mean. But your website stood out, no fancy nonsense, it was down-to-earth. I like that."

Smiling at her words, Ruby resolved to tell Cash as soon as possible about Mrs Lawrence's opinion of his handiwork.

***

Within minutes, Theo, Ness and Cash were piling into Ruby's Ford and making their way to Lailey Way in Crawley. Corinna had offered to stay behind to research Ron Mason and Ruby had gladly accepted, it was one less thing for her to do when she got back. They agreed to discuss her findings when they returned. As they sped along the A27, Theo couldn't resist entertaining them all with an old nursery song, the lyrics slightly tampered with.

"I saw a ghost. Where? There on the stair! Where on the stair? Right there!"

Cash openly showed his amusement but Ness remained as straight-faced as ever.

Stifling her own laughter, Ruby brought them back to the case in hand. "Seriously though, I don't like the sound of this man 'leering' – no one likes to be leered at."

"We'll sort him out, don't worry," said Theo confidently, reprising the song but whistling it this time, fully realising how much she was annoying Ness.

The house in Lailey Way was a mid-terrace, ex-council house, the kind hurriedly put up after World War II. Painted cream, it may have looked smart once upon a time, but now it looked careworn, in need of some serious TLC. One window had a distinct crack in it and the grass in front was patchy in some places, overlong in others; Ruby bet to herself that even in summer no flowers graced the borders running alongside the path to the front door. It was unenticing enough even without its supernatural guest.

Cash grabbed the bag of paraphernalia from the boot of

Ruby's car and followed the rest of the team up the pathway to knock on the door.

"Mrs Lawrence?" said Ruby, stepping forward. "I'm Ruby from Psychic Surveys and this is my team. May we come in?"

The woman in front of her looked harried; her dyed black hair unkempt and her eyes somewhat wild. Although she knew they were coming, she hadn't bothered to dress. She stood there in a night-dress and dressing gown, a cigarette hanging from one side of her mouth.

"Come in, come in," she muttered, not bothering to remove the cigarette.

All the curtains in the house were drawn, something Ruby hated to see during the daytime, believing it imperative to let the light in whenever you can, particularly in a house that was suffering spiritual upheaval. There was also an unpleasant smell in the air, reminiscent of laundry left for too long in the washing machine, its sweet freshness quickly turning sour.

Ruby glanced at the stairs as Angela Lawrence directed them into the living room, where a Christmas tree, haphazardly decorated, stood rather forlornly in one corner – the only nod to the annual celebration that she could see.

"My husband's out," the woman explained quickly. "I haven't told him you're coming. He'll hit the roof if he finds out. You'll have to be quick."

"Why will he hit the roof?" Theo asked, concerned.

"Because he doesn't believe, you see. He thinks I'm round the bend, so do my boys, they can't feel, hear nor see nothing at all. But I can, all the bloody time."

"Just here at home, or elsewhere as well?" Ruby was intrigued.

"It has happened before," Mrs Lawrence admitted – reluctantly, as though confiding a dirty secret. Then with a little more gusto, she declared, "I'm haunted I am, continually haunted and I don't know why. I've done nothing to deserve it."

Another psychic then, thought Ruby, *but one reluctant to*

239

acknowledge it.

"It would help if we opened these curtains," said Ness, gentle understanding in her voice. Clearly she was thinking the same as Ruby. "Do you mind?"

"No," replied Mrs Lawrence, "not at all. I don't know why they're still closed." She did indeed look genuinely perplexed. "I just haven't got round to opening them yet I suppose."

"Not a problem, we'll do it," said Ness, motioning to Cash to help.

Although not a particularly bright day outside, the house felt distinctly better with the curtains open. It was amazing what the light could do, no matter how faint.

"And a window too?" Ness asked. "Can we open a window? It can represent a physical exit to the spirit."

"The locks are a bit stiff on the windows; I keep meaning to get my husband to see to them. I think he painted over them when we first moved in, although he won't admit it, sealed the bloody things shut. A door would be easier."

"The door it is then," replied Ness. "I'm sorry to have to do so; it's rather cold outside."

"It's alright, I understand," said Mrs Lawrence, and Ruby was sure that, on some level at least, she did.

After checking that the woman's two sons were out too, Ruby ran through with her their typical procedure. First, she explained, they would try to connect psychically with the spirit in a bid to persuade him to move on. Then they would cleanse every room with smudge sticks and essential oils to remove any residual energy. Afterwards, she would advise her on the use of suitable crystals. Brown tiger eye was good for protection against unwanted spirits as were calcopyrite and carnelian. Noting a slight frown cross Mrs Lawrence's face, Ruby assured her that stones were relatively inexpensive and could be purchased from a number of places – Ruby's favourite was a crystal shop set beside a tea room in the picturesque village of Litlington, but she reassured Mrs Lawrence that she wouldn't need to go that far. Before Psychic Surveys left, she continued, they would place citrine around her home, a highly effective crystal for soaking up negativity.

As Mrs Lawrence nodded, Ruby asked, "Was it on the stairs that you last saw him?"

"Yes," Mrs Lawrence shuddered. "Leering, like he always does."

"I get that impression too," chimed in Theo. "But I also sense that's all he ever did, leer I mean. He liked the ladies did Cyril, but he wasn't very successful with them."

There came a bang from upstairs, as though a vase or something had been knocked off a table and thrown to the floor.

Mrs Lawrence immediately stepped closer to Ruby.

"That's him," she whispered, clutching at her dressing gown. "You've upset him."

"Don't worry." Ness reached out an arm to comfort her. "We're not in the business of goading spirits to get a reaction. We're here to help them move on, that's all." She looked pointedly at Theo. "Aren't we?"

Theo ignored her and went to stand at the foot of the stairs.

"Can you sense him right now, Mrs Lawrence?"

"I sense him all the time," was the terrified reply.

"Ruby, Ness, shall we try and connect? Cash, perhaps you could stay with Mrs Lawrence in the living room?"

"Sure," replied Cash dutifully.

Standing in the cramped space at the bottom of the stairs, trying to ignore the multitude of coats hanging on a rail beside them and the impressive collection of trainers and shoes scattered at their feet, the trio joined hands.

Before they tuned in, Ness whispered, "You know she's a psychic too, don't you?"

Ruby nodded her head whilst Theo said, "Denial ain't just a river in Egypt, huh?"

"Theo," hushed Ruby, noticing another disapproving glare

from Ness.

"I just meant perhaps we can help her, you know, afterwards, to deal with her gift."

"We can try," replied Ruby, not convinced they'd be able to do so.

A clear image of the man Angela Lawrence was complaining about popped into Ruby's mind. He was in his late fifties, with a face full of bristle, an impressive gut and ill-fitting clothes. It was fair to say he hadn't been one of life's beauties. And yes, Theo was right; he did have an appetite for the ladies, very much so. Sadly his feelings had rarely been reciprocated, the few relationships he'd had ending on a less than happy note. He wasn't a violent man, Ruby sensed, but a very frustrated one – the lack of female appreciation forcing him to become something of a voyeur instead. And although he had created a catalogue of sexual fantasies in his mind, as far as she could tell, they had remained just that – fantasies.

The man, Cyril, was leering at her now, his tongue flicking out between his lips, clenching both hands at her as though he wanted to grope her breasts.

"Cyril, stop it!" said Ruby firmly. "That sort of behaviour does *not* impress me."

Ruby could sense he was taken aback by her admonishment. He quickly recovered though, turning his attentions towards Ness instead and thrusting his crotch at her.

"Charming," muttered Theo. "Leave me out, why don't you? The only broad here you might have stood a chance with."

Humour, Ruby knew, was necessary in dealing with Cyril. He wasn't a bad soul, just wayward. She actually pitied him his frustration, perhaps if the fairer sex had been kinder to him in life, not succumbed of course, but treated him with compassion rather than such obvious disdain, he might have been more tolerable. Instead, she felt overwhelming waves of loneliness emanating from him, a human emotion so strong it anchored him.

"Cyril," said Ruby gently. "You know as well as we do that you have passed. But what you may not know is you don't have to take feelings of loneliness with you into the light, you can just let them go. You don't have to take your physical body either. Leave it behind."

Cyril had stopped leering. He looked confused instead.

Ruby continued, her head still bowed, her hands joined to Theo and Ness.

"Inside, Cyril, you are beautiful, you are magnificent – we all are; every single one of us. You belong to the light and waiting in it are people who love you, the *real* you, maybe even a past love, a woman I mean, someone you met in another lifetime."

Cyril's interest was piqued. He peered beyond them.

A girlfriend?

"Yes, a girlfriend, maybe even a wife, longing to be reunited with you."

A pretty girlfriend?

Ruby nodded her head. "Oh yes, very pretty indeed."

I don't want no-one like me, he said, distrustful suddenly. *She has to look nice.*

"Everyone looks nice in the light, Cyril," Ruby assured him.

Tentatively, Cyril descended one stair.

"That's it, Cyril," urged Theo, "come forward."

He was hesitant again.

Are you sure she's there – this girlfriend?

"You're never going to find out if you don't look." Ruby smiled encouragingly at him.

Another stair descended.

"Open the door wider," Ruby whispered to Ness, before returning her attention to Cyril. "Come on, Cyril, be brave. You need to leave this house now, and this life, it's over, it's done with – just take with you the lessons you've learnt, nothing more. Start again, somewhere else, somewhere better, somewhere you're going to be a lot happier."

He was on the bottom stair now.

And you're sure she'll like me?

Such disbelief in his voice. Had no one *ever* returned his affections?

"She'll *adore* you," Ruby was confident.

He was only inches away now, the look on his face a little more trusting. But again he hesitated.

I don't believe in God.

"You don't have to."

Why?

"You're believed in, that's what matters."

Cyril hung his head.

I'm not a Catholic or nothing.

"I'm not sure God is either."

What is he then?

"Love."

Cyril hesitated no more. Understanding smoothing his grizzled features, lending him an almost serene quality, he walked right up to Ruby and then through her, continuing on his journey at last. As he did so, Ness squeezed Ruby's hand; they both found the moment of releasing someone highly poignant.

Turning slightly, all three watched him take his leave. Not long now and Mrs Lawrence would be leered at no more; another success for Psychic Surveys. In the frame of the doorway the silhouette of Cyril's body was only just visible as the shimmering light started to wrap itself around him.

Moments before he disappeared entirely, he turned to Ruby.

I'd still like to cop a feel of your tits though, he said, and winked at her before fading entirely.

Stunned at first, she soon burst out laughing, as did Theo and even Ness. Some people, dead or alive, were incorrigible.

"Mrs Lawrence now?" asked Ness.

"I think so," replied Ruby.

Chapter Twenty-Six

Although clearly relieved that Cyril had departed, Mrs Lawrence did not take kindly to Ruby suggesting that she might be psychic too.

"Rubbish," she said, anxiety clear in her eyes, "I've been unlucky, that's all."

The rest of the team had moved upstairs to cleanse the bedrooms, deliberately taking their time whilst Ruby persevered.

Sitting at the kitchen table, a mug of tea in hand, she probed again.

"When did you start sensing spirits?"

"I can't remember..." Mrs Lawrence refused to look directly at Ruby. "It wasn't that long ago, I'm sure."

"As an adult? A child?"

A slight tremor ran through the woman opposite.

"Maybe, as a child, perhaps... I don't know. Look, I'm not psychic okay, it's not my fault there are ghosts everywhere I go."

"It's nobody's *fault*," Ruby reassured her. "You have a gift, that's all, you can see beyond what most people see."

"I don't see beyond anything and I don't want to talk about it. I just want to live my life in peace."

Standing abruptly up, she handed Ruby a cheque she had written earlier. "There, thank you very much, I'm very grateful for all you've done but you need to leave now."

"Mrs Lawrence," appealed Ruby. The woman, however, refused to be drawn.

"No, please, I don't want to talk about it, just go. My

husband would have a fit if he came in and found you here. He'd call in the men in white coats I'm sure."

"Is your husband due home soon?" asked Ruby, worried that this timid, confused and frightened woman in front of her was actually cowed by her husband.

Mrs Lawrence glanced down quickly at her watch. "Yes, I'm sure he is. Very soon. You have to go. All of you. Please. I feel so much better now. Really."

Knowing as well as she did that this was a lie, Ruby complied.

"If you do want to talk," she tried one final time, "you have my number. Call me."

"I will, I will, now *please...*"

Sensing the desperation in her voice, Ruby called upstairs to the team to let them know their work here was done.

***

Today was turning out to be far from the rest day the team had planned. As they were travelling back to Lewes, discussing the advantages and disadvantages of having 'the gift', Ruby's car started to shudder violently. She quickly steered it into the hard shoulder before it cut out completely, narrowly avoiding other cars travelling at breakneck speed.

"What the...!" gasped Ruby, staring at the steering wheel, disbelief and shock running through not just her but all four of her passengers.

Silence reigned for a few moments as each and every occupant of the Ford adjusted to the unexpected turn of events. Eventually Cash asked if she had breakdown cover.

"Yes," replied Ruby, coming to.

Digging her mobile phone out of her coat pocket, she rang their number, pleased with herself that she had previously keyed it into her list of contacts. Placing the call, she was told by a very apologetic female voice that all vehicle assistants were unusually busy on account of it being the Christmas holidays, but that they would try to reach her as soon as possible and would keep her updated at regular intervals regarding timeframes.

Knowing it was going to be a damn sight longer than the hour her particular breakdown company promised in the adverts, Ruby wondered if they should get out of the car to seek safety behind the crash barrier, something she had seen numerous people do.

"Most definitely," said Ness, hastily reaching for the door.

Once out of harm's way, Ruby turned to Cash and said forlornly, "Any idea what it could be?"

"Sorry," he replied, putting his arm round her and pulling her close, probably because her teeth were chattering so dramatically. "Cars really aren't my forte."

Despite being pissed off about the car, she couldn't help but appreciate being back in his arms, even if it was in the freezing cold, by the side of a motorway, the day before Christmas Eve. She also couldn't help but notice her two colleagues raised eyebrows that Cash had done such a thing. Amused, she bit down on a smile.

The rescue truck turned up just shy of two hours later, by which time it was completely dark.

"Sorry for the wait," a grizzled looking man said, "we're rushed off our feet."

Securing the car bonnet on its prop and placing an industrial-looking lamp on the side, he stuck his head over the engine, oohing and ahhing dramatically whilst rubbing his chin. At last he walked over to Ruby, the look on his face a decidedly grim one.

"Dead as a dodo, darling, nothing I can do to bring it back to life, sorry. Going to have to call for a tow vehicle."

His diagnosis was met with various groans and it was another hour before the tow vehicle came, driving them straight to Earnshaw's Garage, a good ten minute's walk from Ruby's office. It being Sunday evening, Greg Earnshaw was not in residence. In fact, Ruby suspected he wouldn't be in residence until long after Boxing Day. Hastily, she scribbled a note with her contact details on and posted it through the letterbox. She always went to Greg with car trouble; he would know who she was.

Glumly, all four turned back towards Ruby's office, Ruby wondering how on earth she was she going to get to her Gran's on Christmas Day. Highdown Hall she could get a lift to but Hastings was going to prove more problematic – did trains run on the big day itself? She didn't think so.

Corinna had texted earlier to say she was heading out to the shops to finish her Christmas shopping and that she would return when they did. She had texted again to say she was back at the office and where were they? Ruby explained all as she entered.

"How did it go in Crawley?" Corinna went from being sympathetic to curious.

"Cyril was a bit of a cheeky one!" Theo answered with an amused gleam in her eye. "But he's where he should be, that's the main thing."

Ness immediately set about making tea for everyone. Ruby cursed that she hadn't had time to restock the biscuit tin; if she was hungry, Theo, Ness and Cash must be too – Cash without doubt – lunch had been missed entirely. Despite this, every one settled themselves around the table without complaint.

"So, what did you find on Mason?" Ruby asked, aware that time was ticking on.

"Quite a bit actually, I think I'd score top marks if I ever had to sit an exam on him," Corinna joked. "And absolutely gorgeous he was too, hotter than Ryan Gosling that's for sure."

"Tell us about him." Ness looked genuinely intrigued.

Tossing her long red hair over her shoulder, Corinna took a quick sip from her mug before continuing. "Oh, that's nice," she said, relishing its warmth. "By all accounts Mason was very

248

gifted, he was often hailed as 'the finest actor of his generation'. A bit of a Daniel Day Lewis type, he completely got into his roles; he lived and breathed them apparently. Unfortunately, he was also just as passionate about gambling, drink, drugs and women. Some sources say he never reached his full potential because of such distractions, but in the films he did make the critics seem to agree he was brilliant."

Theo raised an eyebrow. "I must check to see if Sky is showing any of his films this Christmas. I do love settling down in front of a good old black and white."

"But here's the strange thing," resumed Corinna. "He died young too, in 1951, roughly the same time that Cynthia shot to fame. And he died in scarily similar circumstances."

Ruby could feel her eyes widening.

"Really? How?" she asked.

"Well, he was at a wrap party for a film he was shooting in Monaco, doing the usual thing that film stars do I suppose, carousing with starlets and admirers, having a whale of a time. One minute he was there, the centre of attention, the next he had disappeared. He was found in his hotel room the next morning by the maid, he'd been dead for hours."

"A heart attack?" breathed Ruby.

"A heart attack," confirmed Corinna.

Ruby's hand flew up to her mouth. "Incredible."

"Not really," Ness disagreed. "Many health problems are hereditary. It explains a lot."

"It certainly does," added Theo. "In health terms at least, it's important to know your heritage."

Ruby nodded sagely too.

Focusing again on Corinna, she asked, "But did you find anything that specifically connected Mason with Cynthia?"

"I'm sorry to disappoint you, and you know I searched thoroughly, but there was nothing on the net, nothing at all."

"So, whether he *was* her father or not, we still have no idea," Ness said.

Ruby's shoulders slumped. "The only evidence we have that he meant anything at all to Cynthia is the fact she kept an article about him in her box."

"You have to admit though, it does ring true..." Corinna ventured. "Like father, like daughter."

"In more ways than one," Cash responded wryly.

There was silence as all five contemplated the latest twist.

"It also explains where she got her drive and talent from." Ruby said at last.

"And her wild side," Ness added.

"But what I don't understand," Cash looked perplexed, "is what Mary Hart was doing hooking up with a movie star, she wasn't an actress or anything; she was a cleaner."

"Yes," said Ruby, "but perhaps she was cleaning at the Theatre Royal, who knows? Mason may have been involved in a play there and that's how they met. She got lucky."

"Or unlucky," Ness pointed out.

"Or unlucky," Ruby yielded, "depending on which way you look at it."

"So, what do we do now, do we tell Cynthia?" Cash asked.

Theo answered his question with another. "Tell her what? This is all just conjecture. We have no solid proof."

"But it could be her father in the shadows, not Levine," Cash persisted.

"Look, I think we're getting distracted by all of this." Theo looked and sounded slightly exasperated. "Yes, Mason could be Cynthia's father, but even if he is, there is no indication at all that either one knew about the other. An article about the man in amongst clippings of herself proves nothing; all it implies is that Cynthia had an interest in him, perhaps because of his sheer brilliance as an actor, nothing more."

"Or it could have been a subconscious attraction?" Ness offered. "She was fascinated by Mason but without really knowing why?"

"Yes, that's true," Theo nodded at the younger woman, "a

case of like calling to like. I still think, however, our most likely candidate for the man in the shadows is David Levine and that's how I think we should play it. A spurned lover often finds it hard to forgive."

"John didn't," Corinna defended.

"John was exceptional," Theo countered. Looking pointedly at her watch, she sighed again before adding, "It's getting late – very late. We really do need to think about getting some rest. I think we should call it a day before we end up in knots we can't untie."

There were various mumbled agreements amongst the team.

"But before we go, I've been thinking," said Ness quietly, "about tomorrow. To give us the best chance of being successful, don't you think it might be an idea to go back there in the evening? If we went there at about the same time the party would have been going on it would not only give us the best chance of tuning in to all the frequencies and residual feelings, it might also help Cynthia remember too? What do you think?"

"Brilliant idea," said Theo decisively. "That way we could all finish our Christmas shopping and get some rest. This one could take all we've got to give."

Having agreed to meet at Highdown Hall at six o'clock the following evening, Ness was the first to make an exit, bundled up in thick coat, hat, scarf and gloves, a slight, somewhat harried-looking figure. She was followed swiftly by Corinna. Before Theo left she turned to Ruby with a knowing look. "You will get an early night, won't you? It's imperative you do."

"I will," said Ruby, averting her eyes.

"I mean it," said Theo sternly. "And you, young man, you need to rest too if you're going to insist on joining us. We must face tomorrow energised."

"I will, I promise."

As soon as she heard Theo descending the stairs, Ruby turned to Cash, put her arms around his waist and whispered, "Your place or mine?"

"Both," he said, bending to kiss the tip of her nose.

"Ooh, saucy, I like it," Ruby replied, laughing.

"Sadly, you're not going to," said Cash, looking as forlorn as she felt at his words.

"Why?"

"Because I'm going to my flat and you're going to yours. I'm taking onboard what Theo just said, we've got a big day ahead of us tomorrow and we need to rest, especially you, Ruby Davis. I'm not having you going into battle bleary eyed after a night with me."

"Who said I'd be bleary-eyed?"

"I do. If I come home with you now, the last thing either of us will do is sleep. You know it and I know it."

Ecstatic tingles rushed up and down her spine. She started to giggle.

"What about a kiss? Can I have one of those to be going on with at least?" she asked, batting her eyelids coyly at him.

"You can," he said, lowering his lips to hers, "then off home with you, you strumpet, before I lose all control."

After extracting not one but several kisses from him, Ruby reluctantly followed Cash out of the office and down onto the street. From St Michael's Church, just across the road, a carol concert was well underway. Ruby could make out the sound of harmonious voices rising and falling in perfect pitch, *Good King Wenceslas*, if she wasn't mistaken.

Saying one last lingering goodbye, he turned right and she turned left – up the High Street, past the church, past the Fifteenth Century Bookshop with its timber frames and overhanging storeys, like something from the pages of a Charles Dickens book, past Lewes Old Grammar School (its inmates no doubt enjoying a festive break from lessons) and Shelley's Hotel, gearing up for Christmas Day lunches, past St Anne's cemetery, happy to see no souls staring balefully at her, and into Ireland's Lane which in turn led to De Montfort Road and home, all the while feeling as though she were floating on air.

Chapter Twenty-Seven

Christmas Eve

A text message, sent inconsiderately early, woke Ruby the next day.

Remember I'm returning home on Boxing Day with a party of six. I trust the house will be ready for my return.

How much restraint had it taken, she wondered, for Mr Kierney to refrain from adding 'or else'? Clearly he enjoyed wielding his journalistic power – using it to destroy as well as to inform. He could and would do serious damage to their hard-earned reputation if they failed to evict the spirits of Highdown Hall, she had no doubt. Failure was not an option.

Yawning, Ruby attempted to doze off again. But it was no use, sleep was long gone. After less than an hour she gave up trying, her mind too active. Christmas Eve 2012 marked the 54th anniversary of Cynthia's death – a long time to be trapped between here and there. Did it seem that long to Cynthia? Or was time only relevant in this dimension? Somehow, she suspected the latter. Sitting up to stretch, she smiled at Jed, content in his second favourite spot.

"And what about you, boy?" she said. "Are you coming with us today? Mum thinks you should."

Jed looked up, gave one wag of his tail then curled back into a ball.

"Suit yourself," she shrugged, swapping the bedroom for the

kitchen, intent on a serious caffeine hit. Not the instant stuff this time, what with it being Christmas Eve, but a cafetière of something rich, dark and Italian.

After savouring a couple of mugs, she felt ready to eat something. Pouring some Cheerios into a bowl, she fired up her laptop. Her emails were mounting up, the usual spam amongst them but plenty of enquiries too – more and more people, either tentatively or boldly, asking for help with various problems: a survey perhaps, a cleansing, some distance healing. It would take a good day, perhaps two to reply to them all. 2013 looked promising, not just for the spirit world but for Psychic Surveys too – even more imperative then that they should succeed today, that their reputation should not be damaged in any way. No matter how many positives were achieved, it was human nature to remember only the negatives, thought Ruby. Sad, but true.

Instead of a shower, Ruby luxuriated in a bath, filled to the brim with scented bubbles. As the warm water enveloped her, she let her mind empty – all thoughts of everyone and everything pushed temporarily aside. She loved to meditate, trying to reach the calm and tranquillity that existed below the often ear-splitting din of everyday life. Meditation was something she meant to do every day; unfortunately, she didn't always make the time. To do so now was a treat and valuable too, she always felt so much stronger afterwards.

By the time Ruby had dressed it was well after ten o'clock. Should she do more research or just continue to relax? She knew what Theo would advise. She also knew she shouldn't contact Cash before he came to pick her up at five, although she really wanted to. In a bid to distract herself, she decided on Christmas shopping instead and afterwards, once she'd wrapped and tagged everything, watching a film perhaps, or catching up on EastEnders episodes she had previously recorded. Corinna wasn't the soap's only fan.

The day passed quickly. Before she knew it, it was time to get dressed in more hard-core clothing. Restraining her hair, Ruby tugged on a thermal vest, long sleeved T-shirt, woollen jumper, jeans and two pairs of socks, the first pair thin cotton, the second thermal. With the addition of her North Face padded jacket instead of the navy coat she usually wore, she was content she'd be warm enough. Checking her watch, she noticed it was nearly five already. Cash would be here any minute; she'd go outside and wait for him.

"Come on, Jed," she called, watching in amusement as the eager animal flew past her on four furry feet and disappeared straight through the unopened front door.

**

"Aren't you bringing the box with you?" said Cash as Ruby clambered into the passenger seat of his estate car, just as battered as her own.

"The box? Oh God, the box. Sorry, I won't be a minute."

She ran back to the flat and soon returned with it under her arm.

"Did you look through it again today?" he asked once she was settled.

"No, I didn't," Ruby admitted. "I spent the day relaxing instead, trying to keep my mind clear." She thought she'd leave out the bit about EastEnders, she'd only managed one episode anyway before dozing off. "I think we've found what we were looking for anyway."

"Yeah," agreed Cash, "weird or what, huh? About Ron Mason I mean?"

"If there's a link, definitely. But there might not be."

"No, there might not be. Bringing the box with us could be useful; it's another thing that could help to jog Cynthia's memory."

Ruby nodded, it was a sensible train of thought.

Turning round to peer into the back of the car, she smiled.

"Poor Jed, he doesn't look very comfortable perched on whatever it is you've got back there."

"The remnants of my drum kit mainly. And he'll have to get used to it. It's just me and you up front I'm afraid," replied Cash as he put his foot on the accelerator and pulled away.

***

The road that led to Highdown Hall was surprisingly clear considering it was Christmas Eve; Ruby imagined most people must have already gone home to gear up for the big day with their families.

"Did you get a good rest last night?" Cash asked her.

"I slept okay, you?"

"Not so well..." he replied. "Had a few things on my mind, keeping me awake."

"Highdown Hall?" Ruby sounded worried.

He cast a cheeky glance at her. "Oh no, nothing to do with Highdown Hall."

Looking straight ahead, Ruby tried to suppress a smile. She reminded herself that she needed to concentrate on one thing right now and one thing only – sending Cynthia and Co. into the light. It was difficult though, when he was right by her side.

Attempting a stab at seriousness, she said, "Cash, I know I say this every time, but if you don't want to come in, if you're at all nervous, that's fine. You can wait outside."

Glancing at her quickly, this time with no mirth in his eyes, he said, "If you go in, I go in. It's as simple as that."

Ruby couldn't help it this time, she laughed out loud.

"What?" Cash looked genuinely confused. "Why are you laughing?"

"You," she said. "You remind me of Leonardo di Caprio."

"Leonardo di Caprio?" Cash looked appalled. "But I look nothing like him!"

"Not in looks, in what you've just said."

256

"Explain," he insisted.

"You know, in that film, *Titanic,* when he's trying to persuade Kate Winslet not to jump off the ship. He says something like, "If you jump, I jump", have you seen it?"

Cash nodded his head. "Yeah, yeah, I've seen it, an old girlfriend made me sit through it. Such a cheesy film, though I suspect I might be about to develop a new respect for it."

"What you said reminds me of that scene."

"So..." he continued after a moment, "I make you feel like a film star, do I?"

"You make me feel a lot of things," she replied, more serious.

"Ditto," he said, smiling, one hand on the wheel, the other reaching across temporarily to touch hers. "Really though, Ruby, I'm going in with you, to Cynthia's bedroom; don't even think about trying to stop me."

"I won't," she whispered, tingling at his touch.

She couldn't say much more, she thought she might cry if she did. This man sitting beside her, he really was different to any she'd ever known before, so accepting of what she did – promising to stick by her through thick and thin, to watch out for her. It was an all-time first. Historically, and not just in her case but in her mother's and grandmother's too, men didn't stick around. Sooner or later her psychic ability would come between a Davis woman and her man. With Cash though, she seemed to have discovered a new breed of man entirely, someone who was keen to *help* her with what she did. Time would tell, she supposed. But right now, she suspected time would tell only great things.

"It's the next turn off after this," Ruby managed at last, pointing to a sign saying 'Oldlands Wood, 2 miles', which had momentarily shown up in the car's headlights.

"I'm not likely to forget," Cash replied.

***

"Stop! Pull in here," said Ruby, just over a mile away from the gates of Highdown Hall. "I can feel it... This is the place where David Levine passed."

Although the road was empty, Cash mounted the verge, just in case another car happened to appear out of nowhere, desperate to get by. Bringing his car to a halt, he stuck on the hazards, flashing amber lighting up the dark in an almost festive manner. Getting swiftly out, Ruby walked up to the tree that Levine had most likely crashed into, laid one hand flat against its trunk and tuned in. Jed, meanwhile, took the opportunity to cock his leg up against it and have an imaginary wee.

"Anything?" said Cash, coming up behind her.

"No, just residual emotions, like I said before. His spirit, wherever it is, isn't here."

"What can you feel?"

"Anger is the most prevalent... and such extraordinary bitterness, like he was eaten up with it. There's jealousy too. Hmm... I wonder if that was the source of the bitterness?"

"Not a happy man then?"

"Not at all," agreed Ruby.

"Do you think he *is* the culprit? The one terrorising Cynthia?"

Ruby was quietly contemplative for a moment. "It's likely," she eventually replied before turning on her heel. "Come on," she added, "let's go, the others will be arriving soon."

The gates to Highdown Hall drew back slowly, more slowly than ever it seemed to Ruby. Leaving them open so that the rest of the team could follow, Ruby tried to quell a growing sense of unease. Her mother's warning visit, her grandmother's revelation, the attack she'd experienced, they were all affecting her more than she wanted. Although she believed wholeheartedly what her grandmother had taught her, she couldn't help but remember her mother's assertion: where there was good, there was evil, and not just evil acts and evil thoughts, but *pure* evil, as real and relentless a force as love.

They'd already established that what waited for Cynthia wasn't Rawlings' Devil, but what if it *was* a creature from another dimension entirely, what if it had never been human, what if she were putting not only herself in danger, but also, and far more importantly, her dearest friends? Was Jessica right? Was true strength knowing when to retreat? If so, should they retreat now and to hell with their reputation? Let Alan Kierney do his worst?

"You okay?" said Cash as he drew to a stop in front of the house, a house that Ruby thought, by moonlight, looked less like a grand country manor and more like the setting for a Hammer Horror film. All they needed was thunder and lightning to suddenly manifest itself from nowhere, to rip an otherwise benign sky apart, and the set would be complete.

Shaking her head, as though to disperse such thoughts, Ruby replied at last, "Yeah, yeah, I'm fine, just letting my imagination get the better of me."

Leaning over to tuck a rogue strand of hair behind her ear, Cash said, "You're good at what you do, Ruby, bloody good. And Cynthia needs you."

"Your faith in me is touching," Ruby smiled back at him, but it was only a half smile.

"My faith in you is absolute," he answered back, leaning in again to kiss her lightly on the lips.

His words, his touch, helped her, dissolving the fear that threatened to overwhelm her; a fear that could easily be used against her if sensed by an opposing spirit; a fear Gran had always said there was never any need to feel.

Before it could take hold again, Ruby reached for the handle, pushed open the car door and stepped outside, breathing in great gulps of night air. Jed immediately rushed round to her side.

As she straightened up, squaring her shoulders as a soldier might before heading into battle, Ness's car came into view. After crunching to a stop on the gravel, Ness, Theo and

259

Corinna climbed out.

All five turned to stand in a row, staring at the house before them, preparing themselves mentally and psychically for the imminent onslaught.

"Coming, ready or not!" said Theo at last, trying to lighten the atmosphere as she marched up to the front door.

Ruby fell into step beside her, Jed bounded ahead.

The house had been empty for a week but already it had taken on the abandoned air of a property left for much longer. Instead of forlorn and forgotten, it looked slightly smug, as though enjoying its abandonment – wanting to be left to its own devices.

Too bad, thought Ruby. *You belong to the living, not the dead.*

Looking up at the turret that housed Cynthia's bedroom, Ruby thought she could sense movement. Was that Cynthia looking out wistfully across the lake?

"It's just a shade," said Theo from beside her. "A re-run of what happened on Christmas Eve, 1958. Cynthia must have stood and looked out of the window at some point."

"The house is waking up…" It was Ness, close behind them.

"Then let's put it back to sleep," said Ruby, taking another deep breath.

Chapter Twenty-Eight

The big oak door was resistant at first.

"Is that because we're not wanted?" Cash whispered beside her.

"No," said Ruby, imitating his dramatic tone, "it's because the hinges need a good squirt of oil."

"Oh," said Cash, somewhat deflated.

Once inside, Ruby reached for the lights before closing the door and the night out entirely. The Grand Hall lit up before them, the bulbs shining surprisingly bright. Despite her padded jacket, Ruby shivered. She was sure it was colder in here than it was outside. Mr Kierney had failed to leave the heating on, either through absent-mindedness or Scrooge-like stinginess. With him, she suspected the latter and pitied the poor guests arriving on Boxing Day, hoping sincerely they'd bring with them a good selection of thermals and woollen apparel. A house like this would take ages to feel warm again.

Although Cash and Corinna seemed oblivious, Ruby knew that Theo and Ness could also hear the faint sound of music coming from the ballroom – big band music, upbeat tunes; tunes that made you want to dance. And she could sense a large number of people milling about, confined to the ballroom mainly, but also spilling out of the French windows onto the terrace beyond; fur shawls wrapped around the ladies shoulders. Excited chatter and laughter – high expectations of a magical evening to come – filled the air. Not spirits, but shades, emotional echoes of a prominent night replaying.

"Cash, Corinna, would you mind walking through every

room downstairs, cleansing with sticks and oils, opening windows and doors where you can and leaving them open?"

"Of course not," said Corinna, kneeling down by the black bag and unzipping it.

"Start with the kitchen first and then the drawing rooms, leave the ballroom for last."

"What about you?" asked Cash. "You're not going upstairs, are you?"

"Not without you," Ruby assured him.

Looking slightly happier, Cash followed Corinna to the rooms that led off from the Grand Hall, the darkness enveloping them greedily.

Ruby turned to Theo and Ness.

"The ballroom?" she said.

"The ballroom," agreed Theo.

The energy in the ballroom, if not quite at fever pitch, was certainly frenetic. The music was louder here and the shades more dense, almost tangible – dapper gentlemen in black tie, ladies in ballgowns, swirling around the dance floor. Others huddled together in groups, almost conspiratorial. Maids and waiters weaved expertly in and out of the glamorous party goers, proffering an endless flow of champagne. Ruby wondered briefly which of the maids was Esme – although she wasn't dead, the shade of her younger self belonged to this night. She led the other two over to the far end of the ballroom.

"I think this is where John Sterling was standing."

Before them was indeed an outline of a tall gentlemen; the shell of a spirit long gone.

"Dear, oh dear," muttered Theo, but not entirely without amusement. Gazing at him, she continued, "She did taunt him, didn't she? He was madly in love with Cynthia and yet I get the distinct feeling she barely glanced at him all evening."

"She was certainly a player," agreed Ruby.

"But you don't think it's him that haunts her?" enquired Ness. "He's incensed enough to remain grounded."

"Not according to Cynthia," said Ruby. "John wasn't vengeful."

Ness didn't look convinced.

Theo sighed as she looked around. "I'd have loved to have attended a party such as this. Her invites must have been the most coveted in the land."

"I should think the cream of British society was here," said Ness, also looking wistful.

"And American society too," chimed in Ruby. "The jet set crossed the ocean for this."

A sudden banging noise from upstairs put a halt to their musings.

"Madam doesn't like to be kept waiting," said Theo, glancing upwards.

"She still hasn't got used to it." replied Ruby, also turning her head towards the ceiling.

Theo and Ness made their way back to the Grand Hall in search of Cash and Corinna but Ruby lingered for a while longer, walking around the perimeters of the room, searching for something more, but also, if she were honest, reluctant to let go of the scene before her. It would be the only chance she'd ever get to witness such a sumptuous occasion. Just before she reached the door, she stopped.

"Theo, Ness," she called.

"What is it?" asked Theo. "David Levine?"

"I think so," said Ruby, "I'm picking up the same feelings in this spot as at the site of his death: anger, jealousy and triumph. Whoever this is, he was a man with an axe to grind."

"An axe meant for Cynthia?" questioned Ness.

"With luck, we'll soon find out," replied Ruby, leaving with them this time.

***

They all congregated in the Grand Hall.

"We've just got the ballroom to do now," said Corinna, nodding towards it.

"Okay," said Ruby, "while you're doing that we'll spend some time reinforcing everyone's shield – ramp our protection up to maximum level before heading upstairs."

As soon as Cash and Corinna had gone, the remaining three joined hands.

"Remember," Theo addressed Ruby in particular, "we *all* belong to the light."

Ruby nodded at her.

Several minutes later, Cash and Corinna re-joined them, the downstairs cleansing complete. Ruby felt a cold draught; the French doors had been left ajar.

"Are we ready?" Ruby asked.

Four voices assented, not one of them even slightly hesitant, despite another loud bang from upstairs echoing menacingly through the hall.

Jed valiantly led the way.

Chapter Twenty-Nine

Downstairs, the atmosphere had been full of revelry; the same could not be said for upstairs. The atmosphere had always felt increasingly heavy the further up they climbed, as though a great weight was bearing down, the weight of emotions that time could not diminish – fear, anger, grief. At the top of the staircase it was heavier still, becoming even more dense as they ventured towards the turret, bypassing numerous doors, some open, some closed, wanting to peek inside, to make sure that guests from once upon a time weren't inhabiting still. Ruby had checked all of the rooms on first visiting Highdown Hall and found them empty of any spiritual presence, she hoped that was still the case now and no one had decided to return. Perhaps now would be a good time to start cleansing the upstairs rooms, however, another loud crash drew their attention to Cynthia's room. Glancing at Theo and Ness, a silent agreement passed between them: they could not keep her waiting any longer. As they gathered outside her door, a whimper escaped Jed.

"It's alright," Theo soothed. "There's nothing to be afraid of, nothing at all."

Ruby suspected Theo's words were directed at her as much as the dog and she did her utmost to banish the last dregs of fear which insisted on clinging to her heart like a drowning man might cling to the last piece of wreckage. Furtively, she studied the faces of Cash and Corinna, both looked utterly determined. They inspired her.

In contrast to the gates of Highdown Hall, to the oak double doors downstairs, the door to Cynthia's bedroom gave way easily, almost welcoming them in. One spirit at least was glad to see them. They filed in, their jaws dropping in turn as they did so.

"Whoa." Theo looked slightly dazed. "Someone's had a tantrum."

No longer a revered shrine, the room resembled a bombsite. Even in the gloom they could tell quite a bit of damage had been done. The chair by the dressing table was upturned and there were cushions scattered everywhere. On the floor, perfume bottles, combs and brushes lay at random. One bottle had shattered, releasing a bittersweet smell into the air.

Ruby switched on the side lights, the bulbs in the main light had still not been replaced, and walked over to the bed. The silk cover was rent in two. Before she could quash it, another pang of anxiety flared up inside her and almost caught fire.

"Right," said Ness, her practical voice another lifeline. "Gather up all implements that could be thrown to hurt someone and get them out of here."

"Even the crystals?" asked Corinna.

"Even the crystals," confirmed Ness. "And, Cash, see if you can find some way to ventilate this room, perhaps the bathroom window might open?" Thinking about it she added, "You know what? Break it if you have to. The air in here is desperate."

Everyone sprang into action, Ruby as surprised as Ness and Theo that they were not being met with resistance. The room bereft of potential missiles, they re-gathered.

"Join hands," commanded Theo.

Ruby held Cash and Ness's hands. Corinna stood the other side of Ness, in between her and Theo, who also held hands with Cash.

"Jed," called Ruby, "come and sit in the middle."

The dog sloped forwards.

Ruby spoke first.

"Cynthia, we're back. And this time we're not leaving until you've left too. Remember, the light is where you belong and nothing, *no one,* has the power to keep you from it."

Pleased at how confident she sounded, she continued. "We know a second spirit resides in this room. A spirit weighed heavily with human issues." Attempting to address the second spirit, Ruby said, "And I know it was you who attacked me, not Cynthia, but I also know that you did so out of fear and frustration. I don't like being attacked and I'd like you to refrain from doing so again. But I've no hard feelings. I want to help you too."

There was no response, all was silent, but it was a false silence Ruby knew – a predatory silence. There was only one way to break it.

"The second spirit who resides here, we know who you are. You are David Levine."

Ruby was right, speaking his name did indeed provoke a reaction, but not from Levine. Suddenly Cynthia shot forward, stopping short just behind Ruby. In her head Ruby heard her scream at her.

He is not David Levine!

"Cynthia," Ruby endeavoured to explain. "It *is* David Levine. He was a guest at your party; he passed the same night as you, not far from here. His car left the road; hit a tree, the accident was fatal. He returned to Highdown Hall, to the last place he remembered."

He is not David Levine! He is the Devil!

No, they'd established that there was no such creature; they'd *proven* it to her, that Rawlings was a liar and a cheat, no more capable of conjuring up a demon than Cynthia herself had been. Why was she still so insistent?

"Cynthia," Ruby tried again, cursing the slight note of hesitancy that had crept into her voice. "It is not the Devil, it's..."

Before she could finish, Cynthia interrupted.

IT IS!

Ruby gasped. Beside her, Ness flinched.

The energy in the room was building, becoming taut around them like a rubber band, making it difficult to breathe.

Ruby was thankful when Theo took control.

"Cynthia, calm down. I want no more of your childish displays of temper. You might have got away with that sort of behaviour in life, but in the spirit world it holds no muster."

To Ruby's amazement, the energy depleted slightly as though Cynthia had actually taken notice of Theo's admonishment. All five of them inhaled deeply, taking the opportunity to fill their lungs whilst they could.

Deciding on a different tack, Ruby addressed the second spirit again. She could sense he was holding back, but why? Gathering strength for a repeat attack? Just let him try.

"Is what Cynthia saying true? Are you a demon? Perhaps even the Devil himself?"

Ruby sensed rather than saw Theo's look of absolute astonishment that she could ask such a question. But she had to know. Had she been wrong all along? Had Cynthia been right? Her mother too?

An echo of laughter rang out, but it was joyless, containing instead all the dark emotions she had felt both downstairs and at the site of the car crash.

"Please," Ruby beseeched. "Speak to us. Tell us who you are."

As soon as the last word left her mouth, Ruby was torn from the circle and spun violently around, almost losing her footing in the process. Preparing to face David, Cynthia's 'unknown' father, or even Lucifer himself, she was stunned to see Cynthia in front of her, not fully manifested but stronger than she had ever been before.

"Wait," said Ruby, as all four companions rushed to help. "Hold back. It's Cynthia."

Looking at the ethereal face before her, a face that was rapidly gaining in substance, Ruby could see why her beauty had had such an impact on the world; Cynthia was breathtaking, exquisite beyond compare. No photograph, no film could ever do her justice. But that wasn't all there was about her, there was something else, something just as appealing – vulnerability. It was a look she remembered seeing in the eyes of Gayle Andrews in *The Phoenix*, a look that Ruby had thought Cynthia had only adopted for the role. But clearly not, it was very much a part of the actress, it *defined* her somehow. The life-long devotion of Sally Threadgold and John Sterling was easier to understand now. It was a look that made you want to help her, to move heaven and earth to do so.

"Cynthia," Ruby appealed again, but to the film star this time, "help me."

Cynthia's hands, gentle now instead of forceful, moved down to cover Ruby's. They were cold, as light as air and as soft as gauze. As their fingers clasped, the room and those who inhabited it – Theo, Ness, Corinna and Cash – began to fade, becoming no more than shadows themselves. As Ruby entered another world, a glittering world, her heart leapt with elation, elation laced with hope. Had Cynthia Hart, at last, remembered?

Chapter Thirty

Christmas Eve, 1958

A fabulous party! A roaring success! Of course it was. How could it fail to be? She, the great Cynthia Hart, had the Midas touch; she could do no wrong. It was her thirty-first birthday and so many from showbiz and high society were celebrating with her, their generosity unrestrained when it came to lavishing gifts. A steady stream had been arriving at Highdown Hall all day; rubies, sapphires, pearls and diamonds, set in gold, set in platinum – everybody trying to outdo everybody else, to impress her the most. And from John, a Jaguar XK120, sprayed to match the colour of her hair. His valet had driven it to her door this morning; Sally had burst into her room, excited to tell her. How she loved sports cars, John knew that. She owned several of them, but this new addition was the best by far, as beautiful and elegant as she was. She looked forward to racing it along the country lanes, "...but with whom I haven't decided yet" she had deliberately teased when he'd phoned to check her reaction, delighting at how her artful remark had affected him, imagining all too well the frown that would darken his handsome face.

For hours she had lain in bed, flicking through magazines and newspapers, indulging herself in frivolous articles, reserving her energy for the evening ahead. Late afternoon, Sally had drawn a bath for her, deep, warm and scented. She had fussed over her, scrubbing every inch of her back, teasing at her curls, ensuring her fuchsia dress was as smooth as the skin on her mistress's face. She had stepped proudly aside as Cynthia had left her bedroom, watching devotedly as she descended the stairs to greet the anticipating crowds.

As they had marvelled at her, Cynthia couldn't help but marvel too. Before her stood a star cast of her own devising. Faces from film made flesh – but none as famous as her. She was set to soar beyond the stars, higher than even she had dared to imagine, in demand the world over, the lead in the most eagerly anticipated film in cinematic history.

Of course there were those who were jealous, she wasn't stupid, she knew that; the smile never quite reaching their eyes when they greeted her. Young starlets mostly, knowing in their heart of hearts that they would never reach the dizzy heights she had, but occasionally more established actors and actresses too, those who had been eclipsed by her. 'Where has she come from?' she could imagine them whispering. 'Nowhere special,' the reply. That might be true, but she was special now, none could deny it. And she had worked hard to become so – doing everything and anything to shine. Few would have gone as far as she had. She deserved her glory.

She'd noticed David Levine amongst the throng immediately and had shuddered at the sight of him. She hadn't wanted to invite him but had had to concede in the end. He'd written to her two weeks before the party, congratulating her on her forthcoming role in *Atlantic*, informing her that he too was travelling to America to talk with producers, hinting that he might even be working on *Atlantic* itself. When she'd worked with him on *Later in the Day*, he was an assistant to the director, no, not even an assistant, more of the director's pet; she'd found him sly, insidious – a weasel of a man. Thankfully, he was easy to avoid, although at the wrap party, not so easy – he had virtually stalked her, frighteningly so. The last thing she ever wanted was to see him again but, remembering the old adage to keep your friends close but your enemies closer, she had followed its advice. If he was more up and coming these days, if he was going to work on *Atlantic*, she would find out and put a stop to it; she was, after all, the one who called the shots now.

Ignoring Levine, she concentrated instead on her other guests, laughing with them, dancing with them, toying with them. By nine that evening, the party had been truly under way; her guests sipping on the finest champagne, feasting on canapés and fancies sent direct from Harrods. Although she had refrained from eating, she had allowed herself a drink or two, which quickly turned into three or four, the tiny bubbles of champagne bursting inside her like perfect spheres of happiness. And then he had collared her, David Levine – had laid his hand upon her.

"We need to talk," he had whispered into her ear, not seductively as so many had whispered that night but with a harsh edge to his voice.

"Unhand me," Cynthia had hissed back, desperate for such interplay to go unnoticed. Now was not the time to enter into any sort of discussion concerning *Atlantic*.

Levine, however, was undeterred.

In a slightly louder voice, he continued, "Come with me, Cynthia, or I will say what I have to say in public, right here, right now. Destroy you where you stand."

Destroy her? What was he talking about? How could *he* possibly destroy her?

With deliberate slowness, she edged away from the guests she had been regaling with anecdotes of working with Hitchcock. She thought they would be reluctant to let her go, would protest, but their circle had quickly closed again, locking her out. Her surprise that they had done so made her momentarily forget Levine. But soon she became aware of him again, his eyes boring into her. Although she didn't want to, every fibre in her being fought against it, she looked into his face – it had a hardness about it, but also an emptiness too, the latter infinitely more disturbing. How many years had passed since their

272

encounter, she briefly wondered. Four or five? What on earth did he want now? Blackmail? Or worse?

Cynthia's eyes searched desperately for John; suddenly she felt a need for him, a need as strong as a newborn child for its parent. All night long John had followed her with his eyes, silently begging her to favour him, and only him, but now, when she truly needed him, he was staring no more. His attention had finally been captured. Adelaide Dearborn, a British actress, was pretty, but not spectacularly so, not compared to her. Their heads were close together, laughing, their dark hair, Cynthia noticed with a painful stab of jealousy, almost exactly the same shade. A terrible loneliness descended upon her then, the same loneliness she had felt on her first day in London, aged fourteen: the same loneliness that had plagued her ever since and wouldn't let go, that seemed to have caught her in its grip, ensnared her. She also felt guilty. She shouldn't have taunted John tonight, he didn't deserve it, had never deserved it. He was the one she should have kept close, not her enemies. If she had done so, Levine wouldn't have been able to reach her.

There was nowhere private to go except her bedroom. She was loathe to take Levine there of all places, but what choice did she have? Whatever he had to say to her, she didn't want it said in public. Her guests would miss her if she disappeared though, the party would come to a standstill. Surely? She looked about her and was amazed to find everybody looked happy enough, *very* happy in fact. She felt invisible all of a sudden; expunged from centre stage. Even John, faithful John, was ignoring her. Stumbling slightly, she blamed the champagne – just how much had she had to drink? She beckoned for Levine to follow, praying she'd encounter Sally on the way. Sally could run and fetch John, tear him away from the clutches of that two-bit actress. But Sally was nowhere to be seen.

In the Grand Hall waiters rushed past her, intent on keeping the guests' glasses full, just as she had instructed them – under no circumstances was any glass allowed to run dry. As she started climbing the stairs, Levine instructed her to wait. As if in a dream, she watched him retreat. Only seconds later he was back, a brown box clutched to his chest. A non-descript looking object, tatty she would say, why had he bothered to go and get it? Together, they ascended. Where *was* Sally? She hadn't seen her all evening.

Walking slowly down the corridor to her bedroom, Cynthia noticed the sounds of the revellers below becoming increasingly muffled; every step she put between herself and them was rendering her more and more vulnerable. Drawing closer, she was relieved to find anger stirring. How dare Levine think he could treat her so!

Not so much pushing as shoving open the bedroom door with the palm of her hand, she entered the room fully before swinging round to face him, her head held high, her eyes, she knew, firing sparks at him. *Nobody* gave orders to Cynthia Hart.

"I'd tread very carefully if I were you, Levine. Dare to threaten me and I'll bring down the wrath of the entire British judicial system upon your head."

"I'm sure you will," Levine replied, far too coolly she thought. Taking time to survey the sumptuousness of their surroundings, he added, "God knows, you can afford it."

Cynthia was undaunted. "I can ruin you with one click of my fingers, Levine. I am not afraid of you."

"Then why scurry upstairs with me so willingly Cynthia, if you're not just the tiniest bit afraid? Or is it that you simply want a replay of our night together?"

Cynthia started as though she'd just been shot. What night together? Did he mean the wrap party? He must, it was the only time she had spent any extra-curricular time with him. On the night they'd finished filming *Later in the Day*, Levine had been one of several she'd ended up in a hotel room with – how he had managed to inveigle his way in she didn't know – he was

274

nothing but a glorified lackey, but she'd been too preoccupied to question his presence fully. As always, the relief of finishing the picture had prompted a recklessness in her. Pills had been involved, white lines of cocaine, gleaming and endless, bottles and bottles of champagne. Of that particular crowd, she hadn't wanted him to touch her, something about him set her teeth on edge, but she'd had to work hard to avoid him, at every turn he was there. Surely she had managed though? She remembered sandwiching herself between her naked co-stars, Diana Lambton and Oliver Byrne, using them as a form of armour against him. She didn't remember much more than that – the night had passed in a white haze, a blur, but she was sure he hadn't touched her – not him.

She had refused to have anything to do with Levine again after that evening – the very thought of him made her feel uncomfortable. If a film was offered to her that he was involved in, she had simply refused it. When asked why, she would not hide her feelings about him. It was usually enough to have him removed from proceedings, even if she still refused to take the part. The only contact she'd had with him since, his recent letter.

"Get out," she snarled at him. "The sight of you sickens me."

"Oh, Cynthia," he laughed, such a hollow sound. "Are you telling me you didn't enjoy our lovemaking?"

Lovemaking? How dare he even insinuate? They'd done no such thing. She doubted he even knew what love was. About to reply, her eyes fell on the box he was still holding.

"What's in there?" she demanded, a cold fear trickling down her spine. If there were pictures of her from that night, naked pictures, there would be pictures of others too, her co-stars – all of them significant in the film industry, all of them with friends in high places. He wouldn't get far with those pictures – they would ensure the media shunned him.

Coming closer, making her flinch, he placed the box on the edge of her bed.

"I'll tell you what's in that box, Cynthia, but first I have something to reveal to you: my true identity."

Cynthia was taken aback. She hadn't expected this.

"Your true identity? What..."

"I am David Levine."

"I know who you are," her voice was derisive.

"But that's not the name I was given at birth."

"Don't speak in riddles, man, what are you talking about?"

"My real name is Jack Hart, Cynthia. I am your brother."

She stared at him in horror. What nonsense was this? He was nothing like her brother! Levine's hair was dark; her brother's had been fair, not quite blonde but not quite brown either, an in between shade, mousy. Jack had been a scrawny little kid, a snivelling kid, she remembered, whereas this man had a respectable build, as though he were no stranger to fitness. His eyes were brown like her brother's, but it was a common colour, not a clue. Jack had been a boy of eleven when she'd last seen him, almost twelve, clinging to his mother's skirts as he'd done all his miserable life, their mother content to let him, indulging him, Cynthia had often reflected bitterly. Their devotion to one another so complete, it excluded her.

"You can't be... You're *not* my brother," she managed at last.

"Oh, but Cee-Cee, I am."

At the mention of her brother's pet name for her she felt her legs buckle. Her breath caught in her throat and seemed to get stuck there. Quickly, she staggered over to the bed and gripped hold of one of the posts. Jack had called her Cee-Cee since he'd been a toddler, when he couldn't pronounce her name properly. Her mother had called her that too on occasion.

Clearly amused by her reaction, Levine laughed.

"Oh come on, Cee-Cee, are you trying to tell me you really didn't know who I was? You had not the slightest inkling? That it wasn't part of the reason you enjoyed our game of cat and mouse that evening?" More furiously, he added, "I'm your brother, how could you *not* know me?"

"You're not. No..." she continued to deny it; the use of her pet name meant nothing. Perhaps she had revealed it once in an interview and Levine had picked up on it? But scouring her mind, she was sure she hadn't. She had never found it endearing, had wanted to forget it if anything. Forcing herself to look into his eyes, she had to admit, there *was* something familiar about him. Was it the shape of his face perhaps – the turn of his head? She remembered she'd thought he looked familiar when she first met him, but had quickly dismissed the notion, her brother the last person on her mind.

"You can't be," she repeated, the cold fear she had felt earlier turning to ice.

"I can be and I am, sister dear," was his cutting reply.

Cynthia stared at him again. No, it was not the shape of his face nor the turn of his head, it was the look in his eyes that was familiar, the vast swathes of emptiness in them – an emptiness she had always recoiled from as though somehow it could infect her too.

Quickly she tried to recall events in the hotel room. She hadn't slept with him she was certain. She would have remembered. Surely to God she would have remembered. But it was all such a blur, too many drugs, too much alcohol. Panic threatened to choke her.

"It doesn't matter..." she breathed at last. "I didn't sleep with you. I know it."

"You know it?" There it was again, that slyness about him that she loathed. "Cynthia, you know no such thing. You were gone that night, totally gone."

"I wasn't..." she tried to protest. "I... I..."

"Was as drunk as a common whore," he finished for her. "Drug-addled is what you were."

But not drug-addled enough that she couldn't avoid him. She would *know* if he had touched her, she would not have forgotten it. His touch, it would have seared her.

"I DID NOT sleep with you," she screamed.

277

"Maybe you did, maybe you didn't. The fact is you can't be sure. And nor will our good companions that night be either. Everyone was as out of it as each other. Suggestion is a wonderful thing, Cynthia. All I have to do is suggest that we slept together – brother and sister – and people will start questioning – our friends that night will start questioning, imagining things that perhaps never took place. Vile things. And that, Cynthia, is enough."

Cynthia was sure the ground was going to rise up to meet her. "You've got to keep quiet. You can't tell anyone who you are. You can't."

Exposing his teeth, an almost feral expression, he said, "Au contraire, I plan to tell the world *exactly* who I am, about us. I just thought it courteous to let you know first."

"They'll *never* believe you!" she shouted, rallying. "*I* don't believe you. This is some sort of trickery, nothing more. A nightmare I'll soon wake up from."

"Oh, but the world *will* believe me when I tell them about our sweet and humble life together as children, the kind of things a brother *should* know about his sister."

"What things?" she said, testing him. "What do you remember?"

"Our neighbours for a start, how we liked to play together, the games we invented, you were quite fond of Greta's brother, weren't you? You kissed him once, frightened the life out of him I recall, he was eleven, what were you? Twelve? Thirteen? Always precocious. I bet he regrets pushing you off, I bet he wishes he'd let you kiss him now. More than kiss him. What a thing to tell your grandchildren, that you kissed the great Cynthia Hart when she was still young and innocent. They'll remember me too, Greta and her brother, as will many others that we knew, not everyone found me as insignificant as you did."

Cynthia was desperate now, clutching at straws.

"You'll ruin yourself," she pointed out, cursing the catch in her voice.

"Your concern is touching, but alas, the world is not interested in me, only in you."

He was right; it would be her that the media would focus on. Everyone loved a scandal. She'd be ruined, everything she had worked so hard for, had sold her soul for, reduced to ashes. And unlike Gayle Andrews in *The Phoenix*, there'd be no glorious resurrection. She'd be a social pariah, forced into hiding. But hide where? The world wasn't big enough.

Wringing her hands, she couldn't help but rebuke herself. Yes, Jack had changed, but he was her brother, she *should* have recognised him. But then, had she ever taken much notice of him? Had she ever looked at her mother – really looked at her? All she had done was blame them: for the lowly life they lived, for holding her back when she was so much more; for letting her go, so young, into the big, wide world – alone.

"You weren't the only one with ambition, you know," her brother said, as though reading her mind. "I was ambitious too, not pretty enough to be in front of the camera, but I could be behind it. I slept my way up the ranks as you no doubt did, producer after producer using me as they once used you. Perhaps even the same producers? Fancy that? Some of them became quite enamoured with me, you know," he seemed proud, "appreciating a young and supple body to ravish, a male body for a change, a dirty, but oh-so-exciting secret. A secret they wanted to keep; would do anything to hide not only from the public but from their unsuspecting wives. That's how I managed to reach you, how I landed the job on *Later in the Day*. Harry Lord – the director – a family man? I don't think so."

She was sickened by what her brother was saying, by how low his quest for vengeance had brought him. She stopped short. Who was she to condemn?

She struggled to form a cohesive sentence. "Why are you doing this? Why now?"

"Because right now you're the most famous actress in the

world, something I knew you'd be one day. And so I waited, like a good boy, a patient boy, until you had reached the summit. You see, Cynthia, the higher you climb, the further you have to fall."

Leaning forward, one hand clutching at her throat, despair overwhelmed her.

"I don't understand," she sobbed. "I have never wronged you."

At her words, his cool demeanour slipped. Pure hatred seemed to ooze from every pore of Levine's face, congealing to form a greasy layer on the surface of his skin.

"Because you left us, Cynthia. You found fame and fortune and not once did you think to share it with us, to even acknowledge us – your family. You knew how hard mother worked to provide for us, the hours she worked, but you didn't care."

Cynthia rushed to her own defence. "You were never interested in me – you and Mother. You were only interested in each other. I felt unwanted. I *was* unwanted. And when I left, I'll bet you were glad. You never came looking for me, either of you."

"We *couldn't* find you! We didn't know where you'd gone. We went to the police, they weren't interested, they said young girls headed to London all the time in search of fame; that you'd be back when the weather turned. So off we went to London too, to walk the streets, showing your picture to anyone who'd listen. Most didn't. Every time we returned home Mother would cry, it was heartbreaking. And then you started to make a name for yourself. I wanted to make contact then but Mother said no, not after so much time had passed, she said you'd take it the wrong way. She was a proud woman was Mother."

"She was a hopeless failure! She had no ambition; she was content to drudge for others, to do their bidding. I knew I was destined for better things, I wanted a chance at drama school, I would have worked to pay for it too, charred alongside her if I'd had to, but no, she wouldn't let me. She said the film industry would ruin me. Ruin me? What did she know? It *made* me. If you had got in touch, I would have told you both to burn in hell."

"And she knew that, but still she followed your every move, kept track of you in the papers. She was almost obsessive."

Grabbing for the box, he blindly hurled it at her, its contents fluttering to the floor in a strangely graceful manner.

"I told her not to," he was the one screaming now, "I told her you didn't deserve her pride, but she carried on regardless, saving every article she could find about you, placing them reverentially in that stupid treasure box. Yes, that's right, that's what she called it, a treasure box. I couldn't believe it! So damn proud of you she was, winning those awards. My only solace is that she never knew you won an Oscar as well; she had died of cancer before then. Whilst you bathed in glory, she writhed in bed, in agony, unable to afford the care that would have made her last days bearable, the care that you could have so easily provided. I went back, I nursed her, bathed her, cleaned up her shit. You did nothing, yet still she pined for you, her lost daughter, the world-famous movie star."

Cynthia was stunned. Her mother had died of cancer? When?

"I... I didn't know," she started.

"You would have known," Jack took a step towards her, his face so twisted with fury he was unrecognisable again, "had you bothered to keep in touch. That's why I did what I did. I stayed sober that night, Cynthia, I watched you. I planned your downfall. And I did it to bring you back to the gutter, where you came from and where you belong."

Staring at him, at the open box, at the cuttings lying strewn about her, Cynthia caught a movement at the door.

"Sally?" she cried brokenly and then, in horror, "John!"

John Sterling looked as shocked as she felt; he must have heard every word. It was too much. She was damned,

281

earmarked for the Devil with or without Lytton's help.

Her heart lurching violently in her chest, she lunged forward, falling amongst the cuttings, sending them fluttering further. She could barely breathe at all now, there seemed to be a weight bearing down on her, crushing her chest – the pain excruciating.

"Cynthia!" shouted John, rushing into the room.

As he scooped her up in his arms, Cynthia looked into his eyes, those beautiful eyes that had always reflected his belief that there was good in her when she felt there was none. Why hadn't she allowed herself to love him? Love might have redeemed her.

"I'm sorry," she whispered, trying to raise her hand, to touch his face, needing his help to do so. "I'm so sorry... for everything."

"It's alright, my darling," John whispered back. "It's alright, I'm here."

"The world must never know," she gasped as her heart lurched again. If this was to be the end, her legend must remain untarnished.

"The world will *never* know," he assured, kissing her lips as life fled from her.

Chapter Thirty-One

As though waking from a dream, Ruby came to. She swung round to face the rest of the team, waiting anxiously beside her. It seemed like hours had passed but looking around it could only have been minutes – time enough though for Cynthia to reveal the truth.

"It's not David Levine!"

"It's not David Levine?" The shock on Theo's face reflected Ruby's own. "Who is it then? Mason?"

Ruby shook her head vehemently, wild eyes darting from face to face. "No, no, it's not Mason either. The box, it didn't belong to Cynthia as we thought it did, it belonged to her mother, Mary – Jack threw it at Cynthia that night."

Ness stepped forward and gripped Ruby by the shoulders.

"Calm down," she said firmly. "You're not making sense. Tell us what you saw."

"I saw Jack."

"Jack who?" Ness quietly encouraged.

"Jack Hart, her brother. He changed his name to David Levine, but his real name is Jack Hart."

Feeling recovered enough at last, Ruby managed to relate everything that had happened to the others who struggled, like her, to take it all in. Then they quickly joined hands again as Ruby began appealing to the spirit world once more.

"Jack, we know it's you who resides in the shadows. Please don't hide from us anymore. We are not here to judge you; we are here to help you. There is no judgement in the light either, only unconditional love and understanding. Don't be afraid."

No!

It was Cynthia's voice.

He is an abomination! He is damned and in turn he has damned me.

"There is no such thing as damnation, Cynthia," Theo was adamant. "Hell is a concept created by man. Come forward both of you and we'll walk with you towards the light."

No reaction. Perhaps neither of them brave enough to confront their sins?

"The box," Ruby whispered to Cash, "where did you put it?"

"It's in the bag. Do you want me to get it?"

"No, I will. Hold Ness's hand, keep the circle complete."

Ruby went over to the black bag which was lying close to the door and carefully took out the box. Retracing her footsteps, she bypassed the circle and crossed over to the bed. Placing the box down, she tried to match the exact spot it had been placed in by Jack.

As soon as she did so, she felt a rush towards her. Not Cynthia this time, but an altogether much darker energy, a seething mass of bitterness and resentment.

Ruby turned to deflect Jack, but too late, she was knocked off her feet, a cry of surprise escaping her as she fell to the ground, hitting her head against Cynthia's bed. Although she tried hard to hold on, she felt her consciousness receding, only just making out the box being tossed into the air again. It hit Cash as he ran towards her, scattering the contents as they had been scattered once before, across the floor of Cynthia's bedroom.

Throwing himself to the ground beside Ruby, Cash cradled her in his arms. She heard him call out her name, over and over again, as John must have called out for Cynthia, desperation in his voice, but she couldn't respond – he seemed impossibly distant, light years away. She tried to swim back to him, to actually feel the comfort of his embrace, but instead she fell further, into the swamp-like darkness that seemed ravenous for her.

She could sense the energy in the room was at crisis point. It was like some enormous geyser bubbling away just under the surface, ready to burst forth at any given minute, to spew its contents over them all, to burn them, destroy them. She had to surface and fast.

Too late, the geyser exploded. Ness and Corinna were already embroiled in it, their screams piercing the air. Were they hurt? Oh God, she hoped not. Then Theo's voice reached her above the maelstrom. Far from cowed, it was strong and determined.

"White light. Keep projecting white light. A wall of white light, solid and firm, no gaps at all."

Ruby's eyes fluttered.

"Ruby!" Cash sounded relieved. "Are you okay?"

"I... I," she muttered, the worst headache she had ever experienced in her entire life temporarily blinding her, holding her prisoner in the void.

"Where's Cynthia?"

Cash looked angrily around him.

"I don't know, but this Jack character, he's really starting to piss me off."

As she struggled to sit up, Ruby's attention was caught by Jed.

"What's he doing?" she said, screwing up her eyes.

"What's who doing?" asked Cash, confused.

"Jed, he's ferreting about under the bed. What's wrong with him?"

Cash shrugged his shoulders.

"He's out again. He's got something in his mouth."

"I don't..." Cash looked even more confused as a folded piece of paper landed on his lap. He grabbed it. "It's a letter."

"A letter? What letter? Was it in the box? Did I miss it?"

"If it was in the box, *we* missed it, you and me both."

Leaning forward she asked Cash to pass it to her, but her head was thumping so violently she had to hand it back. "You

285

read it... I can't."

Cash held up the paper to what scant light was available and did his best to decipher the jagged handwriting. As he did so his eyes grew wider.

"Right, Jacko," he said, rising determinedly. "Listen up. You too, Cynthia, you're going to want to hear this."

Chapter Thirty-Two

"*Dear Mary,*" shouted Cash. As Ruby had been earlier, now he was wild-eyed, his head thrashing from side to side, looking all around him. "I presume that's your mother, right?"

A hush descended.

"There, that got your attention, didn't it?"

"What are you doing, Cash?" Ruby hissed, afraid for him but intrigued, as intrigued as Cynthia and Jack were, she knew they were listening just as intently as she was.

"*Dear Mary,*" Cash repeated, a little less frantically.

"*My parents don't know I am writing to you. They think they have absolute control over everything I do; well they don't, not always. I wanted to thank you, Mary, for taking my darling baby boy.*"

Cash took a breath, as much for himself as to allow time for the words he had spoken to sink in. After a moment, he continued.

"*I miss Jack every day: the smell of him; holding him close to me. I didn't want to give him up, but you know that. Words can't describe how I feel about him; he is perfect, beautiful. And his smile, I've never seen a smile as sweet. He is so much a part of me; a part I will mourn until the day I die. If only I could keep him by my side.*

"*An orphanage or you – that was the choice I was given. And of course, I chose you. No doubt you were paid an insulting amount for taking him in, but I know money isn't why you did it. You're kind, Mary, I see it in your eyes. You were always kind to me, all the years you worked for us: taking the time to look in on me, to*

287

play cards sometimes or simply sit and talk. I always appreciated it – my mother and father, they're busy people, far too busy to spend time with me. And you have a child too, Cynthia, I've heard you talk about her. I hope she and Jack will become the best of friends, as well as brother and sister.

"I will miss you too, Mary, when we move to America, but at least I can console my poor, broken heart that Jack will be well looked after. He is part of your family now, an ordinary, loving family, not one bound by social constraint. Please treat Jack as your own and don't tell him about me, it wouldn't do him any good. My family will never accept him – especially since he was conceived in somewhat difficult circumstances. But despite that, I love him. I never thought I would, but I do.

"When you kiss him at night, Mary, kiss him for me too. Olivia Aston."

After he had finished reading, there was a resounding silence as everyone in the room, without exception, tried to fit together this latest piece of the puzzle.

At last Ruby spoke, her voice barely above a whisper.

"Can you help me up?"

As Cash rushed to her side, Corinna reached for the box, turning it over and over in her hands as though it weren't so nondescript after all, as though it were a thing of wonder.

"Aston," Ruby repeated. "That name, it's familiar."

"It's one of the families Mary used to work for," Cash hurried to explain. "Don't you remember Esme saying?"

Did she? Ruby winced as she tried to recall. The fog surrounding her brain took a few moments to clear. Yes, that's right; Mary had worked for both the Astons and the Carrs.

As though sensing her confusion, Cash continued, "Olivia must have been a daughter of the Astons. Obviously she got pregnant out of wedlock – a big deal in those days, especially if you're, as Esme put it, 'from the upper echelons' – and she gave the child away – to Mary. And that child, it was Jack, or David as he later called himself."

Corinna stopped looking at the box and looked at Ruby instead.

"So, Jack was no blood relation at all?" she said. "Do you think he knew?"

"Only one way to find out," Ruby replied.

Leaning slightly on Cash, she steeled herself for what was to come.

"Jack, were you aware that Mary was not your natural mother?"

No answer.

"What do we do now?" said Cash, still supporting Ruby. But before she could answer their attention was captured by a light shining through the windows. At first Ruby thought it might be car headlights, perhaps Mr Kierney and his guests returning home early for the Christmas festivities. Quickly, and with relief, she realised it wasn't.

Cash squinted. "Is it my imagination, or has it just got brighter in here?"

The room was indeed taking on an unearthly hue, the light more intense than she had ever seen it before. Unable to help herself, Ruby took an almost involuntary step towards it. It was so warm, so enticing – so *familiar*. She wondered briefly if she were actually dead, perhaps that blow to the head had been far more serious than she'd thought?

She glanced around the room, Theo, Ness and Corinna looked amazed too. But Jed, clever Jed, who had somehow known which piece of paper to seize upon, was wagging his tale frantically.

Ruby sensed movement and turned her head. Just a few feet away from her, facing each other at last, stood Cynthia and Jack. Not demons. Far from it. Just two people.

Cynthia asked the same question Ruby had.

Did you know?

Jack hung his head.

Jack!

Ruby was glad to see fire in her sapphire eyes. Reluctantly, Jack answered.

I... Mother was delirious at the end. She said things. I couldn't be sure.

Looking up, he almost spat his next words at her.

I never had any intention of touching you. What I wanted was to destroy you.

A pause between them.

You didn't know about the letter?

Jack shook his head violently.

That box, why would I look in it? It was all about you.

There was still such bitterness in his voice.

Ruby came forward. "It was about you too, Jack," she pointed out, "you and Olivia. Her treasure box, that's what you said Mary called it, clearly she treasured all three of you."

Ruby wondered briefly whether to mention Mason. After all, he had been in amongst Mary's treasures too. But she decided against it. For whatever reason he was there, Cynthia would find out soon enough.

Jack's eyes locked onto Ruby's – a fire of a different kind burning fiercely in them.

Mary wasn't mine. She was Cynthia's. EVERYTHING was Cynthia's!

"You had everything too. You just couldn't see it."

The cuttings on the floor fluttered ominously. But before his rage could build again, Ruby stepped forward, holding her hand out towards him, trying to reach him, not just physically but emotionally too.

"Mary loved you, Jack. Olivia loved you. Love is everything."

Mary should have told me! The truth might have set me free.

"Why, Jack?" Ruby could guess but wanted him to say it anyway.

He looked lost. He *was* lost.

I might not have felt so... so useless.

The despair in his voice moved her.

"She had promised not to. And from what I gather, Mary was a woman of her word. And you weren't useless, Jack. What you did for your mother at the end was noble."

Ruby's words hit home. The newspaper scraps lay still once more.

There was another pause before he spoke again, subdued.

I'm sorry.

It was Cynthia who stepped closer this time.

I'm sorry too.

Jack reached out to her. Cynthia reached out to him. Their hands connected.

A lifetime wasted.

Ruby was about to interrupt, to try and console Jack further, to tell him nothing in life was wasted, no experience, no emotion, no thought, whether good or bad, that it all had some purpose even if that purpose was never made clear here on earth. But she was stopped in her tracks. A voice, one she hadn't heard before was calling.

Jack.

In the room, those who heard it turned to it.

Who are you? Jack looked frightened as a figure emerged from the light.

The woman smiled at him – a dazzling smile, a smile to lose yourself in.

Jack's face transformed entirely, it wasn't possible to hold onto pain in the presence of such beauty.

Mother?

The woman nodded.

Without hesitation, Jack walked towards her, his image growing stronger as he did so, allowing Ruby a glimpse of the young man he had once been. Pleasant to look at, if a little understated; a fount of hope and promise before anger had stopped him from truly blossoming. As Jack reached the light, Ruby realised it wasn't Mary who had come to reclaim her son but Olivia, reuniting herself with the child that she'd had torn from her.

As Olivia took Jack in her arms, the room glistened as though it were filled with diamonds.

Cash shielded his eyes and Ruby wondered what he could see. She'd have to ask him later. Theo, Ness and even Corinna were rooted to the spot, as if in a trance.

As the two figures faded, Ruby turned to Cynthia.

"There's no one waiting for you in the shadows anymore, Cynthia, it's your turn now."

Cynthia looked downcast.

There's no one waiting for me in the light either.

Turning back to the light, Ruby smiled.

"Oh, I think there is. Look again."

It was John Sterling, striding towards them, faint at first and then much stronger. He was as handsome as Ruby had ever seen him look on the screen or in photographs; his dark hair was neatly greased back, his white shirt open slightly, tantalisingly at the throat.

John... Cynthia whispered, half in disbelief, half in awe.

About to rush towards him, she stopped. Looking down at the news articles Mary had saved, she then looked up at Ruby.

She didn't forget me.

"Nobody could forget you."

She was proud.

"Of *you*," Ruby clarified. "Yes."

Cynthia's eyes clouded briefly but Ruby was not concerned – all earthly sadness, she knew, would soon be resolved. Turning from Ruby, Cynthia looked at John again. A girlish laugh escaped her as she ran across the divide that separated them, hurling herself into the sanctuary of his arms. John was laughing too, a sound as sweet to her as birdsong.

You waited for me, Ruby heard Cynthia say.

I'd wait forever if I had to, replied John.

No more games, said Cynthia earnestly.

Not where we're going, answered John, sweeping her off her feet.

Chapter Thirty-Three

"Mr Kierney?" Ruby waited until she was downstairs in the Grand Hall before phoning her client. "It's Ruby. I think I can safely say you'll encounter no more spiritual upheaval at Highdown Hall."

"She's gone? Cynthia? You've rid me of her?"

And the other one, thought Ruby, but held her tongue. The less Mr Kierney knew the better.

"Cynthia has passed successfully; the house is yours now and yours alone."

"At last," there was a sigh of relief. "You'd better be right though. If I go back... if there's any more nonsense, you and your company, you'll regret it."

"There'll be no more nonsense," Ruby replied wearily.

"We'll see," was his less than generous response.

"Happy Christmas, Mr Kierney," Ruby offered after a moment.

"To you too," he muttered before ending the call.

She turned to the rest of the team, standing waiting for her, all except Jed who was languishing at Cash's feet, and tried to keep the sarcasm out of her voice as she declared, "Another satisfied customer."

"Bastard!" said Ness, surprising them all with the venom in her voice.

"Well it's true," Ness continued, obviously feeling the need to defend herself against their raised eyebrows and opened mouths. "I bet he didn't even say thank you."

"He didn't," admitted Ruby. "But we didn't do it for him,

not really. We did it for Cynthia and, as it turned out, for Jack."

With Ness still looking disgruntled, Theo piped up, "Come on, it's Christmas Eve, a time to rejoice or so they say. And I don't know about you lot, but I've got a date with a rather large glass of sweet sherry – and a mince pie with brandy butter too, I should think."

Her words spurring the others into action, they shuffled their way towards the entrance and out into the night – the stars twinkling merrily in the sky – as if they too were somehow rejoicing. Before closing the door on Highdown Hall, for good this time she hoped, Ruby couldn't resist taking one last lingering look. Tunes were playing, people were laughing – the party was in full swing and this time, *everyone* appeared to be having a good time.

***

Outside on the gravel pathway, the conversation turned to their plans for Christmas.

"I'm off to my mum's," said Corinna, grimacing.

"And why is that so bad, young lady?" quizzed Theo.

"Because all my brothers are going too and, I don't know, when we're all under the same roof as Mum and Dad, we start regressing, behaving like children again. The bickering starts almost straightway."

"Sounds comforting," suggested Theo.

"I suppose," conceded Corinna, before breaking into a wide and excited smile.

"What about you, Ness?" said Ruby, hoping she wasn't spending it on her own again like last year, She was pleasantly surprised when a smile lit up Ness's face too.

"Ness?" probed Ruby, intrigued.

"I'm, er, I'm going to spend it at a friend's," she replied, somewhat enigmatically.

"A friend?" butted in Theo. "Of the male persuasion you

mean?"

"Yes, I do mean," replied Ness, reddening.

Incredibly for Theo, she refrained from teasing her further, the benevolence of the season rubbing off on her perhaps? Instead, they all wished each other a very happy Christmas and exchanged hugs and kisses. Ruby and Cash waited whilst the other three climbed back into Ness's car and then waved at them as they sped off.

"Just the three of us again," said Cash, turning to look at Ruby.

"Yep, you, me and a dog named Jed."

"I think in the song it's 'Me and You and A Dog Named Boo' – a far more appropriate name for a ghost dog in my opinion. But I'll settle for Jed. I just wish I could see him."

"You can smell him," Ruby offered.

"It's not quite the same thing."

"So, what are you doing for Christmas?" asked Ruby, as they walked back to his car.

"Spending it with Mum and Presley," he replied, opening the passenger door for her. "My aunt and uncle are coming down too, from London. The usual houseful. What are you doing?"

"Going back to Hastings," replied Ruby, climbing in and buckling up.

"I thought so. I'll drive you there in the morning."

"Oh no, you don't have to..." she started.

"I'll be at yours, so it's not a hardship. After breakfast, we'll hop in the car and, if you want, I'll come and get you in the evening, or whenever it is you want to come back."

"You'll be at mine?" she said, taken aback.

"Yes, well, that's where we're going now, isn't it?"

"We are?"

Starting the engine, he turned to her and said, "To finish off what we started on Saturday. You've no objections, have you?"

"No," she spluttered, "none at all. In fact, the quicker we get there the better."

"My thoughts exactly," said Cash, switching into gear.

"How fast can you go in this thing?"

"Faster than a speeding bullet, just watch me."

As he sped off, Ruby sat happily back in her seat. In the wing mirror she could see Highdown Hall retreating, getting smaller and smaller. It looked silent and lonely – lonely being a very good thing in this instance. Quickly they reached the spot where Cynthia's brother had died. Ruby wondered if residual feelings still lingered – if they did, they were faint, no shudder coursed through her. Turning her attention to the view in the car's headlamps, excitement was the only emotion that registered. Not just at the thought of having Cash to herself in roughly forty-five minutes time, but the thrilling realisation that she'd finished another successful year in business and also had the prospect of a very promising one to come. She had never felt so happy. She had never felt so proud. She was fulfilling her purpose in life, being who she was born to be. She was Ruby Davis, Psychic Crusader, Believer in Light and Love. With no reason to believe otherwise. Yet.

THE END

Fantastic Books
Great Authors

Meet our authors and discover our exciting range:

- Gripping Thrillers
- Cosy Mysteries
- Romantic Chick-Lit
- Fascinating Historicals
- Exciting Fantasy
- Young Adult and Children's Adventures

Visit us at:
www.crookedcatbooks.com

Join us on facebook:
www.facebook.com/crookedcatpublishing

CPSIA information can be obtained
at www.ICGtesting.com
Printed in the USA
BVOW03s0945161116
468007BV00001B/2/P